PASSION PLAY

"OUTSTANDING...
A mystery superior to most, endowing teachers, teachers' wives, sports coaches, the boys and their girlfriends with an unforgettable reality."

Publishers Weekly

"A genuinely involving and suspenseful 'classic' mystery of the Agatha Christie school... Believable, engrossing... Blain has done a fine, even brilliant job of making the madness, anger and pain these characters suffer seem real... Highly recommended."

Roanoke Times & World-News

"A mystery of originality and power filled with fully realized characters you care about."

Thomas Chastain, author of *Perry Mason in the Case of Too Many Murders*

"Blain keeps the reader guessing... Pacing is quick and boarding-school life is drawn in convincing and often humorous detail... An exciting and thought-provoking debut."

Booklist

"Keeps the action at a fast pitch... A mixture of sex and violence threads through from page one to the end... A highly original book by a fine writer."

Lucy Freeman, Past President, *Mystery Writers of America*

"Touching and thoughtful, sensitive and suspenseful."

San Francisco Chronicle

S0-AXS-071

Avon Books are available at special quantity discounts for bulk purchases for sales promotions, premiums, fund raising or educational use. Special books, or book excerpts, can also be created to fit specific needs.

For details write or telephone the office of the Director of Special Markets, Avon Books, Dept. FP, 1350 Avenue of the Americas, New York, New York 10019, 1-800-238-0658.

PASSION PLAY

W. EDWARD BLAIN

AVON BOOKS NEW YORK

If you purchased this book without a cover, you should be aware that this book is stolen property. It was reported as "unsold and destroyed" to the publisher, and neither the author nor the publisher has received any payment for this "stripped book."

AVON BOOKS
A division of
The Hearst Corporation
1350 Avenue of the Americas
New York, New York 10019

Copyright © 1990 by W. Edward Blain
Map copyright © 1990 by Ann Glover
Published by arrangement with G.P. Putnam's Sons
Library of Congress Catalog Card Number: 89-39052
ISBN: 0-380-71450-7

All rights reserved, which includes the right to reproduce this book or portions thereof in any form whatsoever except as provided by the U.S. Copyright Law. For information address G.P. Putnam's Sons, 200 Madison Avenue, New York, New York 10016.

First Avon Books Printing: August 1991

AVON TRADEMARK REG. U.S. PAT. OFF. AND IN OTHER COUNTRIES, MARCA REGISTRADA, HECHO EN CANADA.

Printed in Canada.

UNV 10 9 8 7 6 5 4 3 2

To those who taught me

ACKNOWLEDGMENTS

Many hands assisted in the production of this book. I am particularly grateful for the suggestions of my manuscript readers, Nat Jobe and Johanna Smethurst, and my editor, E. Stacy Creamer, who prodded me into several crucial improvements. Of course, no one would be reading these words now if my wonderful agent, Nancy Love, had not taken a chance on three chapters that arrived over the transom.

The excellent map of the campus is by Ann Glover.

My family and friends have been astonishingly patient and supportive as I have learned the craft of writing, and my colleagues and students at Woodberry Forest School have provided me the best possible environment in which to work. Thanks to all, and, to echo the final words of the Episcopal Church liturgy, thanks be to God, in whom all things, even the most ambitious dreams, are possible.

W.E.B.

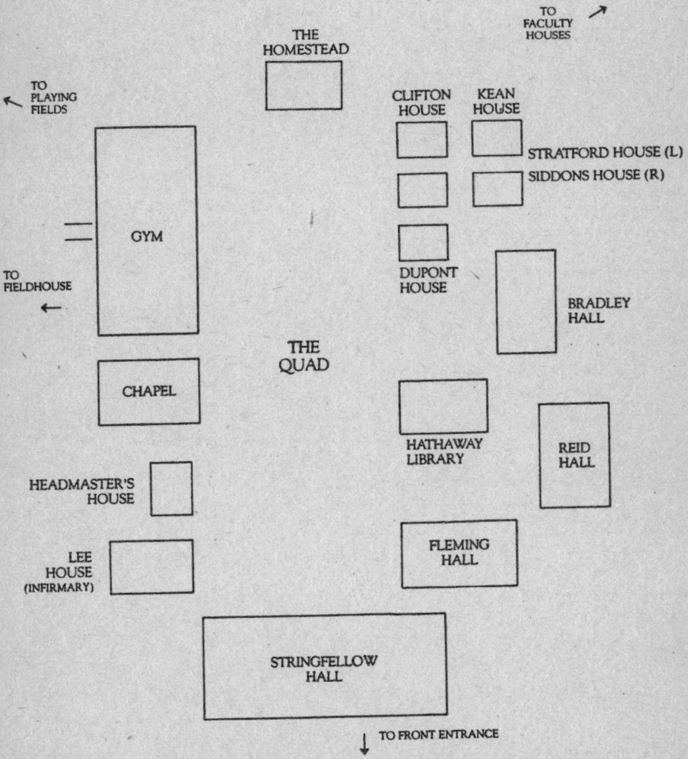
TO FACULTY HOUSES
THE HOMESTEAD
TO PLAYING FIELDS
CLIFTON HOUSE
KEAN HOUSE
STRATFORD HOUSE (L)
SIDDONS HOUSE (R)
GYM
TO FIELDHOUSE
DUPONT HOUSE
BRADLEY HALL
THE QUAD
CHAPEL
HATHAWAY LIBRARY
REID HALL
HEADMASTER'S HOUSE
LEE HOUSE (INFIRMARY)
FLEMING HALL
STRINGFELLOW HALL
TO FRONT ENTRANCE

MONTPELIER SCHOOL FOR BOYS

THE FIRST ACT

He was honestly unaware that a murder would follow the end of the play.

It was cold and growing dark as he emerged from the theater just before 5:00 P.M. in a crowd of dawdling tourists. With a quick dart he sidestepped the slowest pedestrians and hurried east, shrugging into his coat as he approached Seventh Avenue. It was the wrong direction, but at least he was moving. The theater had been too warm, full of vacationers like himself who had purchased half-priced tickets in Duffy Square an hour before the show, and now the contrasting air of the Manhattan streets hurt. The scarf and the hat helped keep back the cold a little. He turned right on Seventh and juggled the small travel bag he was carrying in order to pull on his gloves. Times Square offered a little more light, a little more humanity.

He had expected the musical to cheer him up—the dancing, the glitter, all those smiling faces singing those melodic songs—but it had had the opposite effect. The characters were stereotypes; all the jokes sounded familiar. It had made him feel as though he were watching television, as though he were wasting his life on something utterly mindless, as though he were taking drugs. It was past time to go home.

The theater had been full, but the city was dead. It was the Sunday after Thanksgiving, and he was among the last of the tourists to be pulling out of town. There were probably more people at LaGuardia than there were here in midtown. Well, not really. He'd have to remember that as an example of hyperbole to use for the students. They didn't think of him as knowing much about English, but he did. At the corner the air warmed for a moment as he passed a vendor selling hot chestnuts. What was a chestnut vendor doing at Seventh and Forty-third? He supposed the guy sold them to people like him: tourists coming out of the theater.

At Forty-second Street he saw a subway station, but he was reluctant to enter. It wasn't the same one he'd used to get here; that one had been on Eighth. He turned right on Forty-second, lifted his scrap of luggage, and carried it closer. He knew the city only in an uneasy acquaintance, knew he was safe enough to be walking here at dusk on Sunday afternoon, but he also assumed that it was not an entirely risk-free neighborhood. The pornographic movie houses along this block cast a white light on the few street people milling on the sidewalks, like wares in some block-long K Mart. It was too early and too quiet and too cold to attract many prostitutes or pushers, but he saw one woman in a red satin miniskirt and white boots. She was wearing a fake fur jacket and dangling earrings. How could she stand the cold? Maybe hookers had metabolisms like adolescents, speeded up somehow. He could remember as a boy playing outside when it was ten degrees Fahrenheit. All the parents thought he and his friends were crazy. Now he was reacting like a parent, hiding his face under a scarf and a hat.

He saw the boy in front of a theater halfway down the block. Blond, longish hair, maybe fourteen years old, maybe a little older, brown flight jacket, jeans, Converse basketball shoes. The kid flashed the jacket open and revealed that he wasn't wearing a shirt.

Rage clicked on like a thermostat.

He stopped by the kid. Don't do it, he thought, you have a train to catch, you have responsibilities, you are more disciplined than this. He stopped and looked at the kid. He was not a particularly well-built boy, but he was nice-looking. With his black Converse shoes on, who knows, he could have been an ordinary basketball player from Indiana. He wondered whether the kid would have needle scars on his arms, whether what he was seeing was a facade. He knew big cities just well enough to know that the clichés from television were not to be trusted.

"All the way down for fifteen bucks," said the kid. He had a good voice, the kind of voice that would sound good on a stage. Where had this child gone wrong? The kid shifted his head and looked him over. This boy had the right neck, the right shoulders. Under his coat the man could feel his heart start to pound as the passion surged and took over. Now that it had happened, he knew: whatever he had told himself earlier, this was the real reason he had come to New York. His body was screaming commands; he could not help himself; he would obey. At the ticket booth he bought two tickets for $1.99 each. The boy led the way up to the balcony.

"Up here," said the boy, pushing the man into the back row. It was very dark at first. As his eyes adjusted, he could see that the place was nearly empty. He wondered how many other tourists there were in this kind of theater in New York right now. On the screen in front of him, two naked men were dancing.

He was hot now; the passion was consuming him; he had to finish this.

"First the money," said the kid.

The man pulled his wallet out of his left front trouser pocket. A couple of coins clattered on the sticky floor. He pulled a twenty out of his wallet and gave it to the kid.

"I don't make change," said the kid. The man told him to keep it.

The boy pocketed the money and leaned over the man's lap. As he fumbled at the man's coat buttons, the man firmly took the boy's head in his hands, as if to guide him. With a quick twist, while the boy was pulling at the buttons, the man broke the boy's neck. The boy grunted softly, but his death attracted no attention. They were used to hearing such noises in this theater. He pulled his money back out of the boy's pocket, eased the body down onto the floor, and gave himself exactly thirty seconds to let his heartbeat and breathing return to normal. Now that the passion had fled, he was coldly rational. The coins on the floor should be picked up, even in the filth. He felt and found them, along with his ticket stub from the other theater. For a brief second he was furious with himself for being so careless, but then he forced himself to release the anger. No harm done, after all. He checked carefully for tickets, money, wallet, baggage. All here. Scarf and hat, both gloves. All here. He needed to depart very quickly now. The boy's bowels had probably relaxed. There would be a smell soon.

The man picked up his belongings and left the theater.

Outside, the cold air hit him again. He thought back to the silly musical he had seen. At Eighth Avenue he caught the subway, one stop to Penn Station. He arrived at 5:28, caught his train at 5:40. He read a book on the way to Washington. At 9:00 he was in Union Station. Then he caught a Metro to the parking lot, hopped into his car, and drove southwest. By 11:30 P.M. he was in central Virginia, at home, back on campus.

It was the end of Thanksgiving vacation. He still had his chores to do for tomorrow, when classes resumed. All around him, 360 boys slept or talked or perhaps planned pranks. But none of them, not students or teachers, knew what he knew about passion.

He shivered, but not from the cold.

THE SECOND ACT

Scene 1

Benjamin Warden twitched awake upon hearing the loud electronic pulse of the alarm on his clock radio. It was 6:30 Monday morning, time to get up for school. He had forgotten over the holidays just how much he hated this noise, a peculiar combination of rhythmical beeping and disc jockey chatter, but as he jumped from scatter rug to cold wood to turn off the switch, he permitted a shred of appreciation for how well the damn thing worked. He and Cynthia deliberately left it across their bedroom so that at least one of them would have to get up to shut it off.

Warden hated to start work tired after a holiday. In fourteen years of teaching, however, he had learned to be aware of his fatigue and to discipline himself not to pass it on to his students. Christmas vacation was only three weeks away. With luck he could find some reserves to get him through the next twenty-one days.

Cynthia kept her head on the pillow and watched him stretch his arms.

"Courage," she said.

"Morning." He crossed to the bed, climbed back in, and kissed her. Even when she was ill, she was beautiful. Her hair was exquisitely long and straight, her eyes the color of ripe blueberries, her mouth tiny and turned up in a crescent smile. He loved the dimple at the base of her neck and the others inside her arms and knees, loved to look at the way her breasts swelled so seamlessly outward, loved the firm but soft texture of her skin, loved her smooth parts and her coarse parts, loved her flawlessness, her intelligence, her charity.

"I vaguely remember your arrival last night," she said. "It must have been late."

"Pre-midnight, I believe," he said. "We talked for a minute."

"Was I glad to see you?"

"You were sleepy. You told me that I missed nothing here."

"Did you tell me about your activities in New York?"

He covered the surge of anxiety with a mock shiver. "Cold. Dull without you."

"Did you get to the theater?"

"Joe got me a ticket for a Sunday matinee of *Cats.* I ended up going by myself."

She asked if the play was worth all the Tonys it had won.

"No," he said, "it was actually pretty good."

She laughed.

"For a musical," he added. "Feeling better?"

"Different, anyway," she said, but she turned away when she answered. "I don't think I'd better go in today."

"We can manage."

Warden was chairman of the English department, and Cynthia was its part-time secretary. When she was well, she spent her mornings typing quizzes or running photocopies. She spent her afternoons starting the research for her doctoral dissertation.

Cynthia said she would not fight him for the first shower this morning.

"Stay here," Warden said. "I'll get breakfast." He pushed himself out of bed again, shuffled his feet into his boating shoes. He pulled on a sweater over his tee shirt and a pair of khakis over his boxers.

"Don't you want to eat in the dining hall?" she said.

"No."

She told him that Kathleen Somerville had left some food in the refrigerator.

As he descended the stairs to the living area, Warden could hear the noises of Stratford House through the walls around him. The denizens were up a little early today. Usually even the most punctual boys waited until 7:00 or 7:15 to take their showers in time for the 7:30 buffet breakfast, while some of the older boys waited until 7:55 to get up for their 8:00 classes. Perhaps there was the genesis of a poem here—morning noises, daily routines. Warden imagined them all through the walls, getting ready, the younger ones still learning how to shave, the older ones lying about their sexual exploits over the holidays. Warden thought of them as his family, his and Cynthia's. He liked their youth, liked to say that they kept him young.

He entered the kitchen and turned on the overhead light. It shone down on green Formica countertops, dark green tiles, white appliances. Cynthia's orange gourd and red apple centerpiece remained from Thanksgiving. Beside it was Warden's blue canvas travel bag, which he had simply dropped on the table before climbing up to bed last night. Exactly how late had he gotten in? He couldn't remember. The whole trip back was a blur because he had been playing around with some lines of poetry in his head. He was relieved, in fact, to see that his luggage had made it back to Virginia with him. On a trip last month to read in Massachusetts he had absentmindedly checked his luggage through to Charlotte, North Carolina, instead of to Charlottesville.

He reached into the pantry and took a box of Spoon Size shredded wheat and two drinking glasses. Under the counter he found the frying pan with the copper bottom. It was a wedding present, and therefore just over two years old: twenty-seven months, to be exact. A pang of love and sadness seized him, but he allowed himself to succumb only to a moment of worry. Last week Cynthia had complained of dizziness and blurred vision in her left eye. It had happened before, about a year ago, and again last summer, but both times it had disappeared on its own. Last week, however, she had also developed occasional tremors in her arms, then weakness in her legs. She also had complained of constriction in her abdomen. The local general practitioner had asked them if they had been spraying any insecticides in their home recently, but they hadn't. He had suspected an accidental poisoning or perhaps an allergy and had told her to rest over the weekend, to cancel her trip to New York, and to let him know Monday if the symptoms did not disappear.

On the refrigerator door was a crayon drawing Cynthia had attached with magnets. Warden's four-year-old nephew, Joshua, had drawn it in honor of their first wedding anniversary. Warden envied the child's frankness. There was Cynthia with her long blond hair, wearing a blue dress with a white smear on one side, which Joshua had explained was her handkerchief sticking out of her pocket. And beside her was Warden, long brown trousers, white shirt and blue tie, glasses, and a big red stain down the left side of his face. The kid had a good eye for detail. Warden touched his birthmark before he reached into the refrigerator for the bacon and the eggs on the middle shelf. Even at thirty-five, Warden was not entirely free of his sensitivity over the large rough patch that had covered half his face since he was born. He still felt occasional awe that someone as beautiful and as young as Cynthia would want to marry him, could love him, and yet, he reminded himself, she did.

And what was this in the plastic container? Fried apples. Typical of Kathleen Somerville. He started warming the apples.

Cynthia entered the room. She was dragging her left foot, and she half-fell, half-descended, into the slatted chair at the table. She had put on a blue robe over her nightgown.

"What are you doing downstairs?" he asked. "And why are you limping so badly?"

"Leg's asleep. I want to watch you," she said. "I haven't seen you for three days."

He tore open the plastic packet of bacon.

"I want to hear every little thing about the trip," she said. "How many people were there, how many autographs you signed, how long they applauded, how many job offers you declined, how many women seduced you."

Warden had been reading his poetry at the Ninety-second Street Y.

"I couldn't concentrate on anything but you," he said.

"Oh, come on," she said. "New York? The literati? The Upper East Side? Tell me you were dazzling. Tell me Woody Allen was there. Tell me about the argument Norman Mailer and Susan Sontag got into over which of your poems was better."

"There were maybe 250 or 300 people there," he said. "The term 'famous poet' is an oxymoron, unless you happen to be dead. I wanted to be here with you."

She said at least he'd made both his wife and his agent happy by going.

He told her about signing a lot of books afterward, about meeting reporters from *The New York Times* and *The New Yorker,* about getting a business card from an editor at Farrar, Straus & Giroux.

"Which you immediately passed on to Joe," said Cynthia.

"Of course."

He waved six slices of bacon into the frying pan and punched "2" on the electric stove.

"Did you see anybody from Montpelier when you were up there?" Cynthia asked.

"Not a soul. Should I have?"

"I heard several people on the faculty talking about going. Dan Farnham was, I know."

"Dan Farnham would not waste an evening in New York on me," said Warden. "If you had been along, maybe."

"Aha," said Cynthia. "O, beware, my lord, of jealousy; It is the green-eyed monster. . . ."

He told her to go ahead and finish the speech.

"I can't remember," said Cynthia. "I don't have to. They're not my lines."

"You're not going to do the play still, are you?"

"I want to," she said. "Yes."

Warden punched the button for the hot water and pulled two mugs from the cabinet. Daniel Farnham, one of his colleagues in the English department, had asked Cynthia to play Desdemona in *Othello,* the winter play Farnham was directing here at the Montpelier School for Boys. As department chairman, Warden had advised the choice of another play, one with more parts for the students—*Othello* has the smallest cast of any of Shakespeare's tragedies—but Farnham had insisted that it needed to be *Othello,* that Greg Lipscomb, a black sophomore, was interested in playing the lead, and that all of the boys in the fourth form were reading the play for English class. Warden had not pressed the matter, but he had a sense—a sense that he recognized as paranoid and irrational—that Farnham had a more ulterior motive.

"He chose that play in order to work with you," said Warden. "He's got a terrible crush on you."

"Of course he does," said Cynthia. "They all do. He's just like one of the boys. But I don't have a crush on any of them."

"It's so transparent," said Warden. "Picking the play that you're writing your dissertation on."

Cynthia flicked the zipper on Warden's travel bag on the table. "Is this why you're so lugubrious this morning?" she asked. "Are you really considering Daniel Farnham as a serious rival?"

"When you put it like that, you make me sound like a fool."

Cynthia said she should greet that line with a polite but telling silence.

Warden turned the bacon. "I don't know what it is," he said. He felt robbed of his Thanksgiving holiday. He and Cynthia were going to take a vacation in New York, but then he was forced by agent and publisher to go without her. "This last excursion. It was more work than pleasure." He complained that long trips to read his old material robbed him of time to write new stuff. And now that school was starting up again, his writing time would be diminished even more.

Cynthia reminded him that he could always work down the road at the university.

A delicate subject, one that he wanted to avoid.

"Maybe I should try it," said Warden. "It's just that college students are so sycophantic."

"I beg your pardon?"

It was one of their running jokes. They had met three summers ago, when Warden was teaching a graduate seminar on poetry for the summer session at the University of Virginia and Cynthia enrolled in his class. She had read every one of his books before the course started, and she had startled him by using two lines of his poetry as epigraph to her own work. At first he had been suspicious, but when she had told him that she was merely auditing the course for no credit, he had invited her for dinner, despite his self-consciousness at dating a woman twelve years younger. By the end of the summer, they were married. And they had lived here in their dormitory at Montpelier School since.

He poured hot water over the tea bag in the mug, let it brew for fifteen seconds, and then shifted the tea bag to another mug, which he also filled with water. He took the cups to the table. Cynthia groped for hers and grasped it with both hands.

"You're shaking again," said Warden.

"Yes," said Cynthia.

"Do you really feel all right?" said Warden.

"No," said Cynthia.

"What is it?"

"I'm scared, Ben," she said. "I'm scared of what this is."

"What's the matter?" asked Warden.

"Ever since yesterday afternoon, my left foot has been numb."

Warden heard her as though she were speaking a line in one of his dreams—where a character could surprise him and yet confirm his most dreaded expectations all at once.

He asked her why she hadn't told him earlier.

"Because," she said, "I knew we'd spend the rest of the morning talking about me."

She held her mug in front of her with both hands, as though she were carrying a chalice. He cupped her hands, mug and all, within his large palms.

Her skin felt so cold.

Scene 2

Thomas Boatwright was sitting in English class and dying. He knew this must be what it felt like to die of boredom, because he was doing it. He looked at his watch again. 8:17. Whoopee-do, an entire minute had passed since his last look. They'd been back exactly seventeen minutes from Thanksgiving vacation, seventeen minutes of class for the first time since last Wednesday, and he was dying, dying of boredom, wondering why in the hell he'd ever agreed to attend boarding school, wishing that something would happen to make Mr. Farnham shut up and leave the room.

There were eleven other boys in the class. Their desks were arranged in a semicircle around Mr. Farnham's old wooden desk with GRATEFUL DEAD carved in little tiny letters on the front. Thomas had been staring at the GRATEFUL DEAD for months—it seemed more like years—ever since he'd started school in September and had entered Mr. Farnham's class in fourth-form English. They wouldn't call it sophomore English here at the Montpelier School for Boys; that sounded too American, even though the school was American and everybody sitting here was American and they were, in fact, about two hours away by car from the American capital city, which was where Thomas's family lived and where he'd spent his Thanksgiving vacation and where he ought to be right now, going to Cathedral Academy and getting home at night and away, away, away from this unbelievably boring class.

8:19. His watch had to be broken. Time could not possibly move this slowly of its own volition. They were smart not to put clocks in these classrooms. Sometimes if you didn't look at a watch, you could go into a sort of hypnotic trance and the time would slip away from you. Thomas promised himself that he wouldn't look at his watch for at least another twenty minutes. How would he know when twenty minutes had passed? He would be dead, that's how. He would be dead of boredom. Just before he keeled over, he would look at his watch to see what time he'd expired.

". . . two kinds of love," Mr. Farnham was saying. He was writing on the board. "*Cupiditas* is the bad kind of love, what we would call today 'cupidity' or 'lust.' " He wrote CUPIDITAS=CUPIDITY (LUST) on the board in his usual block letters. "And the good kind of love is *caritas,* what we would call 'charity' or 'unselfish love' today." He wrote another little equation up on the board: CARITAS=UNSELFISH LOVE.

In his notebook Thomas wrote LOVE—2 KINDS. CUPIDITAS BAD, CARITAS GOOD.

"Are those words capitalized?" asked Landon Hopkins, who sat in the middle of the semicircle and was undoubtedly writing down every word Farnham said. Thomas sat on one end of the semicircle, to the teacher's left, because he had read somewhere that teachers don't tend to call on the person situated to one side, that the teacher's attention spreads out in an arc and often misses the people in the front side seats. He looked across the room at Richard Blackburn, his best friend, who rolled his eyes and pretended to draw a gun and shoot Landon under the desk. Richard just killed Thomas. He was the funniest guy ever, starting with his looks. His black hair was shaved close to his temples but was long and floppy on top, and he wore big round wire-rimmed glasses that somehow made him look like Tweety-bird in those old cartoons. Over the holidays he'd had his ear pierced, but Mr. Grayson, the disciplinarian, had spotted the earring at breakfast and had made him take it out. The dress code at Montpelier banned earrings and bracelets and required ties for class. Richard was the best at short-circuiting the rules. Today he was wearing this terrible looking red-white-and-blue tie with Barbara Bush's face in spangles on it. He'd bought it last summer when he was visiting Thomas over the July 4th weekend, when the city just about sank under the weight of the tourists.

"Not necessary," said Mr. Farnham. Boy, had Thomas been wrong about this teacher. Usually when you get a young one, he's pretty cool about getting off the subject and taking the class to the audiovisual center a lot, but not Farnham. He was like Mister Pedagogical Methods, always coming to class with these long lesson plans, which he followed strictly, and never talking about anything but English all day long. He'd taught in some school in Alabama for two years before coming here to Virginia. Thomas guessed it was one of those military training schools where everything had to be just perfect all the time. Farnham wore perfectly ironed clothes, perfectly polished loafers, a perfectly knotted tie, and a perfectly nauseating little mustache the size of a centipede. He was actually pretty nice, Thomas supposed, if he wouldn't lose his temper so much. You do one little thing wrong, like show up without your book or something, and he would spaz for ten minutes.

"One of the great tensions in English literature from the very beginning," Mr. Farnham was saying, "was the tension between *cupiditas* and *caritas.* Everyone knew that *caritas* was the kind of love that God felt for mankind, and that it was the kind of love that we were supposed to feel for each other. But God had also made us as sexual creatures, and so man had to come to terms with the fact that sexuality was in itself a good thing."

Now you're talking, thought Thomas.

"Sexuality was good," said Mr. Farnham, "because it tricked us into reproducing our species. We'd be very unlikely to engage in that particular act if we derived no pleasure from doing so. Think about it."

Thomas thought about it all the time. He was just a couple of weeks away from turning sixteen. Over the holidays he'd met a girl, Hesta McCorkindale, who was a tenth-grader at Mason School and who lived in McLean. She was really nice, he liked her a lot, and when he kissed her it seemed as though somebody had attached a jumper cable to his crotch. He thought about Hesta now, sitting across from him, the school had gone coed or something and so she could be in the class, only she hadn't worn any underwear and he could see—

"Mr. Boatwright," said Farnham. "Near what planet are you orbiting?"

"Sorry," said Thomas.

"Can you tell me what I was just saying?"

Thomas looked at his notes. "Sex is good," he said. The rest of the class started to snicker.

"And why is sex good?" said Mr. Farnham.

"Because," said Thomas. He was nailed. "I'm not sure."

Landon Hopkins raised his hand. "It's good because it encourages us to reproduce our species," he said. "That's what the Pope says, isn't it?"

"Exactly," said Mr. Farnham. "The Pope also says what these old medievalists would say; that is, that when sex becomes the ultimate goal or source of pleasure for mankind, then it has become a form of idolatry. Consider this." He started to draw another diagram on the board. Across the room, Richard mimed laughing at Thomas. Thomas mimed vomiting in response.

"The human soul has three parts to it," said Mr. Farnham, "and the three parts dwell in the liver, the heart, and the brain." Dying, thought Thomas. I am absolutely dying, but he wrote down LIVER, HEART, and BRAIN just in case Farnham called on him again.

He wondered how much Farnham knew about sex. He wasn't a geek or anything. He wore glasses, but a lot of neat people wore glasses. Thomas had worn them himself until he'd gotten contacts two years ago. Hesta wore glasses, in fact, but she wore these really cool wire-rimmed glasses that her aunt had worn during the 1960s.

Living in the 1960s would have been so cool if he could have been fifteen, his age now, back then. He would have dropped out of school to hassle the establishment. He and Hesta would have hung around on the Washington Ellipse in buckskin jackets and stuff, smoked dope all the time, and then every night they would have taken off all their clothes and done everything sexual you could do to each other. Make love, not war. Richard had told Thomas that some people do it in the morning instead of at night. In the morning, that would be wild. Sometimes he was horny in the morning, he had to admit. But he'd always thought that sex was something you did at night. He'd never actually gotten laid himself, but he had consulted many, many pictures and had heard the older guys on the dorm talk about it a lot.

"The heart," said Mr. Farnham, "is the seat of our sensible souls. Now don't get confused when I say 'sensible.' "

Don't worry, thought Thomas.

"I don't mean 'sensible' as in 'showing good sense,' the way we might say that Ford made a sensible decision in pardoning Nixon. I mean 'sensible' in a more literal meaning; that is, in referring to the five senses. The sensible soul is the soul that gives us our feeling, our emotions. There's no logical reason to draw hearts all over the place on Valentine's Day. The heart is just an organ of the body that pumps blood. But when we give each other heart-shaped boxes of candy for Valentine's Day, we are acknowledging a very old tradition that places the sensible soul—that is, the emotions—in the heart."

Landon Hopkins raised his hand for another question. I really am not going to live through this class, thought Thomas. His sister, Barbara, claimed that she had never been bored in an English class. Barbara was a senior at Mason School. She was the one, in fact, whose friends had the party in McLean where he'd met Hesta. He wondered if Barbara had lost her virginity. That was a pretty nasty thought. You don't usually think of your sister as actually being a girl, or rather as being like a regular girl whose panties you'd want to grab. It made him mad to think of Ned Wood or some other guy she'd been out with trying to grab Barbara's panties. On the other hand, was anybody up in McLean getting mad at Thomas now for trying to grab Hesta's panties? Not that he had done so. Hesta didn't have any brothers, only this one sister who was twelve years older and already married now. What if Hesta did have a brother, though? Would he get mad at Thomas for trying to grab Hesta's panties, which he hadn't even tried to grab yet? They'd only been out twice, after all, but he thought about her anatomy almost constantly.

Thomas had a brother himself, Jeff, who was two years younger. Somehow it wasn't so bad to think of your brother getting laid someday, as long as it happened when Jeff was older than Thomas was whenever Thomas lost his own virginity. Across the room Richard pretended to be picking his nose.

"That brings us to the rational soul," said Mr. Farnham, who was drawing arrows like crazy all over the board. "It's the rational soul, seated in the mind, that is superior to the sensible soul in the heart"—he pointed—"and to the animal soul in the liver"—he pointed again. "The rational soul is, of course, the source of our power to reason, and it is reason that keeps humanity from simply behaving like one of the lesser beasts. We do have urges and emotions, but we are blessed with reason so that we may keep those urges under control. We may feel lust for a woman, for example, but we must resist the temptation to indulge that lust. Otherwise, we have committed the sin"—he pointed again—"of *cupiditas,* of letting our natural concupiscence and our God-given sexual desire to become a form of idolatry. Any questions?"

Go ahead, Landon, thought Thomas. Ask him a question. Thomas felt an overpowering urge to look at his watch. Is it too early? Should I or shouldn't I? This conflict would be a good example for Mr. Farnham to spaz about in class, with Thomas's heart telling him to go ahead and look at the damn watch while his brain was telling him to wait, to be cautious.

"All of this," said Mr. Farnham, pulling out his chair and

sitting down at the tidy desk, "is by way of introduction to the next play we're going to read—"

Here it comes, thought Thomas, the bad news. Richard was sitting across from him with his fingers crossed and his eyes closed.

"—William Shakespeare's *Othello*—"

Oh, well. Could be worse. He knew everybody else in the class would be going berserk. They hated Shakespeare worse than anything because he was so hard to read. Thomas kept it to himself that he sort of liked Shakespeare. You don't go telling people that, unless you're some total reptile like Landon Hopkins. Thomas groaned along with the rest of the class, but only so they wouldn't think he was a nerd.

"—for which you are expected to read and outline—did you hear that, Richard Blackburn?—*and outline* the first two scenes for tomorrow. Landon?"

Landon's hand was up. Landon had a complexion like tomato soup before all the soup mix has dissolved and a skinny neck and an Adam's apple that stuck out and bobbed whenever he talked. He was also unbelievably smart because he was unbelievably geeky enough to study all the damn time. "Is that the same kind of outline we did for *Oedipus Rex*?" asked Landon. Mr. Farnham said yes.

"I think you'll enjoy *Othello*," said Mr. Farnham. "It features one of the most evil characters in all of literature, a man named Iago. He looks normal to everybody else, but he turns out to be a sex pervert."

Now he's exaggerating to get us interested, thought Thomas.

"Imagine the tension," said Mr. Farnham. "The audience knows, but the characters don't, that one of them is a dangerously corrupt villain. Only he appears perfectly normal to all the others on stage."

The bell rang.

I do believe in miracles, I do, I do, thought Thomas. He'd been right not to look at his watch. He'd have to remember that in Heilman's religion class, which was even more boring than Farnham's English class. He began to scoop up his other books and notebooks from under the desk.

"Mr. Boatwright, could I speak to you before you leave?" said Mr. Farnham.

Damn. You can't get away with a thing in here. Mr. Farnham would be all right if he'd just loosen up once in a while. So a guy daydreams for a minute or two during a lecture. So what? Nobody pays perfect attention to everything.

He approached Farnham's desk with books in hand and coat on. Richard bumped him on the way out the door, and Thomas responded with an elbow. Farnham waited until everyone was out of the room before he spoke.

"Do you have a class next period?"

"Geometry."

"I won't keep you long. Did you know that I'm directing *Othello* as the winter play? We go up in early March."

"Yes sir." How the hell could he not know it? Farnham had been advertising auditions for a week before Thanksgiving.

"Have you given any thought to trying out for a part?"

No, he hadn't. "I just made the basketball team," said Thomas. "JV, I mean."

Farnham nodded. It seemed as though he'd rehearsed every gesture. "You'd be good at basketball, I imagine," he said. "You're tall, well built."

This was a little embarrassing.

"What about doing both?" said Farnham. "You could take a small part in the play, something like Desdemona's father, and only rehearse once a week."

"I don't know," said Thomas. He really didn't know. He did like to act; he and Barbara and Jeff had been doing their own shows at home in the living room ever since they were little kids. But the guys who did theater here were sort of on the fringe of things. Thomas wanted to fit in.

"Your father was excited about the idea of our doing Shakespeare when I spoke with him over Parents' Weekend," said Mr. Farnham.

"Oh," said Thomas. So that was it. He wanted Thomas in the play because he happened to be the son of Preston Boatwright, who happened to be the drama critic for the biggest newspaper in Washington.

"Don't get all down in the mouth," said Mr. Farnham. "What did I say?"

"You're just asking me to be in the play because my dad was pushing you to."

"That's not true." He pulled his chin up a notch. Farnham was a small man, 5′6″, 130 pounds. He looked like he shaved around that mustache maybe once a week, and with his short brown hair and his tortoiseshells he could pass for a sixth-former.

"He's always prodding me to be in the plays here," said Thomas. "What did he say, that he'd give you publicity in the *Post* if you gave me a part?"

Mr. Farnham's face flashed red as though a spotlight had hit it. "What he said," said Mr. Farnham, "was that you were good."

Thomas was surprised, then pleased. It was pretty neat to hear even a secondhand compliment from his dad.

"I don't know," he said. "Coach McPhee says we'll be pretty busy."

"Come by the theater after basketball practice this afternoon. We can talk about a part then."

Thomas had to go to class.

"I don't know, Mr. Farnham," he said, as he backed toward the door.

"Just come by anyway," said Mr. Farnham. He smiled. "We can just talk. You can tell me about your Thanksgiving holiday."

"Yes sir," said Thomas. Dammit to hell, can't he understand when somebody says no? Be polite anyway. "Did you have a good holiday?"

"I had an excellent holiday," said Mr. Farnham. "I went to New York."

But Thomas did not have time to hear about some boring trip to New York.

Scene 3

Benjamin Warden looked down at the papers in front of him. It had been a cheap trick to assign some writing in class on the first day back from vacation, but it had kept him from having to run the class. Now, however, he had to grade the results.

It was 10:15 in the morning. Three class periods had already met, and now it was recess, a half hour for the boys to clean their dormitory rooms for inspection. Warden was trying to keep his mind off Cynthia and on schoolwork, but his thoughts refused to be so tractable.

As department chairman, Warden taught three sections, two of which were electives in creative writing, where he worked with the most gifted seniors. These papers, however, were from his class of sophomores, his only section that happened to meet on Monday morning—and his only problem class. They were the remedial section of fourth-form English, still working on grammar and the most elementary principles of composition, though Warden was eager to get them into writing poetry and spending more time on literature. Today he had forgone grammar and had given the class six words, all six of which they were to use in a poem. He had allowed them forty-five minutes—the entire period—to work.

The six words, which embraced at least four parts of speech and three of the five senses, were "muffin," "licorice," "blithely," "strummed," "squeaky," and "moist." Robert Staines had written the poem on the top of the pile:

My mother baked,
A licorice muffin,
It tasted like turkey,
Without any stuffin',

The inside was moist,
The outside was squeaky,
I strummed when I ate it,
Delicious and blithely.

Warden had watched Staines work. The boy had taken five minutes to dash off the writing, and then he had doodled until the end of the period when his classmates turned in their papers. What annoyed Warden was that Staines's poem was actually all right, if only by accident. He had produced some startling images—"the outside was squeaky" and "I strummed when I ate it"—but Warden knew the boy was unappreciative of his own inadvertent imagery. It was the old dilemma of the English teacher: to praise work for what he saw in it, or to nail the student for not taking the assignment seriously.

Warden knew that he was supposed to be objective about all his students, and he could usually find something likeable about everyone in a class. Not Staines. There was something shifty and arrogant about Staines. He was a good athlete, but he was absolutely uninterested in anything academic. In his poem, for instance, he hadn't even tried to find out what the words meant. "Delicious and blithely": that was an accidentally interesting line. Warden supposed that he should give the boy some credit for the clever feminine rhyme of "muffin" with "stuffin'."

Why hadn't anybody called from the doctor's?

Warden had wanted to summon an ambulance this morning, but Cynthia had stopped him. She had already arranged transportation with Kathleen Somerville last night, and she had told the doctor she was coming. She had also accused Warden of missing too many classes with his readings anyway. He had allowed her to prevail, and now he felt guilty and frustrated for doing so.

What was the diagnosis?

He hunted through the pile of papers until he found the Lipscomb boy's work. This one was likely to be quite good. The boy had no business being in a remedial English class; he was there only because he was a sophomore newboy and Sam Kaufman insisted idiotically that all new sophomores take remedial English until they pass a grammar competency exam. In October he had told Kaufman, the academic dean, that Lipscomb was far too bright to be in a remedial section, but Kaufman had refused to budge until he'd seen the results of the exams in January. Warden wondered whether Kaufman was prejudiced. The Lipscomb boy was black, one of only a handful of minority students at Montpelier.

Greg Lipscomb had written the following:

I fear the white folk
Who want to nibble my skin like licorice;
Peel my ebony armor down
To where it's squeaky white bone;
Cook my heritage until it's as tame as a muffin
They can dip moist in their milk
And blithely swallow in torn pieces;
Boil my muscle into ukulele strings
To play my life like a jingle
Strummed on a cooking show
On color TV.

It was an astonishing piece of work, an angry voice of black indignation, fright, and cynicism. Warden said so in a comment on the paper and hoped that perhaps with enough encouragement the boy would start to believe in his own capabilities. So far Warden had not been able to establish any rapport with him. He did his work faithfully and beautifully, but he seemed to mistrust Warden's praise of his accomplishments.

Warden was alone in his classroom on the third and top floor of Fleming Hall, the academic building. Daylight from the large arched windows helped the overhead neon lamps to brighten and cheer the place, despite the gloom of the winter clouds outside. Cynthia's touches were everywhere in this room—in the geraniums by the windows, in the neatly tacked posters of the English Lake District on the bulletin board, in the postcards of Jane Austen and the Brontë sisters she had taped to a couple of windowpanes. Through those high windows in his corner room he could survey the elliptical lawn around which the school was built, the lawn known on campus as the Quad, even though it was more rounded than quadrangular. He had brought her to this room on her first visit to Montpelier in June two years ago. She had laughed aloud with the delight of seeing the place, and she had made him laugh, had made him see the school afresh.

Ostensibly he had been the one giving her the tour of the campus, but it had been she, not he, who had led them from building to building. His classroom in Fleming Hall was in the lower southeast corner, at 5:00 if the Quad were a clock face. Next door, sprawling from 5:30 to 6:30, was Stringfellow Hall, the main building that housed a bit of everything—the headmaster's office, admissions, alumni relations, the dining hall, the student activities rooms, the post office, the laundry rooms, the school store, and, upstairs, even some dormitories. They had walked clockwise around the campus: at 7:00, Lee House, the infirmary; at 8:00, the headmaster's residence; at 9:00, the chapel; at 10:00 and 11:00, because it was so big, the gym and its various appendages; at 12:00, the Homestead, the squat frame house remaining from Montpelier Plantation, where the Stringfellow family had lived when the school was born, and where Warden's friends the Somervilles lived now.

Cynthia had stood on the white-painted wooden steps of the Homestead in the summer humidity and had seen everything, had admired the jonquils bordering the sidewalks as well as the Blue Ridge Mountains on the western horizon, had noticed the symmetry of the trees on the Quad and the evenness of the roof lines and the way the brick on all the buildings, new or old, matched up perfectly with that of Stringfellow. She had insisted upon visiting every building on the Quad, even the dormitories: Clifton House and Kean House, back to back at 1:00 on the imaginary dial; Stratford House and Siddons House at 2:00; Dupont House at 3:00, and behind it, Bradley Hall, the large arts center built in the late 1960s. At 4:00 Hathaway Library, and, directly behind it, providing a jowl or sideburn to the oval face of the campus, Reid Hall, the science building. Then they had walked the entire course again, this time on the outside of the Quad. She had held his hand and tugged him along the vaguely circular road that divided the central campus from the playing fields, tennis courts, maintenance buildings, faculty houses, parking lots, and woodlands that constituted the rest of the school grounds. They had finished their tour at his home, which then happened to be the smaller of the two apartments in the gym.

It was quiet here in Fleming during recess. He could hear noise from the English office down the hall, where somebody was using the loud clackety printer for their computer. The term "word processing" sounded dreadful to Warden, who refused to use anything but his electric typewriter. Cynthia had bought a computer with some money they had received as a wedding gift. Cynthia. He could not help worrying over her, and yet he felt foolish for not using the time she had given him more productively. He was impressed with how easily he could sit here at his desk and at least appear, despite his distracting anxiety, to be following his normal routine. It was remarkable that the human soul continued to function even in the face of despair.

Now he sounded like an English teacher, a trite one.

Warden stood up and walked down the hall toward Horace Somerville's classroom. Horace was Warden's best friend in the world, though Horace was a generation older and had once terrified Warden as his European history teacher. Warden had been Horace's student in this very building, back when the floors were of dark tile rather than brown carpeting, when the hall lights were white globes suspended on black cords rather than these banks of fluorescent lamps stuck into the ceilings like inverted ice cube trays.

Still, despite its renovations, Fleming Hall remained for its inhabitants in the English, history, and foreign language departments the more distinguished of the school's two academic buildings. Reid Hall, home of the math and science departments, was built only three years ago to provide modern laboratories and antiseptic classrooms, but already the building required major structural repairs. It was sliding down the hill that Montpelier School was built upon. That was the way Warden felt this morning: as though the ground beneath him had started to slide away.

A boy passed him in the hallway and greeted him by

name, a nice-looking boy with longish-blond hair and an armful of books.

"Now your name is—," Warden said. He did not know the boy.

"Russell Phillips." A thin boy, but looking fit.

Warden asked why he wasn't on dorm.

"I cleaned my room before breakfast," said Russell Phillips. "Too cold to walk back to Kean House."

Warden teased him by pointing out the healthful benefits of a brisk walk in chilly weather.

"I'd rather die," said Russell Phillips. Then he continued on his way to the stairs.

The words startled Warden so much that he forgot momentarily where he was going.

Scene 4

Although Horace Somerville had happily occupied the same classroom in Fleming Hall for all thirty-eight of his teaching years at Montpelier, this morning he felt the sameness wearing him out. He was tired of looking at that same map of the ancient world he'd brought down with him from Boston in 1952, those same portraits of the Civil War generals he had put up in 1960, the same cracked old blackboard where he continued to scrawl his assignments. All the fresh paint and the new carpeting (never mind that the carpet was new ten years ago; a decade was still new for Montpelier and for Somerville) and these fancy metal desks that slid around the room instead of remaining firmly planted like the old benches: all this modernism was just superficial cosmetic change. Somerville was having the same damnable conversation he'd had with slovenly students every week of his life since the year Eisenhower was elected president. He was tired of these lazy little ignoramuses who refused to listen to his advice, which at the moment he was dispensing with increasing asperity.

"Learn the dates!" he said for the several dozenth time to the boy in front of him. "Learn the dates! Then you can get to the fun part of history." Little bastard was practically yawning in his face. Somerville would wake him up with a cattle prod.

"Yes sir," said the boy. He was a third-former named Wallace, with straight brown hair cut as though someone had put a bowl over his head and a necktie carelessly tied with the knot too big, the back strand longer than the front. Somerville himself was wearing a starched white shirt and a knit tie. For a while in the 1960s he had gone through a bow tie phase because he'd hated the paisley alternatives. Now he was happy to see the world returning to something resembling sartorial common sense, though this boy had obviously never shined his shoes since the day his extravagantly indulgent mother had bought them for him.

"We offer a fine version of this course in summer school," said Somerville.

"Yes sir."

He was glad to see Wallace squirm a bit, but then the boy astonished him by picking up his books as if their conference were over. Somerville impounded the books and placed them on his desktop, then stared at his student as if the boy were some particularly grotesque piece of unidentifiable offal dragged home by a hunting dog.

"Don't 'yes sir' me. Just learn the dates."

"Yes sir."

It was 10:25, ten minutes into the mid-morning recess. Somerville knew what a charming sight they must make for the random observer, the mop-headed little ninth-grader slouching a bit ("Sit up, boy!") in the straight wooden chair beside Somerville's desk, the experienced old instructor—bright eyes, thick-lensed reading glasses, thinning white hair, basset hound jowls, and overgrown ears—patiently working him through his lessons. Those officious imbeciles in the development office were frequently sneaking photographers over here to catch him in a Norman Rockwell pose, the archetype of the gruff but loving grandfather. Hogwash.

Somerville had kept Wallace after class for failing to do his homework assignment over the Thanksgiving holiday. There was nothing wrong with this boy that a little grit and motivation and intellectual awakening couldn't fix, but the child seemed perfectly content to accept Somerville's finest invective with only a token bit of cringing. Somerville wondered whether he was losing his touch.

"You're probably ready to go now, aren't you?" he said to Wallace.

"Yes sir."

"You'd like to get to your room before it's inspected."

"Yes sir."

"Before somebody sticks you for demerits."

"Yes sir."

"1485."

Somerville noted with pleasure that the boy seemed to lose some height as he realized that he was not yet free.

"Well?" said Somerville.

The boy hesitated. "The Battle of Hastings?" he said.

"That was 1066. 1485."

"The end of the Wars of the Roses?"

"Correct. What was the battle?"

Ben Warden interrupted by knocking on the open door. The boy looked to the doorway at Warden and grinned.

Damn, what a time for Ben to appear. "Answer the question," said Somerville.

"Shrewsbury?"

"That was 1403! Learn the dates!" said Somerville. "Now get along off to your dormitory. You're lucky I need to see Mr. Warden."

The boy picked up his books and passed Warden in the doorway. On the threshold he paused and turned back to Somerville. "Well, what was the battle?"

"That's what I'm asking you!" said Somerville. "Learn the dates!"

Unfazed, the boy turned and asked Warden.

"I believe it was the Battle of Bosworth Field," said Warden. "That's what Shakespeare tells me, anyway."

Somerville rewarded both his auditors with a miniature explosion.

"It wasn't Shakespeare who taught you that date," he said. "I did." He told Wallace that Warden had been his history student in this very course twenty years earlier. "And he was just as miserable at history as you are until I shook some sense into him."

"Neat," said the boy.

"What was that?" said Somerville.

"Yes," said the boy. "Yes sir."

"Get out of here, Wallace, before I tie you up and horsewhip you."

"Yes sir." The boy skidded down the stairs. Likeable little kid, Somerville had to admit, despite the vacuity of his cranium.

He turned his attention to Warden, who indeed had stood many a day in that same doorway. He knew why Warden was there; this morning Kathleen, Somerville's wife, had driven Cynthia Warden—with what sounded like a potentially dangerous neural disorder—to see a doctor in Charlottesville. Warden was a model of disorder himself, looking as unraveled as the threads on his old corduroy trousers and as ragged as the collar on his shirt. Somerville had always admired Warden's well-preserved youth, down to the carelessness of his attire. Despite fourteen years of boarding school life, Warden had retained his trim undergraduate figure and his thick black hair; it was as though the birthmark on his face had absorbed all the other ravages that time might inflict on a human body. But this morning he looked as tired of life as Somerville was of adolescent lassitude.

Warden sat in the chair recently vacated by Wallace, the third-former. Somerville sat beside him and waited. They had shared this routine many times over the years. One of them would seek counsel, and the other would provide it.

"They're on to you," said Warden. "Everybody knows you're all bark."

"I've got a few teeth left," said Somerville. He had liked Warden from the moment he'd met him all those history lessons ago.

Warden asked if Kathleen had called.

Somerville shook his head. He said he would not expect

them to call, but simply to drive back to the campus when the examination concluded.

"Unless they send her to the hospital," said Warden.

Somerville sat with a hand on each of his knees. His gray flannel trousers were perfectly pressed. He reminded Warden that waiting rooms were notoriously slow. All of them on the faculty had taken turns over the years at driving injured boys to doctors' offices and emergency rooms in Charlottesville, forty miles away. With 360 boys enrolled, and all of them required to participate in athletics, one was always requiring X rays or stitches or plaster.

"I should be with her," said Warden.

"My wife is acceptable company."

"I'm scared she has cancer," said Warden.

It was a word Somerville hated to hear. His son Alfred had died of intestinal cancer twenty-nine months ago, just before Ben's wedding to Cynthia. Alfred had been thirty-one years old. But Somerville accepted Warden's amateur diagnosis. He and Kathleen had discussed Cynthia's symptoms and had speculated the same conclusion. "She might," he said. "I pray not."

"What should I do?" asked Warden.

"Wait. Hope. She's a young woman," he said. "Don't bury her yet."

Warden said that was exactly what he had been doing—acting as though her death were already decreed. "What are the five stages you're supposed to go through? Depression, anger—?"

Oh, Lord, he's been reading those pop psychology books. Somerville had tried that route himself a few years ago, but he had found that the Episcopal Book of Common Prayer was sufficient psychology for him. (And then they changed the prayer book!) He forced himself to concentrate on Warden. "Denial is the first stage," said Somerville. "Anger, depression, bargaining." How many times he had searched those books for some source of comfort. "Finally you get to acceptance. It took me a while to reach that last stage."

Warden asked him the difference between denial and optimism.

Somerville did not answer. He stared at the three-year-old calendar on the white wall of his classroom and sought a fresh way of articulating the peace that accompanied religious faith. It was one of their favorite topics of argument.

Warden must have misunderstood his silence. "I'm afraid I've dredged up some sad memories, Horace," he said. "I'm sorry."

"Don't be foolish," said Somerville. "Alfred had a good life, no matter how short." He wanted to stress the positive. "He went out with dignity, and knowing we loved him."

"At least he died quickly," said Warden.

"Yes," said Somerville, "it would have been much worse to watch him . . ."

"Linger," Warden finished the sentence for him.

Damn it to hell, that was careless. Somerville knew Warden had watched both parents die very slowly over the past five years. "It's my turn to apologize, Ben," he said. "I shouldn't have said that." But he was silently annoyed with Warden for trapping him into a faux pas.

Warden waved his apology away.

"I came in here to be distracted," he said. "You're doing your best."

Somerville asked him about his trip to New York.

"Absolutely uneventful," said Warden. "Nothing newsworthy happened at all." But as he sat with his friend, Warden recalled uneasily that something indeed had happened. Something he could not mention to anybody.

Not yet.

Scene 5

As a junior varsity basketball player, Thomas Boatwright practiced in the old gym. The varsity teams—basketball, wrestling, swimming, and indoor track—got all the locker rooms and the facilities in the huge new sports complex called the Fieldhouse which was built out the back of the old gym, but Thomas did not especially mind. There was something nice about the traditions attached to the older building. He stepped into the vestibule of the gym and immediately turned down the stairs to his right. All the locker rooms were on the same basement level. He supposed they'd have to change that if the place ever went coed.

Angus Farrier was pushing a dustmop down the smooth concrete halls as Thomas approached the door to the JV basketball locker room.

"Use the handle," said Angus, which was his way of telling Thomas that he had just cleaned the glass of the door and that he didn't want fingerprints on the surface.

"Window open?" asked Thomas.

"Them's already in there," said Angus. "Had some help."

Thomas had never seen Angus dressed in anything other than what he had on now: a white tee shirt and clean olive trousers. Angus was thin and tall and very strong, with white hair in a crew cut and wrinkles all over his face. His eyes were a light blue, his skin doughy white, as though he never emerged into the sunlight. Some of the boys said he never did, that he lived in his lair in the basement all the time, where he kept an old desk beside the furnace and the boiler. He had probably been working at the school ever since Mr. Stringfellow started the place a million years ago. Everybody knew Angus. He ran the gym, kept it clean, washed all the uniforms and practice equipment, and prepared daily the 350 rolls of jocks, socks, shorts, shirts, and towels nearly every boy on the campus would use in the course of a practice. Sometimes, when he had fewer chores on a given day, he would distribute the rolls to each boy's locker in each locker room, rather than wait at his wire-mesh window for the boys to pick them up.

Inside the locker room bright fluorescent ceiling lights shone on carpet the color of ripe watermelon and on dark green benches. One row of lockers ran along the walls, and another group was clustered in an island in the center of the room. The lockers were not actually lockers, but wooden cubicles, also painted green. Thomas's was just to the right of the door. A white adhesive tape strip saying BOATWRIGHT ran across the top of Thomas's locker. He was proud of it. On the shelf at eye level was a rolled-up towel containing all his practice clothes.

Ralph Musgrove was already in the locker room and getting dressed for practice.

"Hey, Tom."

"Hey, Ralph."

Ralph was the starting center, five inches taller than Thomas, 6′5″ as opposed to 6′0″, and he was stockier, stronger, and quicker. He had a great shot, too, and he could zip passes through all kinds of traffic. His only weakness was that he couldn't dribble with his left hand. Thomas was the second-string point guard, but he would soon be third-string if his shooting did not improve.

Robert Staines entered the locker room while Thomas was getting undressed. Staines was a starter at wing.

"Hey, Musgrove. Hey, Boatwright."

"Hey."

"Hey."

Staines was the kind of person who seemed like the greatest guy in the world for the first thirty seconds. He looked just like one of those surfers in the Pepsi ads on TV. He had blond hair that flopped just above his ears and perfect teeth, which he was always showing you in a big grin. He was a couple of inches shorter than Thomas, but much stockier. He probably weighed twenty pounds more, and he looked older, broader-shouldered, thicker in the chest.

"You have a good holiday, Ralph?" asked Staines as he stripped off his clothes. Staines was the fastest dresser you ever saw.

"Pretty good."

"I got laid so many times I lost count."

Ralph said it wasn't too hard to count to zero.

"How about you, Boatwright? You get your paddle wet?"

"Not really." Same old conversation.

"You're not aggressive enough," said Staines. "You got to know what you want, and go after it."

Thomas had roomed with Staines during their freshman year and had hated his guts most days of the week. Staines was never, ever serious about anything except sports. Not that Thomas was some big study fish or anything, but Staines was a ridiculous goof-off. For the first month of school they were always getting demerits from Mr. Delaney, the house master over on Kean House, where most of the ninth-graders lived, and a couple of times they got called into Mr. Grayson's office for playing their stereo during study hours. Mr. Delaney, who was also the varsity basketball coach, liked Staines because Staines was a good athlete; but Delaney was also fair, and finally, after about a million times of his walking into their room and finding Thomas lying in bed with a history book open and Staines lip-synching in the middle of the room to his Springsteen album, Delaney realized that maybe these guys weren't equally responsible for the noise. So Staines started going to the disciplinarian's office alone, and then, when his fall trimester grades came out, he started going to required supervised study hall during the evenings in the big lecture hall in the basement of Fleming.

The problem with Staines was that he would never shut up. Study hours ran from 7:30 to 9:30 every night, Sunday through Friday, and about the only time the room was quiet for Thomas was the time that Staines was required to be in supervised study hall. As soon as the bell rang at 9:30, Thomas would leave his room and go next door to visit with his friend Richard Blackburn, who'd gotten stuck rooming with the geek of all geeks, Landon Hopkins. Since most of the freshmen didn't know anybody else coming to the school, it was a waste of time for them to request roommates, so they just got matched up by Dean Kaufman. Dean Kaufman was a dork.

He had been able to escape Staines until 10:00, when all the freshmen were required to be on dorm and in their rooms. They had to have their lights out at 10:30, which had given Staines thirty minutes to talk Thomas's buns off. He would talk about two subjects—sports and sex.

"Are you a virgin?" Staines had asked him once early in the year in one of his rare nonrhetorical questions.

Thomas had said, yeah, sure, of course he was, he was only fourteen years old.

"Hell, I lost it in the eighth grade," Staines had said. "My girlfriend used to come watch my football practice. . . ." And he had been off and running down the field of his story.

He was always claiming to be unable to keep track of his own exploits.

"I got laid so many times over Christmas I lost count," he'd say, or "Did you have a good spring break? I got laid so many times I lost count."

Finally Richard Blackburn had suggested that he get a pocket calculator, to which Staines had replied by punching Richard on the upper arm, for which Richard had retaliated later by going into Staines's dresser drawers and putting Ben-Gay in Staines's jockstrap. The result, when Staines finally had put the damn thing on, was that he had done this weird little dance all the way down the hall to the shower. That had inspired Richard to call him The Big Blond Gorilla. Staines had responded just by pounding the hell out of Richard.

But that was all last year. They were old boys now.

Staines tied his white Converse basketball shoes with double knots and headed for the bathroom.

"You know what your problem with girls is, Boatwright?" he called from the urinals. His voice echoed off the tiles. "No offense?"

Thomas knew that whatever followed was going to be highly offensive. People like Staines thought they could say any damn thing they wanted to, as long as they prefaced it with some disclaimer.

Staines did not wait for a reply. "It's probably some unconscious hormone they smell," he said. "I noticed a certain odor in your dorm room last night."

Thomas said he hadn't noticed any smell.

"It's nigger," Staines said. "You probably can't smell it. You live with them, you start to smell like them, too."

That can't be true, Thomas thought. I lived with you all last year, and I never smelled like an asshole. He felt like saying he was tired of Staines's bigotry and boorishness and didn't want to hear the guy's voice again.

But, as usual, what he said instead was nothing.

Scene 6

Practice was terrible, partly because Thomas Boatwright had not worked enough on basketball over the holidays, and partly because he was so distracted by Robert Staines. The guy had called his roommate a nigger. What a jerk. And Thomas had said nothing about it. What a bigger jerk.

Many times Thomas had practiced the speech he was going to make to Staines one day, the speech in which he would tell the guy just what a cheese-brained, smelly-footed, hormonally imbalanced, white-supremacist ball of kitty litter he really was. Thomas polished that speech constantly. One day he would have the nerve to deliver it.

Staines was intimidating. He seemed so socially sophisticated, so well coordinated, so comfortable with what he wanted out of life. He was a great athlete, and most of his friends were upperclassmen. Thomas regarded Staines with equal measures of envy and scorn. The problem was that Thomas did not want to receive the scorn of Staines in return. So he kept his mouth shut and told himself that Greg wasn't worth the hassle anyway.

The whole day was turning out to be a pain in the posterior.

It was nearly 6:00 in the afternoon and had been dark for over half an hour. Thomas was freezing as he walked from the gym across the Quad to Bradley Hall, where he'd promised Farnham that he'd come by about an audition for *Othello.* His head was still wet from the shower, and the wind was blowing so hard that he thought his hair might freeze. Out of the pocket of his trench coat he pulled a blue knit stocking cap and tugged it all the way down over his ears. There were too many damn things going on around this place at the same time. Farnham wanted him in the play; McPhee knew that practice was supposed to be out at

5:30 but kept everyone back shooting free throws; Hesta was counting on him to call her sometime this afternoon; and he still had all that Shakespeare to read.

Bradley Hall was one of a row of buildings behind and parallel to the buildings lining the eastern edge of the Quad. It was built in the 1960s, with glass doors and lots of floor-to-ceiling windows in the entrance hall. All the lights were still burning in the plaster-and-marble lobby.

When he was still fifty yards away, Thomas saw someone emerge from the building through the big glass doors, lurch, stagger, and then limp on off into the darkness, heading north, toward the dorms. It was a figure so bundled up against the cold that he could not tell who it was, or even how old. It looked like the person was drunk.

"Richard?" Thomas called. The person did not answer, but hurried off into the darkness.

Richard had signed up to be on the technical crew for the play on the grounds that it would be the easiest, warmest, most convenient way to spend the winter. That would be just great, thought Thomas, if Richard got himself thrown out of school for partying down at the theater. Dr. Lane, the headmaster, was so strict about enforcing the rules banning drugs and alcohol from the campus that hardly anybody took the risk. It was easy enough to get away for the weekend, where school rules didn't apply. Whoever this was at Bradley had been heading off toward the dorms on the eastern Quad, one of which was Stratford House, which was Richard's dorm. Don't be stupid, Richard, thought Thomas as he entered the warm brightness of Bradley.

The foyer was a large room with a couple of sofas and an Oriental rug and portraits of famous alumni on the walls. Straight ahead were the doors to the bathrooms. To the left was the hallway leading to the rooms for studio art and music and the backstage area. To the right was the entrance to the auditorium itself. Thomas heard noises to the left and headed down the hallway for the backstage area. He could hear a regular thwacking sound, as if someone were trying to open a crate by throwing it regularly onto the floor.

Hardly any lights were on in the hall, just every other ceiling spot shining out through the white acoustical tile. The door to his left led to the gigantic art studio, which was now dark. There were two doors to his right. The nearer door led backstage, which was also dark. Thomas did not see anyone in the building, but he assumed somebody was here. He saw a light and heard noise coming from the door to the scene shop. His basketball shoes were quiet on the sleek green linoleum as he approached the open door.

In the scene shop Thomas could see Mr. Farnham standing with his back toward him. Farnham was wearing an old sweater and paint-speckled blue jeans and Adidas running shoes. He was holding a two-by-four about three feet long—holding it with both hands, raising it over his head, and bringing it down hard onto the concrete floor, as if it were an axe and the floor were a tough log. As he swung, he grunted wildly, almost as if he were the one being hit. Thomas watched him swing it three times. He grunted louder and louder and swung harder and harder with the board until it splintered and broke off at the end.

There was an energy in the air that made Thomas shudder. Anger was radiating out of Mr. Farnham like light from a torch, and Thomas could feel it, sense it. Mr. Farnham took the broken board and threw it hard against the cinder-block wall. Then he turned toward the door. Thomas himself spun away out of the light of the door and ran back down the hall to the exit. He did not want Mr. Farnham to know that he'd been there, that he had seen the teacher acting like King Kong on speed.

No winter play for me, he thought, thank you just the same.

It was time to go home.

Scene 7

Thomas Boatwright and Greg Lipscomb lived in a typical dormitory room, nearly a perfect square, symmetric, with a single bed on each side of the room, two desks between the beds, two dressers at the foot of the beds, two closets facing the dressers, the entrance to the room between the two closets. There was one big window over the desks. They had an oval hooked rug in the middle of the floor and posters of everybody you've ever seen all over the walls. Greg had a stereo next to his dresser with tapes and albums, but half of them—Thomas couldn't believe this—were sound tracks to Broadway musicals or, even worse, classical music.

Greg was lying on his bed and reading a paperback when Thomas entered the room. The stereo was playing something by Bach or Schubert or somebody. Thomas turned it down.

"Hey," said Greg. He looked at Thomas over the top edge of his book.

"I got to ask you about Farnham," said Thomas. He took off his hat and coat, sat on his own bed, and faced Greg. "What kind of mood was he in at play practice this afternoon?"

Greg had on white socks, jeans, and a thick yellow wool sweater. His skin was the color of black coffee, and his fuzzy hair was cut to within an inch of his head—a small Afro.

"Just fine," said Greg. He did not look up from his book.

"Something weird happened just now," said Thomas, "when I went over to talk about the play."

"You're going to be in the play?" Now Greg looked up at him. The whites of his eyes looked faintly yellow in the light of the study lamp.

The way he said it pissed Thomas off a little. "Maybe," he said. "If I want to be in the play, I'll be in the play. What's the matter with it?"

"It's fine." Greg turned back to his book.

"You know," said Thomas, "maybe I'd talk to you more if you gave me some kind of reason to start a conversation."

Greg kept his eyes on the page. "You told me Staines got on your nerves last year for talking. Now you say I don't talk enough. Staines is right next door if you want somebody to talk. I don't."

Screw this. Thomas walked out of the room. On his way, he turned up the stereo to louder than it had been before.

"Hey," Greg yelled. Thomas kept walking. Maybe it did stink a little in their room. Maybe Staines wasn't so bigoted after all.

Next door, Staines had his own stereo cranked, playing brassy pep songs from the University of North Carolina. Somehow he was tying his necktie for dinner at the same time he pretended to play the drums. He lived in a single, which meant that his room was the size of a good walk-in closet. Nevertheless, he was so wound up in his own performance and so deafened by the music that he did not notice Thomas's entry at first.

Staines was from Morganton, North Carolina, and if he wasn't discussing sex, then he was likely to be talking the same kind of trash about the University of North Carolina's basketball team. Dean Smith, the four corners, Carolina Blue, Blue Heaven, Tar Heel born and Tar Heel bred—Thomas had gotten tired of the spiel by October, before the basketball season had even started.

This is what you wanted to get away from, Thomas thought. He had made a mistake to come here. Staines was no guy to confide in about anything. But before he could leave, Staines saw him in the mirror, boogied a little, then turned down the stereo one notch.

"Are you trying to drown out my music over there?" Staines yelled.

"It's not me," Thomas yelled back.

"What?" yelled Staines.

They might have gone hoarse if Mr. Carella hadn't burst into the room on them. He didn't say anything. He just turned off the power switch on the stereo. The record croaked to a stop.

Mr. Carella was the dorm master on their floor and lived in the faculty apartment at the end of the hall. He was the same age bracket chronologically as Farnham, but he seemed about fifty years younger. Not only was he the perfect dorm master—young, funny, and hardly ever around—but he was also the first good science teacher Thomas had ever had in his life.

"Sounds of silence," said Carella. "Lipscomb's Mozart is better than your Tar Heel crap, but my first choice is to hear nothing but my own stomach growling."

It was quiet next door, too. Carella must have stopped there on the way over.

As usual he seemed to be like a truck idling, slightly

bouncing with all that potential energy. He was short and broad and muscular, with a head one size too big and black hair that curled down over his ears. He was barefooted and had his tie halfway on.

"I have some bad news for you, gentlemen," said Mr. Carella.

Staines interrupted him. "No demerits," he said. "Not with the mixer this weekend."

"No demerits this time," said Carella. "Schoolwork. I have posted a change in the biology syllabus on the bulletin board downstairs. Your lab reports are due tomorrow instead of Wednesday."

"Because of a loud stereo?" said Staines.

"Of course not. This assignment is for the whole class," said Carella. He was a new teacher who wasn't very well organized.

They both protested.

"I know, I know, things are rough all over," said Carella. "Spread the word to the others. I'll make an announcement at dinner tonight. Lab reports due tomorrow."

He slapped Thomas on the shoulder as if he had just delivered a baby and then left. Thomas was shell-shocked: quadruple damn it to hell's shit supply; that was all he needed, more schoolwork to do.

"Have you started your lab report yet?" said Staines.

"Hell no."

"You want to work together on it?"

"I don't know," said Thomas. "I've got so much to do tonight." He knew that working with Staines meant that Thomas would do the work and Staines would try to copy it. You just couldn't trust him. Montpelier operated on an honor system, and Staines was always pushing it to the limit. At basketball practice he would call you for stepping out of bounds when you didn't, or call you for a foul when you hadn't touched him. There was talk on the dorm last year when Staines came into a good bit of cash at the same time that Landon Hopkins missed the money he'd gotten for his birthday. And once in October Thomas had surprised Staines going through Greg's dresser.

"You've got to do the lab, too, don't you?" said Staines.

"Maybe I'll do it in the morning."

It wasn't ever quite enough to call in the honor council, but it was enough to make you want to move off his dorm, which is exactly what Thomas tried to do at the end of last year. And now here was Staines as his closest neighbor. Maybe he should just live in the damn gym like McPhee and Farnham. Dean Kaufman could move Farnham onto the dorm to work with Greg on the play, and Thomas could take over his apartment.

"I need to work on that lab with somebody," said Staines.

"Ask Greg," said Thomas. "He's in the class."

"Boys like Greg are for cleaning up labs, not writing reports on them," said Staines.

It was enough to drive Thomas back to his own room.

Scene 8

Thomas's problems with Greg went back a long way.

Montpelier School for Boys was over a hundred years old, but it had been racially integrated for only about twenty years. They still had a hard time recruiting blacks. This year, for instance, there were only five black guys in the whole school.

One of them was Thomas's roommate.

Dean Kaufman had called Thomas in last spring at the end of his newboy year to ask him if he'd be willing to room with a new black student.

"He's very interested in theater," the dean had said. "And considering your background, I thought . . ."

Finish your sentence, Dean Kaufman, Thomas had thought. That was a running joke around the school, the way the dean never finished his sentences. Kaufman the Clueless, everybody called him.

"I was going to room with Richard Blackburn," Thomas had said. He hadn't wanted a black roommate. Not that he was prejudiced. He'd gone to school at Cathedral Academy with black kids before he'd come to Montpelier and believed in affirmative action and equal opportunity and civil rights. Still, there was something unsettling about rooming with a black guy, a total stranger and all.

"You and Richard could still be very good friends," Dean Kaufman had said.

"Could we be on the same dorm?"

"Sure, sure," Dean Kaufman had said. "Of course you could. And I think you'd really enjoy Greg. He'll be a fourth-former, like you, and he's from Baltimore, so maybe during vacations, I don't know, since you're from Washington, maybe you could, you know . . ."

"Get together."

"Exactly."

Dean Kaufman was such a loser. Everybody called him Bozo because of his thick black glasses frames and his frizzy brown hair he combed straight back off his high forehead.

What else could Thomas have said except sure, he'd be glad to? When he'd told his parents, they'd been very happy—good opportunity, high tribute to you, son, and all that other stuff. So he'd written Greg Lipscomb a letter over the summer, and Greg'd written back in that really tidy block print he always wrote in, and in August Greg's mom had driven him down to Washington in their new Honda Civic, and they'd spent the weekend messing around in Washington just to get to know each other before the fall.

Greg had really been fun that weekend, cracking hilarious jokes and eager to do anything anybody'd suggested. Thomas had been looking forward to rooming with him. And in September, when they'd moved into their room on Middle Stringfellow, things had been nearly perfect at first. Thomas had been mad that Richard Blackburn wasn't living on Stringfellow at all, that Richard and Ralph Musgrove, his roommate, had been put in a room all the way over on Stratford House. It was so typical of Dean Kaufman to screw everything up. That was still okay, though, because Thomas went over to Stratford House a lot anyway to see his advisor, Mr. Warden, who lived there in one of the apartments. And it turned out that Thomas and Richard were in a bunch of classes together anyway, and they were both third-string on the JV football team.

At first Greg had fit right in. You would have hardly thought he was a newboy at all, the way he learned his way around the school so quickly—not the geography so much, which was easy, but the other stuff, the stuff you never see written down but just understand somehow, like always standing up at the dinner table until the master of the table arrives, or letting the seniors break in line at the snack bar during study hall break.

Then something had changed. It was gradual, though, for Thomas couldn't pin it down to a particular day or incident. Maybe it was when they'd found out that Greg was going to audition for the fall play instead of go out for a sport. Everybody at Montpelier had to participate in athletics all year long—football, basketball, baseball; or cross-country, wrestling, track; or soccer, swimming, tennis; or some other combination—but you could get out of sports for a season if you were involved in a play. They said the play was equivalent to the athletic commitment. That was true enough as far as the time went; those guys spent hours over at Bradley getting ready for the performances. The students were wary, however, about drama. You had to be careful about which play you were in. It was okay to be in the spring play, because a bunch of seniors usually went out for parts just to say they'd done it before they graduated. It was even okay most of the time to be in the winter play, as long as some cool people were in it. But you never, never went out for the fall play. Fall was football season, and football was king of the sports; you were considered a geek if you did drama in the fall.

Especially if you were a good athlete, like Greg. He was big, around six feet tall and 170 pounds, and he was only fifteen years old. They'd shot some basketball on the tiny little court Thomas's dad had put into their backyard at the townhouse in Georgetown, and Greg had eaten Thomas up. He'd killed him. He could catch a football, too, as they'd seen within a day or so of his arrival at school, when a pass from a pickup game on the Quad had gone wild and from the sidewalk Greg had just snared it with one hand, with one single hand, and had flipped it back about forty yards to the players. He was an awesome athlete. Thomas just couldn't understand it when he said he wasn't going out for football.

"I didn't come here to play football," Greg had said. "I could play football at home."

"Yeah, but you could probably make the varsity. You could still go out for a play in the spring."

"I'm playing tennis in the spring," Greg had said.

Thomas had warned him that nobody would think he was cool.

"I didn't come here to be cool," Greg had said.

Thomas had said he didn't understand why a person would deliberately sabotage his chance to fit in.

So Greg had done a dinky little one-act play in the fall, and then damned if he hadn't gone out for the winter play as well. He'd even asked Farnham to do *Othello* so he could be the star.

Thomas had begged him to go out for basketball. "We need you," he'd said. "We don't have a single black guy on our team."

Greg had just shaken his head in that irritatingly stubborn way of his.

After that day, they hadn't done much talking. Greg spent most of his time reading or studying by himself. Sometimes an entire evening in the room would pass without either one saying a word to the other.

And just before Thanksgiving, Thomas had arranged to room with Richard Blackburn for the next academic year.

Scene 9

A tumor.

Cynthia and Benjamin Warden sat side by side on the sofa in their living room. It was 7:15 P.M., and the dormitory around them was noisy in the last-minute rush before study hours began at 7:30. It had been their decision, though, to live in such turmoil. When they were married, Eldridge Lane, the headmaster, had offered them a quiet, private house outside the perimeter of the central campus, but Cynthia had objected on the grounds that she would not have been as active in the life of the school. In typical fashion, she had demanded to participate. So they had taken Stratford House on the Quad.

Tonight was the first time Warden had regretted their choice of housing. Cynthia, trying to rest, had her eyes closed and her head back on the corduroy slipcover.

"It's the oddest sensation," she said. "Like falling but never hitting the bottom. I'm falling to the left."

Degenerative nerve disease.

Warden told her that she should be in bed.

"I could just go to sleep right here."

"Why don't you, then?"

"Because we have to talk about Christmas."

Warden thought it was crazy for them to be sitting here having such an ordinary conversation under such extraordinary circumstances. Cynthia had come home at 3:00 in the afternoon exhausted from tests and doctors. She was to check into the hospital for more tests tomorrow.

"Shouldn't we wait to find out what's making you sick?"

"Maybe we should," she said, "but Margaret deserves a reply to her letter."

Margaret was Warden's sister-in-law, married to his brother Lawrence. They lived in Atlanta with their son, Joshua, who had drawn the decoration for the refrigerator door, and they had invited the Wardens to stay with them for Christmas. Harold Cunningham, Cynthia's father, had also issued an invitation for them to spend Christmas with him on his farm in Warrenton.

A stroke.

Dr. Manning had sent her from his office to that of a neurologist. The specialist had told her that he wasn't sure of what she might have; it could be anything from a freak viral infection that would pass from her system to something more serious: a growth, a stroke, cancer.

Cancer.

Warden was trying to sensitize himself to the word, the ugly, hard, cutting syllables with the serpent's hiss at the end. He was playing over and over all the dreadful possibilities.

But, he reminded himself, it could be nothing serious.

"I vote for a holiday here," said Warden. "Start our own traditions. Atlanta is too far. Harold could come visit us."

"Dad doesn't leave the farm."

"Not for ordinary events like our wedding. But maybe he'd come if we invited him for Christmas." Maybe, he thought, if Harold knew his daughter was dying. Harold had raised Cynthia on his horse farm single-handedly since the divorce almost two decades ago. Cynthia's mother had bred dogs. Upon discovering that she liked dogs better than babies, Mrs. Cunningham had moved away when Cynthia was three, taking all the dogs and leaving her only child. Cynthia had stopped hearing from her mother after her sixteenth birthday.

"Dad's been trying, Ben," said Cynthia. "It's just taking him a long time to get used to having his daughter married, that's all."

"To having his daughter married to a freak," said Warden. He touched his birthmark.

"A poet."

"An imperfect foal."

"Go to, sirrah," she said. "He invited us for Christmas. That's progress."

He said he would go if she wanted, would do whatever she liked. "Tomorrow I'm going to wake up and this whole thing is going to be a dream. It's going to be last week again, and we won't have had Thanksgiving yet, and I won't have gone to New York, and you won't have gotten sick."

"We're not going to advertise this trip to the hospital," Cynthia said. She looked so beautiful with her head laid back on the sofa, with her blond hair loose and fanning behind her face. It was like the hair of Ophelia in Holman Hunt's painting Warden had seen in the Tate Gallery. A painting of double death: Ophelia died before the play was over; Hunt's model for the painting, his lover, caught a cold from lying in water to pose and also died.

Warden reminded her that the Somervilles knew already, and that the inevitable rumor machine at Montpelier would undoubtedly circulate the news.

"I was thinking of family," said Cynthia. "People who aren't here. My dad. Your brother. They don't need to be worried unnecessarily."

Warden agreed.

Cynthia held his hand in her lap palm up, as though she were reading it. "I'm only twenty-three years old," she said. "That's too young to be seriously ill."

"Of course it is."

"Only it's hard to deny this sense of free-fall." She pulled his hand up to her face. "It helps to know you're falling with me."

Warden encircled her with an arm and held her to him.

"We are not accomplishing anything except to tire you out," he said. He accused her of suffering a classic case of psychological denial; she had insisted upon dining with the boys tonight.

Cynthia said he was right, that she'd been unwise. "I just want life to be exactly the way it had been before," she said.

But how is that, thought Warden. No day is like the previous one. The earth is slowing down, the sun is burning out, the universe itself is expanding so quickly that eventually it must tear itself down the middle like a patch of putty.

They had gone to the dining hall early, at 6:15 for the 6:30 dinner, so that the boys would not see Cynthia limping to the table. They had remained at the table afterward until the room was clear.

"I start feeling so sorry for myself," said Cynthia, "and then I look around at your advisees, and I wonder what kinds of trouble they're suffering. You know how awful life is when you're that age."

"My advisees are privileged little preppies. The worst trouble they have is getting through *Great Expectations* without using Cliff's Notes."

Cynthia said he was wrong. "Tonight I was watching Thomas Boatwright," she said. "Did you notice him before we ate? He stared at Chuck Heilman the whole time Chuck was saying the blessing. He was oblivious."

"And why did you not have your own eyes closed during the blessing?"

"Because I was watching Thomas Boatwright," she said.

"And what was so fascinating about Thomas Boatwright?" said Warden. He accused her of mental philandering.

"What was so fascinating," she said, "to anyone who happened to notice, was that Thomas Boatwright was obviously troubled. Once in a while you should open your eyes yourself."

He let it go. He could not tell her all his reasons for being preoccupied. He needed to work them out.

"Maybe I should go check on young Boatwright tonight," said Warden.

"Do you have to go out?"

"I have to get some papers graded by tomorrow," he said. "I left them over in my classroom."

But the papers were upstairs in his briefcase.

Scene 10

It was 7:35 P.M. and Thomas Boatwright was supposed to be studying in his dormitory room. Quiet hours were from 7:30 to 9:30, and unless you were really dumb or your advisor hated your guts, you could work in your room. Otherwise you were assigned a seat in the supervised evening study hall. Thomas was not dumb, and his advisor, Mr. Warden, was a nice guy, and so Thomas was allowed to study in his room on Middle Stringfellow, which was the dorm on the middle floor of Stringfellow Hall. But Thomas was in Richard Blackburn's room all the way over on Stratford House, where he sat on the bright patchwork quilt that covered Ralph Musgrove's bed and talked with Richard, who sprawled on his own bed, and with Ralph, who sat at his desk with a book open in case somebody came into the room.

"I can promise you it wasn't me," said Richard. "You really think somebody got drunk before dinner? That would be suicide."

"He was walking like a drunk would on television," said Thomas. "You know, lurching around, having a hard time keeping upright."

"Maybe it was somebody from off campus," said Ralph. "Some townie."

"That's not as weird as what you told us about Farnham," said Richard. He leaned back on the bed and propped himself up with his skinny, pointed elbows. The light glinted off his round wire-rims and made him look like what Thomas imagined as a starving Communist intellectual.

"I swear to you he was pounding the floor like there was a snake on it and he wanted to kill it," Thomas said. "He threw the stick away, and then he turned; I thought I was next."

"He saw you?" asked Richard.

"I don't know," said Thomas. "I didn't hang around. But I bet you if he had seen me, he'd have killed me."

"Farnham is Jekyll and Hyde," said Richard. "He was nice as hell at play rehearsal today. At least for the first part, when I was there."

"I know why he was mad," said Ralph. Ralph was from Mississippi and spoke very slowly. His hair was the deep red of an Irish setter, his eyes brown, his face freckled. He wore a tee shirt with Jimmy Buffett's picture on it. The tee shirt was too small for Ralph's 6′5″ frame.

"Why?" said Thomas and Richard.

"Because Dean Kaufman doesn't want to let my advisor help out with the play."

"Dean Kaufman," said Richard.

"He says Mr. Dickinson is too busy," said Ralph.

Out of fifty people on the faculty, Peter Dickinson was the only black member. He taught one history class and worked most of the time in the admissions office, where he recruited minority students. He traveled all over the place trying to talk black kids into coming south for a private education. Just recently he had been meeting with a group in Baltimore.

"What was Mr. Dickinson going to do in the play?" Thomas asked.

"Guess," said Richard. He asked him how many parts for black guys he thought there were in the play.

"Othello?"

"Very good," said Richard. He tried to imitate Farnham's tone in English class.

Thomas said he thought Greg, his roommate, was going to be Othello.

"Greg's been pathetic in rehearsals," said Richard. "Hasn't he told you about it?"

"We don't talk much," said Thomas. He told them about Greg's surliness this afternoon. It had not improved when Thomas returned to get ready for dinner. Just thinking about it was irritating.

"Farnham's been pulling in faculty members all over the place," said Richard. "He wants Dickinson to play Othello and Mrs. Warden to be Desdemona."

Ralph said from the desk that he'd shave his legs if he could be in a play with Mrs. Warden.

Thomas would do more than that. Sometimes he thought about Hesta McCorkindale and how they would probably be intimate someday, but sometimes, without anything ever really triggering the thought, he imagined walking into the Wardens' apartment to see his advisor and finding Mrs. Warden in the shower, where she would slide back the curtain, her body all wet, and pull him in to join her. He thought she was the most beautiful woman he had ever seen in his life.

"Is he going to put any students in the play at all?" Ralph asked. "Besides the usual geeks?"

"He asked me to be in it, don't forget," said Thomas.

"I said besides the geeks."

Richard said that Nathan Somerville was in the play.

That was news. Nathan Somerville was not only the grandson of Mr. Somerville, the legendary history teacher, but Nathan was also the head councilman, which meant that he held the most prestigious position in the student body. He ran the whole honor council himself, and whenever there was a potential honor violation, it was Nathan

Somerville who decided whether it was worth convening the council over. He was a great athlete and about the smartest person in the world, taking all AP courses and applying early to Princeton. Plus, even though he was a senior and eighteen years old, he was really friendly and nice to the underformers. He lived on Upper Stringfellow Hall, one floor up from Thomas.

"How?" said Thomas. "I thought he was playing varsity basketball."

"Not as of this afternoon," said Richard. "He said he was tired of getting yelled at by Delaney and wanted to do something different."

The prospect of participating in the play had now become much more attractive. Being a member of a cast that included Mrs. Warden and Nathan Somerville could turn out to be the most prestigious thing Thomas had ever done in his life.

"Maybe Farnham was just testing some wood for the play or something," Thomas said.

"Or maybe he's just crazy," said Richard.

The door to the room opened and Mr. Heilman, the school minister, stuck in his head. All they could see was a face like Humpty Dumpty's and wispy brown hair and glasses as thick as paperweights.

"What're you rascals up to?" he asked. That was so typical of him to call them "rascals." Mr. Heilman was almost as big a nerd as Dean Kaufman. Heilman was afflicted with what Thomas called School Minister's Disease, which meant that he went out of his way to convince everybody that he was really a normal person even though he was a minister. So he was always dicking around, telling dirty jokes, and trying to be one of the guys. But he wasn't. He was thirty-eight years old and married and had only been a minister for about five years; before that he'd been a guidance counselor in some public school in Richmond. He was not exactly fat but was heading that way and his hobby was to go to the movies. He and his wife were always departing for "the cinema" somewhere, which meant that his side of Stratford House had to be supervised half the time by Mr. Warden, who lived on the other side.

All three boys said hi to Mr. Heilman.

"I heard voices," he said. "And you know what the rules are about visiting during study hours." He practically sang it, as if he were talking to people maybe six years old.

"Sorry, Mr. Heilman," said Thomas. "I had something on my mind, and I just couldn't wait until 9:30."

"Would you like to come talk to me about it?"

No, no, no, no. "That's okay," said Thomas. "I think I've got it all straightened out."

No counseling, no sympathy. "Get on back to your dorm, then," said Heilman. "And if the DM catches you, so much the better." He pulled the door hard to close it.

Thomas wished he had just stayed on his own dorm and risked a phone call to Hesta. Now he was going to have to cross the campus during study hours, and he was sure to get caught.

"Who is the DM anyway?" asked Thomas.

"McPhee," said Richard.

"Great," said Thomas. Just what he needed, to get into trouble with his basketball coach. Next to Mr. Warden and his dad, Coach McPhee was the adult Thomas admired most in the whole world. Unlike Coach Delaney, who stalked the sidelines and ranted and kicked the bleachers once and supposedly got called into Dr. Lane's office for doing so, Coach McPhee never lost his temper. You would have expected an Irishman from Boston to rage, but even when somebody royally screwed up, McPhee would never yell. You could tell he was mad, of course, by what he said and by the flush of his face, but he had a knack for never making you feel worthless or stupid. He just made you want to do better.

"You better go," said Ralph.

"Yeah," said Thomas. Why was it that the more he had to do, the less he wanted to get started? He stood up slowly and put on his coat.

"Don't let Farnham get you with a stick," said Richard.

"Don't let McPhee stick you," said Ralph. That was a joke. "To stick" at Montpelier meant to issue demerits.

"Don't let your roommate talk you deaf," said Richard.

"How can I walk back if I'm laughing this hard?" said Thomas. "You guys are the funniest people I've ever seen in my life."

Back in the cold, he walked south on the sidewalk bordering the Quad. It was only 100 yards or so to Stringfellow, but he was sure that McPhee would catch him off dorm during study hours. Or if not McPhee, some other duty master. The faculty here was unbelievable. Some of them were completely out of it, like Heilman; when he was on duty, you could practically light up a joint in the dining hall and he wouldn't notice. But most of them seemed to have radar.

He went up the back stairs of Stringfellow. Damn, it was cold outside, and very warm in here. The building was shaped like a U, and Thomas had just entered the left-hand prong. He was in the administrative wing, but that was okay, since nobody would be in the offices at night. He still had to make it around to the lobby in the base of the U and then up the stairs to his dorm. But he was lucky. Although frequently masters on duty sat in the lobby, nobody was there tonight. Thomas was feeling uneasy. If the Stringfellow duty masters weren't in the lobby, that meant they were probably circulating around the dorms, so he was just as likely to get nabbed in the hallway. And there was always the slight threat of the omnipresent day master, in today's case McPhee, who wandered all over the campus and checked not only on the students, but on the faculty members who were supposed to be checking on the students. If Thomas got caught for being off dorm, he'd get stuck for five demerits, which would be enough to put him in Saturday night demerit hall from 7:30 to 9:30. That would be very uncool, since this Saturday night Montpelier was having a mixer for eight girls' schools, and Hesta was coming down. He could imagine himself sitting in D-hall while Hesta was at the mixer without him, with all those other horny guys around asking her to dance and talking to her. What if somebody like Robert Staines tried to move in on her? Thomas crossed the lobby and headed up the stairs praying for luck. He just couldn't get caught, not tonight.

There was nobody in the hallway on Middle Stringfellow. The gray carpeting muffled his footsteps, though the bright overhead fluorescent lamps made him visible from probably 200 miles away. Why the hell did Montpelier have to be so rich? The building was practically older than *Beowulf*, but they remodeled the place eight years ago and put in new bathrooms and new closets and stuff and these damn big lights. Of course, they also carpeted it, which was working to his advantage. Everything was absolutely quiet. In the spaces under the brown wooden doors of the rooms he was passing, he could see lights on. Every-the-hell-body on campus was studying now, and he would be, too, in just a few more minutes.

First, though, he was going to let his roommate have it. Nobody had the right to be as rude as Greg had been this afternoon. You don't ignore people because you happen to be reading.

He turned a corner, and there it was, his room, just a few yards away. I'm going to make it, he thought. Boatwright, you lucky bastard, you prime-cut devil you, you did it. He turned the knob on the dark wooden door and fled into the lighted interior as if he were being pursued by Nazis.

The first person he saw was Greg, sitting with his back to the door at his own desk with the study lamp on. The second person was Mr. McPhee, the DM, sitting at Thomas's desk next to Greg.

Mr. McPhee was looking straight at him.

Scene 11

"Where have you been?" said Coach McPhee.

Thomas told him. There wasn't any choice under the honor system, but Thomas would have told him anyway. Coach McPhee listened with his long legs stretched out and his ankles crossed and his hands locked behind his head, his elbows sticking out like Dumbo's ears. He dressed like an adult version of a Montpelier boy: lace-up leather moccasins from Bean's, khaki pants, a white shirt with loosened tie and collar, and a Carolina-blue sweater. The difference was that he still had his coach's whistle on a cord around his neck. Because Coach McPhee had really thick black curly hair in ringlets around his head, you would have thought he was younger than late thirties, except that up close you could see the permanent wrinkles around his eyes. His eyes were bright green, and they never seemed to wander or even to blink while Thomas talked.

"So you had this really important subject you just had to discuss with Richard Blackburn," said Mr. McPhee.

"Yes sir."

"You can't tell me what it was, but you had to tell Richard right away."

"I just had to tell somebody."

"So why didn't you talk it over with your roommate?"

I tried, I tried, Thomas wanted to shout. Coach, can I help it if my roommate is a jerk? "I guess I figured I could talk it over with him anytime," said Thomas.

Greg was motionless at his desk. He had changed from dinner clothes into a red tee shirt from the University of Maryland.

Mr. McPhee asked Thomas if he was planning to quit basketball to take a part in the play.

"No," said Thomas.

"Because Mr. Farnham asked me after dinner what time I let you out of practice today. He said he was expecting you for an audition."

"It wasn't anything as formal as an audition," said Thomas.

Mr. McPhee said nothing.

"Believe me, Coach," said Thomas, "if I do take a part in that stupid play, it's just going to be a little one. I want to play basketball."

"I believe you," said Mr. McPhee. "But I don't like to hear you use the word 'stupid' so carelessly." Mr. McPhee still spoke with the Boston accent he'd grown up with. Everybody in Virginia said it was a New York accent, but they said that about every Yankee, even the ones from Ohio. Mr. McPhee, who had played basketball for Boston College, was the only major college basketball player Thomas had ever met.

"Tell you what," said Mr. McPhee. He uncrossed his ankles and pulled down his hands and stood up. "I've got to make my rounds. I'm not going to stick you tonight, Boatwright."

Thomas was ready to start believing in God.

"But I'm going to check back here later," said Mr. McPhee. "You need to get two things accomplished before lights out tonight. Are you listening? I want you to do all your homework. And I want you to find out about your roommate's art project. He and I were just having a very interesting conversation about all sorts of things. You talk to him after study hours are over. You understand?"

"Yes sir."

He picked up his hat, coat, scarf, and gloves from Greg's bed and left.

Thomas sat down at the desk next to Greg and pulled out his heavy black Pelican edition of Shakespeare, just in case McPhee decided to pop back into the room immediately. Greg was sitting and staring straight ahead at the open notebook in front of him.

To hell with waiting until study hours were over.

"What's the problem?" said Thomas. "I come into the room before dinner, I want to talk with you, and you act like I'm poisonous."

Greg didn't answer.

"What's wrong with you?" said Thomas. "Why have you turned into such a snob?"

Greg stared hard at the switch on the light in front of him. Thomas assumed he was not going to answer and opened his Shakespeare anthology. At least he had covered his agenda.

"I guess maybe I'm jealous," said Greg.

That was not what Thomas had expected to hear.

"Jealous of me?"

"You got it so good here," said Greg. "You do what you want, nobody tries to pigeonhole you."

Thomas asked him what in the hell he was talking about.

"Everybody pressuring me to play on your football team and your basketball team. Everybody pushing me to perform."

Thomas argued that they merely wanted him to be one of the guys. "Everybody else plays basketball. You're good at it. Why shouldn't you play, too?"

"I play."

"On the team, I mean."

"I don't like the way your team operates," said Greg. "All

you care about is a winning score. You don't care about the people at all."

Thomas said that wasn't true, they were all friends on the basketball team.

"You and Robert Staines? You can't stand the guy, but you put up with him because he's good," said Greg.

"So?" said Thomas. "Being on a team is all about getting along with other people."

"I'm not talking about just getting along," said Greg. "You let the guy run without a leash because he's the best player. Whatever he does, whatever he says, nobody confronts him. If you guys didn't care so much about winning, you'd tell him to go to hell."

Thomas reminded him that the coaches were in charge of picking the teams and keeping the players disciplined.

"I mean off the court," said Greg. "After practice. On the dorm. You treat Staines like he's some royal prince nobody can contradict."

"Staines does plenty of stuff I can't stand," said Thomas. He was dodging the issue.

"You never tell him so," said Greg. "You just go along."

That was true. It had happened this afternoon. It happened all the time. A couple of days into the school year, Thomas and Greg had been playing a pickup basketball game with Staines and some of the other sophomores. After Greg had blocked one of his shots out of bounds, Staines had thrown the ball straight into Greg's face. That had started a fight, which had broken up only when Coach McPhee, who lived in one of the gym apartments, had heard the ruckus and come in to break it up.

Thomas had stood by with the others and watched. He was embarrassed to remember.

"I've always been sympathetic with you over the way Staines acts," Thomas said. Since the fight Staines had behaved as though Greg were invisible. He wouldn't make eye contact with him in the halls, wouldn't speak to him, wouldn't acknowledge him.

"Why don't you show it once in a while?" said Greg. "Why don't you tell him?"

Thomas was exasperated by the question; it was exactly

what he had asked himself earlier in the day. Moreover, it was none of Greg's business to be questioning how he got along with people at school. Thomas sure as hell had a lot more friends than Greg did. "Staines was here before you were," he said. "We can't just turn on an old boy because he starts a fight with a newboy. You handled him okay. You shouldn't have let him run you off."

"You think I'm afraid of him?" Greg asked.

"No," said Thomas. It couldn't be a matter of fear. Greg still played in pickup games every Saturday and Sunday. He could guard anybody, go anywhere, try any move. He could probably have played varsity if he'd wanted to. "I mean you let him run you off from the team."

"It wasn't Staines," said Greg. "It was everybody else on the team. All you other guys who defer to him."

That lofty moral tone irritated Thomas. "That's your opinion," he said. "You're the one to miss out."

"Miss out on what?"

"Earning our respect," said Thomas. That one would hurt. Not being respected was the worst thing Thomas could imagine. "We respect people who have a talent and aren't afraid to use it." That will get him, Thomas thought. But Greg just scoffed.

"How about people who stand up for their own principles?" he asked. "Do you guys have any respect for them?"

Thomas asked if Greg thought of himself as the Man of La Mancha.

But instead of getting mad, as Thomas had expected, Greg became calmer. "Let me spell it out for you in large print," he said. "I don't want to be known here for being good in sports. Everybody takes it for granted I'm a good athlete because I'm black. I make a good catch or a good shot, they figure it's because sports come naturally to me. That's not respect. That's spectating."

Thomas had never heard anything like it. "Are you some crazy militant or something?" he said. "People admire good athletes. It's hero-worship." He pointed out the recent Olympics in Seoul: Carl Lewis, Florence Griffith-Joyner, Greg Louganis.

"You admire Carl Lewis because he trained so hard,"

said Greg. "You see him setting a goal and then reaching it."

"Exactly." Thomas hated it when somebody stated his argument better than he could.

Greg said his own goal was to be a good actor. "Why should you and your friends decide otherwise?" he said. "Why do you keep tying me down to athletics?"

"Nobody's tying you down."

"No? Then why haven't you ever congratulated me for getting cast as Othello? Why do you keep picking at me about basketball?"

Thomas started to respond but halted when Greg's words registered. He could think of no good answer. He had never met somebody with a two-foot vertical jump for whom drama was more important than basketball.

All of a sudden the momentum had shifted. For the first time in his life, Thomas considered that perhaps talent alone was not enough for some people, that maybe being naturally skillful did not automatically make you naturally satisfied. "You're gifted at sports," he said finally. "You could make a name for yourself in sports."

"There you go again," said Greg. "Why do you keep suggesting that my only chance to make a name for myself comes through the athletic department?"

Thomas hesitated again. Was it true? Was he writing Greg off as a good athlete? As nothing but a good athlete?

"Okay, correction," Thomas said. "Sports are not the only way you can be prominent around here. They're just the most logical way. They're the easiest for you."

He thought that was a good response until Greg's comeback: "So how can taking the easy way earn me anybody's respect? How could I respect myself?"

Thomas realized with discomfort that he was getting his consciousness raised. It didn't feel so great to have all your assumptions dismantled, but he had to consider Greg's argument. You watch a pro athlete—black or white, it didn't matter—make a great play, and you admire his skill, but you don't actually respect him for it. You respect him for his dedication and his character and his reputation after the contest is over. Thomas had thought he was going to demolish verbally this arrogant roommate of his. Instead, he was getting taken to school. He had served up what he'd thought were killer points, and Greg had smashed every one back into his face.

"I guess 'respect' was the wrong word," said Thomas.

"It's exactly the right word for what I want," said Greg. "But I need to earn my respect. The hard way. By succeeding in theater."

It was time for one attempt at self-defense. "Don't you think it's unusual for a good athlete not to play a sport?" said Thomas.

"Yes," said Greg.

Thomas was encouraged. "So can't you see how weird it is for you to ignore me when I ask you to go out for basketball?"

"No," said Greg, "not when you ask me to play because there isn't a single black guy on the team."

He could remember saying that. And an hour ago, if somebody had asked him what was wrong with it, Thomas would not have been able to say. He had thought of it as a compliment, an appeal to racial pride based on the assumption that everybody knew black guys were the best basketball players. He'd never considered that being a good basketball player wasn't necessarily every black person's goal.

Oh, hell. It was like asking a guy to be club treasurer because he's Jewish, or hiring somebody to be your cook because she's female. It was the worst possible reason.

Thomas felt like a toilet seat.

"I never meant that to be a racist remark," he said.

"What else could it be?" said Greg.

What else indeed.

"I apologize," Thomas said. "I see your point." He could see several points. "All this time I thought you were being moody. You've been as mad at me as I've been at you."

Greg said he just wondered how Thomas had been so brainwashed by Robert Staines.

"I wasn't brainwashed," said Thomas. "I was just, I don't know, unobservant."

Greg said he had been wondering why Thomas had changed so much from last summer.

"That's exactly what I was wondering about you," said Thomas.

They sat and stared at each other for a moment. It was much less awkward than their previous silences.

"I guess I overreacted," said Greg. "I mean, it's not just because I'm black. I heard the varsity guys were putting a lot of pressure on Nathan Somerville to drop the play."

Thomas could still recognize a gesture of friendship.

"I'm sorry for being so stupid," he said.

"I'm sorry for being so silent," said Greg. "I was interpreting everything you said in the worst possible way. I'm not a good mind reader."

"How could you read something as narrow as my mind?" said Thomas.

The tension in the room had dissolved.

Thomas was impressed with his roommate's ambition and abashed over his own failure to comprehend. "So you act because it's a challenge," he said. "Because it's tougher for you than sports."

"Yeah," said Greg. "Only it's not working out too well." He confirmed that Coach Delaney, the varsity basketball coach, had been furious about the defection of Nathan Somerville from his team, that he had come over to rehearsal today and had yelled at Farnham for stealing good athletes.

"So that's why Farnham was so crazy this afternoon," Thomas said. He reported what he had seen in the scene shop. "I bet he was imagining Delaney's head under that two-by-four."

Greg was not finished. "After rehearsal," he said, "Farnham called me aside and said to consider the choice between sports and theater carefully. Promised me he'd understand if I wanted to quit the play. I got the message."

Thomas could guess the message but asked anyway.

"The message that I wasn't any good," said Greg. "He was telling me that I couldn't handle the part."

Thomas had heard the same thing from Richard a few minutes ago. In the light of the desk lamp he could see Greg's eyes wash into wetness.

"I can memorize the lines just fine," said Greg. "It's that I don't understand them."

Thomas said nobody could get Shakespeare without the footnotes.

"This is worse," said Greg. He kept his voice very low. He

said he had never read Shakespeare before in his life. "I read it and reread it, and I'm not sure what it says. What if I can't ever catch on?"

Thomas said he could always do something else. Mr. Dickinson would step in if they needed a substitute.

Greg clenched his fist hard around the pen in his hand. "If I can't understand Shakespeare, then what am I? What if I really am just a dumb, stupid black boy good only for catching balls for the white folks? I want to be more than that."

Thomas was dumbfounded. It was the first time in his life he had encountered firsthand such a passion to succeed. He tried to smooth matters over. "It would be just like me getting cut from a team," he said.

"Not when the coach of the team is begging other people to try out," said Greg. "They try to talk me out of my part, and they're calling people like you in to audition. Everybody in this school wants me to play sports. I'm not doing it. If I can't do Othello, I'll go home."

Thomas knew that he meant every word. He also knew that he did not want Greg to go home. Not now. Thomas felt protective.

"Is that what McPhee was doing in here? Recruiting you?"

Greg shook his head. "He was cool about it. He said stick to the play."

Thomas knew what he would do in Greg's position. He would quit the play and go out for basketball, where he would get a starting position and lots of acclaim among the students. But then what? Wouldn't he always assume from then on that he couldn't measure up intellectually, that Shakespeare and the rest of those guys in English literature were over his head? And was that fair? Mr. Warden was always raving at the dinner table about how talented Greg was. And Thomas knew from biology class that the guy was smart as hell. Coach McPhee had charted the course; Thomas would sail it.

"You can do it," he said. He was not at all sure it was true.

"I don't think so," said Greg.

"It just takes getting used to the language," said Thomas.

"I don't have time to get used to the language."

"I'll help you," said Thomas.

"What do you know about Shakespeare?"

"Are you kidding?" said Thomas. "All those nights at Arena Stage, all those summer festivals? I probably know more about Shakespeare than Farnham does." A little exaggeration was acceptable.

"Why do you want to help me?" said Greg.

A good question. Maybe to appease his conscience. But maybe also because he admired Greg's convictions. He wanted to see the guy make it.

"It'll be a trade," said Thomas. "I help you with Shakespeare, you show me how to shoot a left-handed hook."

Greg did not answer at first. "I don't know," he said. "I feel like I ought to do it on my own."

"You'll be doing it on your own," said Thomas. "If you think I'm putting shoe polish on my face and choking Mrs. Warden on that stage, you are one crazy roommate."

Greg said nothing. But for the first time in what seemed like months, he laughed.

Scene 12

Warden pulled his scarf closer to his face and walked through the cold to Fleming Hall. It was 8:30 P.M. The campus was quiet, all the boys in their rooms. His wife was at home in her room, in her bed, listening to music. His duty was to be with her.

And yet he had to get away. Seeing her so ill was stirring up dirty old sediment in the estuary of his mind. He groped to define his malady: Helplessness? Despair? Denial, anger, depression, bargaining?

Not acceptance. He would not accept the decline of his wife without a fight.

From the moment he had started to love Cynthia, he had been afraid of losing her.

He used to dream as an adolescent boy—and still did—that

his face was whole and that women were drawn to him for his looks. In high school he had never gone on a date. Girls were mysterious creatures who married Prince Charming, not boys with permanent acne, and it had been easy, here at an all-boys' school, to get involved with sports and studies and writing for the literary magazine. His favorite play then was *Cyrano de Bergerac.* He had read it again and again and had cried at the end, had cried to think of the beautiful Roxane loving the man for his words and not for his looks. That was when he had started writing poetry.

Eventually, though, he had learned that girls—just like boys—did not always look merely at the face when they were sizing up a prospect. They also liked the body. His parents had always encouraged both him and Lawrence to play sports. He had loved football from the first time he'd played it at age eight, not only for the fun of hitting, but for the anonymity bestowed by the helmet; in uniform he looked like everyone else. In baseball he always played catcher, so that he could wear a mask. And when he enrolled at Montpelier in the ninth grade, he was delighted to discover wrestling, a sport where he could also wear a mask. Warden was not a great athlete, but he was a willing one. He completed his workouts the best he could and considered himself just an average performer with below-average appearance. Hence he had been astonished during his junior year at Montpelier to overhear some girls behind the backstop talking about what a good build he had. He had liked that and had never forgotten it. At mixers, too, he had learned that he could make girls laugh by saying funny things about the chaperones out on the dance floor, but that it was easier to be funny with a group of girls, because as soon as he was alone with just one girl, he found himself helplessly speechless, and that a girl alone with him would eventually invent a clumsy excuse to leave.

Sewanee had offered him the same environment as Montpelier, but the difference was the automobile and the freedom to purchase a pint of whiskey from the bootleggers down the road and to spend a Saturday evening in Chattanooga. In those days he had discovered women who would consort with him, who would gladly go for a date if he had a ten-dollar bill or even a drink to offer them. They would dance at the roadhouses and laugh and sit in the car on country roads for quick, satisfying trysts. But he rarely had seen the same woman twice, and he had needed a drink or two of bourbon before he could relax enough to talk.

In his senior year of college he had found his Roxane. Her name was Elizabeth, and she was beautiful and bright and attentive. She had come up as a blind date, the friend of the girlfriend of Warden's roommate. She went to Converse College in South Carolina, almost too far from the mountains of Tennessee, but Warden's roommate had a car, and he was perfectly willing to drive across the mountain to visit the ladies at Converse. The four of them—Warden's roommate, the roommate's date, Warden himself, and Elizabeth—had become a regular set. Warden at last had understood what being in love meant. Elizabeth had been the woman with whom he had wanted to spend the rest of his life, and late in May, just before graduation, he had asked her to marry him. She had put off her answer. A week later, she had married his roommate.

He enjoyed telling the story now as a joke on himself. But it was a rueful joke. It had hurt at the time, and he had always assumed that the fault of losing her was his own.

Elizabeth was the last woman Warden had allowed himself to love until he met Cynthia. After Sewanee he had deliberately returned to Montpelier, to the monastic existence where he could be free of the distractions of women, but he had found women everywhere—other men's wives, the nurses, the secretaries, beautiful women strolling along the sidewalks. He had kept himself in physical shape, had understood the benefits of exercise on the libido. At night he had dreamed—delicious, tantalizing, excruciating fantasies of himself with all sorts and conditions of women.

Even after he and Cynthia were married, he experienced random moments of wonder that she could really be his wife—and stray moments of dread that, like his happiest dreams, this interlude of joy would end.

And now Cynthia was ill. It was his greatest fear come true. He had initially assumed that the thief would be a younger man with handsome face, but over the past two years, Cynthia had nearly convinced him that such fears were silly, possessive, childish. He had taken to worrying over her being in an automobile accident whenever she commuted to Charlottesville to meet with the director of her dissertation. He had failed to consider sickness even last summer, when she had suffered the first of these brief episodes of blurred vision.

He wanted to protect her from whatever assault she faced. Maybe the boys on the dorm were using some kind of incense to which she was allergic. Or maybe they had transmitted to her some obscure virus, one to which males were naturally immune.

He was tempted to fall into a metaphysical depression. Was he himself the cause of her troubles? By flouting the gods, by marrying this lovely young woman, had he aroused their anger, triggered their punishment? Which old culture warned that it was unwise to find a perfect love, for such a love would make the gods jealous?

Not fair, he corrected himself. Theirs was not a tragic story of star-crossed lovers; it was about the princess who kissed the frog. She kissed him and found that he remained a frog, and she married him anyway. The conventions of the story demanded that she get well.

Or at least that she avoid suffering.

The worst would be some lingering illness. Horace Somerville had spoken to Warden's most private fears today when he had talked about the speed of his son Alfred's death. To watch Cynthia gradually fade, to lose her beauty and her spark, that would be unbearable. Warden had been through that with both parents in the past decade—the months of increasing debilitation, the convulsions, the trips to the hospital, the remissions, the many false assumptions that at last it would be over this time, the final relief mingled with guilt and grief and emptiness.

Denial, anger, depression, bargaining.

What kind of bargain would he make to get her well? Sell his soul, like Faustus, to the devil? If only he believed in voodoo or black magic, then he could track down the shaman who was responsible for Cynthia's illness and steal his magic. Instead, he had to rely on the local witch doctor.

Upstairs in Fleming Hall he sat at his desk and stared at the empty surface. What was he here for? Had he meant to come here, or was he going to the gym for his workout? He would remember in a moment. Right now he wanted to start a poem, something about superstitions and scapegoats.

Something religious: death in life, the dying god.

The death of one so that another might live?

Scene 13

At 9:15 Thomas Boatwright finished Act I of *Othello* and should have started on his biology lab report. He and Greg had spent an uninterrupted hour studying. It had been a comfortable silence between them, and Thomas was ready for a break. He opened his desk drawer and pulled out a bag of corn chips.

"Less than an hour till I can call Hesta," he said.

Greg put down his pen and took some chips. "She called you before study hall," he said. "I meant to tell you earlier."

The heart did the usual double-pump, and then the disappointment took over. Damn, if he'd been on dorm, he could have talked to her. "What'd she say?"

"Nothing. Said she'd call back."

"Who's on duty in this building tonight?" Thomas said.

"Nathan Somerville."

That was a relief at least. The fifteen seniors on the honor council were dispersed among all the dormitories. They were almost like faculty members at times, making sure rooms stayed clean and rules got obeyed, but since they weren't faculty members, they tended to go a little easier on you if they caught you breaking a rule. If you were on the phone during study hours, say, and somebody like Mr. Somerville was on duty, he would stick you with demerits for sure, but if it was his grandson, Nathan, you'd probably get by with just a warning. You were also supposed to consult with your councilman if you ran into any trouble on the dorm. It was the biggest honor at Montpelier to be a councilman—and also the biggest pain, since the faculty expected you to be a perfect citizen and the students expected you to cut them a break.

"You think I should ask Nathan for permission to call Hesta?"

"You won't be able to get through at Mason anyway," said Greg. "They got study hours, too." He took more chips.

He was right. And if Coach McPhee came back through on his rounds and saw Thomas on the phone, he'd probably kill him on the spot.

"You know what Mr. McPhee was telling me before you came in?" said Greg. "He and his wife split up."

"She's not living here anymore?"

"That's right."

"What about Michael?"

"She took him, too."

"When?"

Greg told him that it had happened over the Thanksgiving holidays. She'd taken off and gone back to Boston. She'd packed up all her clothes, too, and her books and her pictures and all her cameras, and she'd already found some work in Boston back at the photographer's studio where she used to work before they got married.

"Why'd she leave?" asked Thomas.

"He wouldn't say. He said he'd flown up to Boston over the weekend to try to talk her out of it."

Thomas considered the implications. "I bet it was because of Michael," he said. "I think Michael was really jealous of him. He didn't like Coach McPhee much."

"That boy was crazy. He had himself the perfect stepdad." Everybody knew about McPhee: how he'd played college ball and then pro ball in Italy. He'd come back and gone to grad school at Georgetown and had started coaching basketball at Capital City Prep. Two years ago he had come to Montpelier, and everybody said he was a better basketball coach than Mr. Delaney. Just last summer he'd gotten married to a widow from Boston with a fifteen-year-old son, a guy nobody knew very well.

"Michael was weird," said Thomas. "I asked him if he'd

be going out for basketball one time. He said he'd deflated his basketball and thrown it away after he'd moved to Montpelier. Like this was some big statement."

Greg agreed that the coach was much more likeable than the kid. "I talked to him once," he said. "The guy complained because he didn't have a dorm room. I'm talking like, boy, count your blessings. Can you imagine not wanting to live in that apartment? No phone restrictions, TV anytime?"

"They should have sent him to another school," said Thomas. "We don't need guys like that here."

Then Thomas started to think: What if Hesta had been calling to tell him that she couldn't come down this weekend after all? What if what had happened to Mr. McPhee and his wife were part of some epidemic or something, with all women breaking up with all men?

Greg brushed the chip crumbs off his fingers and began to unroll a blueprint on the desktop. Thomas asked him what it was for.

"Art," said Greg. "This is my project. You recognize the building?"

Thomas couldn't recognize anything. It seemed to be about five buildings, all the same shape, like a stretched-out, squared-off horseshoe. Then he realized that it was five stories of the same building.

"It's Stringfellow," he said. "Where's our room?"

Greg pointed to a small square on the right-hand wing of the third horseshoe.

"There's the bathroom," said Greg. "And there's the common room. You notice something funny here?" He pointed to a large open space at the end of the hall.

"Where's Mr. Carella's apartment?"

Greg said that was the point. These blueprints were from 1928, and Mr. Carella's apartment hadn't been carved out yet. "That was a reading room and a library," said Greg. "Mr. Delaney told us about it today in class."

That was pretty interesting, Thomas had to admit.

"So what's your project?" he asked.

"Architecture," said Greg. "I'm supposed to figure out from the plans of the buildings on campus where a secret escape tunnel might be built."

"A secret escape tunnel?"

"Sure," said Greg, "in case the Indians or the slaves or the Revenuers started getting too close to home."

Thomas was starting to remember something. He didn't reply.

Greg spoke in the same neutral tone. "Slaves, man. That was a joke."

"Sorry. I was thinking about Revenuers."

Greg said the tunnel was supposed to connect Stringfellow Hall with the Homestead.

"Under the Quad?" said Thomas.

"That's what Delaney said."

They looked at the blueprint for half a minute in silence.

"So," said Greg. "There's my art project. Why are you thinking about bootleg whiskey all of a sudden?"

He told Greg about the staggering figure leaving Bradley Hall this afternoon. "It looked like he was drunk. You don't think Farnham was drinking, do you? A surly drunk?"

"Get real," said Greg.

"It's possible."

"Somebody looked drunk?" said Greg. "Somebody not walking right?"

"Yeah, that's it."

"All bundled up in a bunch of clothes?"

"That's him," said Thomas. "You know who it was?"

"Yeah," said Greg. "It's not a him. It was Mrs. Warden. She got there at the end of rehearsal. Everybody else was gone. Farnham was talking to me about working on my character, but when she showed up, he sent me on home."

"But why would Mrs. Warden be drunk?"

"She wasn't drunk," said Greg. "She just wasn't walking right."

"You think she hurt herself?" said Thomas.

"Maybe so."

"Or," said Thomas, "maybe she'd been down there earlier, and Farnham had blown up and had hit her with a board, and she was limping because of the injury."

"Get real."

"Well, it's possible," said Thomas.

"Maybe she told him something that got him mad," said Greg. "Maybe she told him she didn't want to be his lover anymore."

"She's not his lover," said Thomas.

"It's possible," said Greg.

"She's not his lover."

"Okay," said Greg. "Don't get mad."

Thomas had surprised himself with the vehemence of his response. "I guess we'll never know," he said. He pulled out his book of lab reports.

"Did you finish Act I?" Greg asked him.

"Yeah."

Greg paused. "So when Iago says that stuff about 'the beast with two backs,' is he talking about, you know, doing it?"

"You got it," said Thomas.

"I couldn't believe Shakespeare would talk so much about sex," said Greg. "I thought it meant something more serious."

Thomas said he thought there was nothing more serious than sex.

"Tell me about this speech here," said Greg, "where Desdemona is talking to her father."

Thomas said he'd be glad to.

And he was pleased to realize that he meant it. Coach McPhee would be proud when he returned to check on them. He had asked Thomas to do his homework and to find out about Greg's art project, and Thomas had followed his orders.

But Patrick McPhee did not return to speak to them that night. He got sidetracked by the death of Russell Phillips.

Scene 14

My noble father,
I do perceive here a divided duty:
To you I am bound for life and education;
My life and education both do learn me
How to respect you; you are the lord of duty;
I am hitherto your daughter: but here's my husband,

And so much duty as my mother show'd
To you, preferring you before her father,
So much I challenge that I may profess
Due to the Moor my lord.

Warden was reading the lines to Cynthia in their bedroom. He was fully dressed in gray woolen trousers, white shirt, and tie, while she wore a blue flannel nightgown. He sat on the bed and leaned back on the headboard while he read; she lay supine beneath the covers. The bright, hard winter sunshine of Tuesday morning provided plenty of light for the reading.

"My noble father," echoed Cynthia, "I do perceive here a double duty—"

"Divided duty," said Warden.

" 'I do perceive here a divided duty,' " said Cynthia. "I should have known that from the meter. Da dum da dum da dum da dum da dum. Da. Iambic pentameter with a little extra syllable at the end."

"Go on."

"My life and education both do teach me—"

"Learn me," said Warden.

"No wonder the neoclassicists rewrote Shakespeare," said Cynthia. "His grammar was terrible."

"Start again."

She said the speech aloud and corrected those errors but committed two others.

"Not bad," said Warden.

"She sounds like Cordelia," said Cynthia.

"So she does." This was *Othello,* and Cordelia was in *Lear,* but the principle was the same: a daughter who understood love better than her father did, and who was soon cursed by her father for her supposed disloyalty and ingratitude. And both died at the end of their plays. The canniness of his wife's insight was what hurt Warden the most. She was so talented, so smart, so good; she should be finishing her doctoral dissertation on Shakespeare and publishing and acting and enjoying life till she was a hundred fifty years old.

"How much time do we have?" Cynthia asked. The question startled him. Then he realized that she was asking about their departure.

It was 8:45 A.M. "Another forty-five minutes," he said. Montpelier School was on a rolling schedule stretching over six days of the week, so that no class met at the same time each day. Warden's first class on Tuesday did not meet until 9:30, when he would walk over to Fleming Hall, tell the students their assignment, and then drive Cynthia to the hospital.

"Did you finish grading your papers?" she said.

"Finally this morning, yes," he said. "I spent an hour looking around that classroom for them, and they were here all the time."

She reminded him that he had already told her about his error twice. "Are you tired of reading?" she asked.

He said he was absolutely not tired of reading. How could he be, when he was reading his favorite writer to his favorite audience?

She had waked with blurred vision in both eyes. They had not panicked; she was going to the hospital soon, where the doctors would make her well. In the interim, she was going ahead with learning her lines. She was not going to allow her eyes to prevent her from playing Desdemona.

"Do you know why I'm writing about this play?" she said.

"Why?"

"Because it reminds me of us," she said. "The father who objects to his daughter's marriage, the older man marrying the younger woman."

Warden had not missed the parallels himself. "The fair young woman marrying the man with the sooty face."

"Your face is not sooty," said Cynthia. "It's rubicund."

Warden touched the mark on his face without thinking. "I was paranoid when I first met you," he said. "I thought you were trifling with me. I assumed you had some ulterior motive."

Cynthia reached up and took his hand from his face. "What do you mean?" she said. "I had a very ulterior motive. I wanted to marry my teacher." She kissed his open palm.

"I hate my face," said Warden. "I wish I could give you a face you deserve."

" 'I saw Othello's visage in his mind,' " said Cynthia. "Desdemona and Othello truly loved each other, didn't they?"

"Yes."

"And we truly love each other, don't we?"

"Yes," said Warden.

"Then how could he kill her? Could you even imagine killing me?"

"Stop it," he said. He pulled his hand away.

"I'm sorry," she said. "It's this vertigo. It makes me just the tiniest bit off plumb."

But her question brought the play into focus for him as if he had never understood it before. Othello adored Desdemona, and she him. And yet he killed her. In their bed. At night, when he should have been making love to her. The scene of her death was as familiar to Othello and Desdemona as this bedroom was to Warden and Cynthia, the most intimate, the most private, the most personal room of the house. Desdemona lay in bed and begged her husband to investigate her story, to believe her, to trust her as she had trusted him, but he proceeded to kill her nonetheless. He was jealous, under the spell of the green-eyed monster that lurks in wait to feed on love. He loved her so much that he killed her.

Warden thought of Browning's poem "Porphyria's Lover," told by a madman who killed his mistress at the moment she expressed her greatest love for him, so that such a love could never be diminished. He imagined himself even now putting down the book, leaning over and taking his wife's throat in his own large hands and squeezing the life out of her. Would she fight? Would she protest? Or would she simply look at him in understanding that he was killing her because he loved her so much, because he could not stand the thought of her living with some terrible virus inside her, nibbling away at her insides, stealing her energy away. The sickness knew her in a place where even Warden could not go. He was jealous of her disease.

He shuddered.

"You have given me the worst sorts of nightmares," he said.

"I'm sorry," she said.

It was warm and bright in the bedroom. He lifted the white-covered Signet paperback and looked for his place. Cynthia interrupted him.

"Othello must have killed people in the course of his career, don't you think?" said Cynthia. "He was a general. He had had a long life of adventure. It was hearing about all those adventures that attracted Desdemona to him. She was attracted to him because he was a killer."

Warden accused her of deliberately misreading the text.

"She was attracted to him because of his nobility, his courage, his valor," he said.

"So killing people was noble?"

"For the right cause, of course."

"Would you kill someone for the right cause?" she asked.

"It would have to be a very good cause," said Warden.

"Would you kill someone if it would cure me of cancer?"

"Cynthia."

"I'm sorry," she said. "I'm doing it again. We don't know that it's cancer."

Warden reached over and caressed her neck.

"It could be nothing," he said. "Some tropical bug you got off a papaya in the Safeway."

"I want to get back to work," she said. "I think of the poor English department, all those vocabulary quizzes you're having to photocopy by yourself, those grades that need recording, those book orders."

"They can all wait."

"And the mixer this Saturday. I should tell Sam Kaufman he needs to get somebody else to be in charge. I've taken on too much." Cynthia was also director of weekend activities at Montpelier.

Warden said she suffered an excess desire to take part in the daily workings of the school. "This mixer can take care of itself."

"It certainly cannot," she said. "I have to be there. I have to check on the bands and make sure that all the chaperones are there and check in the buses from the girls' schools."

Warden told her that he would help.

"I should still call Sam," she said. "Only Sam Kaufman is the biggest gossip on campus."

"So we won't tell him," said Warden. "How do we explain your absence?"

"I'm going to be back before they notice," she said. "I'm going to be back by tomorrow."

He continued to read to her until the telephone rang and pulled them both back to their bedroom. Eerily, it was Samuel Kaufman, the dean of students, and for a moment Warden wondered whether Kaufman was calling to confirm the rumors he'd heard about Cynthia's illness.

"Is Cynthia available to do some substitute teaching?" asked Kaufman.

Warden said she was not.

"Then you're going to have to find somebody to cover Patrick McPhee's classes this morning. He can't make it. We've got this . . ."

"What's the matter?"

"He found a boy dead last night. We've had a suicide."

"Who?" It was the only word Warden could manage.

"A newboy third-former. Russell Phillips. Apparently he jumped off the roof of the gym."

"Sam," said Warden. He started again. "This is horrible news."

"It was awful," said Kaufman. "Pat McPhee found him around midnight. In the fall his neck had been twisted all the way around so that his face was looking backwards."

Warden said nothing.

"I have some other calls to make," said Kaufman. "So you'll be on your way to Fleming now?"

"Yes. Sure."

He hung up and told Cynthia the news.

"Who is Russell Phillips?" she said.

Warden said he had met the boy only yesterday. "A newboy," he said. "Didn't like cold weather."

"Was he depressed?"

Warden shrugged and began to dial the telephone. Be home, Kathleen, he thought. On the third ring she answered.

He asked if she could drive Cynthia to the hospital.

"Yes," said Kathleen. Her voice was broken, as though she were choking.

"Have you heard the news about the boy?" asked Warden.

"Oh, yes," said Kathleen. "He was one of our advisees. Horace and I are both sick about it." She said she would come for Cynthia in half an hour.

He hung up. Cynthia asked him why the boy would jump off the roof of the gym.

"It's the highest building on campus," said Warden. "Next to Stringfellow. And Stringfellow would be too crowded."

Cynthia exhaled impatiently. "That's not what I mean," she said. "Why would he want to kill himself?"

Warden was pulling his navy blue blazer out of the closet. "I don't know," he said. "Only it bothers me that we've been talking about death all morning and that we now have a real death. There's been too much talk about death."

She could not relinquish the subject. "What would he be doing at the gym at night, anyway?"

Warden explained that the boy was on the wrestling team. The wrestlers held extra training sessions in the evenings after study hall.

Cynthia twisted onto her side and lay with her head on the pillow. "I can see two of you," she said, "like on a bad television picture. I wish one of you could stay here with me while the other goes off to work."

"I'll stay," he said.

"No," she said. "It was only a silly thing to say, not a real wish. I don't want to waste a real wish on having some company for the morning." She held up one arm. He bent down to kiss her quickly and then stood up.

"The school will be in complete turmoil," he said. "We'll probably have a special schedule for the day."

"I'll be all right," she said. "In a minute I'm going to get up and get dressed."

"Do you want some help?"

"Of course not."

"All I have to do is tell Sam Kaufman you're sick. He'll let me go with you."

"They need you here," said Cynthia. "I'll be all right with Kathleen."

"I'll try to call at lunch," he said.

"Poor Russell Phillips," she said. "From the roof of the gym."

"Yes," said Warden.

"I wonder if Dan Farnham heard anything last night," she said. "He lives in the gym."

"I'm sure I'll find out in a few minutes," said Warden. He held a scarf and a stack of folded papers in one hand.

"You didn't notice anything unusual last night, did you? When you were out?"

"Not at all," said Warden. "I was in Fleming Hall. I wasn't near the gym." He started for the door and then paused. "Why do you ask?"

"I don't know," she said. "The gym roof. The neck twisted around. It sounds weird, like something supernatural."

"I'll find out all I can," said Warden. His heart was sprinting.

Scene 15

It had been so easy with Russell Phillips. The wrestlers had been following their usual fanatical training schedule, working out after study hall at night, running up and down the stairs of the old gym, down to the basement and the locker rooms, up to the top floor and the rooms for wrestling and lifting weights. Russell had been bench-pressing some weights himself. And running. He was a little zealot, Russell, a bantamweight who wanted to get lighter.

It was such a kick to watch them all running the stairs, sweating through their gray tee shirts, encouraging one another with breathlessly muttered monosyllables. There must have been twenty or so at first, but most of them had disappeared after the mandatory fifteen minutes. Russell Phillips had stayed.

And so had he. It was perfectly natural for him to be there, after all. So when all the boys had left, save Russell Phillips, he had sat down on a bench in the weight room on the third floor of the gym to watch Russell finish his set. The kid had longish blond hair that was stringy with sweat and a red pimple on the back of his thick neck. The hair reminded him of that other hair. And when Russell had asked him for permission to stay just a bit past on-dorm time, he had granted it. Why not? It was within his authority to do so.

"You're dedicated, Russell," he had said.

"Yeah, well, it's about all there is to do here," Russell had said. A bit cocky, this boy.

"Did you work out over the holidays?"

"I worked out with my girlfriend," he'd said. Sure of himself, almost disrespectful. "In fact it was sort of in this position."

The words were outrageous, but he masked his reaction.

Even as he spoke to Russell, though, even as he uttered the words that reassured the boy that staying off dorm a bit late would be all right, he felt the passion return, felt his heart lurch and then flare into pounding, as though it had jump-started itself on a steep hill. While the boy was running more stairs, he toured the building: all dark in the furnace room, which contained an old desk and a cot, and which everyone called, to his amusement, "Angus's Lair"; all quiet in the basement, where a shiny concrete floor opened onto sets of locker rooms and a training room and coaches' offices; all quiet on the main floor with the basketball court and the trophy-lined lobby; all quiet in both faculty apartments.

Should he check the tunnel? No, that was a secret. No one would be in there at this hour. The only noise was upstairs; when he returned, he found that Russell had finished in the weight room and was now next door in the wrestling room, head down on a mat and serving as pivot as the boy spun and writhed and worked himself through an imaginary contest. This was a comfortable room, this box about twenty yards square, covered with mats on the floor and the walls, extra rolls of mats stored vertically like tree trunks against one wall.

"You scared me," the boy had said upon his return. "What are you doing here, anyway?" And then, before any chance for a response, the boy had added, "Sorry. Stupid question."

He had felt the heat pump into his face and had heard his own pulse in his ears.

"Let me show you a special move, Russell," he had said, and the boy had let him. Why not? The boy had sat on the mat and had let him kneel down behind and take the boy's head in his hands. Russell Phillips was strong, but he was tired, and he was not prepared anyway for a familiar adult to twist his neck suddenly and break it.

The boy had not died right away, and that part was bad, the eyes accusing him and the voice trying to speak but only choking. He had removed the boy's shoes and socks from the motionless feet and then had replaced the shoes, retying them patiently, all the while listening to that increasingly labored breathing. Once done, he had gone next door for a barbell and had climbed the stairs and broken the lock on the door to the roof. Then he had dragged the limp boy up the stairs, still coughing and choking and gasping at first, but then finally quiet, and had thrown him off the roof.

Now that it was over, he was all cool reason again. And yet he nearly vomited when he remembered the boy in the theater in New York. That had been only yesterday, though it seemed so much longer. He was going to have to control himself. It was wrong, giving in to this passion this way. He would be strong. He would resist. He would try.

THE THIRD ACT

Scene 1

Eldridge Lane, Ph.D. (economics, Rice University), for fifteen years headmaster of the Montpelier School for Boys, was furious.

"No one connected with my school is a murderer," he said. "No one. The very idea is preposterous."

Carol Scott said nothing. She looked like a bank officer calling to sell him a loan, with her gray wool suit, light makeup, short black hair pulled back with a gold barrette. She even carried a leather briefcase, which now rested on the patterned carpet at her feet. But Carol Scott was not a bank officer; she was an investigator with the county sheriff's office, and she was willing to wait for Lane to finish his tantrum. She cut her eyes over to Horace Somerville, the only other person in Lane's office. Horace Somerville was a vestryman at the Episcopal church in town where Carol Scott's children went to Sunday school and where she and her husband sang in the choir. She had greeted Horace a few minutes ago by noting that his tie had its knot uncharacteristically lopsided. He had surprised her by straightening it quietly instead of excoriating her.

Carol Scott sat beside Horace Somerville in front of Eldridge Lane's desk wishing she had not drawn this assignment. She knew Lane well and didn't care for him at all. He complained too frequently about the way she did her job, particularly when it meant adverse publicity for Montpelier School. It was a great school, sure, with a national reputation, but that didn't mean that the boys didn't try to buy beer with fake ID's from time to time, or that an ounce of coke didn't end up in somebody's dorm room on occasion. Lane treated every one of her visits as an intrusion. Maybe she intimidated him. She was 5′10″, the same height as he. She guessed that he had probably parted that silvery hair of his on the same line for every one of his fifty-nine years, and she could not imagine him wearing anything but the traditional attire he had on today: charcoal gray suit, white shirt, striped tie, black tasseled loafers. She figured him as the type who didn't like changes, including changes in the gender of the workplace.

It was clear that nothing had changed since the last time she had been in this office, which was what? five or six years ago? Six years, she remembered. It was a hazy June day when she had arrested Lane's youngest daughter, then seventeen, for possession of marijuana. Carol Scott had only been twenty-two then; it must have been one of her first arrests. She had made a special trip out to tell Lane in person that she thought the girl was probably dealing it, though she didn't have any hard evidence. Back then Lane had sat behind the same expansive desk, had swiveled in the same green leather chair, had adjusted the position of the same brass desk lamp, had ranted just as vehemently. He'd been livid that they had actually arrested his child without telephoning him first. In the end, his daughter had managed to get by with a fine and probation. The experience had seemed to straighten her out, for Carol Scott had seen her picture in the paper last summer, bride of some lawyer in Chapel Hill.

"This school exists because of the trust that parents place in us," said Lane. "A false rumor could do serious damage to our admissions program, not to mention our fund raising."

It was 9:00 in the morning, Tuesday, November 30, and Carol Scott was tired. She'd been called out here last night late to check on a corpse and had settled for five hours of sleep.

"We plan to operate with discretion," she said.

Behind her she heard a knock on the door. She turned to see Felix Grayson bearing down on her.

"Hello, Carol," said Felix Grayson. "Out here to discuss that Phillips boy, are you?" He was fifty years old, bespectacled with bifocals, and very large. He wore steel-toed work boots, khaki trousers, a plaid shirt, and a black knit tie. He stood 6′7″ and carried 230 pounds of muscle. He eased into the one chair remaining in front of the desk, right ankle resting on left knee, hands clasped and resting on his stomach. Grayson was the school's disciplinarian, and once in a while he had occasion to converse with the local police.

"You explain," said Lane to Carol Scott.

"I was on my way out here this morning anyway," she said, "just to look around one more time in the daylight. Then I got a call from a very nice man in New York."

She said that the New York police had found the receipt from a Montpelier School Store on the floor of a movie theater off Forty-second Street. It had been lying one row away from the body of a young male prostitute whose neck had been snapped by brute force.

None of the men spoke.

"Now it could be that this boy's death last night was a suicide," she said. "I think it's unusual to have a suicide so quickly after a vacation, but it's possible. What makes me uncomfortable is the way his neck, too, is twisted."

"Couldn't that happen when he fell?" said Lane.

She admitted that it could.

Grayson asked her what she wanted them to do.

She said she wanted a yearbook with everyone's picture in it to send to New York. The ticket salesperson at the movie theater might be able to make an identification. She also wanted a sample cash register receipt from the school store to send up for comparison.

"This receipt was not in particularly good shape," she said. "It had been stepped on and spilled on. The part with the items purchased and the date seem to be gone forever. But they could read the name Montpelier."

According to the police in New York, there were twenty-seven schools in the country called "Montpelier." No one had learned yet how many of the schools had their own supply shops.

"It couldn't be ours," said Lane. "And even if it were, we can't assume that a member of our own community is responsible for these deaths. We get people through here all the time—tourists, salespeople. We send off mail orders all over the country."

"I agree that the possibility is remote," said Carol Scott.

"Still, I would like to get the names of everyone on your faculty and all of your students who visited New York over the Thanksgiving holidays. I would also ask that you take some precautions with security. Don't let these boys walk around the campus by themselves."

"They have to walk around the campus by themselves," said Lane. "We have 500 acres of land here. How can I control the behavior of 360 boys?"

"You'll think of something," said Carol Scott. "Tell them that you've put in a new rule."

"How can I do that without arousing suspicion or starting a rumor?" said Lane.

"It's all right with me if you want to treat this death like a suicide," said Carol Scott. "Tell the boys that they need to look out for one another. That they need to be 'buddies.' I don't know. You know your students better than I do."

"How long will we have to go through this charade?" said Lane.

She said it would be at least until Montpelier School for Boys was clearly not tied to the death of the kid in New York.

Then she picked up her briefcase and left.

Horace Somerville waved her a silent good-bye. He liked Carol, knew Eldridge would, too, if he could make the effort to get acquainted. Somerville and Eldridge Lane had known each other since they were thirteen years old, when both of them had enrolled at Montpelier as third-formers. Somerville had been on the search committee that had nominated Lane as headmaster sixteen years ago, when Horace was academic dean. But Somerville had stepped down from that job three years ago, when he'd noticed himself slowing down. It was better for somebody younger like Sam Kaufman to have the position, even if Kaufman was an idiot. He wondered if perhaps Eldridge should have made the same move two or three years ago. Eldridge was slipping, Somerville thought, worried more about appeasing the board of trustees and keeping up the image of the school than he was about keeping in touch with the actual community.

Lane pulled a Hershey's Kiss from his jacket pocket and pulled at the silvery foil wrapper. "So where do we go from here?" he said. "You two are here to counsel."

"It wouldn't be out of line to send the boys home early for vacation," said Somerville.

"On what grounds?" said Lane. "If nothing got settled over the holidays, would they all then stay at home? Should we close down the school?"

"I say we wait for the police to finish their investigation," said Grayson. "They said they wanted to look at our yearbook and our cash register receipts. Let them."

"I agree," said Lane.

"Shouldn't we call a faculty meeting?" said Grayson. "Tell everyone to be on guard? Inform them that the police think it might not have been a suicide at all?"

"I'm considering that," said Lane.

"Why hesitate? We need the extra security. We could have fifty vigilant adults on campus with their eyes open."

"Horace has already advised me otherwise," said Lane. "Though I do not think his reasoning is sound."

Horace Somerville spoke before Grayson had an opportunity. "I believe that Russell was murdered. He was my advisee and I knew him, and I don't believe he was a candidate for suicide. But we can't tell the faculty that."

"Why not?" said Grayson.

"Because," said Somerville, "I'm worried that the killer is somebody on the faculty."

Lane said that was ridiculous.

Grayson did not appear rattled by the suggestion.

"Why on the faculty?" he asked.

"Because we are isolated and rural and do not have strangers wandering around our campus at night. We notice them."

Grayson said that strangers were on the campus all the time.

"They don't congregate at the gymnasium," said Somerville.

"Why not a student?" asked Grayson.

"Exactly," said Lane. "Why not somebody on the staff? Why not a friend of the school from town? Say it's not a suicide. That's some leap in logic to assume automatically that he was killed by a member of the faculty."

Somerville said he was going on instinct and hoped he was wrong.

"But who? Who on the faculty could it possibly be?" said Lane.

It was Grayson who answered. "McPhee."

"Why McPhee?" said Lane.

"He found the boy. Pretty convenient for him just to stumble onto a body at the side of the gym at midnight."

"Pat McPhee was the day master," said Lane. "He went looking for Russell Phillips when the boy was reported missing from his dormitory."

Grayson continued. "Plus an ex-professional athlete? You know he's in good shape. And he lives in the gym. Easy access."

"What a miracle that Carol Scott didn't arrest him on the spot," said Lane. "Why are you so eager to convict McPhee? Where were you last night when the boy died?"

"I'm not accusing," said Grayson, "just playing along. I heard McPhee went chasing off to Boston over the holidays and came back without his wife or her son. I imagine that must have rattled him some."

"So he starts killing our students?" said Lane.

"They were married just last summer," said Grayson. "I bet he's still got his honeymoon hormones."

"Don't waste my time, Felix," said Lane. "Are you seriously suggesting that Patrick McPhee is capable of murder?"

"No," said Grayson. He turned serious. "I think Horace, here, is cuckoo."

"Is there anyone on this faculty who is capable of murder?"

"No," said Grayson.

"I agree," said Lane. "Let's not complicate matters with rumors and innuendoes."

"If you think it's so silly," said Horace Somerville, "why did you ask our advice? Why take any precautions whatsoever?"

This time Eldridge Lane said nothing. He knew of at least two members of the faculty who had been in New York on Sunday.

Scene 2

By the end of second period, everyone on campus knew that one of the newboys had committed suicide.

Thomas Boatwright learned about it between classes from Richard Blackburn.

"They said he broke the lock on the rooftop door with a hammer and dived off the roof," said Richard. "I heard it was because he couldn't make weight for the wrestling team and was depressed."

Thomas said he couldn't believe it. "I sure as hell wouldn't kill myself if I got cut from the basketball team."

"That's because you don't understand the mind of your basic wrestler," said Richard. "They're all crazy. They're obsessed with themselves. They're narcissistic and anorexic all at the same time."

"Did he leave a note?"

"Hell, no," said Richard. "Wrestlers can't write. I've got to go."

They were standing in the brightly lighted cinder-block and tile hallway of Reid Hall, the science building. It was 9:30, third period, time for biology. Montpelier's weekly schedule was pretty neat except for the part about going to classes on Saturdays. Your classes were always rotating around, so that you didn't have the same class at the same time of day every day. English, for example, met Monday at 8:00 but didn't meet Tuesday until 2:15, after lunch, and it didn't meet at all on Thursday. Biology, on the other hand, didn't meet on Monday, and Spanish didn't meet on Saturday. Nobody had classes at all on Friday or Saturday afternoons so that all the athletic teams could play games without missing classes. It worked pretty well, so you didn't get stuck in a rut with the boring classes like English and religion as your first thing to look forward to every day of the week, and the fun classes like biology and Spanish sort of got sprinkled through your schedule like candy.

Science was usually Thomas's worst subject. He just couldn't keep all those terms straight.

"Where's the carotid artery?" Richard would ask him.

"In the thigh," he'd say.

"No."

"The lungs."

"No way."

"Where, then?"

The carotid artery was in the neck. Richard would laugh at him for always forgetting, but Thomas couldn't see what difference it made where the damn carotid artery was.

But Mr. Carella made biology class lively and fun. He was Italian and from the North and talked really fast and always cut jokes in class and on dorm, where the worst thing he ever did to you was to ask you to turn down your stereo. He'd played football and wrestled on the varsity teams at Union College, and he was also excellent in basketball, tennis, and lacrosse. On weekends he took groups kayaking and rappeling.

Thomas always looked forward to biology class the most, but today he was dreading it.

Carella helped coach the JV wrestling team. Russell Phillips had been one of his wrestlers.

Instead of being depressed, however, Mr. Carella was his usual upbeat self.

"Boatwright, Boatwright, can't even float right," said Mr. Carella as Thomas entered the biology lab. He was sitting on a gray metal lab stool behind the long black lab table at the front of the room, and the biggest surprise for Thomas was that he was so dressed up, in blue slacks, a white button-down shirt, and a tie. Carella didn't even wear ties most days; instead he wore open-necked shirts, jeans, and sneakers. One day he even wore a Redskins tee shirt, but Dean Kaufman saw it and made him go back and change.

"Boatwright doesn't even have to come to class today," said Mr. Carella. "He knows all about sex already."

Then Thomas noticed the two big plastic models on the black-topped table in front of Mr. Carella. One was a big limp penis with scrotum, all made of ribbed beige plastic and hinged so that you could open it up and see everything inside. It was open now, and Thomas could see a bunch of red blood vessels and blue tubes and green globules and a bunch of parts he couldn't identify. The other model Thomas did not recognize at first, but then he realized with a jolt that it was an equally gigantic uterus and that it, too, was hinged and open so you could see all the places inside. Thomas laughed involuntarily and blushed.

He piled his flat lab report on the stack at the corner of the front table. There were already a dozen reports in the pile; Thomas was one of the last people getting to class. He took his seat at one of the smaller student tables next to Greg, who told him Hesta had called during first period.

Damn. They'd been missing each other's calls since Sunday.

"Let's get started, fellows," said Carella.

A second later Robert Staines skidded into the room.

"Sorry I'm late," he said. He took it for granted that Carella wouldn't mind.

"Where's your lab report?" asked Carella. He was all business.

"Yeah, right, the lab report," said Staines. He motioned to the disorderly load of spiral notebooks, loose papers, and textbooks under his left arm. "It's in here somewhere."

"Put it in the pile and sit down."

"Actually," said Staines, "it's not exactly finished."

"See me after class," said Carella.

Staines said he had to clean his room after class. During the 10:15 recess your room got inspected by one of the teachers on duty, and if it was messy, you got demerits.

"You should have cleaned your room this morning. See me after class."

"You've got to be kidding me," said Staines.

"Watch your mouth," said Mr. Carella. "Sit down and shut up."

"Didn't you hear what happened? One of the newboys jumped off the gym roof," said Staines. He was looking particularly blond and gorilla-ish today, with scuffed old cordovan loafers on his tiny little feet that everybody said were like pigs' feet, jeans with a tiny hole in the crotch, and a gigantic gray and red ski sweater. His nose was running, and he hadn't shaved, so that light glinted off the stubble on his face.

"Sit your buns down, Staines, and plan on staying for a while."

Staines took his seat at a table behind Greg and Thomas. There were four pairs of the black-topped tables in all, with seats for sixteen, but there were only fourteen boys in the class. The walls of the lab were covered with charts—the periodic table of elements, the different eras of prehistoric existence, human anatomy, and the parts of a cell.

Mr. Carella started the class with a little speech. He said it was in honor of Russell Phillips that he wore his best clothes. "Russell died, and I'm sick about it, and when I go to mass in Montpelier, I'm going to light a candle for Russell and pray that his soul finds peace. Have any of you guys prayed for Russell? Maybe you should."

Everyone was very quiet. He told them nobody was going to use this death as some lame excuse for not doing his homework, that Russell was dead and we were alive, that we were in biology class to study life. He said they were starting a unit today on the life force, the sex act, and that they were going to treat it seriously. The room was quieter than the library.

"I hope that if any of you guys get depressed, you won't hesitate to come and talk to me or to your advisor or to somebody," said Mr. Carella. "We care."

His eyes got very bright and wet, and he brushed them with quick light flicks of his fingers.

"Let's do some biology," he said.

And they did biology for the rest of the period. They talked about the male reproductive system and the female reproductive system and estrogen and testosterone and ovulation and penetration and masturbation and herpes and gonorrhea and AIDS. At first Mr. Carella was really clinical and serious about the whole thing, but after a while he started joking around in his usual way and made everything fun.

"This is that thing you've been dreaming about, fellows," he said. He had his hand on the big plastic vagina and was rubbing it in a really seductive way. "White women, black women, even Italian women, they've all got the same thing. It's not so mysterious when you look at it in biology class, is it? Well, tomorrow I thought I'd ask my friend Jamie Lee Curtis to come in from Hollywood and show us a real one."

Mr. Carella was just a killer in class.

Robert Staines raised his hand and asked whether Mr. Carella thought it would help some of the less experienced boys at Montpelier if the school went coed.

Mr. Carella pretended to go berserk. " 'The less experienced boys,' Staines?" he said. "You have plenty of experience yourself, of course, is that it?"

"Lots of fun over the holidays," said Staines.

"The holidays," said Mr. Carella. He stood and thought for at least a minute without saying anything. When he spoke again, he had switched tones back to the serious one. "We joke too much," he said. Then he went into a speech about how sex was a very powerful, very dangerous force to abuse, how it was what generated life and was a gift from God that deserved respect. "We can identify every fluid and every organ and every step of the process, gentlemen, but we can't explain that incredible urge or that explosion of power we get from sex. I can't teach what passion is, boys. But I can sure tell you not to treat it lightly."

The bell rang. That was the way it always was in biology class, over before you were expecting.

"Hold it," said Mr. Carella. He read from a piece of paper announcing a special assembly in the chapel at 11:30. Typical of the school to choose a time when nobody would miss any classes. At 11:30 you had consultation period, where teachers could yank you into their rooms for individual tutoring.

"Dismissed," said Carella. "Except Staines."

Everybody gathered his books to leave. Robert Staines tugged on Thomas's sweater. "Wait up," he said. "I've got to talk to you about the mixer this weekend."

It suited Thomas to wait. He and Greg always cleaned their room before breakfast.

In fifteen seconds the only people remaining in the classroom were Staines, Thomas, and Mr. Carella. Thomas sat on top of a student table while in the front of the room Carella dissected Staines without a knife.

"You are the most irresponsible, arrogant, flippant, disruptive student I have ever seen," said Carella.

"And you love it," said Staines. The guy was incredibly brazen. And the thing was, Carella did love it. He laughed.

"Where's your lab report?" he asked.

Staines said he hadn't done it.

"None of it?"

"I put my name on it."

Carella shook his head as though Staines were his mischievous little brother and told him to get the report done by tomorrow. It made Thomas a little mad. Everybody else had to get his work in on time. But that was typical of Robert Staines. Somehow he charmed people into letting him get away with felonies.

"I got to have some coffee," said Mr. Carella. "You boys keep the place clean." He took the stack of lab reports and left the classroom.

Staines swaggered back to where Thomas sat.

"I've got that guy completely figured out," he said. "If you're a good athlete in his class, you've got it made."

Thomas asked him what he wanted.

"Your sister's at Mason, right?" Staines asked.

"Right," said Thomas. Hell, Staines had only been his roommate for a whole nine months last year. They'd only talked about fifty million times about how Barbara was a student at Mason School.

"She knows Katrina Olson?"

"I don't know," said Thomas. "Probably." Barbara knew Katrina Olson. Everybody at Mason knew Katrina Olson. Even Hesta, who was new at the school this year, knew her. Katrina Olson was nicknamed the Bay Bridge Tunnel because of all the traffic that entered her.

"I'm trying to get the Kat-woman to come down for the mixer Saturday," said Staines. "You know how it is when you get the urge."

"Yeah," said Thomas.

"You know, passion," said Staines. "Like what Carella was talking about."

"Yeah." It was a tribute to Mr. Carella that even Staines listened in his class.

"You think your sister could set it up for me?"

Thomas did not want to get into the pimping business. "I don't know," he said. "I don't know if she knows her that well."

"I could probably just call old Katrina myself," said Staines.

"Yeah."

"What about you? I hear you've got a girlfriend up there now," said Staines.

Hell. "Sort of," said Thomas.

"Just get her to ask if Katrina's got a date already," said Staines. "If she doesn't, then I'll call her."

This was his chance to tell Staines no for once. "Yeah, okay," said Thomas. "If I can ever get Hesta on the phone myself."

He started to leave. Staines drifted back to the front of the room and walked around to the teacher's side of the large lab table.

"You coming to the dorm?" Thomas asked.

"Yeah," said Staines. He started opening drawers under the lab table. Thomas was appalled. Teachers' desks, closets, and drawers were strictly off limits.

"A teacher's desk is Red Flag," said Thomas. "Are you crazy?"

"He doesn't care."

Staines continued to open and close drawers. He asked if the lab report had been difficult.

"Not really." Not if you knew the carotid artery was in the neck.

Staines asked where Carella kept the sample lab reports. He said that over the holidays he had forgotten the format they were supposed to use to write them. It was a ridiculous excuse, since the class had been writing lab reports by the same format every week since September. But Staines was just stupid enough for it possibly to be true. He moved to the teacher's desk beside the lab table.

Thomas was getting uneasy. Breaking a Red Flag was a very serious offense. He wanted both of them to leave.

"You aren't going to find the answers," said Thomas.

"I'm not looking for answers," said Staines. "That would be cheating. Just some examples to get me started."

He opened the middle drawer of Carella's desk and froze.

Thomas asked him why he did not bring up the sample reports when Carella was still in the room.

Staines did not answer. He reached into the open desk drawer and pulled out something metallic.

"Now what do you suppose Carella would be doing with these?" he said. He held up a pair of shiny handcuffs.

Somehow it was funny as hell.

Scene 3

At 11:30 the whole school assembled in the chapel. Dr. Lane, the headmaster, sat beside Mr. Heilman behind the lectern. Heilman was in his vestments; Lane was in civvies. Thomas and Richard sat together toward the back. It was very quiet, and Thomas felt himself getting sad. He hadn't even known the boy Russell Phillips, and yet now that he was here in the chapel, with its familiar white walls and clear windowpanes and huge marble altar with a dark blue rug running up the aisle to it, Thomas felt himself ready to cry. Somebody who was alive yesterday was no longer alive today. What if Thomas's parents died suddenly? Or Barbara? Or Jeff? What if Hesta died?

He looked around for Greg but didn't see him. Nathan Somerville was dressed in a black robe at the altar and lighting the candles with a long brass taper. When he finished, he went down to the front pew and sat with his grandfather. There was no choir, but Mr. Carson, the music teacher, was playing some quiet improvisation on the organ. He saw a couple of boys with tears on their cheeks. Thomas felt his own throat start to tickle and felt embarrassed. This was stupid, a conditioned response. He glanced to his left. Richard was dry-eyed but looked very solemn.

Mr. Heilman stood up, called the assembly to order, as if it needed to be, and told them what they already knew: that Russell Phillips had taken his own life last night. After he read a passage from the Bible and said a long prayer that melted into the Lord's Prayer, he started talking about getting in touch with your feelings and dialoguing, and the proper ways to grieve, and all the other stuff he was always tossing around in chapel services. Thomas thought the assembly would have been better without Mr. Heilman involved.

Dr. Lane spoke next. Thomas didn't know Dr. Lane very well. As headmaster, he was distant from the students most of the time. Often he was off in New York or Atlanta or somewhere trying to raise money for the school. He didn't teach any classes or coach any sports, and he handled only the most serious disciplinary cases and the honor offenses sent to him by the board of councilmen. He spoke in an elegant Richmond accent, in which "house" rhymed with "gross" and the final "r" on words did not exist.

He told them something that they did not know.

"I do not wish to add to your grief," he said, "but I have spent the morning talking with Russell's parents in Louisiana and to his roommate and to several of his teachers. These people have indicated to me that Russell was not at all obviously suicidal. He had been planning a skiing trip to Colorado for the Christmas holidays, and he was preparing for the big wrestling tournament on Saturday afternoon. He even had a date for the mixer."

He paused. "What I'm saying is that you can't take anything for granted. Somebody who seems perfectly happy on the surface can be miserable underneath. I am therefore asking you in these next months at school to make a conscious effort not to let anyone be alone. No boy is to be alone on the dormitory during the academic day, and no boy is to walk the campus alone at night. Let's stick together. Let's behave with thoughtfulness toward one another. And let us make no mistake about my words. This is not a suggestion, but a new school rule: no boy is to be alone on this campus after dark."

Thomas felt the unpleasant churn of annoyance transform his grief into exasperation. That was so typical of the school, to lay down another rule on the students just because of one special case. He didn't like the way Dr. Lane had implied that one of them might have prevented Russell's death if they'd been more attentive. Why the hell does everything always have to be the students' fault? From the murmuring and the hum of tension he knew that others in the chapel felt the same way.

"Dr. Pain," said Richard. He got shushed by one of the teachers sitting behind them.

Dr. Lane went on to say that all faculty advisors should be available for any boy who wished to come by to discuss Russell's death.

"Otherwise," said Dr. Lane, "I urge you to get back into your routine as quickly as possible. It may seem difficult at first, but I assure you that it's the best thing. Classes will meet this afternoon as usual, but any boy who would prefer to meet with Mr. Heilman will be allowed to do so."

That was shrewd, thought Thomas. He gives us a choice between bullshit for credit and just bullshit. Thomas preferred to get credit.

On his way out, at the back of the chapel, Thomas saw Angus Farrier, same old crew cut and same old olive trousers, but, unbelievably, wearing a tie and a jacket instead of the usual tee shirt.

"You hear that new rule, Angus?" he asked. He was referring to Lane's demand that nobody be on campus alone after dark. You could usually count on Angus to say something funny about Dr. Lane, but today he was all business.

"Maybe it'll help," said Angus. He was looking down at his shoes as he spoke. "I can't do it all by myself."

"What're you talking about?" said Thomas. People were crowding by him to get out of the chapel.

Angus shook his head and departed for the gym. Thomas went on to lunch. He figured Angus had misunderstood his question.

That afternoon he made an even greater mistake.

Scene 4

Only three hours had passed since the special assembly this morning. To Thomas it seemed like a million years. One minute to the bell, and it would be three o'clock, and classes would at last be over. The rotating schedule had rotated English class into last period today. Of course Farnham had gone right ahead with *Othello* as though nothing unusual had happened at all. He was jabbering on about major themes, and he was pointing to where he had written in big block letters APPEARANCE on one side of the board and REALITY on the other.

The whole class sat in silence. Everybody had closed his notebook and had piled his books on the desktops. Half a minute to go, and Farnham was acting like somebody who'd just translated the Rosetta stone.

"Othello starts off as a military hero, but he ends up as a *tragic* hero. He makes a terrible mistake, but he learns from that mistake. He achieves self-recognition at a terrible cost. Thomas Boatwright—"

Saved by the bell. Almost.

"—see me after class. The rest of you are dismissed." Across the room Richard stuck his teeth out and made his samurai face, stolen from the old clips of John Belushi on "Saturday Night Live."

Mr. Farnham was erasing the board. "Why didn't you come by for an audition yesterday?" he asked.

"I did come by," Thomas said carefully, "but I didn't see you on the stage." That was true enough, but Thomas knew he was quibbling with the truth, and hence was violating the spirit, at least, of the honor system.

"Do you still want to try for a part? Mrs. Kaufman is coming by to read for Desdemona today."

Thomas said he thought Mrs. Warden had that part.

"She does if she can manage it," said Mr. Farnham. "She's been ill."

Thomas had seen her at dinner last night. He asked what was wrong.

"Nothing major, I'm sure." Why did adults always think they needed to protect you from bad news?

Thomas said he'd decided to try out for a part, but that he wasn't interested in Brabantio. "I don't want to be an old man."

"You could read for Roderigo," said Farnham. "He's young. You and Nathan Somerville could rehearse on your dorm, couldn't you? Nathan's playing Iago. And Roderigo's a good part."

"What's so good about it?" said Thomas. "He's pretty stupid, isn't he? Isn't he the one that doesn't know what's going on?"

"It's fun to play stupid people," said Farnham. "Besides, you get to die."

Thomas thought about the conversation on the way to practice. They'd decided that Thomas would come by the auditorium if he got out of practice before 6:00. "You get to die." That was supposed to be the big drawing card, getting to gasp for breath, choke, stare in shock off into the middle distance, then slump to the stage. Thomas had seen a lot of stage deaths in his life. Three years ago his father had taken his family to England, where they'd gone to see *Hamlet* in Stratford. Thomas had been disappointed to see both Hamlet and Laertes breathing heavily at the end of their sword fight even after both were supposed to be dead. He had pointed it out to his dad.

"Being dead is hard," his father had said, "though I don't think those actors were giving it their best."

At the end of a Shakespearean play, nearly everybody important ended up dead. He figured it was the same way in *Othello.* But who could tell? The only one he was really sure would die would be Desdemona, since he'd seen posters of Othello strangling her ever since he was a little kid. Maybe after what Farnham was saying today about reversing your expectations, it would turn out that Othello would get to live. What if the bad guy turned out to live at the end? That was the neat thing about Shakespeare; even when you anticipated exactly what was going to happen, he twisted the formula just enough to keep you surprised.

As usual, Robert Staines was running his mouth in the basketball locker room.

"Hey," said Staines, "you hear about the cops being out here? They say there's something weird about Russell Phillips's death."

Ralph Musgrove asked him what he was talking about.

"They said his neck got twisted completely around, like in *The Exorcist.* I say it was one of the niggers on campus practicing voodoo spells."

Coach McPhee's voice came from the other side of the room, from behind the island of lockers hiding him.

"That's the stupidest comment I've ever heard," he said. He walked out from where he'd been sitting and rolling towels to help Angus. "You don't know what the hell you're talking about, Staines." He said Staines was lucky there weren't any black kids on the team to overhear him. He was angry, and the whistle he wore around his neck bounced against his white coach's shirt. "You weren't there. I was. His neck twisted because he hit his head on the side of the building when he jumped, and because he landed on a guy wire supporting a telephone pole down below. You are not going to turn this tragedy into some stinking racist propaganda. You understand me?"

Staines was staring at the carpet. He said he understood.

"You better have a hell of a good practice today, Staines," said McPhee. "And that means I don't hear your voice."

And Staines did have a good practice. They all did. Somehow every time Thomas touched the ball, Staines or Musgrove had broken free under the basket where Thomas could hit him. He was handling the ball well, dribbling with either hand automatically, working the ball around the perimeter and then zipping it inside or even shooting once in a while when he was open. Everything went well until the end, when they got to the free throws. They paired up at the six different baskets in the gym, Thomas with Ralph Musgrove. Thomas hit only five of ten shots.

"Concentrate," said Coach McPhee, who seemed able to

watch everybody at the same time. "Do your routine, Boatwright. Two dribbles only, look at the basket, bend your knees, and follow through."

At 5:30 Coach McPhee called them all together. "It's getting dark outside," he said. "You remember what Dr. Lane told you today. Nobody walks around the campus alone after dark. Pair up when you leave the building."

"We're not depressed, Coach," said Staines.

"Yeah, Mr. McPhee," said Ralph Musgrove. Everybody on the team reacted with him.

"We can look after ourselves."

"I'm not afraid of the dark."

"If some guy wants to be alone, he'll find a way."

"It's stupid."

"We're not babies."

"That's enough," said Mr. McPhee.

Everybody got still. "Not babies," said Mr. McPhee. "No, you're not. Babies like to have somebody look after them. Adolescents want to get on with their own independent lives." Thomas had never heard him sound so bitter. "Let me tell you something about babies, gentlemen. I had a baby brother who drowned in a bathtub because his sitter was careless. His teenaged adolescent sitter was given a responsibility, but he didn't take it seriously, and my baby brother drowned." He paused. "And gentlemen, I was that babysitter. I was your age, and I thought I had better things to do than to look after a two-year-old kid in a bathtub."

He seemed to be staring at each one of them at the same time. Nobody said a word. Thomas looked away, down at his shoes.

"Think unselfishly," said Coach McPhee. "Try a little self-discipline. Your duty is to look out for each other. If I catch you breaking that rule, I'll see to it that you get plenty of demerits and plenty of time to sit on the bench for Saturday's game. Dr. Lane is serious about that policy, and so am I."

So Thomas ended up walking back to the dorm with Robert Staines. They agreed that the new policy was dumb.

"It's just another damn excuse for them to take away some of our freedom," said Staines. "I should have gone to Exeter or Andover."

Why not just straight to Harvard, Thomas thought. Staines had never earned over a C in any course since he had been here.

Back on the dorm they split up. "Good practice," said Staines.

"Yeah, good practice," said Thomas. Staines was actually behaving like a human being.

The room was empty. It was 5:45. At the same moment he realized Greg must still be at play practice, Thomas remembered his appointment with Mr. Farnham. If Coach McPhee had not just lectured them, he would have ignored the new rule and walked over to Bradley Hall by himself. That story about his little brother was horrifying. Maybe Staines would go with him. He hurried next door to Staines's room, where Tracy Chapman was blasting on the stereo.

Staines was getting high.

He had taken a can of Right Guard and put a towel over the nozzle. When Thomas walked in, Staines was huffing the aerosol spray coming through the towel as the deodorant liquid got filtered out by the terry cloth. Supposedly the chemicals in the aerosol spray got you stoned; Thomas had heard about the procedure but had never seen it before. He knew only that it was illegal at school. He turned around immediately to leave, but not before Staines grabbed him and pulled him back into the room.

"Hey," Staines said. "You're going to be cool about this, aren't you?" He was swaying as he held Thomas's arm. He held it hard, and he shouted because of the volume of the music.

"If you want to rot your brain, that's your problem," Thomas shouted back. There weren't all that many drugs at Montpelier, not at least in comparison with a lot of schools, because Dr. Lane was so strict about kicking you out even for possession. But some people tried getting off on "legal" substances like aerosol sprays, glue, and record cleaners. Carella had told them in biology class that such stuff could eat your brain cells, and Thomas had believed him. Hell, Thomas had never even smoked pot before.

"You want to try it?" said Staines.

"How could such a good athlete—" Thomas started.

Then Mr. Carella was in the room. He was still wearing

his sweats from wrestling practice. At the sight of him Thomas nearly hyperventilated. Staines let go of Thomas's arm and casually tossed the towel with the Right Guard can onto the bed.

Carella turned down the volume to nothing. Then he looked at them both. He said he could hear the noise all the way downstairs in the lobby. He looked at them hard. "Anything going on here?" he asked.

"Nothing," said Staines.

"Thomas?" said Mr. Carella.

What could he say? Mr. Carella was a cool young teacher, but he was still a teacher, and he was fanatic about eliminating drug abuse.

"I'm just talking to Robert," said Thomas.

"Nothing illegal going on here?"

"No sir," said Staines.

Thomas thought carefully. "Talking's all right, isn't it?" he said.

Carella looked at them in silence for several seconds. "Fine," he said. "Just remember the rules about noise."

He left. Thomas started to follow him out the door.

Staines grabbed him by the arm again. "Where are you going?" he said.

"Back to my room."

"Back to narc to Carella, you mean."

That wasn't true. "Let me go, Staines," said Thomas.

Staines said they needed to talk. "Look," he told Thomas, "this is the first time I've ever done anything like this. I was depressed after McPhee jumped all over me before practice. I was trying to cheer myself up."

It was all bull. But so what? If only Thomas were better at making quick decisions. He was not sure of what to do.

Staines was encouraged by the silence. "Be cool," he said. "I promise you it will never happen again." He released Thomas's arm and picked up the towel and the can from his bed.

He put the Right Guard into his top dresser drawer and tossed the towel into his open closet. "Now let's think about this," said Staines. "There's nothing illegal about spraying a can of deodorant. Remember that. There's no rule against it."

Thomas knew the rules. There was a rule against getting high.

"Everything's fine," said Staines. "I learned my lesson. Boy, what a stupid stunt for me to pull."

"Are you talking about discipline or honor?" said Thomas. Honor violations were different from disciplinary infractions. You lied, cheated, or stole, and that was an honor violation. Then you had to appear in front of the honor council. Convicted, you could get one of two punishments: immediate dismissal or honor probation. People on honor probation could remain at Montpelier, but they were automatically dismissed if they were ever found guilty of a second honor violation. If, on the other hand, you broke a regular old school rule—like a rule about drinking or going off dorm or staying up after hours—that was a disciplinary matter. Breaking a rule in the disciplinary code could get you kicked out of school too, if it was serious enough, but it would not be considered a moral blemish, the way an honor violation would be.

The distinction in this case was moot. As Thomas saw it, Staines had violated both codes: the disciplinary rule about intoxication, the honor rule about lying.

"What about honor?" said Staines.

"What you told Mr. Carella. That wasn't true."

Staines hit him hard on the shoulder with his open palm. It was a half punch half slap that forced Thomas back a step and rattled him.

"I don't remember what I told Mr. Carella," Staines said. "You can't remember either, can you?"

Thomas had never seen Staines so angry. His shoulder hurt. "It all happened fast," said Thomas.

Staines relaxed a little. "That's right," he said. "It all happened so fast, none of us can remember what we said."

But Thomas could remember plenty. "I think it was deception," he said. "You lied to him."

Staines hit him again the same way. "Be careful about bringing up deception," he said.

Thomas's shoulder throbbed. He was getting angry. "Don't hit me," he said.

"Don't accuse me," said Staines.

For a second it was a standoff. Thomas wanted to be sensible. "Let's just go talk to Mr. Carella," he said. Staines exploded all over again.

"You want us both kicked out of school?" said Staines.

Of course he didn't want them kicked out of school. He reminded Staines that if you turned yourself in, you were often acquitted. The very worst you could get was probation. They liked for you to be honest.

"Probation, hell. I'm already on probation," said Staines.

Thomas was shocked. He had lived either with Staines or next door to him since they had enrolled at Montpelier, and he had never known about an honor trial. "What for?" he asked.

Staines said never mind. He was blocking the door so that Thomas couldn't leave.

"You be damn careful about what you say," said Staines. "If I'm guilty, you're guilty too. Remember that. You're guilty of an honor violation. I go down, you go down, too."

"I haven't deceived anybody," said Thomas. But he was not sure whether that was altogether accurate.

"No?" said Staines. "Mr. Carella left this room with the impression that nothing illegal had been going on. Did you contribute to that impression?"

"I just wanted somebody to walk with me over to Bradley," said Thomas. "You can't get me involved in this."

Staines said it was too late, that the only way to handle it was to keep quiet. "You say nothing, I say nothing, nobody suffers."

Thomas knew this was the time to blast him, to turn him in, to let the school authorities handle it. But what would people say? He didn't want people like Mr. Warden and Mr. McPhee and his parents hearing about his having to go before the honor council. And what would his teammates say if Staines got dismissed? The honor system was a funny mechanism. You were supposed to be honest, but there was also an unwritten code that said you gave a fellow student the benefit of the doubt.

But he shouldn't have any doubt. Staines was already on probation.

But if he went to the honor council, he would have to

testify in front of all those seniors. And what if he turned Staines in and they acquitted him? What would it be like to live next door to the guy then?

Thomas said he would think it over.

But what he really wanted to do was to die.

Scene 5

Dean Samuel Kaufman was in a snit.

All this whispering, all these surreptitious meetings all day, and nobody included him in a thing. Why was he academic dean, if he was constantly to be excluded? He had just about had enough of this high-handed Eldridge Lane and his breach of protocol. Maybe it was time to resign.

Well, no, actually it was time for cocktails before dinner. Not time to resign; time for a drink. He admired himself for being able to make a play on words despite such a humiliating day.

It was 6:00 P.M. Kaufman was at his home on campus waiting for his wife, Virginia, to get home from that outrageously long play rehearsal Dan Farnham had begged her to attend. Had anyone asked Dean Samuel Kaufman to take a part in the play? Of course not. But they'd asked his wife. She was going to be Iago's wife, Emilia, the lady-in-waiting to Desdemona. Ginny was far too old to be making a spectacle of herself in some high school play, but since it was Shakespeare, Kaufman supposed it was all right.

It was getting on toward dinnertime. Surely Ginny would be home in a minute. Kaufman poured himself a nice tall bourbon and ginger ale and turned on the television news. If they had anything adverse about the school on television, it wouldn't be Kaufman's fault. He'd had nothing to do with any of this mess from the moment Pat McPhee had discovered the body. Eldridge Lane had handled the entire matter himself from the beginning, just exactly like some . . . Kaufman wasn't sure what he was like, but it was tacky.

Lane's handling of the situation irked Kaufman to no end. The police coming out here last night and again this morning, the assembly today before lunch, the telephone calls to and from the parents of Russell Phillips: had Kaufman been invited to any of it? Not at all.

"Just mind the office, Sam," Eldridge Lane had said. Mind the office! As if he were the secretary!

Kaufman was forty-five years old and had taught intermediate Latin and third-form English grammar before his promotion to the deanship. He held advanced degrees in educational theory, and he was a very respected member of the academic community—at least in *some* circles. Just last year he had published an article in a regional educational journal on how to teach Latin vocabulary with a rotary dial telephone, but did anyone at Montpelier School even mention it? No matter. Someday all his labor would be recognized. He had shaped up the Montpelier curriculum very nicely in the three years since he'd taken over as dean. They now offered an elective course in philology (why, oh, why wouldn't any students at least try it?), and the individual classroom teachers never *ever* ran out of chalk or grade report forms now that Kaufman had moved in. Did anyone utter a word of thanks? His predecessor, Horace Somerville, had not cared a whit about chalk and grade report forms. Horace Somerville was a crusty old charmer of a character to have on the faculty, but that office had been in absolute shambles until Kaufman had come along.

That first drink went down too quickly. He'd have to nurse the second or he might cause a scandal in the dining hall by showing up tipsy. He checked for his travel-size spray of Binaca mouth freshener in the pocket of his sports coat. It was there. He carried it with him everywhere.

Kaufman's back was bothering him. It always did when he felt too tense. He supposed a little more medicinal bourbon could help relax those muscles. Damn Eldridge Lane to hell, and damn all his cronies, too. If he wants to have secret meetings with that policewoman and invite Horace Somerville and Felix Grayson, that was just fine with Dean Samuel

Kaufman. He would run the school while they were off playing at espionage.

Ginny came home at 6:15. She looked flushed and happy, almost like a little girl, even though her hair was half gray and she was two years older than Kaufman.

"That walk in the cold air feels so good," she said. She turned down the volume on the television set and sat down beside him on the love seat.

"Why were you so late?" he asked her.

"They had me reading for Desdemona. What a wonderful part. And I found out a secret."

Kaufman was immediately alert.

"What?" he said. He loved a secret. Knowing it was almost as fun as telling it.

She prolonged his excitement. "Dan Farnham slipped up and told me after rehearsal," she said. "He wasn't supposed to reveal it."

"What is it?" said Kaufman.

"Not even the headmaster knows," said Ginny.

Kaufman begged her to tell him immediately.

"Cynthia Warden is in the hospital," she said.

"In the hospital?" He had called the Wardens this morning, and Ben had said nothing about taking Cynthia to the hospital. Shouldn't the academic dean have been informed? Was there some enormous conspiracy among the faculty members to exclude him from everything? No matter; he had found out anyway. "What's her trouble?"

Ginny said nobody knew.

"She's in for tests," she said. "Dan Farnham made me promise not to tell a soul. Nobody's supposed to know. It could be dreadfully serious."

"How awful," said Kaufman. It was wonderful. A fresh piece of gossip that not even the headmaster knew.

He could hardly wait for dinner.

Scene 6

Mrs. Warden was in the hospital.

Thomas had been desperate to talk to his advisor tonight, and he had gone to dinner early hoping to set up an appointment for afterward. But Mr. Warden had never appeared. Instead, Dork Kaufman had come over to their table and had said that Mr. Warden was probably at the hospital with his wife who was having tests and that the boys shouldn't worry about her and not to say anything because it's supposed to be a secret.

It wasn't all that rare for faculty members to miss meals. They were not technically required to be in the dining hall ever, but most of them ate there because the food was free. Still, Mr. Warden was faithful about appearing whenever he was not off campus for a poetry reading. And tonight of all nights Thomas had needed his advice.

It was 7:15 P.M. Thomas lay on top of his bed alone in his dorm room and replayed the whole incident again and again.

Was it an honor violation or not?

He hadn't exactly lied to Mr. Carella. On the other hand, he hadn't answered his question, either.

But Staines *had* lied, hadn't he? By going along with Staines, Thomas himself was guilty of deception.

Maybe it wasn't really deception. Mr. Carella hadn't asked exactly the right question. If he'd asked, for example, if Staines was huffing Right Guard to get high, then they would have had to answer him directly.

Bull. He had asked them if anything illegal was going on, and they had implied that it wasn't. Plus, the way he had looked at them was a sign that he knew they were lying. Maybe he was on his way to see the councilmen right now. Maybe there would be an honor hearing Sunday, and Staines and Thomas would both be thrown out of school.

Maybe not. Maybe the luck would be with them, and they would get away with it. If they did, Thomas swore that he would never, never fail to tell the truth again. Thomas promised God that if he could just escape this time, he would never fail to be forthright again.

But what about Mr. Carella? He had looked at Thomas so funny. He had known Thomas was lying to him. What would he think from now on? Would he think Thomas was some sneak like Robert Staines?

There was only one thing to do. He had to go down and talk to Mr. Carella. He had to tell him the truth.

But if he told him the truth, then he would be narking on Staines. Staines would get booted for sure, if not for lying, then for getting high on the dorm. Everybody would hate Thomas for getting one of his classmates kicked out of school.

Or would they? Staines wasn't all that popular. And he was violating the rules. Thomas would just be doing his duty, wouldn't he?

Or was he just going to get Staines kicked out in order to save his own hide? His shoulder ached where Staines had hit him. Isn't that what it came down to—Thomas wasn't supporting the honor system for the sake of honor, but for the sake of his own peace of mind?

Thomas had a chilling thought. What if Staines was down in Mr. Carella's apartment confessing, and then Thomas got booted for not confessing with him? Or, even worse, what if Staines told Carella that it was Thomas who was huffing the aerosol, so Thomas got blamed for everything?

But would Mr. Carella believe that?

Nobody was on the hall. Such vacancy was unusual during the few minutes before study hours started; Thomas took it as a sign. He walked down to the opposite end of the hallway and knocked on Mr. Carella's door. No answer. As usual, the door was unlocked. Thomas knocked again and opened the door.

"Mr. Carella?" No answer. He could hear the shower running. Mr. Carella was a nut for cleanliness. He seemed to be always taking showers. Thomas let the door close behind him. While he waited inside the apartment, he rehearsed what he was going to say.

Mr. Carella, I need to talk to you. You know just now when you were in Robert's room? Well, I'm not sure whether it was illegal or not, but . . .

Was it an honor violation or not? Staines was not using some drug, after all. There was nothing in the rule book about deodorant. It probably didn't make you that high, anyway. It just rotted your brain cells so quickly that you thought you were high. So if Staines was not doing anything illegal, then they really hadn't deceived Mr. Carella, and then the councilmen and everybody would keep Staines in school, and a whole big production would be made out of nothing because Thomas had panicked.

He needed to think this over some more.

He heard the water go off in the shower and the squeak of the hooks as the shower curtain got drawn back. Thomas let himself out the door quietly and walked quickly back to his room. Two boys emerged from a room three doors down, but they had not seen him come out of Carella's apartment. Staines would kill him if he found out about the visit.

Within just those few minutes, Greg had returned from his meeting with the yearbook staff after dinner. Oh, hell, it was club night. That's why so few people were on dorm. Thomas had missed his meeting of the Spanish club. Big deal. What could they do—kick him out of school for it?

"Hey," said Greg. He sat down at his desk. "Why didn't you come to rehearsal?"

"Something came up here." Should he tell Greg or not?

Greg pulled a handwritten note out of a cream-colored envelope on his desktop. "I've been invited to tea at the Somervilles'," he said.

"Good deal," said Thomas, but he felt a tiny lurch of envy. It was almost getting to be funny; just when he thought he was as miserable as he could possibly be, something else went wrong.

Tea at the Homestead was a Wednesday night ritual with the Somervilles. Each week they invited ten or so different boys over to drink coffee or tea and eat finger sandwiches before dinner. Every boy at the school got invited sometime during his stay, but you never knew when the invitation would come. It was a huge honor to be invited, and you never turned them down. And the boys who got invited more than once usually turned out to be councilmen or editors of the newspaper or other big wheels on the campus. It was almost like a screening process. Thomas had never been invited.

"Good deal for both of us," said Greg. "You got one, too." He pulled out a sealed envelope and handed it to Thomas. In black ink his name appeared in a thin wiggly script.

"Where'd you get this?" Thomas asked.

"On your desk," said Greg. "Haven't you done any studying today?"

Thomas opened the envelope. "Mr. and Mrs. Horace Somerville," he read, "request the honor of your presence for tea, Wednesday, December 1, at 5:30 P.M."

Greg put the note aside and unrolled the blueprints he'd been looking at last night.

"Mr. Delaney says that nobody has found any secret tunnel in the twenty years he's been making the assignment," said Greg.

"Then why does he assign it?" He wanted to scream Greg listen to me can't you see I'm going nuts what the hell am I going to do?!?! But he sat there like it was any old ordinary day and they were having an ordinary old conversation.

"He says it should be there," said Greg. "There's a story of old Mrs. Stringfellow escaping some marauders by leaving through a secret tunnel."

Maybe he was worrying over nothing. Maybe Staines had really done nothing wrong. He could feel it out with his roommate.

"Look," said Thomas. "Suppose you found somebody huffing Right Guard deodorant on the dorm. Would you consider that a violation of the drug rule?"

"Yes," said Greg. "Who did it?"

He should not have asked Greg. Of course the answer would be yes; now the guy was waiting to find out what was up. Should he tell Greg or not? Telling him would bring another person into the incident and triple the complications. But Greg was reliable. He could keep a secret. But of an honor violation? Thomas needed to talk to his faculty advisor before he spoke to any other student. This was becoming too confusing. "I was just wondering what you'd say," said Thomas. "Hypothetical case."

Greg looked at him funny, turned back to the blueprints, and rested his hands like blinders on the sides of his head.

Thomas left the room without speaking again. A newboy was using one of the pay phones in the hall. The other one was free. He tried to call Hesta. She was at consultation with her math tutor. He tried to call Mr. Warden. There was no answer. He couldn't leave the dormitory because he wasn't supposed to go outside alone. He couldn't go back to his room because he didn't want to talk to his roommate. He couldn't go to Mr. Carella's because he wasn't sure of what he wanted to say.

He could see why Russell Phillips might want to throw himself off the gym roof.

Scene 7

At 10:15 on Wednesday morning Benjamin Warden sat in the English office with Daniel Farnham and tried to prepare a lesson for his 10:45 class. He had spent all of yesterday afternoon and evening with Cynthia at the hospital, and now he was scrambling to catch up with his work. So far the medical tests had produced no clear diagnosis, but more would be run today. There was nothing Warden could do for her this morning; it was time to concentrate on *Othello*.

"You could just cancel the class," said Farnham. He sat in a ladder-backed wooden chair next to Warden's cluttered desk. "None of the students are going to want to discuss English anyway." Monday night's death of Russell Phillips was still generating much conversation on campus.

But Dr. Lane had made it clear that he wanted life to go on as normally as possible.

"I don't like to cancel a class," said Warden. "If the students want to talk about this boy's death, I'll let them. Still, I should be prepared to talk about Shakespeare." Who could ever tell with adolescents? Every class had a separate personality, as fickle and prone to mood swings as that of any person.

"What I'm doing with mine today is to look at expectation versus actuality," said Farnham. "We just started the play this week, and I thought I'd present some history about Elizabethan stereotypes of blacks."

That sounded good to Warden. He had to respect Farnham for knowing his stuff. Here was Farnham, twenty-five years old and with less than three years of experience, giving advice to the chairman of the department. If only he didn't wear that ridiculous little mustache. Groucho Marx had more hair in one eyebrow.

Warden had hired Farnham last year on the strength of his resume and the quality of his instruction, which Warden had seen firsthand when Farnham had taught a sample class as a part of his interview. The man was good, and he should have been, having graduated from a strong prep school in Chattanooga, finished high in his class at Bowdoin, done a master's in one year at Duke, and taught for two years at the Spring Hill Day School in Montgomery. Yet Warden had a hard time warming up to Farnham. The fellow was always trying too hard to be perfect. Warden suspected that he suffered from a sense of inferiority over his lack of height; Warden, at 6′ 2″, was eight inches taller. Farnham compensated for his shortness by lifting weights and jogging and playing squash and even basketball. He had requested an apartment in the gym, and Dr. Lane had obliged him. There was no arguing Farnham's fitness. At a party for the faculty last fall, Warden had seen him win a bet by bare-handedly twisting a soup can into a shape like a bow tie.

There was no question of his competence in the classroom or outside it. His students complained that he was tough; Warden liked that. Better to be too tough than to pander to students' taste the way that new biology teacher, Carella, did. Farnham was professional enough to know that he wasn't here to pal around with the students, but to guide them. His work in the theater was impressive, too. Last fall, with nearly every student who could breathe already signed up for one of the football teams, Farnham produced a clever pair of one-acts by Chekhov.

It bothered Warden that he couldn't like Farnham better. Farnham was reliable, intelligent, talented, good for the department and for the school. Warden knew enough about psychology to realize that what he found distasteful in others was probably a mirror of his own weaknesses. And Warden himself was susceptible to feelings of inferiority, a physical inferiority with which he had been born, this red patch on his face, but also an academic inferiority, the result of his having grown up just down the road in Charlottesville, attending Montpelier School, and then earning a B.A. from the University of the South. He had no master's degree himself. Even as a publishing poet, he could not get away from his disdain at his own flimsy academic pedigree. When Cynthia had announced her intention to go on for a doctorate, he had been pleased, of course, but he had also recognized a slight dismay that his wife would have a degree so much higher than his own.

He picked up a paper clip and began to straighten it.

As Farnham talked about his approach to Othello, Warden wondered what he found so threatening about this earnest young man. Was it his job? Farnham was ambitious. He would make a good department head someday, Warden suspected; he was organized where Warden was haphazard, punctual where Warden was likely to forget entirely about a meeting he'd called himself. Or was it Cynthia, for whom Warden sensed Farnham had a powerful attraction? His job and his wife. How about your money or your life, Warden asked himself. He found his own behavior ridiculous.

"You disagree?" said Farnham.

"Not at all," said Warden. Farnham had been talking about what, the appearance versus reality motif?

"It's just that you started looking disgusted."

Warden was embarrassed. "Not with you. I was distracted."

"About Cynthia? Sorry she's ill. I was quite upset when I heard," said Farnham.

Warden assumed Farnham had heard from Sam Kaufman, who somehow had got wind of the news and had alarmed everyone on the campus. "We're still hoping it's a trivial illness," said Warden.

They spent a few minutes talking about the typical Elizabethan image of a Moor: lascivious, passionate, dangerous.

Warden hadn't taught *Othello* for years, and he'd never approached it as a play about stereotypes. But there it was: Othello defies the audience's expectations at the beginning of the play, then confirms them when he becomes the excitable and lusty African, then recovers his dignity at the end.

"That whole motif of expectation versus actuality runs through the whole play," said Farnham. "We've got honest Iago, who turns out to be dishonest in the extreme, and Othello the Moor, who turns out to be noble, and then we've got the added problem of Desdemona, who turns out to be exactly what she appears to be—chaste and virtuous. Shakespeare plays around so much with his audience's expectations that he makes it easier for us to believe Iago's duping of Othello with a handkerchief."

Farnham was warmed up, and he went on. Warden found himself drifting back to Cynthia, who was so damned stubborn about insisting that he carry on with his normal routine. He should be with her now. She was having a spinal tap this morning, then X rays and a myelogram.

"Mr. Warden?" The voice came from the doorway. It was his advisee, Thomas Boatwright. "I was wondering if you were busy."

"Of course I'm busy," said Warden. That was so typical of these boys, to interrupt an essential conference and then plead ignorance. "Mr. Farnham and I are talking."

"Sorry," said Boatwright. "I just had something on my mind."

Terrific. It always transpired this way; when he was most pressed for time, the most interruptions occurred. Warden did not want to be a counselor this morning. He did not want to be a teacher. He wanted to flee: to exit the office, jump into his car, drive to Charlottesville, or perhaps elsewhere.

"Wait outside," said Warden.

"That's all right, Thomas," said Farnham. "I can leave."

"Why should you leave?" said Warden. "Let him wait."

"I ought to be inspecting the dormitories anyway," said Farnham. "We've covered enough for you to wing it."

He noted the boy's failure to meet Farnham's eyes as the man passed him in the doorway. Obviously there was something troubling young Boatwright. Cynthia had said he looked anxious at dinner Monday night, and Warden had never followed up. He felt vaguely ashamed and selfish.

"Sit down, Thomas," said Warden. "I shouldn't have snapped at you." Boatwright was a nice boy, a little undisciplined academically, perhaps, but a right-minded person. Amazing how he had developed physically since last year: still slender, but more muscular, broader in the shoulders, taller—at least six feet tall now. He still had the freckles and the bright brown eyes; the black bangs still stopped well short of his eyebrows; the upturned nose was still a shade too large, but his face would surely grow around it; he still probably shaved only twice a week.

It was as though Warden had not looked at him for several months. Boatwright had grown into a very nice-looking boy.

Warden caught himself. His mind had wandered enough this morning.

Scene 8

Thomas sat in the chair and looked at his advisor and wondered how to begin. Last night he hadn't slept, hadn't been able to concentrate, hadn't been able to function. Every time he had seen Nathan Somerville on the dorm, he had felt his heart pound and his bladder fill. But nothing had happened. No councilman had come knocking on his door. Staines had passed by him in the hall and had acted as if he didn't even know Thomas's name, hadn't even looked at him. At dorm check-in, Mr. Carella had acted normal enough. The only problem was that Thomas's conscience was torturing him. He couldn't stand it. He had to tell his advisor.

All night he had rehearsed what he was going to say, how he was going to come in and ask Mr. Warden about a completely imaginary, totally hypothetical case of one student's finding another student sniffing aerosol spray and then getting confronted by a teacher. But now that he was here, he could not get started. It didn't feel right. Mr. Warden was tense, probably worried about his wife, and Thomas would only present another irritation to him.

Mr. Warden spoke first. "What's on your mind?" he asked. "Your grades?"

That was a big joke between them. Mr. Warden was always kidding him about how Thomas worried over everything but academics. He made Bs and Cs and could do better if he studied the way Landon Hopkins did.

"My grades are the same."

"A mother lode of mediocrity," said Mr. Warden. Other times he had said "a cornucopia of the commonplace" and "a masterpiece of moderation."

They often bantered at the beginning of a conversation. "I'll try to bring them up before you run out of alliterations," said Thomas.

Mr. Warden said any fourth-former who could speak intelligently about alliteration should be on the high honor roll. He broke off a piece of paper clip and let it drop to the desk. "So what's the trouble?" he asked.

Hell, now what? Conversations between advisors and advisees were supposed to be strictly confidential. Advisors, however, were still adults and still members of the faculty. Now that they were actually face-to-face, Thomas could not bring himself to tell Mr. Warden about last night's episode on the dorm with Robert Staines. He knew already what the teacher would say: turn himself in to the honor council. But if he turned himself in, he might get dismissed from school. If he turned Staines in, then Thomas might get Staines kicked out of school. He would hate to be responsible for another student's expulsion. And if he turned Staines in and Staines somehow beat the rap and remained here, then that might be the worst of all. It was so easy last night to tell Mr. Warden when Mr. Warden wasn't really there. Today he had initiated the conversation, he had told him there was a problem, and Mr. Warden was waiting to hear what the problem was.

"I've been thinking about going out for the winter play," said Thomas. It was a legitimate concern, he supposed. "I'd like to be in a production with Nathan Somerville and Mrs. Warden, but I'm not sure I can handle it and still keep up with basketball."

Mr. Warden said he thought being in the play was a wonderful idea. "You aren't going to study in your free time anyway," he said. "Not unless you undergo a radical personality change."

If they were pursuing this subject, Thomas might as well speak all his worries. "The thing is," he said, "I'm not sure I want to work with Mr. Farnham."

"Why not?" Mr. Warden perked up a bit.

"It's his temper," said Thomas. "You never know when he's going to spaz."

"I beg your pardon?"

Mr. Warden knew the expression but insisted that his students use standard English.

"I never know when he might erupt," said Thomas. "Last Monday night I was down in the theater and saw him really go berserk." He told Warden about Farnham's furious pounding of the floor of the scene shop with a board. "Of course, to be fair, I guess I could understand that one."

Warden asked him how so.

"Because your wife had just been down there," said Thomas. "He was probably mad because she was going to miss rehearsals."

"What do mean, my wife had been down there?" asked Warden. He was perturbed. Had she been out on Monday afternoon before they went to the dining hall? If so, she had not told him. "She wasn't at the theater Monday," he said.

"Yes she was," said Thomas. "Greg saw her down there before he left rehearsal. I saw her myself. She was limping away really badly."

Damn it to hell, what was this all about? Warden did not like this at all. Cynthia had asked for secrecy over her hospitalization, and then she had sneaked out for a tryst with Farnham. But that was silly. She was an adult. She didn't need to check in with Warden each time she left the house. He filed the irritation away to consider another time.

Thomas saw no need to continue this meeting. If they weren't going to talk about the real issue, the honor issue, he did not want to stay. Besides, he was upsetting Mr. Warden in talking about his wife. "I hope she gets well," said Thomas. "She's one reason I would consider the play."

"Go out for the play," said Mr. Warden. "And let me know if Mr. Farnham's temper does not improve."

Mr. Warden was a good advisor. Thomas left the room grateful for a friendly adult. He ought to be thinking about Christmas presents for Warden, McPhee, Carella, and the other teachers he liked.

But then it hit him all over again that he might not be here at Christmas. And if he and Staines did get away with it and nobody found out, then Thomas would be here because of a lie. That hurt most of all.

Warden watched his advisee leave and noted that the boy did not appear to feel relieved. Did he know more about Cynthia and Farnham? Of course not. There was nothing to know.

The bell rang. It was time for class. Warden was supposed to be talking about *Othello,* and he did not know one damn thing to say. He could think only of his wife, sick in a hospital bed forty miles away, a beautiful young woman with a mind and a will and a life of her own.

Why had she struggled down to that theater without telling him?

Scene 9

Thomas would do anything to avoid being in trouble. He could not understand why Richard Blackburn would seek trouble out.

Mr. Farnham nearly imploded in English class when he

found out Richard had glued together all the pages of Landon Hopkins's Shakespeare anthology.

Richard had done it yesterday afternoon during play practice, when Landon was working on setting some lights. There had been a big bucket of glue in the scene shop and a paintbrush, and there had been Landon's book, and it had been too much to resist. Landon brought the remains to class today looking like some black-and-white patio brick, every page stuck together. Farnham was short, but he had no trouble hefting that book and sticking it up into Richard's face.

"Do you have any idea of what such an act of vandalism signifies, Mr. Blackburn?"

Richard said yes, he did.

"Please explain."

Richard said he thought it signified Landon was becoming too sexually excited around Shakespeare.

Farnham went berserk, threw him out of class and sent him to Mr. Grayson and fired him from the play crew all in about three seconds of rage.

Grayson gave Richard twenty-five demerits—enough to keep him in Saturday night D-hall for the rest of the term—and told him to buy Landon another book. He also sent a letter home to Richard's parents.

Later in the day Richard appeared in the gym at the end of basketball practice. It was around 5:30, and he said he wanted to talk to McPhee about being the manager for the JV team. Thomas was getting dressed in the locker room while Richard interviewed. At first it seemed to go well.

"I do need a manager," McPhee said.

"Perfect," Richard said.

"But why you?"

They stood just inside the glass door of the locker room.

"I'm the perfect man for the job," Richard said.

"Are you dependable?" Coach McPhee looked sweaty but relaxed as he leaned on the door jamb and grilled Richard, who looked bouncy and confident.

"Very dependable."

"Then why are you here at 5:30 instead of at 3:30, when practice began?"

And with that McPhee put Richard through a verbal Veg-

O-Matic. He accused Richard of trying to get himself a free afternoon. All the boys at Montpelier were required to participate in an afternoon activity. Richard had been fired from the play crew but hadn't started looking for a replacement until the afternoon was over.

"Well," Richard said, "I did have a lot of work to do."

"Like gluing the pages of books together? I don't need a manager who shows such little respect for other people's property. Especially for a book. I am an English teacher, too, remember."

"Yes sir."

"So I think you'd better find yourself something better to do with your time this winter," Coach McPhee said.

"Yes sir." Richard's head was hanging.

Coach McPhee excused himself and said he was going home, which for him was just down the hall through an inside door. Angus Farrier opened the door and told everyone to hurry up, that he wanted to lock up the building.

"Bunch of terrapins," Angus said. He asked Richard to move on, then proceeded down the hall. Instead of obeying, Richard wandered over to Thomas in disgust.

"McPhee dies," he said to Thomas. "And so does Farnham. I am going to get both of those guys so bad that they'll never recover." He threatened to blow up the whole gym and all the inhabitants with it.

Thomas didn't know how to proceed. Richard was his friend, but the way he was acting was so childish.

"Why not just let it go?" Thomas said.

Richard stared at him. "You're acting like somebody's dad," he said. He zipped up his ski jacket, elbowed the door open, and left.

Thomas was glad to see him go.

Last week Richard had been his best friend. Today he could not remember why.

Scene 10

Somehow Thomas Boatwright had survived the past twenty-four hours; he was now worried that he would never make it through the next twenty-four minutes.

It was 5:45 P.M. on Wednesday afternoon. He sat in a circle of chairs arranged in the living room of the Homestead while Mrs. Somerville, who looked really elegant with her snowy hair pulled back in a tight bun, poured tea into fragile teacups that Thomas was sure he was going to break. She asked each boy in turn whether he wanted cream or lemon, one lump of sugar or two, and she responded seriously to the boys' self-conscious, half-mumbled replies. Mr. Somerville was talking to Greg about music stores in Charlottesville. Nobody else said anything. The students fidgeted and tried to figure out whether they should wait for everybody to be served or should go on and drink from their cups. If this was what tea at the Homestead was all about, then it must be some huge practical joke on the whole school: everybody talked about what an honor it was, and nobody really knew why.

Thomas needed to get this business with Staines cleared up. It was interfering with everything in his life: classes, basketball practice, paying attention to his manners here at the Homestead.

Little grains of tea were floating around in the bottom of his teacup. That wasn't normal, was it? Did the Somervilles have holes in their teabags? Maybe this was just an extraordinarily bad Wednesday for everyone.

Wednesday was Hump Day out in the real world. If you could get through Wednesday, you were over the hump, and you had only two more days till the weekend. Here at Montpelier, though, Wednesday was just the third day in the week. When you have classes on Saturday morning, it's hard to find a Hump Day.

Today, however, was significant in one way: it was Wednesday, December 1. November was over for good, and there were only sixteen more days, not counting today, until Friday, December 17, when Christmas vacation began. And only fifteen days, not counting today, until Thursday, December 16, when Thomas Boatwright turned sixteen years old. He liked the idea of turning sixteen on the 16th. It was an event he'd looked forward to all his life. Maybe the driver's license was it, or maybe the driver's license was just a sign that you were more independent and more grown up. He'd been practicing his driving and studying his handbook during the Thanksgiving holiday, and thought he had both the driving and the rules down pretty well. Of course, the way Montpelier made you wait until Friday the seventeenth to get out for the holidays, he'd have the weekend to practice up before he went down to the Division of Motor Vehicles to get his license. Years ago they had dropped a requirement for you to parallel park, but Thomas could parallel park anyway. As soon as he got his license, he was going to drive his mother back home, drop her off, and drive over to Hesta's house, where he'd pick her up, and they'd go off to some secluded spot and park and then, just to make the day complete, they'd go all the way and make passionate love.

That was his favorite fantasy lately. The problem was that there weren't too many secluded places in northern Virginia, and he wasn't at all sure that his mother would just let him drop her off and solo like that on his very first day with his license, even though he knew perfectly well that he was an excellent driver. It just had to work out that way. Monday, December 20, was going to be the real Hump Day.

"Thomas?"

He realized that Mrs. Somerville had just spoken to him. Greg and all the other guys and Mr. Somerville were staring at him like he'd just had an epileptic seizure or something. It was quiet as hell, but you could see the guys getting ready to laugh. He hated it when he was caught daydreaming.

"I'm sorry," he said. "Would you repeat the question?"

Then all the guys did laugh.

She hadn't asked him a question. She had invited him to try one of the scones on the table next to him.

"Thanks," he said. He picked up one of the flat brown

biscuits and popped the whole thing into his mouth. Everyone in the room laughed again. Even Mr. and Mrs. Somerville cracked a smile. Thomas realized he was the only one in the room eating a biscuit.

"Perhaps you'd like to pass the plate to the boy on your left," said Mrs. Somerville. Thomas knew as he passed the plate that this would be the last time he was ever invited to tea at the Homestead.

Greg stepped in to rescue him. "Mr. Delaney told us there was a secret tunnel from this building to Stringfellow Hall," he said. "Does anybody here know where it is?"

Horace Somerville reacted immediately. "I don't have much patience with that kind of speculative history," he said. "We've had tales of secret passages around this school since I enrolled here over fifty years ago, but I've never seen an actual tunnel. There's plenty of documented campus history here. Learn the facts."

It sounded as bad as class, but then Mrs. Somerville told her husband not to be so harsh with their guests. She asked him to entertain them with some tales.

Mr. Somerville was more inclined to lecture than to entertain. "There used to be three buildings where the gym is now," he said. "Up at this end, where the boiler room and Mr. McPhee's apartment are, used to be the old kitchen for the Homestead." He said the kitchen had been outside for safety, in case there was a fire.

"The lobby of the gym is the old caretaker's cottage," he said. "You can still see the old brick fireplace and the remains of the chimney on the outside. And at the south end, at Mr. Farnham's apartment, is the site of the original school library."

Greg asked why they tore down all those old buildings.

"Didn't tear them down entirely," said Mr. Somerville. "Swallowed them up. You can still see some of the old foundations if you go snoop around in the basement over there."

He spoke specifically to Thomas. "Ask your advisor about it," he said. "Mr. Warden used to live in that south apartment before Mr. Farnham moved in. Ask him about the old brickwork in the fireplace and the chimney."

The sound of a siren interrupted him. Everybody jumped.

"It's coming from next door," said Mrs. Somerville. It was the fire alarm for the gym.

"We'd better see," said Mr. Somerville. They all put down their teacups, some on the end tables, some on the Oriental rugs on the floor, and they ran to the front porch of the Homestead. At a school like Montpelier a fire was the most frightening prospect possible. You could lose a whole building as well as a bunch of lives.

From the porch they could see people from all over the campus rushing to find out what was wrong.

The gym was by far the largest building on the Quad, a huge box of brick and glass and white columns. Decorative white trim outlined the tall windows of the basketball court where Thomas had just been practicing. Below the middle windows was a squat cube of a lobby jutting like a wart from the rectangular face of the building. That was the old caretaker's cottage Mr. Somerville was just telling them about, with its truncated chimney barely reaching over the roof line of the lobby. It looked odd, now that Thomas knew what it had been, like a Rubik's Cube attached to a shoe box. The building was dark except for the lights on in the two faculty apartments at each end. Everyone speculated loudly over where the first flames would appear.

In a couple of minutes he heard the long, low hoot of a fire truck. The alarm system at Montpelier automatically notified the fire department and the sheriff's office in town. Soon three fire trucks were lined up on the Quad in front of them.

But it was a false alarm. People came and went from the Homestead, Mr. and Mrs. Somerville included, and gradually the news drifted back to Thomas and Greg on the porch. Information at Montpelier spread almost instantaneously, as though all of them were psychic. Someone had pulled the alarm on the basement level, the locker room level. The doors had been shut and locked, Angus Farrier would swear to it.

Mr. McPhee's front door on the north end of the gym was only twenty yards away, and they could see him on the threshold talking to some firemen. What had Mr. Somerville said about this end of the gym? It used to be the old kitchen for the Homestead.

"It's weird to think of going outside to your kitchen," said Thomas. Mr. McPhee's chimney was a little more than a free-throw shot's distance away from them. "Don't you think the food would get cold when they brought it over?"

"It's not that far," said Greg. "I can believe in an outside kitchen easier than I can believe in a tunnel from here to Stringfellow."

Directly across the Quad they could see the lights of Stringfellow Hall. It looked far away in the dark and the cold, a couple of football fields from them.

"There's no way somebody could have dug a tunnel that far," said Greg. "Look at it. The grass would all be dead, or the ground would be sunken. It would have collapsed somewhere."

"Does that mean you've stopped looking?"

"As long as Delaney is offering extra credit," said Greg, "I'm still in the tunnel business."

It was 6:15. They just had time to get back for dinner at 6:30.

They walked together across the Quad to Stringfellow Hall. Greg pointed to the lights on in Farnham's apartment.

"That place is awfully small to have been the library," he said. "They must not have had many books in the old days."

Thomas was not listening.

"Hey," said Greg. He poked Thomas in the arm. "Tune in to my station."

"Sorry," said Thomas. "What'd you say?"

"I said that looks like Richard on top of Farnham's chimney," said Greg. "He's got a handful of dynamite."

Thomas looked. There was nobody on Farnham's chimney.

"That was a joke," said Greg. "This is called Getting Your Friends to Relax."

Thomas said he was too busy to relax.

"You want to talk about it?" said Greg.

Yes, he did. "I can't," said Thomas.

"How long are you going to keep this up?" said Greg. "It wasn't too long ago when you were on my case for keeping too quiet."

Thomas promised Greg it had nothing to do with him.

"I know," said Greg. "It has to do with somebody huffing aerosol on the dorm."

Thomas kept walking.

Greg said he was in the school store today when Robert Staines bought himself a new can of Right Guard deodorant.

Thomas was afraid to say anything.

"Seems to me old Robert runs through quite a load of that stuff," said Greg. "What a coincidence."

Thomas took a breath. "Are you sure you want to get involved in this?" he said.

"Bring it on."

Thomas told Greg all about Staines and the deodorant spray and the question of honor and standing in Mr. Carella's apartment and then leaving when he changed his mind.

"What do I do?" said Thomas.

"You know what to do," said Greg.

"No, I don't," said Thomas. "I've been worrying about it for twenty-four hours."

"You mean you've been talking yourself out of it," said Greg. "You know what to do."

Yes, he did.

"But can I do it?" said Thomas.

"Yes," said Greg. "You're going to do it right after dinner."

Yes. It was a relief. He was going to turn himself in to the councilmen as soon as the meal was over.

Scene 11

Warden felt cold in the car as he drove in the darkness to the hospital in Charlottesville. There was too much to think about. He did not want to ask Cynthia about her meeting with Dan Farnham, not when she was in the hospital. She was his wife, she loved him, it was not healthy for him to be so possessive. And yet the knowledge of that meeting nagged.

It was one of several competing distractions. Until his return from New York, his life had seemed headed in the proper direction, toward improvement. They had liked his poetry at the reading. Some people from Columbia had even paid him a compliment. But he had not been able to do any decent work since. Monday night's attempts at writing had resulted in confused, incoherent gibberish, from which he could never get a grip on his ideas. Cynthia's illness was infecting his own muse.

Tonight, however, he had an idea. It was merely an image, that was all, but it fascinated him. He saw an attractive middle-aged woman standing in front of a large fire. She was disillusioned. Why? He did not yet know. But he had a couplet:

Why am I bitter? Here's a cryptic hint:
The hottest fire springs from the coldest flint.

He very desperately wished he had the opportunity to sit and write and get to know this woman better. For him writing was a discovery, and it was also an addiction, a craving he had to satisfy. But there was no time. He owed Cynthia a visit.

The results of the tests were coming in, all of them negative. No cancer. No brain tumor. No masses anywhere. It was strange how the relief was replaced so quickly by frustration. What was it, then? They were both hungry to know the name of this enemy that was attacking them. Today they had given her a myelogram. She had to drink as many liquids as possible in order to foreshorten the dehydrating effects of the drug she'd get. Then she'd have to sit up in bed for hours in order to keep the dye in her spinal column from trickling into her cranium and giving her a headache.

It took fifteen minutes to find a parking place near the university hospital in Charlottesville. He finally found a meter on Jefferson Park Avenue and walked a quarter mile. The hospital was dreary, clean but cold. In the white-tiled lobby he had to pick up a visitor's badge and wait for an elevator. It was after 7:00 by the time he reached Cynthia's room on the eighth floor.

The wide wooden door was open when Warden approached her room, number 816, a private room for which they paid an extra fifteen dollars a day. Cynthia was propped up in the bed to a sitting position with her head supported by an extra pillow. Her hair swirled on the linens like that of Botticelli's Venus. She looked very tired. Warden went to her and kissed her lightly.

"They say I should sit up all night to be safe," Cynthia told Warden. He pulled a chair up to the side of her bed. She told him about the myelogram. "Russell Phillips was on the television news," she said. "I could hear it. Everything still looks blurry."

Warden had not known. They did not own a television set.

She told him she had called her father. "He was ready to drive down here tonight," she said. "I talked him out of it."

"By telling him I'd be here," said Warden.

"I didn't need to mention anything that horrible." Her tone helped to relax him.

He asked whether the doctors had predicted when she could leave.

"Not at all. They want to do a CAT scan tomorrow." She asked him to warn Sam Kaufman that she might not be on campus for the mixer this weekend.

He told her Sam Kaufman already knew.

She gently scratched the top of his hand. "Tell me what you did today."

Warden told her about the special assembly, then about his chance to meet with Thomas Boatwright.

"He wants to audition for the play," said Warden. "That was his big concern."

"I'm sorry you can remember it all so clearly," said Cynthia.

"Me too."

They joked about his memory lapses, which were nearly always the function of his best writing. Warden was never so absentminded as when he was working on a poem. When he was at the height of his concentration, he could blank out several hours of the day. He'd been known to hold classes, drive to the grocery store, even sit through a dinner party, and have no memory whatever of the events later.

"Let me tell you about my meals," said Cynthia. "In the beginning, there was Jell-O." She tried to make him laugh for a half hour before she gave up. "Don't be so glum," she said. "I'm the one in the hospital, remember."

Warden apologized. He did not want to tell her everything on his mind.

"I got a rejection today," he said.

"Oh, those silly, silly editors," she said. "What else is competing with me for your attention?"

What else, he thought. Shall I tell her what else?

"Dan Farnham helped me plan my classes today," Warden said.

The expression on his face helped her guess immediately why he had broached the subject. "He told you I'd been down to see him backstage before dinner."

"He did not tell me. Thomas Boatwright did."

"But of course you did not become anxious or jealous or peevish because you understood that I had to tell him where I would be," she said. "I had to let him know why I wouldn't be at rehearsals. The telephones backstage were busy, so I walked down before dinner."

Warden admitted to becoming peevish, but not terribly so.

She looked at him straight on with her wobbly eyes. "Is that an improvement?" she asked.

"I just don't understand why I couldn't deliver the message for you," he said.

"Ben, it's the same conversation every six months. Will you please stop worrying about younger men? There are too many of them out there for you to compete against. You just have to trust me."

"I trust you," he said.

"Then stop imagining that I've packed a suitcase to elope every time I speak to another male."

The hyperbole made him smile. "I don't think he's a healthy friendship for you to cultivate."

"You think he's going to pounce on me?" she asked.

Warden said he thought Daniel Farnham was too unstable. "He's going to explode someday," he said. "The boys already talk about his temper. I don't want you to be there for the eruption."

Cynthia had seen Farnham's temper quite recently. She had survived. "So now you're pretending to protect me?" she asked.

"I do want to protect you."

"But you can't. Something has already got me."

Both were silent.

"It's because I love you," he said.

She knew, she knew.

"This is not 'The Miller's Tale,' " she said. "You are not an old cuckold. I am not a young flirt. One foolish young woman dumped you a long time ago. Don't hold her mistake against all of us."

"I do trust you," he said.

"Then let me breathe."

The evening had almost ended well. But outside, alone and in the cold, he realized that he'd forgotten where he'd parked the car.

Scene 12

Nathan Somerville was about the nicest guy Thomas had ever met. You're supposed to be nice if you're the senior councilman, but Thomas figured Nathan would just be nice anyway. As the councilman on Upper Stringfellow, he was responsible for running Thomas's dorm. He was hardly ever irritable, even in the morning. If you walked into the bathroom and caught him putting in his contacts or shaving, he would make some joke or give you some greeting that sounded like he was really glad to see you. It was good, sort of like having your dad or a big brother there. He was one of the few seniors who would actually be friendly to the underclassmen and not beat on them for entertainment, and he was always willing to help you out if you were having trouble with algebra or Spanish.

Thomas knocked on the door and figured that with the worst possible luck, Nathan wouldn't be in, but his roommate, Ned Wood, would be. There was nothing really wrong with Ned Wood; he was just always hitting you in the arm or calling you some obscene name. He could actually be pretty funny at times. But the voice that said "Come in" was Nathan's voice, and when Thomas entered the room, he saw Nathan was the only one there.

"Boatin' Shoes," said Nathan. "I bet I know why you're here."

Thomas nearly lost his dinner. It was too late. The councilmen already knew. He was going to be tried for an honor violation and dismissed before his sixteenth birthday.

"How'd you find out?" Thomas said.

"Farnham told me."

Mr. Farnham knows too?

Nathan pulled loose his tie and stepped out of his loafers. His hair was blond and on the short side, just over his ears, and he blinked a little more frequently than usual because of his contact lenses. Everybody kidded him about it, but he just smiled it away. He was always smiling, it seemed, except for now, when he looked at Thomas, read his expression, and told him to sit down.

"What's the matter?" said Nathan. "Aren't you here to talk to me about taking a part in the play?"

Instant relief.

"No," said Thomas. "I'm here to turn myself in."

He told Nathan how he had walked in on Staines, what had been said, and how he had panicked.

Nathan listened without interrupting. Then he blinked his eyes and looked Thomas square in the face and said, "You screwed up."

"I know."

"You should have talked to Carella right away."

"I know."

"You shouldn't have let so much time pass," said Nathan.

Thomas knew all of it. "I just wanted to tell you," he said. "Greg, my roommate, is the one that advised me to come."

"Greg's a good friend," said Nathan.

"Yeah," said Thomas. It was true. "Yeah, he is."

Then Nathan said it was a complicated issue, with both the drug rule and the honor system involved. The honor council did not handle drug cases, which went to the disciplinarian and the headmaster.

"It's going to be trouble for Staines," said Nathan.

"What about for me?"

"Maybe," said Nathan. "The good part is that you've turned yourself in."

Nathan would talk to Mr. Grayson, the disciplinarian, and then to Dr. Lane. "Lane's leaving campus tomorrow for a few days," he said, "but the councilmen can go ahead and investigate the honor part at the regular meeting this Sunday night."

That was bad news. "You mean I have to wait until Sunday to find out what happens?"

"You'll have to testify. It'll be your word against his, if he decides to deny it. Are you ready to go through with that?"

Hell no. "Yes," said Thomas. He squirmed. "But it's going to be so damn hard to do."

Nathan agreed. "You'll be nervous at first," he said. "Just tell the truth."

Thomas asked him what penalty to expect.

Nathan could not predict. "But," he said, "it seems to me that you haven't violated the honor system as much as you've endorsed it."

"Do you think I'll get the boot?"

Nathan was certain he would not. "Whatever happens, you'll still be here," he said. He urged Thomas not to say anything to Staines or anybody else about this conversation with him. He wanted to see if Staines would confess on his own. "If he comes to you and says he's changed his mind about keeping quiet, then encourage him," said Nathan. "That would help him."

Thomas said he'd already tried that once.

"You maybe ought to clear things up with Mr. Carella," said Nathan. "I'll talk to him, too. We don't want him to think of you as dishonorable."

Thomas said he would talk to Carella after class tomorrow.

Nathan said that was okay. "Now get out of here, Boatin' Shoes," he said. "I got studying to do, and so do you."

Now that his conscience was clear, Thomas felt a million times better, except that he hated the idea of spending the next four days living next door to Staines in limbo. Four days was such a long time. So much could happen.

And so much did.

Scene 13

Carol Scott was in a staring contest with Eldridge Lane. It was 10:00 P.M. on Wednesday, December 1, and she had never felt so tired in her life.

Eldridge Lane blinked first.

"I will say it one more time," he said. "It was a false alarm. There was nothing sinister about it."

"It was in the gym, though," she said. "That's the same place the boy died."

"Coincidence."

"It will not be coincidence if the New York police find a match between the paper they found on the floor of the theater and the sample register tape I mailed them yesterday," said Carol Scott.

Eldridge Lane said he was leaving early in the morning for Philadelphia and wanted this interview over.

"You had eight students in New York over the Thanksgiving holiday," said Carol Scott. "Here are their names." She handed Lane a list. "However, all of them were with their families throughout their visit. I think we can rule them out."

"You certainly can," said Lane. "These are some of the most prominent families in the Southeast."

Carol Scott was taping this conversation with a small portable recorder. She had told Lane that it was easier than taking notes. The truth was that she wanted to play it back to Stuart, the sheriff, to show him what an asshole Lane was. She pulled out another slip of paper.

"You also had three members of the faculty in the city over the break," she said. "Carella, Farnham, and Warden."

"Benjamin Warden is a nationally prominent poet," said Lane. "He was there for a reading."

"He has no alibi for Sunday afternoon," she said. "He says he went to the theater alone."

"He has been here as long as I have, and I trust him completely," said Lane.

"And the other two?"

She noticed that Lane was less positive about Carella and Farnham.

"They're fine men," he said. "Relatively new to the faculty, but first-rate, solid people. Came to us with flawless recommendations. We don't just hire anybody here, you know."

She knew. Montpelier School dominated the community. It was the largest employer in Montpelier County. Back in 1968, for its centennial celebration, *The Washington Post* had done a feature article.

"Carella says he was visiting a friend, and that he and his friend walked around the city all weekend, barhopped, that sort of thing. The New York police are checking with the friend. Farnham says he was in the Metropolitan Museum on Sunday. He went on Sunday and paid nothing, so he doesn't have any ticket as evidence of a visit there."

Lane said he hoped she was not browbeating his faculty.

She explained that she was asking questions about Russell Phillips, was he depressed, how well did they know him. The information about people's whereabouts at Thanksgiving was emerging from casual conversation. That's why it had taken her so long to interview everybody.

"After meeting these people, are you not satisfied that they are reliable?" said Lane.

"I liked them," said Carol Scott. "But most people get very charming when they find out they're being interviewed by a cop."

She wished he would take the hint.

"So where are we?" said Lane.

"I would like for you to cancel your mixer scheduled for the weekend," she said.

"Not this again," said Lane. "To do so would raise too many questions."

"You can do it out of respect for the dead," said Carol Scott. "You just had a boy die on your campus."

"We have acknowledged the death of Russell Phillips. Now we are returning to life as usual. You simply do not understand the dynamics of boarding school life. These boys have forgotten all about Russell Phillips, those few who knew him. Adolescents need something cheerful to look forward to. They don't need to be reminded of how depressed they're supposed to be."

She had to grant him that. She had a son and a daughter, ages six and four.

"Then please," she said, "promise me that your gymnasium will be secure."

"The gym will be locked," said Lane. "And I will see to it that a faculty chaperone patrols there as well."

It was awfully late.

"All right," said Carol Scott. "Then everything should be fine."

But she hoped, just for the sake of this jerk, that it wouldn't be.

Scene 14

The next two days passed quickly. On Thursday morning the student grapevine reported that Richard Blackburn had set off the fire alarm in the gym the night before. He had propped the back door open with a little pebble so that it had looked closed, and then he had waited until the building was clear, sneaked in, pulled the alarm, and exited the way he'd come in. On the way out he had kicked the pebble into the grass.

"I was outside in the dark by myself," Richard told Thomas at the 10:15 morning recess. "And you know what? I never once felt the least bit depressed." He said Lane's rule about being alone after dark was unenforceable and ridiculous.

The most amazing quality about Richard was that he had no conscience at all.

Thursday after class Thomas told Mr. Carella what had really transpired in Staines's room.

Carella was understanding about it. "I thought you acted guilty that day," he said. "Good for you. It's only the truly corrupt who can look clean and innocent all the time." He promised that he wouldn't confront Robert Staines about the incident until after the honor council had held its hearing on Sunday night.

On Friday they had an abbreviated basketball practice because of the game the next day. They could start practicing at 2:00 because classes ended at noon every Friday (but resumed on Saturday morning), and athletic practices were supposed to be done by 3:30. Thomas, however, screwed up his free throws and had to stay after.

"You're not following a set routine," Coach McPhee said. "Sometimes you dribble the ball once, sometimes twice, sometimes not at all. Do the exact same thing every time you step up to that foul line. I don't care what it is. Make it comfortable for you. But make it the same routine."

Thomas shot fifty free throws and made thirty-two of them.

"You're going to be making forty-five out of fifty before the season is over," said Coach McPhee. He took the ball from Thomas and stood at the line. He took two bounces, looked at the basket, bent his knees, shot, followed through. Swish. Ten in a row.

"That was great," said Thomas.

"You'll do that, too," said Coach.

After he got dressed, Thomas went over to Bradley Hall, to the theater.

He was expecting a bunch of people there, but the only

ones present were Mr. Farnham, Landon Hopkins, and Nathan Somerville. The cast had had an early practice too, and everyone else was gone.

The seats in Bradley Hall were in six sections. They were divided into thirds longitudinally by two aisles extending from the stage all the way to the back of the auditorium. They were also divided in half horizontally by another aisle that stretched from one side of the room to the other. Thomas stood at the intersection of the two aisles closest to the lobby door and watched Nathan read from the white-covered Signet paperback. Landon read along with him. Mr. Farnham watched. All three were on the stage.

"But we have reason to cool our raging motions, our carnal stings or unbitted lusts, whereof I take this that you call love to be a sect or scion," said Nathan.

"Si-on," said Mr. Farnham. "The 'c' is silent."

"Scion," said Nathan correctly.

"It cannot be," said Landon, reading.

"It is merely a lust of the blood and a permission of the will," said Nathan. "Come, be a man! Drown thyself? Drown cats and blind puppies!" He stopped and lowered his book.

"That's good," said Mr. Farnham. "Why stop?"

"He's here," said Nathan, and he pointed his book outward toward Thomas.

"Terrific. Come on up here, Thomas."

Mr. Farnham was wearing his usual white shirt and tie, but he had switched from loafers into Adidas running shoes. Nathan had on an Izod under a button-down shirt—the layered look. You weren't required to wear a tie between the end of class and dinner, and after dinner you could also remove your tie. Nathan gave Thomas a grin as he walked up the side stairs onto the stage. It made Thomas feel better. He had been in this room a million times, but he'd never stood up here on the stage before. The room looked a lot smaller, the seats closer to the stage. He felt a little scared. But he also felt more important.

"You recognize where we are?" said Mr. Farnham.

Thomas did not.

"You mean you haven't memorized the whole play yet?" said Nathan. He grinned again. Unlike his grandfather, Nathan had a real Southern drawl. Today he was not wearing his contacts, but some round wire-rims, like Richard's, only bigger.

"I'm not even sure I'll get a part," said Thomas. But he'd spoken words up on the stage, and that was enough to relax him. Mr. Farnham explained that they were reading one of the scenes between Roderigo and Iago, where Iago is reducing love to mere lust.

"It's a perfect example of the corruption of reason by passion," said Mr. Farnham.

"I remember now," said Thomas. "We did it in class. It's that place where Iago talks about our bodies being like gardens."

"Yes, yes, exactly," Mr. Farnham said. He laughed gleefully as he said it. Mr. Farnham was odd. He was so damn moody. Everything was either a total crisis or the greatest event in history.

Landon handed Thomas the paperback and showed him what page they were on. Mr. Farnham said he didn't want to do that scene for the audition.

"Roderigo doesn't have many lines there," he said. "Let's do the opening scene instead."

Thomas turned to Act I, Scene 1 and realized that Roderigo had the very first lines of the play. If he got the part, he would be the first person in the whole cast to speak.

"Just stand there," said Mr. Farnham. "Turn out a little. I'm going to go out to the seats to listen and to watch." He hopped down from the stage and moved out to the middle of the house. "Whenever you're ready. Landon, read Brabantio. Use my book. Plenty of volume, Thomas."

"Tush! Never tell me; I take it much unkindly/ That thou, Iago . . ." Thomas began to read the lines. At first it was awkward, but then he started to enjoy it.

" 'Sblood, but you'll not hear me:" responded Nathan as Iago. "If ever I did dream of such a matter,/ Abhor me."

"Thou told me thou didst hold him in thy hate," said Thomas, and he felt a rush of frustration, doubt, and petulance—but not, he realized at once, as himself. He was becoming Roderigo. He understood these lines. They read up to the part where Brabantio calls for torches.

"Good," said Mr. Farnham from the seats. "Now read the last scene for Roderigo. One we haven't gone over in class. The one where Iago kills him."

It was Act V, Scene 1.

Nathan was scary in that scene. It was as though he had decided to reveal some cruelty that he had kept hidden away for as long as Thomas had known him. He had a power about him, an evil determination that built Thomas's own dread and anguish. When Thomas read his last lines—"O damn'd Iago! O inhuman dog!"—he found a loathing and a recognition and a horror in his voice. It was absolutely exhilarating.

Mr. Farnham geeked a little by jumping out of his seat and applauding wildly, but it was okay. Thomas and Nathan knew it had clicked. Even Landon was awed.

"That was really good," said Landon. He sounded astonished.

"That was marvelous," said Mr. Farnham. He climbed the stairs and joined them on the stage.

It was more than marvelous for Thomas. It was fun.

"Could I have the part?" he asked. "I'd really like to do it."

Mr. Farnham said of course he could have the part. The question was only a matter of when he could rehearse.

"Tomorrow's bad," said Thomas. "We've got a game and a mixer."

"What about Sunday?"

Nathan said Sunday was okay with him.

"Sunday at 3:00, then," said Mr. Farnham. "We can rehearse the bits with Iago and Roderigo, and figure something out about the crowd scenes later on. This is going to be a memorable production."

He was standing between Nathan and Thomas on the stage. With one hand he gently pinched the back of Nathan's neck, and with the other he did the same to Thomas's. Then he patted them both on the back. It was the first display of affection Thomas had ever seen from him.

Scene 15

When Cynthia awakened early Friday evening, her first thought was that she was glad to be home. She had been here now for six hours, and she had slept for five of them. The hospital had been exhausting. All the jokes about being awakened to get a sleeping pill were true. And even though they had tried to keep news of her hospitalization quiet, people had come. Dad had to be there, of course. And Ben; she had really needed to see him. But not people like Chuck Heilman. He was such an oaf. He'd popped in on her early on Thursday evening while she was listening to a concert on PBS. He'd said he was going to see Meryl Streep in a new movie. He had stayed for almost half an hour, reciting his platitudes about persevering and centering and coming to inner peace in order to make outer healing possible.

On his way out he had asked her why she was in there.

"They're not sure," she had said, and later, after Ben had arrived, she had cried over how selfish Chuck Heilman had been.

"He was here to kill time before his damned movie," she had said. "And to find out the latest gossip."

"He's a poltroon," Ben had said.

"I was spiteful. I wouldn't tell him what was wrong."

But they knew what was wrong. The doctor had confirmed it on Thursday afternoon, and she had been the one to tell Ben when he came down on Thursday night.

Multiple sclerosis.

"The odd thing is that I feel better," she had said. "I'm stronger, and I can walk better. My vision is clearing. I thought I was getting well."

Ben had held her hand and had said nothing.

She was going to see a doctor in Washington next week for a second opinion, but she was already letting the news settle into her life, like a dye into cloth. Dr. Manning had been nice about explaining the disease. He had suspected it when she had reported her first episodes last summer, but the diagnosis depended largely on eliminating other possibilities. The good news was that she did not appear to have the type of MS that ran its course quickly. In these early stages, especially, she could look forward to remissions. There could be times when she felt well and could certainly go back to her work. Finish her dissertation? Absolutely. Play Desdemona? Of course, if she felt like it.

It was the later part that he had played down, that she and Ben had avoided discussing themselves. The doctor said there were all kinds of new treatments involving diet and water therapy. It was not at all a bleak prognosis, he suggested. But bleakly was how the Wardens had reacted. It could take as few as five years or as many as thirty, but eventually she was likely to become more and more debilitated, less and less able to move or to speak, and she would very slowly die.

She should not be dwelling on the future. It was 8:00 on Friday evening, and she lay in her own roomy, comfortable bed. She stared at the digits on the face of the alarm clock across the room and realized that she was seeing clearly. Her double vision was gone. She cautiously emerged from bed. Yes, the eyesight was clear. Her left ankle was still a bit shaky, but it, too, was improved. She wanted so much to believe that it had all been a mistaken diagnosis, that she was actually well, and that the aberration of the last week would not visit her again. She could not do it, though. As much as her heart wanted to pop champagne corks and toss confetti, her head stood sternly by to remind her that she was suffering from a devious, unpredictable disease. She was sick with multiple sclerosis. There was no cure.

And the facts made tonight that much more precious to her. The poisons in her system had lost their power for the moment. It was low tide. She slipped out of her cotton nightgown and into some jeans and a tee shirt. She was twenty-three years old, and she felt good. She liked the feel of the jeans against her bare skin, liked the unrestraining tee shirt. The instant after she pulled it on, she wanted to pull it off again. She was doused in desire to make love to Benjamin Warden, who sat and wrote in the study next door.

Ben was working on a poem. He had been working on it since Wednesday, and it was giving him trouble. He was struggling to fit the information into the fourteen lines of a sonnet. Cynthia had known better than to ask why it had to be a sonnet. Ben was no more free to manipulate the shape and the structure of a poem than a mapmaker was to change the contours of a landscape. Ben had told her more than once that revising his work was just a matter of listening for the finished version of a poem, the version that had existed all along.

The building was quiet. The boys were studying in their rooms. She walked out of their bedroom to peek into Ben's study and saw him facing away from her, leaning back in his swivel chair and reading a piece of typed paper. That was good. Perhaps he was finished. If he were in the middle of a problem, he would be hunched over the keyboard or pacing.

In a moment she would interrupt him, but just for now she took the pleasure of observing him. He was twelve years older than she, but he was still so much like a boy. She loved to look at his shoulders, at the shape of his dark hair on the back of his neck, at the long lobes of his ears, at the way he sat back and still kept his feet propped up on their toes. He might have been eighteen years old from the back. And from the front he was many ages at once. The crimson blotch down the side of his face gave him the aspect of a hideous demon, one of Satan's minions that had plagued the earth for centuries. It was his eyes and the kindness of the other side of his face, however, that redeemed his appearance. He was so loving, so kind. She thought of his birthmark as a mask that had not yet crumbled entirely away. It was to her a lovely metaphor for the body and the soul—the ugly physical shell beneath which dwelt the splendid countenance of love.

She did love him. She wished he would simply relax into her love for him instead of listening to the doubts that attacked him like viruses from time to time. This latest crush on her from Dan Farnham was no more serious to her than a third-former's would have been. But it was anguish to Ben.

Was it fair to interrupt him now? Perhaps she should resume her own work. Cynthia had a study of her own, but whereas Ben's was messy with unanswered letters, stacks of papers, open books on the desk and on the chairs and on the floor, hers was tidy and even dusty. His was a working study; hers was a museum. She would let herself rest through another weekend, and then she would return to her work. She needed to pick up her research again. But later. Tonight she sought other satisfactions.

"Are you at a good stopping place?" she asked from the doorway.

He swiveled to face her. "You're up," he said. "I heard nothing."

"You were with the virgin at the homecoming bonfire," she said. "I should be jealous."

"You should not," he said. "The virgin is a bit too dense, I fear."

"Let me see."

"Can you?"

She told him that her vision had cleared. He waved the paper toward her, and she came forward to take it. She read:

THE VIRGIN ALONE AT THE HOMECOMING BONFIRE

The pagans knew a thing or two of fire.
(I'm not about to make a study list
Of functions: heat, light, cleanliness. Let's kiss
The lesson plans good-bye for half an hour.)
I mean more primitive matters still:
The way it flickers, seduces the eye,
Pumps sparks deep into the hard night sky,
Bonds us together, obviates my chill.
It's life, they said, that elemental heat
(Combined with earth, with air, with wetness) makes.
We celebrate that life-heat now. It aches.
The sparks spill past the stars, die at my feet.
Why am I bitter? Here's a cryptic hint:
The hottest fire springs from the coldest flint.

"You've got some syntax problems," said Cynthia.

"Yes," said Warden. "How do you read the situation?"

"She's a frustrated old maid," she said. "Not that old an old maid, but never married. And she teaches, and she's attending the homecoming bonfire, and she's bitter because she seeks sexual fulfillment and she can't have it."

Warden smiled. "That's very good," he said. "You don't think I need to put some lively teenagers in there anywhere? Cheerleaders with their skirts flying up, strapping football players with bulging crotches?"

"It's very sexy now," she said.

"So are you."

He stood up and held her to him.

"Leave the lights on," she said. "Just pull down the shades."

Instead he dropped to his knees, lifted her tee shirt and kissed her midsection. She felt a surge of heat and slid down onto the carpet with him. She pulled at his shirt. He unbuttoned her jeans.

"Is this wise?" she giggled. She did not stop what she was doing.

"No," he said. "I love you."

"Love you," she said. She was kicking now to get the jeans off when they heard the door to their apartment slam downstairs. "Mr. Warden?" came the voice from the living room. It was a student. She froze.

"What?" called Ben. His voice was shaky.

"It's Robert Staines," came the voice. "I was wondering if I could ask you about the grade on this poem."

"Hell," said Ben. "What's he doing off his dorm during study hall?"

"We should have known better," she said.

"Mr. Warden? Is it okay?"

Ben was sitting up and tucking in his shirt. "I can't come downstairs right now, Robert," he called.

"No problem," came the voice. "I'll be right up."

"No!" they both shouted at once, but it was too late. He was Robert Staines, star athlete, and he took the stairs three at a time. Cynthia was struggling to pull her jeans back on and to hide her most private parts behind Ben on the floor when he saw them.

"Oh. Mr. Warden. Mrs. Warden."

"Go downstairs, Robert," said Ben.

"Yes sir."

"Leave the apartment."

"Yes sir."

"Do not interrupt my wife's physical therapy exercises again."

"Yes sir. I'm really sorry, Mr. Warden."

"Just leave now. I will meet you in the common room."

Robert Staines left even faster than he had appeared.

Cynthia lay on the floor and laughed. She had never felt so humiliated.

"I will never, never set foot in the dining hall again," she said. "I will never be seen on this campus by anyone ever again."

"That bastard came charging up here deliberately," said Ben.

"No."

"Yes," said Ben. "I know that boy. He's devious."

" 'Physical therapy lessons'? Do you think he'll believe it?" Cynthia laughed helplessly at how awful it all was.

Warden started to laugh with her.

"It was our own fault for acting so impulsively," Cynthia said. "I'd just like to die right now, that's the only problem."

Warden stood up and finished tucking in his shirt.

"Mr. Staines is going to wish he were dead after I finish talking with him," he said. "He's supposed to be studying in his room, not traveling around the campus. And not by himself."

"Don't be too long with him," said Cynthia. "Walk him back to his building and then hie thee hither."

"You're awfully forgiving this evening."

"Not at all," she said. "I just want to finish my therapy."

Scene 16

The number rang eight times before somebody answered.

"McBain House."

"Is Hesta McCorkindale there, please?"

"No, Thomas, she's in the library. Some people are serious about their studies, you know."

"Hi, Susie." He hadn't recognized her voice. It was Susie Boardman, Hesta's roommate.

"She's going to be so angry when she finds out you called and she missed you." Susie had this funny voice, clipped and sort of British-sounding. Hesta said she was hyperintelligent. Thomas had never met Susie face-to-face; they were telephone acquaintances.

"What time is she getting here tomorrow?"

"Dinner, I suppose. Isn't that when the bus is to arrive?"

"Yeah," said Thomas, "but can she get a ride earlier?"

"Sorry about that. She's got a swim meet."

Damn. Thomas had forgotten about her swim meet.

"You can entertain me until she gets there," said Susie. Then she laughed, but Thomas felt a pleasant stirring. What was he, some rock star or something? All these women seemed to crave his body.

He had one distasteful chore to perform. Was Staines still expecting him to arrange a date for him? And should he? Wouldn't he be acting like a hypocrite, arranging a date for the guy he had just turned over to the councilmen for an honor violation? On the other hand, if Staines got acquitted, wouldn't setting him up with a date show that Thomas had no personal grudge against him?

"Susie?"

"Yes?" she said, in her mock operator voice.

"Do you know Katrina Olson?"

"What do you want with her?"

"This guy I know at school wants to go out with her."

"It's too late," said Susie. "She's got a date with all of the Washington Redskins."

"That's fine," said Thomas. At least he had tried.

"I'm kidding," said Susie. "Actually she's going to be down at the mixer this weekend with Stud-of-All-Studs Robert Staines."

"What?"

"He called her last night. You should have heard what she promised to do to him. Such a nasty, nasty girl."

"He was the one that wanted to go out with her," said Thomas.

"He got his wish," said Susie.

"Yeah," said Thomas. "And he'll probably get herpes on Saturday."

Susie giggled. They hung up the telephone anticipating a memorable weekend.

Susie thought about what she would wear. Thomas thought about what he would try.

Scene 17

Thomas had thought his morning classes were dull, but they were nothing compared to having to sit and listen to Robert Staines at the training meal on Saturday morning.

"You should see her thighs," he said for the fifth time. "The thighs are perfect. And you should see her smooth stomach muscles."

It was 11:30 on game day. The twelve guys on the basketball team were eating roast beef on bread with gravy, mashed potatoes, and canned peas. It was the meal every athletic team at Montpelier ate before a game. They would play at 2:00 today. The varsity would play afterward at 3:30. Thomas was nervous. It was their first game of the season. Coach McPhee had told him that he wouldn't be starting but that he'd probably play a lot. He had taken maybe two bites of roast beef and had stirred the gravy around in his potatoes, but he couldn't remember what it was like to be hungry. He just wanted the game to get here. And now Staines was telling the same story about catching Mr. and Mrs. Warden in the act last night. It was all getting on Thomas's nerves.

"Why'd you go upstairs?" asked Ralph Musgrove.

"That's where they were," said Staines.

"I never would have gone upstairs in a teacher's house," said Ralph.

"I thought he was alone. Everybody was talking about how Mrs. Warden was in the hospital. So when I heard his voice up there, I just ran up the stairs. You should have seen old Red Label squirming around trying to cover up the old secret spot."

"Shut up, Staines," said Thomas.

Staines asked what his objection was.

"Just let somebody else talk for a while, okay?" Thomas wanted to say that he liked the Wardens, that he didn't like to hear Mr. Warden's birthmark made fun of, that he didn't like to hear Mrs. Warden discussed in such vulgar terms. But he couldn't say all that at the damn lunch table in front of everybody, and he couldn't sit there and listen to any more of it either.

"Okay," said Staines. "Only you seem to be the only one here who's complaining."

Nobody else at the table spoke.

"You make it sound like Mrs. Warden is a whore," said Thomas.

"Let me tell you something about women, Mr. Rogers," said Staines. "They all want it. You hear all these fairy tales about beautiful princesses saving themselves for the handsome prince who will marry them? That's bull. They'll tell you they don't want it, but they do. And old Red Label was about to deliver the pepperoni when I interrupted."

"They're married," said Thomas. "You make it sound like animals breeding."

"Marriage doesn't matter," said Staines. "You think it's some spiritual experience? My dad's been married four times. He's taught me all about women. You know how you daydream about it? Girls dream about it too. They spend their lives waiting to get popped."

"Not all girls are like that," said Thomas. He wished somebody else at the table would speak up.

"Maybe the ones you hang around with," said Staines. "No wonder you're still a virgin, Boatwright. You hang around with den mothers."

Thomas replied that he ought to hang around with Staines's mother if he wanted to get anywhere.

Staines lunged for him, and they would have gotten into a fight right there if Mr. Delaney and two councilmen hadn't been at the next table.

Thomas spent the next hour in his dorm room fantasizing about pounding Staines's face in. Apparently the stupid beanie-brain had forgotten all about the Right Guard episode. Staines thought he was safe. He'd find out differently Sunday night. Thomas was glad the councilmen knew. And even if Staines did get acquitted and did get to stay at school, Thomas could live without the guy's approval.

In the locker room nobody said much while they were getting dressed. Coach McPhee reviewed the offense and their starting defense with them, and then it was time to warm up, and then the game started.

They were playing Albemarle Academy. Thomas got into the game in the second quarter but got yanked for not passing to Staines, who was open on a back-door twice. Coach McPhee was furious at halftime.

"Man's open, you pass him the ball," he said to Thomas in front of the team. The boys sat on the benches in the locker room while the coach paced. "That ball isn't your private property."

"Sorry, Coach." They were down by three points.

"Sorry, nothing. You play ball the way we practice it."

In the second half Thomas got into the game again. He passed the ball inside to Staines, but the pass never arrived. Albemarle was ready for the back-door play and stole it. Coach McPhee said nothing the first time it happened. The second time he pulled Thomas out again.

"See me after the game," he said.

Staines got hot in the fourth quarter. He hit two shots from outside and stole a pass for a lay-up, and Montpelier was ahead by one with thirty seconds to go. Coach McPhee signaled for the four corners slowdown.

"Make them foul you," he yelled. But with fifteen seconds to go, Staines got the ball on the baseline, drove toward the basket, and put up a fifteen-foot jump shot that missed. Albemarle got the rebound and scored at the buzzer. Montpelier lost by a point.

"I got fouled on that shot," Staines said in the locker room afterward.

"You never should have taken it," said Coach McPhee. "We didn't play smart ball today, boys. We didn't use our heads."

"If I'd gotten the ball more, we could have won," said Staines.

Coach McPhee grabbed a ball and threw it hard into Staines's chest. It bounced off on the floor. Thomas was shocked to see Coach McPhee lose his temper, but glad to see Staines as the target.

"You don't make excuses," Coach said. "We lost as a team. We didn't play well as a team." He left them alone.

The coaches' office was across the hall from the locker room. After Thomas dressed, he dragged himself over. He wished that he could start the day all over again, beginning with lunch.

Coach McPhee was there alone. You could tell he was peeved about the loss, but he wasn't going to hit Thomas with a ball or anything.

"What was the matter with you today?" he said. He pointed to a wooden chair across the desk from his own. Thomas sat.

"I wasn't concentrating," said Thomas.

"What were you and Staines spatting about?"

"Sir?" It amazed Thomas how teachers seemed to know everything.

"The passes that didn't get thrown or got thrown a second too late, the looks, the comments. You think I'm Helen Keller?"

Thomas told him about the argument at the training meal.

"Let me get this straight," said Coach McPhee. "Staines

supposedly popped in on the Wardens and caught them in the middle of doing what husbands and wives do?"

"He said that. I think he was exaggerating."

"And he said some nasty things about them?"

"He called Mr. Warden 'Red Label,' " said Thomas. "I hate that."

Coach McPhee said he hated it, too.

"Let me tell you something, Boatwright," he said. "When I was fifteen years old, my parents left me to baby-sit for my two-year-old brother. It was just the two of us alone in the apartment. I was supposed to give my brother a bath, and then dress him, and then put him to bed. You got the picture so far?"

Thomas did. He had heard this story before, but he dreaded it nonetheless.

"I was too preoccupied with my own little world to look after my baby brother properly," said Coach McPhee. "He drowned in the bathtub, Boatwright. I was irresponsible. I left him alone in that big claw-footed bathtub, and he drowned. Not a day in my life goes by without my thinking of that little boy in that pool of water. I should have been there, and I wasn't. You understand why I'm a teacher now? You understand why I'm a coach? I owe a debt. I had a responsibility, and I blew it. You had a responsibility today, and you blew it, too. The difference for you is that it was only a game. But responsibility still matters. Your responsibility was to the team."

Thomas felt like a cockroach in front of a can of Raid.

"All right, Boatwright, get out of here," he said. "You need to learn how to overcome your personal grudges."

"Yes sir."

"And I'll talk to Staines later on."

But Coach McPhee never spoke a word to Staines again.

Scene 18

On the evening of Saturday, December 4, the only adult in the dining hall at Montpelier School who was clearly enjoying a good mood was Kevin Delaney. His varsity basketball team had won by ten points over Albemarle Academy, and he was now undefeated for the season. One win, zero losses.

Delaney was a big man, pumpkin-sized head on top of a weather-balloon-shaped torso, arms reminiscent of fireplugs, and thighs like tuba cases. His mood tonight was as expansive as his body. His boys had won—even with the defection of Nathan Somerville to that damn Shakespearean production going on, they had won in double figures—and Delaney was proud of himself.

Delaney's spirits withered quickly, however, after five minutes of sitting at the table with four other adults and waiting in vain for a compliment on his victory. Felix Grayson, the DM for the day, was griping because eight bus loads and a couple of vans were bringing almost 250 girls to the campus and he knew that he wouldn't be able to supervise the place properly. Dean Samuel Kaufman was complaining of a dull ache in his lower back, brought on by a visit this afternoon from Benjamin Warden, who wanted Robert Staines dismissed from school for entering a faculty apartment without permission. Cynthia Warden, who sat at the head of the table, was angry because one bus load of girls had arrived an hour early with a chaperone who refused to drive three miles into the town of Montpelier for dinner. And Patrick McPhee was gloomy because his JV team had lost their basketball game by one point as a result of undisciplined play.

"Those sophomores always get jittery," said Delaney. McPhee did not answer.

"I was happy that my boys seemed to adjust to playing

without Nathan Somerville," Delaney said to everyone at the table. He waited for a response.

Sam Kaufman, whose wiry pompadour was uncharacteristically unkempt tonight, paid no attention to Delaney and asked Cynthia where her husband was.

"He's at home. He's writing," said Cynthia.

Delaney wished Kaufman would go to hell for ignoring him. Cynthia Warden was a more promising prospect for generating a conversation about basketball. She might have been one of the high school girls up for the mixer herself, in a striped skirt, blue knee socks, black lace-up shoes, and a white turtleneck under a sweater. Her hair was thick and freshly washed and fanned across her shoulders.

"You look very well, Cynthia," said Delaney. "Did you make it to the games today?"

Cynthia said thank you and that she did not. Delaney wrote her off and decided to try one of the men.

They occupied a rectangular mahogany table for twelve in the center of the dining hall, a large trapezoidal room with plaid carpeting and brass chandeliers. On the table were plastic trays containing varying remnants of lasagna, salad, and canned peaches. On Saturdays at Montpelier the meals were always buffet. There were probably a hundred boys and another forty visiting girls dining at other tables in the room, which could seat five hundred persons at capacity. Many of the other students had decided to take cabs into town to eat in the local restaurants. They were permitted to do so, as long as they returned by 9:00 P.M.

Grayson complained that the school would resemble a commune of anarchic hippies by the end of the evening. "Everybody's going to be doing his own damn thing. Supervision will be just a word in the dictionary."

"Did the wrestlers win?" asked Delaney. He thought maybe he could divert the conversation to basketball indirectly.

Grayson ignored him. "I'm the day master, and I can't find half my duty team," said Grayson. "Has anybody here seen Carella or Farnham? Neither one has shown up for dinner, as far as I know."

Delaney was annoyed with his colleagues. Everybody had

his own agenda tonight. Nobody was listening. He considered going back to the serving line for a fourth helping of lasagna and starting a food fight. That would get Felix's attention.

"Let's hope I have a quieter night than you did, Pat," said Grayson to Patrick McPhee.

McPhee rubbed an invisible spot on his water glass and did not appear to hear.

"You're in high brood tonight," said Delaney. "You'll win the next one."

McPhee worked up a rueful grin. From a pocket he pulled out his coach's whistle on its cord and blew one quick shrill tweet. Everyone in the room fell quiet and looked over.

"Time out," McPhee said, and then he left.

Conversation in the dining room resumed. Those remaining at the faculty table were nonplussed.

"He's had a bad week," said Felix Grayson. "You know he always takes his duty rotation so seriously."

Cynthia asked if there was any word from Diane.

"She's gone for good, I hear," said Grayson.

"Good riddance if you ask me," said Kaufman.

Delaney's shoulders slouched a little closer to the floor. Here we go, another dish of dirt from the talking tabloid.

"I heard she was using him just to get a free education for that introverted son of hers," said Kaufman. "Married him last summer and then turned cold. Pat got tired of it and threw them both out at Thanksgiving."

"That's preposterous," said Cynthia. "He went to Boston over Thanksgiving to see her."

"All I know is they slept in separate bedrooms," said Kaufman. He'd heard it directly from the business manager's secretary, whose office was right next to bookkeeping, where one of the accountants was good friends with a lady who worked for the housekeeping department. "Draw your own conclusions."

"I conclude that he's miserable," said Cynthia. "I think he's amazing to cope so well."

"And on top of everything else," said Delaney, "he lost his game by just one point today." Nobody took his cue.

Grayson asked Cynthia if she was back to full strength.

"Not quite yet," she said. She had taken a long nap that afternoon to prepare for supervision of the mixer this evening. An hour ago she had checked on the bands, both of which were on campus. Now she was hoping that all the members therein would remain sober and play when they were supposed to. "But you can expect me to help tonight." She said she was the culprit who planned the evening and therefore surely should help supervise.

"Welcome aboard," said Grayson. "I'll be glad to use you at the mixer."

"If you're well," said Kaufman. "Do they know yet . . . ?"

"They're running more tests," said Cynthia. She and Ben had agreed not to release any news until she had a second opinion.

Grayson said Dr. Lane had requested that a duty man check the gym during the evening.

"Lots going on at the gym this afternoon," said Delaney. No reaction. Was he not speaking loudly enough? Was he invisible? He was now thoroughly disgruntled. His team had won, damn it, but you'd think it was a feat no greater than sweeping the gym floor. "Not many spectators, though."

"People were afraid of scratching your floor," said Cynthia.

Delaney knew she was teasing. She had asked him about having a dance in the gym, but he had forbidden it on the grounds that the basketball court would be ruined. He had given her permission to use the art studio instead.

"I thought our boys might burn a hole in that floor with the fast break," said Delaney.

"Don't talk about burning," said Grayson. "After this fire alarm thing the other night, we want to make sure the gym stays locked up. Too many cubbyholes for people to get into trouble. Sam, you cover the gym."

"I'm not on duty tonight," said Kaufman. His glasses sat a notch too low on his nose. "I traded my duty with Horace Somerville." He announced he was going home to put some heat on his back. Kaufman was trying to decide whether to look for Robert Staines tonight or find him tomorrow. In addition to Ben Warden's complaint about his barging into the apartment during study hours, there had been talk of an honor violation. Kaufman hated to have to confront the boy on Saturday night, but perhaps he should.

"I need somebody to tour that gym," said Grayson again.

Delaney wanted revenge. They had just arrived at talking about his game when Grayson had steered them elsewhere.

Cynthia said she would check it.

Grayson hesitated.

"Don't you think a woman is capable of handling the athletic building?" she asked.

"It's not that," said Grayson.

"What is it, then?"

"I'm thinking about your health," said Grayson.

"I'm antsy from lying around for so long," said Cynthia. "There are plenty of chaperones for the mixer. I'll help patrol the gym."

"You don't have to patrol like a cop on a beat. Just make sure it's locked up and nobody's in there. But I can find Farnham to do it."

"You don't trust me."

Delaney watched the conversation and wondered why Felix was so reluctant to accept her offer.

"I trust you," said Grayson. "It's just that I don't want anything to happen to you. You might faint out in the cold by yourself. Besides, I don't have an extra key for you." He wanted to steer her away from campus duty politely. He was not thinking primarily of Russell Phillips's death and Horace Somerville's suspicion that the boy had been killed. The police had publicly declared it a suicide, and that was sufficient for Grayson. However, he proudly considered himself old-fashioned, and he did not like the idea of sending a woman out unescorted at night to patrol the grounds or the buildings.

"We can find a key," said Cynthia.

"I have to keep my own," said Grayson. "I don't know of an extra."

Kevin Delaney reached into a pocket and pulled out a large ring of keys. "You want to borrow my pass key to the gym, Cynthia?" he said. "I won't be needing it."

"Thank you very much," said Cynthia. She took the key. "I'm covering the gym now, right?"

"Right," said Grayson. He was clearly annoyed at being outmaneuvered.

Delaney picked up his tray and left the table. His high spirits were restored. Maybe he would celebrate his victory by getting some beer and watching the tube tonight.

He could tell that Felix didn't like Cynthia's having a key. Good. That's why Delaney had given it to her.

Nothing put him back into sorts faster than spreading some aggravation around.

Scene 19

Cynthia Warden returned to Stratford House after dinner. Going to dinner had not been so bad. She had not noticed any leers or smirks from the boys, and the faculty seemed utterly ignorant that she and her husband had been caught *in flagrante delicto* the evening before. The toughest part had been leaving Ben at home and entering the dining hall by herself. It had been a solo flight, and she had landed safely.

She found Ben in the study, staring motionless at his poem.

"I brought you a plate of lasagna," she said.

He jumped, as though he had just awakened. "I missed dinner?" he said. "I'm sorry."

"I knew you were concentrating," she said. She carried the Styrofoam plate to his desk.

"Your hair is wet," he said.

"It's been raining," she said. "You really have been absorbed, haven't you?"

"I'm thinking maybe it should be a double sonnet," he said. He noted that rain should help with supervision for the mixer, because the students would be more likely to remain inside. Cynthia disagreed.

"They'd sneak off during an earthquake if they had to," she said.

Warden pulled the aluminum foil cover off the plate. "Yes, that's the Montpelier lasagna," he said.

Cynthia dug through the pockets of her raincoat. "I have some other goodies here somewhere," she said. She pulled a canned Coke and a napkin out of one pocket. "Can't forget your silverware." From the other pocket she removed a handful of metal and laid it on his desk.

"Stealing from the dining hall?" asked Warden.

"Those are ours," she said. "I stopped in the kitchen on my way upstairs."

"What's this?"

"Kevin's key to the gym," she said. "I'm going to dry off." She bent and kissed him on the top of his head.

"Thanks for dinner," he said. "I've been off with the virgin all day."

"I'll be glad when your fling with her is over," said Cynthia. She departed for the bedroom.

Warden ate the lasagna and stared at the key on the desktop before him.

Scene 20

It was drizzling rain, it was cold, it was the kind of nasty December evening that made Irishmen drink and octogenarians move to Florida. But for Thomas Boatwright, it was Easter morning: Hesta had finally arrived.

He was waiting for her in the common room of Stringfellow when she walked through the door. He could tell it was Hesta even though she was practically invisible under the hood of her yellow rain slicker. She saw him and pulled back the hood and ran over to him all at once. His heart nearly pounded out of his chest, and then a gigantic grin suddenly stretched across his face as though somebody were pulling his mouth with rubber bands. He stood up and wasn't sure of whether to shake hands or hug her wet rain slicker or just say hi, when she leaned forward and kissed him quickly on the cheek. Then he went warm and thought that if fifteen Iranian terrorists walked through the door right now with machine guns he would fight them all off with one hand to protect Hesta. It was love.

She laughed and shook herself out of the rain slicker.

"Isn't this great?" she said. "I got it from my brother. He used to wear it when he was a traffic safety patrol."

Hesta was beautiful. Her body was rounded where it ought to be and slender in the right places. Her blond hair fell down like a poodle's in bangs across her forehead and around her ears. She had on some new oval-shaped tortoise-shell glasses, a big red cardigan sweater, and a navy blue corduroy skirt. She wore white socks and Bean hunting shoes, and she was just an inch shorter than Thomas. The braces on her teeth emphasized the warmth of her huge grin. She was the best-looking girl on the campus, even when she wore something as goofy as a safety patrol boy's raincoat.

"I'll hang it up," he said, and he took the parka from her, turned his back, and walked to the coatrack by the door. He knew it looked awkward just to leave her in the middle of the room like that, but he couldn't help himself. He had to be in motion. He felt the crazy urge to go shoot some baskets in the gym with her, or to read her his part from the play, or to show her how much he could bench-press.

She waited for him in the center of the room.

"I'm sorry we were late," she said.

"It's only 7:30. The bands haven't even started."

They paused, both of them grinning at each other. Thomas was glad that nobody else was in the common room.

"You want something to eat?" Thomas asked.

Hesta said they'd stopped at McDonald's on the way.

"Susie's around here somewhere," said Thomas.

"I see her all the time," said Hesta. "Let's just sit here and catch up."

So they sat on the couch and talked until 8:30, when it was time to go to Bradley Hall for the mixer. People came and went from the common room, but Thomas noticed only vague motion from the corner of his eye. He was with Hesta, and the entire universe had rolled into a ball that encompassed just the two of them.

And yet even in the perfection of it all, even in the wonder of being with her and touching her fingers and laughing with her, in the back of his mind, like the hiss of a snake, Thomas heard the words of Robert Staines. "She wants it," said the voice. "They always act like they don't, but they do."

And Thomas's heart throbbed a beat quicker.

Scene 21

Cynthia put on a dry Montpelier School sweatshirt over her blouse. She had changed skirts and knee socks and had found some boots. She patted her hair dry with a towel and reentered Ben's study. He crossed an entire line out and tapped the paper with his pen.

"It's 7:30," she said. "I'm going over to the mixer."

Ben said nothing. He had not heard her.

She approached his desk.

"Ben," she said, as she touched him on the shoulder.

"Yes," he said without looking up.

"Have you seen Kevin's pass key to the gym?"

Then he did look up.

"What?" he said.

"The key. Have you seen it?"

He shuffled some papers on the desktop. "It was here," he said. "I wonder what I did with it."

"What did you do with your trash from dinner?"

"Trash?"

"The Coke can and the lasagna plate," Cynthia said. "The silverware."

Warden looked around the room, then into the wastebasket half filled with balls of paper.

"I have no idea," he said.

Cynthia found the Styrofoam plate and the empty Coke can in his bottom drawer. Their silverware was in the wastebasket.

The key apparently had disappeared.

Scene 22

Greg Lipscomb was the only student in Hathaway Library. He was also the only male and the only black person. He was, he teased himself, the only person, unless you wanted to count Mrs. Shepherd, the librarian, who was an old white bag (she was at least forty-five years old), who talked on the phone, laughed a lot, and was always asking you what you were reading.

He'd checked out the buses when they arrived. There had been only two black chicks in the whole load, both of them with boyfriends here. The white folks' schools were trying, he supposed, but that didn't make it any easier if you were one of the trailblazers.

To hell with them. He'd come over to the library to browse around in the Archives Room, which Mrs. Shepherd was delighted to open for him after she'd gone through the usual jive about his social life.

"Why aren't you at the mixer tonight?" she had said. "You might be able to meet a girl."

He hated the way she emphasized her key words. Why is the library even open tonight, he'd wanted to say to her, but instead he'd said something about going over to the dance later on. That was so typical of the way these adults operated. They open up the library, but then they act surprised and start messing with you when you go there. It was 8:30. He'd been here for half an hour, and he had ninety minutes to go until Mrs. Shepherd finished moving magazines from one stack to another and closed the place down.

He was sitting at a rectangular plastic-wood-covered table

with a large folder the size of an artist's portfolio open in front of him. Beside him in a chair he had dumped his hunting cap and his damp green ski jacket which his parents had given him at Thanksgiving as an early Christmas present. He had on a white button-down shirt and a good pair of jeans; he was dressed for the mixer anyway. But for now he was looking through old blueprints. The one Mr. Delaney had given him for art class had dated from the 1920s. Greg wanted to find one from an earlier era.

The diagrams weren't just of Stringfellow Hall. He'd already run into some interesting floor plans for Hathaway Library, from before the time they'd added the periodicals wing and the audiovisual center, and for Stratford House, which apparently was exactly the same since they'd built it in the 1940s—thirteen rooms for twenty-six boys and a faculty apartment tacked onto each side.

Somebody had stuck in with the plans an old clipping from *The Washington Post.* It had a big picture of Stringfellow Hall and a smaller picture of Mr. Somerville in front of the Homestead and another one of some boys playing lacrosse. It was a big feature article, over half a newspaper page long, all about the school, and Greg read part of it with a mixture of pride and embarrassment over being a part of the place:

> Before Montpelier Plantation became a school in 1868, it was a working vegetable farm. The old wooden Homestead had been the original farmhouse since the previous century, but in 1858 Virginius Stringfellow had started to build himself an extensive plantation house two hundred yards away. He and his sons had raised the walls and the roof and had roughed out the interior just before the Civil War started, and the house had stood like a ruin until 1868, when ex-Captain Stringfellow, his men, and their families decided that if the South was going to rise again, it needed to be well educated.
>
> The first schoolboys lived in the old brick-and-log kitchen while the unfinished Big House—now re-

named Main Hall—was completed. It took five years for Captain Stringfellow, his fiv› sons, and the schoolboys to get the place habitable, a big square three-story box of a building with a dozen classrooms and a barracks dormitory in the attic. In 1905 the enterprising Stringfellow clan added a wing and built a modest library; in 1920 they added another wing; and in the late 1920s, just before the stock market crash of 1929, they completed a major capital campaign that raised the roof of the entire building, added another entire floor plus an attic, and modernized the plumbing, wiring, and heat. That same campaign was responsible for the building of the current library building and a mammoth gymnasium, which subsumed several of the older outbuildings on the property. (Lost to the gym were the original library and the old kitchen, the school's first dormitory.) It was the last great triumph for Captain Stringfellow, who died riding a horse in 1930 at the age of 90. He had been the school's only headmaster for 62 years.

During the 1930s Montpelier School did little building, but it accomplished something much more important: it established a reputation. By now it had a student population of 150 boys in grades 7 through 12. Talented alumni who could not get good jobs came back to the school to teach, and before long word spread through Virginia and the Carolinas, then later to Georgia and Tennessee, that Captain Stringfellow's school was a good one. For years graduates of the school had attended colleges like the University of Virginia and the University of North Carolina, but by 1940 Princeton, Williams, and Yale were attracting Montpelier alumni. In the 1940s and 1950s the school built a series of residential houses and expanded its student population to 300. It reached its current size of 360 students and 50 faculty members in the mid-1960s. And now with graduates enrolling in every school in the Ivy League, the Montpelier School is one of the most prestigious boarding schools in the country.

It sounded good on paper.

Clipped to the newspaper article was what looked at first like a large piece of scrap paper. When he looked again, Greg could see it was an old blueprint. Or rather it was a copy of an old blueprint, with which somebody had done a lot of work. It had round brown coffee stains around the edges, penciled computations, and all kinds of lines drawn from nearly every corner and every wall. Most of the lines were scratched out or partially erased.

The drawing itself was of two rectangular rooms, the ground floor and the basement of one building. The dimensions were 20′ × 30′. The upper floor was dominated by a gigantic fireplace along what Greg assumed was the northern wall, since it was at the top of the page, with a door on the east wall, and a total of three windows in the other two walls. Opposite the fireplace stairs led down to the clearly labeled cellar, a room with no windows and only one door.

He looked at that door in the cellar more closely. Where the hell could it be leading? It opened onto a little hallway of some sort, one that peeled off toward the left-hand corner of the page—southwest if the top of the paper was north. But the strange thing was that the hallway seemed to just open up into the ground. Was it a larder of some sort? He turned the sheet over to look for some kind of identifying label on the plans, and what he read momentarily confused him. Someone on the back had written in pencil GYMNASIUM.

He looked back at the drawing. This couldn't be the gym. The gym was huge. Had there been an old gym at Montpelier? Why would they have a fireplace in the gym?

Oh, yes. He had it. Why would somebody clip this drawing to that article if there weren't a connection? What he was looking at, he realized with delight, was one of the older outbuildings absorbed by the new gymnasium.

The old caretaker's cottage. It had to be. The dimensions were right, and the place still had a fireplace. And that hallway leading off from the cellar could be a closet, or it could be a larder.

Or it could be a tunnel. His heart went into a tap dance.

Okay, okay, now don't panic. Think clearly.

What if it was a tunnel? What would the tunnel connect? He closed his eyes and pictured the fireplace in the lobby of the gym. It was on the south end. So if he twisted the drawing around with the fireplace on the south, then the tunnel led off across the Quad toward Stratford House.

That made no sense.

Why would the caretaker's cottage have a tunnel at all? And why would it lead to Stratford House? The outer houses weren't even built until twenty years after the gym got finished.

For a moment he was dejected. Then he realized that it didn't have to be the caretaker's cottage at all. There were two other outbuildings swallowed by the gym. And one of them was the old kitchen for the Homestead. Sure, that was it. They would want a kitchen to have a tunnel so that the food would stay warm in cold weather. Mr. McPhee's apartment was right on the site of the old kitchen, according to Mr. Somerville, and he had a good-sized fireplace.

But there was another problem. Mr. McPhee's fireplace was on the east side of the gym, bordering the Quad. Greg looked at the plans again. If this were the fireplace in Mr. McPhee's apartment, then the tunnel in this blueprint would lead off toward the athletic fields, directly away from Stringfellow Hall and from the Homestead. Would they want a kitchen with a tunnel leading to the outside? Maybe.

But there was another fireplace in Mr. Farnham's apartment on the south end of the gym. Mr. Farnham's fireplace was on the west wall. So if you consider the fireplace in this drawing to be on a *west* wall instead of a *north* one, as Greg had assumed at first, then the tunnel led off not to the southwest, but to the southeast. Straight to Stringfellow Hall. Greg turned the blueprint ninety degrees counterclockwise and imagined the fireplace as Farnham's. That was the one. The tunnel—if it was a tunnel, he reminded himself—connected Farnham's apartment with the main building on campus. And Greg had found it.

He had maybe conceivably possibly found the secret passage Mr. Delaney was talking about, and it was right in a teacher's home. It made so much sense. The reason nobody had been able to find the tunnel before was that it didn't connect the Homestead itself with Stringfellow; it connected the old *library* of the school with Stringfellow. Sure, they would want to be able to get to the books if it snowed or something.

Greg was having a good time playing with the possibilities.

The gym was built so that when you entered the building from the Quad, you were actually on the second floor, the floor with the basketball court. The tunnel, being in the cellar of the old library, would then be on the basement floor, the locker room level of the gym. Was it behind a closet? Or maybe it was still open, with a piece of furniture in front of the entrance. Could Mr. Farnham know about it?

He closed the blueprints carefully back into the large folder and left it, as he had been told to do, on the table in the Archives Room. Through the glass separating him from the library's office, he could see Mrs. Shepherd typing index cards. He knocked on the glass and waved a combination thank-you and good-bye to her, grabbed his ski jacket, and ran out of the building. He could get into trouble for being out on the campus alone at night, but it was just a short run down to Bradley Hall. Thomas would want to hear about this. Maybe Mr. Farnham would even let them into his apartment to look.

A tiny voice of misgiving—that it had all been conjecture so far, that he could be making a mistake—whispered to him to slow down. He ignored it and ran for Bradley Hall, to the mixer.

Scene 23

Cynthia Warden ran into the towering Felix Grayson in the lobby of Bradley Hall. Noise from both sides of the building indicated that the bands were indeed performing as promised.

She explained that her husband had lost Kevin Delaney's key and that she needed some way of getting into the gym.

The information did not improve Grayson's mood. "I sure as hell hope none of these kids find it," he said.

"It's at home somewhere," she said.

He asked her if she had seen Kemper Carella, one of his missing duty men.

"No," she said. "I've been trying to find someone who could let me into the gym." She had tried to call Pat McPhee but had gotten no answer.

"Farnham's back in that scene shop," said Grayson. "He's spent his whole duty day over here. Get a key from him."

Cynthia hesitated. "I don't want to bother him if he's working," she said.

"Bother him," said Grayson. "He needs to clean himself up and start acting like a chaperone."

"Would you like to walk back with me?"

Grayson looked to see if she was joking. "I'm getting some air," he said. "The eardrums can stand only so much."

They stood in the tiled lobby as students passed them going to and from the auditorium on the right and the art studio on the left off the hallway behind the stage. The idea for two bands had been Cynthia's. One group played on the stage as a concert group; the other band was set up in the large art studio for dancing. Her plan had been to achieve intimacy in the dance space and still to provide an open concert atmosphere for those who wanted to sit and listen. From the traffic it seemed that all students wanted merely to move from one band to the other.

Cynthia turned away from the auditorium and maneuvered down the crowded backstage hallway. In the scene shop she found Daniel Farnham staining the frame of a four-poster bed. Farnham looked like one of the boys in his jeans and his old green Izod. Even the little mustache gave him the appearance of an adolescent who had not yet started to shave. Despite the closed door between stage and scene shop, they struggled to communicate, even with shouting. The conversation would have required mime and lipreading had the neighboring band not decided to take a break.

"Isn't it terrific?" said Farnham, pointing to the bed. "I got it in a junk shop in town. Just finished sanding it and putting it together this afternoon."

"Wouldn't it be better to stain the pieces separately before you join them?"

"Yes."

Cynthia laughed. "But you're doing it this way."

"Nobody in the audience will be able to see my mistakes anyway."

Cynthia liked the bed. It was a queen-size, with four tall posts rising at each corner and a sturdy wooden headboard at one end. There was no mattress or box springs.

"That's my next step," said Farnham. "We want something comfortable for you to lie on before you die."

"I've been studying lines," said Cynthia. "I want to come back to rehearsal next week."

Farnham said that was the best news he'd heard since Grayson had told him the mixer would be over by 11:00.

"The good Mrs. Kaufman is willing, but not able," he said. "We need you as Desdemona."

"I need to do it," she said.

Farnham brushed the wood of the bed a few more times. "Do they know what's wrong?" He did not look at her when he asked.

"We have to get a second opinion." Cynthia watched him brush more stain onto the frame. She said she had never delivered a line lying down before.

"It's tough. You have to practice the breathing."

Farnham dipped the brush into the can of stain and applied more to the darkening surface of the wood. They spoke simultaneously, then paused.

"Go ahead," said Cynthia.

Farnham shook his head.

"I was wondering if you were planning to go home soon," said Cynthia. "I need to get into the gym."

"I'll be there in an hour or so. Grayson told me to change before I took a turn in the noise inferno." He asked her why she needed to go to the gym.

"I'm inspecting to make sure no miscreant students sneak in," she said.

"I could do that for you."

"I want to do it," said Cynthia. She was both amused and annoyed with all the male chivalry.

"You want to go now?" said Farnham. "My apartment is unlocked. You can cut through to the trophy room."

"It's not a good idea to leave your apartment unlocked," said Cynthia. She was remembering Robert Staines's visit to her home yesterday.

"There's nothing to steal." Farnham continued to stain the bed. "I didn't think you'd be back here after Monday night," he said.

"Dan, drop it."

"I don't know how I could lose my self-control like that. I promise you it won't happen again," he said.

"I'd better go," said Cynthia.

"My feelings just got the best of me," he said.

Cynthia said she was leaving now.

"Cynthia," he said, "give me a chance to apologize."

She buttoned her raincoat and pulled a plastic scarf over her head. "Your apology is accepted," she said.

After she left, Farnham continued his brush strokes on the bed for half a minute. Then he hurled the brush at the cinder-block wall, where it left a brown smear and fell with a faint clatter to the floor.

Greg Lipscomb, who watched from the doorway, had arrived just as Cynthia left the room. He saw Farnham throw the brush, then stare, motionless, at the bed in front of him. Greg could see that the man was mad. Damn. He was dying to investigate this tunnel business, but not when Farnham was on the rampage. He would have to pursue it some other time.

Scene 24

The rain had let up by the time Cynthia emerged from Bradley Hall around 8:45 P.M. She moved against a wave of boys and their dates just arriving for the extravaganza. Thomas

Boatwright and a cute girl in a yellow rain parka passed her on their way in. Thomas looked cute, too, in his blue ski jacket, plaid flannel shirt, and blue jeans. The hillbilly look had arrived among the preppies. She caught his eye and he greeted her shyly, but he did not stop to introduce his girlfriend. Cynthia had grown accustomed to such mannerisms among the Montpelier boys. They never thought it was necessary to make introductions across generational borders.

A damp mist permeated the campus. As Cynthia walked toward the gym, a wave of fatigue hit her and nearly knocked her down. She had to stop and lean against a tree. You're trying to do too much, she thought. Go home and go to bed. Go see your husband.

But she continued to walk toward the gym. Dan Farnham's apartment door was on the south end of the building. It was strange to be entering another person's apartment. Over the square concrete stoop a bulb shone, illuminating harshly the door in the surrounding gloom. As Farnham had promised, the wooden door was unlocked. Inside it was warm. She clicked on a ceiling light; she had not been in this apartment since Ben had moved out and Farnham had moved in. The place was furnished with institutional-grade stuff provided by the school—heavy-legged tables, fake-leather red sofa and chairs, even the generic ducks and hunting scenes framed on the walls. She saw *Harper's* and *American Film* stacked neatly on the coffee table, but aside from the magazines and one small bookshelf containing paperbacks, there was no sign of Farnham's personal life whatsoever. All his secrets had been tidied and tucked away. She snooped a bit. The efficiency kitchenette was antiseptically clean, only orange juice and beer in the refrigerator. The single bed in the bedroom was neatly made. The bathroom was spotless.

The attack of lethargy had passed, and so she resisted the temptation to sit and rest in one of the chairs. But at the thought she felt her innards squirm with a startling excitement. I'm like Goldilocks in the house of the three bears, she thought. A voyeur. Or would that be feminine, *voyeuse*? Who's been sitting in my chair? She could barely help giggling. Who's been sleeping in my bed?

She took the stairs down to explore the rest of his home.

A study, another bathroom, a guest room. Everything was so tidy. On the interior wall was a large metallic door. She walked across the beige carpeting and opened it. In front of her, lighted only by the exit signs over the doors at each end of the hall, lay the long slick concrete flooring of the locker room level of the gym. She found a light switch on the wall and clicked on a row of lamps across the ceiling. Then she entered the hallway.

The gym is lovely, dark, and deep, she thought. She had never been out here in the locker room level. She was amused at how much it turned her on. It was a schoolgirl fantasy, to be sneaking around in the place where boys took off their clothes and splashed around in the showers. Past the locked glass doors of the darkened locker rooms, past the coaches' offices and the training room, she approached the stairs at the opposite end of the hall. Two doors on the far wall had clumsy signs taped at eye level. MCPHEE APT., KNOCK 1ST, the door on the left said in black Magic Marker. The other, fifteen feet to the right, said in different writing, BOILER. RED FLAG. KEEP OUT. It was signed ANGUS. Cynthia's fatigue had disappeared. She felt privy to all sorts of secrets, roaming here in the bowels of the gymnasium. At the same time she felt guilty. Was this why she had insisted upon taking this duty? Did she have some unconscious urge to pry?

It was time to move upward into the airier spaces.

The stairs were dark too, lighted faintly at the landings by windows, through which a dim glow from the campus sidewalk lights filtered. One flight up, at the basketball court level, Cynthia saw nothing. Up another flight, and she was at the weight room and the practice room for the wrestlers. A padlocked chain secured the door to the weight room.

The door to the wrestling room was open.

She did not know that this was the room where Russell Phillips had been killed earlier in the week. She was not even sure of whether the room should have been locked or not. What attracted her was the sight of the soft foamy mats across the floor. A floodlight outside the window threw a soft reflection on the dark blue vinyl of the mats. Inside the room other mats, rolled and stored vertically like columns, lined the walls. Three ropes hung from beams on the ceiling, and attached to one wall she saw a pegboard. She felt tired again, now that she had climbed some stairs and had dissipated the adrenaline surge of exploring the lower depths.

She was unaware that someone was in the room with her.

Cynthia took off her plastic scarf and raincoat, folded the coat, and used it as a pillow as she stretched out supine on the mat, facing the window, leaving the door and the rolled columns of mats behind her. Little black scarabs of blindness floated skyward in front of her. She began to weep, not gradually, but at once in one surprising sob. It was so unfair, this waxing and waning of the life force in her. There was so much she wanted to do, and her body was betraying her. She retained the urges but lost the energy, kept the will but lost grip of the means. Self-pity surrendered to anger. She would not succumb to a virus. She would play Desdemona, and she would finish her dissertation, and she would continue with student activities here at Montpelier. Fumbling in the coat folded under her head, she found her handkerchief and dried her face.

Pulling herself up to her knees, she faced the window as if in supplication, arms out, pleading. She no longer saw spots in front of her eyes. Instead she imagined Othello, advancing on her, carrying a lantern and also a determination to kill her. She spoke her lines from memory:

That death's unnatural that kills for loving.
Alas, why gnaw you so your nether lip?
Some bloody passion shakes your very frame:
These are portents; but yet I hope, I hope,
They do not point on me.

Behind her she thought she heard a noise. She turned to see what it was.

"Angus?" she said.

Scene 25

Richard Blackburn sat in demerit hall in the basement of Fleming Hall with two books open in front of him. The book visible to an onlooker was a Dick Francis thriller, still number one on the best-seller list and a perfectly respectable volume for him to be perusing on this Saturday evening.

It was not, however, the book he was reading. Tucked inside was *The Fuck Book,* which Richard had found over the Thanksgiving break in the bus station and snagged to bring back to school. It was all about sex, some of it stuff that Richard had never even heard of before. It made him a little uncomfortable.

It was five minutes until 9:00. Another thirty-five minutes to go. The wooden seat was uncomfortable, and the ancient graffiti carved in the desk in front of him were as familiar as his own fingernails. There were twelve boys in D-hall tonight, a small number. Since it was just after a holiday and the beginning of a new term, fewer people than usual had had the opportunity to build up enough demerits to qualify for Saturday night detention. They were spread over the large study hall room, six rows of desks, twelve desks in a row, all desks bolted to the floor, all facing the proctor's desk in the front of the room, all perfectly visible under the bright neon lights.

He looked up from his books at the dark windows splattered with rain. Immediately he heard Chuck Heilman clear his voice at the front of the room. He turned to see Heilman staring him down and shaking his head. They were supposed to study for two solid hours, not behave like normal people and look out the windows. Talk about cruel and unusual punishment. And then they pick the geekiest, stupidest teachers to be the supervisors, so if you do look up, you have to look at somebody like Heilman, whose fat fingers delicately flipped through a book of famous quotations as he worked on tomorrow's undoubtedly tedious sermon.

Richard was angry at Landon Hopkins for crying about his stupid Shakespeare book and angrier at Daniel Farnham for sticking him in here. That was all right. He was going to get his revenge soon enough. Setting off the alarm in the gym had been just a warm-up exercise. Tonight came the coup de grace.

Outside in the bushes Richard had hidden a black plastic garbage bag. Inside the black plastic was a brown paper grocery bag. Inside the grocery bag was a dead squirrel.

He had found the squirrel this afternoon in the middle of the road surrounding the campus. Immediately he had known that the squirrel would end up as a major inconvenience to Daniel Farnham. He had kicked it off to the side of the road, where he had come back after dark with a couple of bags and some sticks and had scooped it up. He'd been planning to leave the squirrel in a burning grocery bag on Farnham's front porch and ring the doorbell. Farnham would come to the door, see the fire, and stomp it out. He'd get squirrel all over himself.

The problem was that Farnham was supervising the mixer. So he wouldn't be home. It was beginning to seem like a silly, risky plan anyway, with all these people all over the campus. Maybe he would just leave the squirrel in Farnham's car. Or hide it somewhere in the scene shop. By Monday it would stink like hell. What he'd really like to do is leave it in Landon Hopkins' bed, under the pillow. Too bad he didn't have two dead squirrels to play with.

Heilman was clearing his throat again. Richard looked up.

"There's a movie on television tonight that my wife and I really want to see," said Heilman. "You know what I'm going to do with you rascals? I'm going to let you out of here half an hour early. Now scoot."

Scoot. *Madre de Dios,* but Heilman was such a nerd. Still, Richard scooted himself right out that door and down to the mixer at Bradley.

It was cold and damp outside, but Bradley Hall was steaming. Richard left his coat on anyway. The place was packed.

He paused in the foyer and then turned left, toward the art room, and tried to spot Farnham.

Thomas was in the hallway with his girlfriend, Hesta. She was pretty nice, Richard supposed, but he couldn't see anything special about her. For Boatwright she was like Venus. Richard thought girls were interesting in a clinical sort of way, but he didn't have time to pursue a regular girlfriend. He saw himself as too busy to fool with them. He also found them a little scary.

"What are you doing here?" Thomas asked him.

"Heilman decided to act human."

"Susie Boardman's here without a date," Hesta said.

"Yeah," Richard had said. "Well, I'm waiting for some people."

Boatwright and his bimbo went inside the art studio to dance.

Down the hall was the scene shop. Richard could see that the light was on. He unzipped his coat and moved down to scope the place out. There were people constantly in motion in the hallway, so it was easy for Richard to approach the door and take a casual peek inside as he strolled by. Someone was inside, all right. But it wasn't Farnham; it was Greg Lipscomb.

Richard walked into the scene shop. "You seen Farnham?" he said. The band on the stage was on break, so they could talk without screaming.

Lipscomb was pacing around the bed frame in the middle of the room like some guy in the movies whose wife was about to have a baby. "He just left," he said. He was acting as though Richard were some mosquito.

"What's your problem?" said Richard.

"Nothing. You seen Tom?"

"Just a second ago. He's with Hesta." Richard didn't have anything against black guys, but he couldn't stand it when somebody had a secret and obviously kept it from him. "Look, I'm not here to bug you. I just want to find Farnham."

"I wouldn't try talking to him now if I were you."

"I don't want to talk to him. I just want to know where he is."

"Farnham went flying out of here," Lipscomb said, "after

doing that." He pointed to a brown stain on the cinder-block wall and the glistening damp brush on the floor that had made it.

"What's he mad about now?"

"Who knows? Something to do with Mrs. Warden, I guess."

"She was in here with him?" Richard could imagine what was going on. Apparently Mrs. Warden was some nymphomaniac, if you could believe what Robert Staines said about finding her on the floor with her husband, but he couldn't conceive of a wimp like Farnham ever actually doing it with her.

"She was here, she left, he went crazy, he left. I was here to ask him a favor, but not when he's throwing paintbrushes."

Throwing paintbrushes. Crud. He could be anywhere. Richard should leave Boatwright's roommate to paint the bed or whatever he wanted to do. Lipscomb sure was jumpy.

"Why are you so skittish?" Richard asked. He did not really expect an answer.

Instead of shrugging him off, Lipscomb surprised him. "I'm about to bust to tell somebody," he said. "Can you keep a secret?"

Richard said he was practically a priest.

"I think I've found that secret tunnel Delaney's been talking about."

"Bull."

Greg told him about the drawing in the library and his theory that the tunnel led from Stringfellow Hall to the basement of the gym. "Do you think it makes sense, with the chimneys and all?" he said.

"It makes a hell of a lot of sense," said Richard. Ideas exploded like popcorn. Oh, yes, yes, yes, it was perfect. To think that he had been getting tired of the whole project, that he had been on the verge of leaving the squirrel on McPhee's door, McPhee who was also a jerk, but the squirrel seemed so right for Farnham, who was so tidy and picky and perfect.

Richard shrieked with his most contrived mad-scientist-sounding laughter. Several people from the hallway looked inside the scene shop, then moved on.

The band started to play again, so Richard had to shout. "Show me this blueprint," he yelled. "We have an early Christmas present to deliver to Mr. Farnham."

Scene 26

This was the best night ever. All the problems from earlier in the day had disappeared. Hesta looked great, the bands sounded great, everybody was having a good time. Thomas couldn't believe he was at Montpelier with all of these girls around. They were everywhere: tall girls who stooped over self-consciously, short girls with cute little doll faces, hefty girls who laughed a lot, skinny girls whose eyes dared you to try them out. Thomas loved the way girls behaved, the way they linked arms with each other or danced with each other, the way they sat with their backs so straight, the way they shook their hair back from their faces like beautiful horses. It was almost too much for him, all these curves and mounds and valleys vaguely concealed by a few millimeters of cloth. Even if Hesta had not been there, it would have been wonderful.

But it was for Thomas as though he and Hesta were the only two people in the room. Or as though the other people in the room were not capable of understanding what kind of electrical connection Thomas and Hesta were making. He had this stupid grin on his face all the time, and she was smiling, too, and they were talking in spite of the loudness of the music about everything in the world. Thomas had never felt so happy.

The Prodigals were playing a bunch of oldies—stuff by the Four Tops and the Beatles and the Beach Boys. It was as though every song were played for them. He was loose. His body just moved to the beat of whatever tune they were playing, and Hesta, well, Hesta was always a good dancer. He loved to watch her shake her head at him during a fast song while she still kept her eyes on him. And when they played a slow song, and he and Hesta got up close and actually touched all the way down their bodies, that was it, that was paradise, that was the ultimate merger of body and soul.

Yet the longer they danced, and the more they touched, the more Thomas was aware of the heat pumping through his veins, of the quickness of his breath, of the growing throbbing energy in his loins. He wanted to kiss her so badly, but there was no way here, not with all the guys around, not on the dance floor in front of all the teachers.

He remembered Robert Staines in the locker room talking about how all girls wanted it really, about how you had to be aggressive, and he thought about how Staines was like some damn dog that needed to mount something every week or so. He wondered confusedly, though, whether maybe Staines could be wrong even if he was successful. Thomas knew what he desired, knew what he was going to do if he got the opportunity, and knew that the moment of truth had arrived. He would ask her a question, and if she turned him down, then fine, it wasn't meant to be.

He was going to ask her if she wanted to leave the mixer. She would know that he was asking her to go fool around, and it would be all up to her. Surely she must feel the same way he did, where everything was just so right and so true. Surely she wanted to as much as he did. And if she didn't, well, that was it then, they would stay here.

"Do you want to go outside?" he whispered in her ear. Then he pulled back his head and looked at her eyes.

She looked straight back at him. He knew what she was going to say before she spoke.

"Yes," she said.

His excitement grew.

Scene 27

Richard was sold absolutely.

"You're a great detective," he said. "This has got to be Farnham's apartment, and this has got to be a tunnel leading to Stringfellow."

They were back in the Archives Room looking at the blueprint. Richard was convinced that Greg had made a significant discovery. But the more Richard raved, the more dubious Greg became.

"It's just a couple of lines running off a basement," Greg said. "We can't be sure it's the old library."

"Of course it is," said Richard. He pointed out the scrawled identification "GYMNASIUM" on the back of the drawing. "There are three fireplaces in the gym, correct?"

"Correct."

"It can't be the lobby fireplace. That's the old caretaker's cottage, where the fireplace is on the south side of the room. You can see very clearly in this diagram that the fireplace is at the top of the page and the tunnel runs off toward the left-hand corner. In which case the tunnel would lead across the Quad toward buildings that went up a zillion years after that cottage was built."

"I know," said Greg. "I'm the one who told you."

"McPhee's fireplace is on the east side of the room, so if this is a drawing of the old kitchen, then the tunnel leads away from the Quad and into the playing fields."

Greg said it was possible to have an outside escape tunnel. He had seen them at plantations along the James River.

"Yeah," said Richard, "but remember the legends. They always mention the Homestead and Stringfellow Hall. They always talk about tunnels from building to building."

Greg said they were making too many assumptions.

"So what do you want to do?" said Richard. "Go back to the dorm and study?"

Greg admitted that he had nothing better to do on a Saturday night with no date.

"The worst we can be is wrong," said Richard. "We can have some fun, kill some time. Maybe pull the ultimate prank. And if we don't find a tunnel, we don't tell anybody how we spent our evening."

"Let's make a copy and get on with this," said Greg.

"Yeah," said Richard. "The squirrel in this bag will thaw."

They contributed a nickel each to the Xerox machine, made a copy of the drawing, replaced the original once again, and left the library. They went not to the gym, but to the northwest entrance to Stringfellow Hall.

Richard wanted to find the entrance in Stringfellow, take the tunnel to sneak into Farnham's apartment, and deposit his dead animal.

"What if there's something blocking the door?" Greg asked.

"We leave it behind the door. It'll still smell up the place. That'll be even better. He'll never get rid of it."

"And how are we going to find the tunnel in Stringfellow?"

That was the tricky part of Richard's plan. He hoped to use the blueprint to show him the precise angle at which the tunnel left the gymnasium. He would then follow that angle with his eye. Where his eye met Stringfellow Hall, he hoped to find the entrance to the tunnel.

In the cold mist the boys stood at the corner of Stringfellow and looked carefully at the dark gym. The only lighted windows were in the far left side of the building.

"Farnham's at home," said Greg. "Let's just go ask him if we can look around."

Richard held up the bag with the squirrel in it. "Why not just ask him to stick this squirrel under his refrigerator for us and leave it for a month? The whole idea is secrecy, you moron."

Greg tried to guess how far it was from Farnham's apartment to Stringfellow. The first building next to Stringfellow was the infirmary; then came the headmaster's house; then the chapel; and finally the gym. The south end of the gym was closer to them than the Homestead was, but the place was still a long way from where they were standing. It seemed impossible that the Stringfellow family would dig a tunnel over a hundred yards long just to get to the library.

But Richard was busy checking the blueprint. The parallel lines indicated the tunnel veered off from the building at a forty-five-degree angle.

"Farnham's apartment doesn't stretch the width of the building," said Greg.

"I know, I know," said Richard. "It ends before the side stairs to the locker rooms."

They traced an imaginary line from Farnham's apartment to Stringfellow.

"Right in the middle of this building," said Richard. "That makes sense."

"But it's one floor below us," said Greg. "What's down there?"

"That's what we're about to find out," said Richard.

Scene 28

Thomas and Hesta walked out of Bradley Hall into the misty silence of the night. He had his arm around her shoulders; she had both her arms around his waist in an awkward hug. It would have been hard to walk that way if they had been in a hurry. But part of the mood was to wait, to see, to let build whatever volcanic explosion Thomas was anticipating. They turned left when they emerged from the building and walked past Reid Hall, the science building.

Thomas wasn't sure where he was going. If it had been warm and dry weather, they could have stayed outside. Or if it had been warm and wet, they could have managed by finding an unlocked car belonging to the faculty. There were stories all over the school about where you could take girls. You were crazy if you tried to sneak a girl back onto your dormitory. There was always some resident master or a DM prowling around, and for big dances they recruited other members of the faculty and even faculty wives to help supervise. Part of the game was to see where you could find to take a girl, and then to see how far you could get with her once you'd arrived.

"It feels good out here," said Hesta.

"Yeah. That room gets hot." It felt good to be touching her. They walked past Fleming Hall, where Thomas had English class, and he thought for a minute about taking Hesta up to Farnham's classroom. That would make a good story, but the problem was the furniture. The teachers had nothing but desks in their classrooms. But the teachers' lounge had a couch.

"Let's go in here," said Thomas. They cut in through the entrance to Fleming and scampered immediately up a flight of stairs. They dropped their arms from around each other, and Thomas took Hesta by the hand to pull her along. Now it was urgent. The teacher's lounge was the first door on the left. Thomas pushed it open and nearly ran into Mr. Somerville.

"Boatwright," said Mr. Somerville. "I thought I heard footsteps in the building." He was in a sports coat and tie as usual, as if it were Monday morning instead of Saturday night.

Thomas wanted to turn and run.

"This is Hesta," he said. He was grateful for the habit of manners, which gave him some time to think.

Mr. Somerville took her hand and said he was delighted to meet her.

"I was just showing her around the campus," said Thomas.

"Indeed," said Mr. Somerville. "This room seems to be a popular stop on the tour tonight. I encountered my own grandson with a young lady earlier in the evening."

That was good. At least he wasn't getting mad.

"We'd better go," said Thomas.

"Yes," said Mr. Somerville. "Have a nice visit, Hesta."

Outside again they were walking.

"We were lucky he was mellow tonight," said Thomas.

"He seemed like a nice man," said Hesta. She put her arm around his waist.

She was so warm. He suggested that they cut across the campus.

"Where are we going?"

"The chapel."

"Isn't that sacrilegious?" she said.

He did not think so.

She asked him what they would do if it was locked.

"Then we'll go next door," he said, "and sneak into the gym."

Scene 29

They were very scientific about the whole thing. First they paced off the distance on the outside of the building. Starting at the west end of Stringfellow, they carefully counted their footsteps to the point in the middle of the building where the angle to Mr. Farnham's apartment in the gym matched the angle on the diagram. If the angle was drawn wrong on the blueprint, then they were in trouble. But they were assuming the angle was accurate.

Then they went inside to the ground-floor hallway and measured off the same number of paces. The ground floor of Stringfellow Hall consisted mainly of two hallways that met at a T intersection in the middle of the building. Off the hallways were doors to offices and storage rooms and the bookstore and the game rooms and the laundry room. You had to go up one flight to get to the main floor of Stringfellow, with the carpeted lobby and the portraits on the walls and the big triple-sashed windows.

Despite his doubts, Greg was becoming excited. The blueprint might, after all, turn out to be legitimate. It was possible that they may have found a tunnel forgotten for decades.

Richard counted out loud, and Greg paced, making sure that he kept his stride at exactly the same length as outside. It was bright down here in the tiled hallway, but there were few people around. Up ahead they could hear the click of billiard balls hitting one another, and to their left they noticed the quiet rumble of a washing machine. Nearly everybody on campus was at the mixer.

"Thirty-four, thirty-five, thirty-six. Stop," said Richard.

Greg was already stopped. They were in front of a smooth wooden door with a bright steel knob. There was no sign on the door.

"This is it," said Richard. "Now watch the door be locked."

The door was not locked.

They opened it and saw a flight of wooden stairs descending into the dark basement. Greg found a light switch on the wall and flicked it. A bare bulb at the bottom of the stairs shone on a splotched concrete floor. They descended the stairs and paused at the bottom to get their bearings.

"We need to go straight ahead," said Greg.

"I know, I know," said Richard. "I've just never been down here before."

There was not much to see. The room they were in did not undergird the entire building. It was perhaps twenty-five feet wide and thirty feet long, with walls of white brick and an open ceiling exposing beams of 2′ × 10′ lumber. Some old furniture, stuff that you might have seen in a common room years ago, was stacked over to the left side of the room. Beside it was a pile of thin mattresses, the kind they used on the dorms. A metal door to their right was labeled FURNACE. And in the wall directly in front of them, they saw a planked wooden door.

Greg suddenly felt as though he had to go to the bathroom. He couldn't see Richard's eyes behind the glint of those round little John Lennon glasses, but he could tell that they were focused on the door ahead. The two boys didn't even speak; they simply ran over to the door in front of them and then paused, instinctively drawing the occasion out for the most dramatic moment.

"This has got to be it," said Richard. The damp plastic bag in his left hand quivered in his clutch. "You do the honors."

"What if it's locked?"

"If it's locked, we break it down," said Richard. "We are not stopping now."

"We should have brought flashlights for the tunnel," said Greg.

"Just open the damn thing."

The door was not locked. Greg put his hand on the old-fashioned metal latch and pressed down. The door swung open toward them.

They heard the breathing before they saw who it was inside.

Scene 30

Heilman is so stupid, Thomas thought, as he and Hesta walked quietly down the aisle of the darkened chapel. He leaves the door to the building open any-old-time so that any-old-body can wander in. And here we are.

He held her hand in his, and he thought she had to be able to hear his heartbeat. He was afraid to talk because he knew his voice would sound strangled. They were walking down the aisle, just like a couple about to be married, only they were skipping the marriage part and going straight to the honeymoon. Tonight's the night, Thomas thought. Tonight I'm going to find out what it's really like.

They could hear the creak of wood from somewhere off in the left transept. Another couple, maybe more than one, was undoubtedly here with the same idea, seeking a quiet sanctuary from the noise and the rain and the cold. Thomas could see only dimly in the darkness of the chapel, but he knew its geography well. At the end of the nave they climbed three stairs, and then they were in the choir. A small door, shorter than his waist, swung open to give them access to the cushioned pews.

Hesta was hardly breathing. "It's so weird to be in a church," she whispered.

They sat next to each other. Thomas had his right arm around her shoulders. She was right. He had never sat in the choir before, and in the dark and from the new angle the entire building looked different, like a haunted barn. The creak of wood told him that somebody else was moving toward them. Hell, they should have gotten a reservation. The shape of whoever it was moved off to the right transept.

"Do you want to go?" he asked.

She snuggled up against him. "We just got here," she said. "It's nice."

There was a part of Thomas that was delighted simply to sit here with Hesta and enjoy her company. To have her pressed up against him, to feel her hand gently caressing his fingers, to hear her whispering an occasional question, to which he could whisper a reply—that was good, that was terrific, that was so damn much better than the boyish pranks of people like Richard.

And yet there was another part of him that kept hearing Robert Staines in the locker room. Thomas and Hesta murmured small talk while all the time he listened to the whisper of desire, the urgent suggestive voice that insisted he now succumb to the delicious instinctive possibilities. He knew what he wanted. Only he didn't want to spoil this moment either. How do you know when the other wants it? And then Hesta turned her face up toward his, and even in the dimness he could see her remove her glasses, could see her eyes shine in the faint light, and almost as though he were watching somebody else, he turned his head and kissed her.

Scene 31

Greg nearly wet his pants when he realized someone was behind the door.

It opened to reveal a large walk-in closet, like a pantry. The place was lined with shelves, mostly empty, except for the three candles burning on the lowest shelf near the floor. On the floor was a mattress partially covered with an old bedspread. A sofa cushion was at the head like a pillow.

And lying on the mattress were a girl and Ned Wood. Both of them were naked from the waist up. Greg saw the girl's conical breasts, glimpsed clothes tossed randomly on the mattress, before Wood jumped up and pushed him and Richard back out the door and shut it on the girl behind him.

"What the hell is this?" said Wood. "Junior narc squad?" His blubbery torso was splotched red and white as though he had a rash, and his blondish hair swung across his forehead.

"We didn't know," said Richard. His face was bright red. Greg was glad that he himself couldn't blush.

"What are you doing here?" said Wood. He pushed Richard and glared at Greg.

"We were looking for a tunnel," said Greg.

"Holy crap," said Wood. "The Hardy Boys back at the ranch."

"We won't tell," said Richard.

"We won't tell anybody," said Greg.

"The hell you won't. It'll be all over the school tomorrow."

"Not from me," said Richard.

"I don't talk," said Greg.

"What the hell have you got in that bag?" said Wood. "Beer?"

Greg felt like an eight-year-old.

"Nothing," Richard said.

"What's in the damn bag?" said Wood.

"A dead squirrel," said Richard.

Wood started to deliver a complicated set of instructions involving the squirrel, a hot tire iron, and several of Richard Blackburn's bodily orifices.

Then all of them heard the faint sound of a siren outside.

Scene 32

She was struggling silently, pushing him off, and he was struggling just as silently. He was stronger than she, but she was no weakling, and she was more desperate.

"Stop," she said. "Stop it now."

Thomas could not answer and he could not stop. The delight of their first kiss had broken majestically over his body like a perfect wave on an empty beach. But this force was different, an exquisitely dangerous undertow. He would stop in a minute, in just another moment he would regain his footing, but not now not now not quite yet just another moment, another gasp, another thrill.

"You can stop," she said, and she raised her knee hard into his groin. He shuddered with the pain, and she pushed him off with her arms and her leg and sat up in the choir pew. Then she did something he hadn't expected. She started to cry.

"You hurt me," said Hesta. "Why?"

Thomas was angry with pain and shame. "How was I supposed to know?"

"How were you supposed to know what?" said Hesta. "That this was wrong? Because I told you, that's how. Because I said no. Because I pushed you away." She sobbed. Her voice was louder.

"I didn't think you really meant it," said Thomas.

In the distance they could hear a siren approaching. Neither paid attention to it.

"Say that again, please," said Hesta.

"I thought you wanted me to. I'm sorry," said Thomas.

"Wanted you to?" she said.

"I didn't understand. Now I do." He buckled his trousers. Nobody in the locker room ever mentioned anything like this.

Hesta's sobs changed key, from fear to rage.

Flashing lights caught the clear glass windows on the wall of the right transept and splashed colors momentarily over the wall of the chapel. Thomas barely registered the event. He focused entirely on Hesta.

"I understand, too," said Hesta. "I understand that everything I've heard about men is true." She grabbed her rain slicker and was up and moving before he could react.

"Wait," he said, as he pushed open the little door to the choir. It hurt him a little to stand. Hesta was already down the three stairs of the apse and into the center aisle of the nave. She did not wait. He caught up with her at the door.

"I'm sorry," he said again. He was not angry now, but ashamed.

"I'm going back to the mixer," she said, and she pushed open the door to the chapel. She had her slicker halfway on.

"Just wait a second for me to explain," said Thomas. He tried to put on his jacket and hold the door and grab her elbow all at the same time. But Hesta was not even looking at him. She was looking next door toward the gymnasium. Two police cars and an ambulance had parked right on the grass of the Quad in front of the gym. Red and blue lights flashed on her face. Thomas saw a large pack of students, boys and girls, moving across the grass in front of Stringfellow.

"What's going on?" he called. One of the boys, a newboy, stopped and located Thomas by the sound of his voice. Thomas could see the boy grin in the foggy light, and he realized how obvious it must look to everyone that he had been fooling around in the chapel. He felt embarrassed, but also a bit proud, and then he felt ashamed for feeling proud.

"Everybody's going over to the gym," said the newboy.

"What for?"

"Somebody's dead," said the boy.

"Who?" Thomas called. Hesta lifted the hood on her slicker.

"I heard it was Robert Staines," said the boy, and then he ran ahead.

Scene 33

At the sound of the sirens, Horace Somerville put down his magazine and stood up in the teachers' lounge in Fleming Hall. He did not know why there were sirens on campus; he knew only that there must be trouble. He put on his raincoat with the furry lining and his floppy rain hat and gloves, and then he picked up his oversized golf umbrella in the Montpelier navy blue and white and departed the building in the direction of the noise. He felt faintly guilty for riding out his chaperone duty in the quiet of the teachers' lounge, but he had excused himself by rationalizing the need for chaperones in the less public parts of the campus. Already in the course of the evening he had thwarted three couples looking for privacy. Still, he was relieved to note that the sirens had not stopped at Bradley Hall, where he was supposed to be, but had halted in the opposite direction. Helped by the occasional walkway lights on campus, Somerville joined small groups of people moving west. It took only a couple of dozen yards for him to see that the trouble was over by the gym, where all the lights were on.

Somerville could remember hearing his older brother Virgil talk about when this gym was built back in the mid-1920s. Virgil had been a third-form newboy and had owned a box camera with which he had taken photographs of the construction to show his family. Virgil had been thirty-one years old when it was Horace's turn to enroll at Montpelier, but he had pulled out the photo album and had shown Horace all his pictures from his days at school. What had stood out most vividly was the memory of all the rubble associated with the building of the gym. A decade ago they had built the huge, bulbous fieldhouse out behind the old gym—new basketball courts, swimming pool, locker rooms—but for Horace the gym was always the old gym, the building that to his young mind had seemed as big as the Waldorf and as grand as Madison Square Garden.

A mob of students and adults milled around in the mist outside the building. It wasn't a fire, then; they wouldn't have been so close, and of course he would have smelled the smoke or seen the flames. There was the Boatwright boy talking pleadingly with the girl in wire-rimmed glasses and the yellow rain mac. What was her name? From the way the girl's lips were set, it looked as though young Boatwright was losing his argument. The young people were always finding some way of breaking each other's hearts. Somerville turned to look for some adults. He wondered if Kathleen had come out to check all the commotion. Then he saw a clutch of his colleagues over by the main lobby door to the gym. One policeman stood in front of the door; several more moved around inside. He caught the flash of a camera from inside the building despite the glare of the fluorescent lights. Was it a robbery? He would not allow himself to consider any worse possibilities.

Somerville strolled over to the circle of adults huddling under umbrellas. He recognized Ben Warden and Dan Farnham, and the third was Carella, that young fellow teaching science.

"Gentlemen," he said.

Warden and Carella greeted him by name.

"You haven't seen Chuck Heilman or Sam Kaufman, have you?" asked Ben Warden.

"Neither since dinner."

"Dr. Lane wants to find somebody who can address the students in chapel tomorrow. It might turn out to be you."

"What's the trouble here, Ben?" Somerville asked.

"It's bad, Horace," said Warden. "We've got another boy dead."

"Who?"

"Robert Staines."

"The fourth-former," said Somerville. He tried to assimilate it. Had Staines been one of the boys he had chased away from the teachers' lounge earlier? "Not another suicide?"

"No," said Warden. "It's looking as though the first one wasn't suicide, either."

Somerville nodded. "Tell me what happened," he said.

Warden knew few details. "His girlfriend found him dead inside the gym," said Warden. "She roused Pat McPhee out of his apartment with her screaming. He's the one who raised the alarm."

"Patrick McPhee again," said Somerville. "He's having a bad week."

"What terrible luck," said Warden.

"Very bad luck," said Somerville. Warden looked like a man fighting off a collapse—understandable, perhaps, given the pressures he had been resisting recently. What would it take to make a good man go bad? Or to go under? Somerville felt a trickle of dread make its way down his neck, and he was aware of being very tired, as if he had stayed too long at a party and regretted not leaving an hour before. "Where's Cynthia?" he asked.

"Inside," said Warden. "They won't let anyone else enter the building. I've tried."

"He was my student," said Carella. "This is the second one I've lost this week." He had tears in his eyes.

"Mine, too," said Warden. "This isn't the way teaching usually is, Kemper."

Carella wiped his eyes like a little boy on the sleeves of his blue Montpelier sweatshirt. He had the hood up, but little tufts of hair popped out from beneath the edges. He held an umbrella in one hand and shook.

"You need a proper coat there," said Somerville.

"This is plenty warm," said Carella. "It's a wrestling warm-up. I'm not shivering from the cold." His voice broke. Somerville observed with distaste Carella's lack of self-control.

A policeman walked out to the group from the gymnasium. "Has anyone here seen a man named Angus Farrier?" he asked.

No one had. The policeman moved to another group.

"Why do they want Angus?" said Warden.

"Maybe he saw something. His car's here," said Carella.

Somerville considered Farnham, who stood in an ordinary trench coat with both hands in the pockets and wore a short-billed cap that did little good against the rain. Farnham hadn't said a word since Horace had arrived, but stared into the gym.

Not shivering from the cold, thought Somerville. Neither am I, my boy. Neither am I. What is happening in this place? What is happening to my school?

Somerville's heart nearly broke as he accused himself of dereliction of duty. If he had been at the mixer, if he had been more attentive, perhaps this latest catastrophe could have been prevented. At least he could make sure that the rest of the students were safe. Where was Felix Grayson, the day master? Someone needed to take charge.

He roused Warden, Carella, and Farnham. "Let's get these boys onto their dorms and out of the cold," he said. They looked at him stupidly.

"Right now," he said. "It's not safe for them to be out here."

The men started to direct pedestrian traffic—all but Daniel Farnham, who stood silently and stared at the gym.

Scene 34

Inside the gym Katrina Olson fought off hysteria.

She had silky blond hair, the color of imported mustard. Her eyes were blue and just a fraction too close together, and her nose rose at a slope distinctively beautiful. She wore a gray Montpelier School sweatshirt over her white blouse and the top half of her navy blue skirt. Her legs were bare down to her wet lace-up moccasins.

She sat on the beige corduroy sofa in Patrick McPhee's apartment. Cynthia Warden was next to her. McPhee himself sat in a wing chair to the left of the sofa. Felix Grayson sat in an easy chair to the right.

It was 10:15. Carol Scott, the police investigator, sat directly in front of Katrina Olson in a straight-backed chair borrowed from McPhee's dining room.

"We had come here to the gym to talk," Katrina Olson said through tears. She held the handkerchief she had borrowed from Cynthia and wept into it like an actress.

"Take your time," said Carol Scott. "How did you get into the building?"

"Around the back," she said. "There was a door propped open with a little pebble. Robert said he'd arranged it all earlier in the day."

"Why?"

Cynthia Warden thought the investigator in charge was too striking to be on the police force. This Carol Scott was clearly under thirty years old and under six feet tall, though barely in both cases. She wore her dark hair in a pageboy with a gold pin on one side, and she had on one thin bracelet, a gray woolen suit, black nylons, and low-heeled shoes. She had removed her plain blue cloth overcoat and her fake-fur Russian hat. Cynthia had seen her in town a few times at the dry cleaner's, but she had not known the woman was a cop.

"Robert told me he knew of a quiet place where we could be alone out of the rain," said Katrina Olson. "Mixers are so noisy, you know?"

No one answered. Cynthia knew that what they were about to hear would be close to the truth but not the truth, that the truth would not emerge in this first telling of the story, and that if it emerged at all, they would hear it because they had first persuaded Katrina Olson to stop concealing whatever it was that she and Robert Staines were doing in the gym. Smoking pot, making love—whatever it was didn't matter as much as finding out how Robert Staines ended up with his neck twisted so that he appeared to be looking backwards.

Katrina Olson coughed out more sobs, as though she were coming to the end of her supply. She did not want to tell them the next part of her narrative. She spread Cynthia's handkerchief on her lap.

"Pretty monogram," she said. "What does the middle C stand for?"

Cynthia said her maiden name was Cunningham. The girl was stalling.

"What happened next?" asked Carol Scott.

"He took me upstairs to the wrestling room," she said. "It was dark, but you could still see once your eyes got adjusted because of the light coming in through the windows. It was strange to be the only people in the whole building. At least I thought we were." She was on the verge of breaking down again.

"What time was this?" asked Felix Grayson. He was still in his raincoat and floppy rain hat, even though it was warm in Patrick McPhee's apartment.

"About 9:00, 9:15," she said. "We went to the wrestling room for about half an hour. All we did was talk."

All knew she was editing her story.

"I had to go to the bathroom," she said. "I wanted Robert to go with me, you know, because it was so scary and dark, but he was tired and wanted to rest on the mats on the floor."

It was sex then, thought Cynthia. Though it might have been drugs, too. She couldn't smell any alcohol or smoke on Katrina Olson, but of course they could have been doing pills.

"He told me where the ladies' room was in the lobby. I found it okay, and then when I came back up the stairs, I could see him sprawled out on the floor. I could tell there was something wrong just from the way he was lying, but then I turned on the light and saw the way his neck . . . I must have screamed a thousand times."

Carol Scott took notes. She also had a small tape recorder, the size of a transistor radio, on the coffee table to her right.

"I heard her from in here," said McPhee. "I was asleep in that easy chair and then I heard a girl screaming outside my door. I thought it was a nightmare."

They had covered this part already. McPhee had rushed outside through one of his interior doors to the gym, had found Katrina Olson and Robert Staines, had determined that Staines was dead, and had brought the girl down to his apartment. He had called Grayson first, and then he had called the police. Grayson had just talked to the headmaster in Philadelphia.

Carol Scott turned to Cynthia. "You say you were here earlier," she said.

"Yes. Around 8:45."

"You patrolled the entire building?" said Carol Scott.

"I didn't rattle every doorknob," said Cynthia, "but I checked the place thoroughly."

"Are you the one who unlocked the wrestling and the weight rooms?" asked Carol Scott.

Cynthia said the wrestling room was already unlocked. The weight room had been padlocked.

"You didn't unlock the weight room next door to the wrestling room?" Carol Scott said again.

"No," said Cynthia. "I didn't have a key."

Carol Scott said somebody did, because the weight room was unlocked when the police arrived.

"And you didn't see anybody?" said Carol Scott.

Cynthia said she didn't see anybody except Angus Farrier.

"He's the janitor?"

"More than that, really. It's hard to explain his status here. He runs the gym."

Carol Scott nodded. She had interviewed him a couple of days ago. He had told her he had gone hunting alone over the Thanksgiving holidays. "You saw him upstairs in the wrestling room," she said.

"I was rehearsing my part in the play," Cynthia said, "saying my lines and working on my posture, and Angus surprised me."

"What do you mean by 'surprised'?" asked Carol Scott.

"I mean he startled me," said Cynthia. "I didn't hear him coming up the stairs, and all of a sudden he was in the room with me. He said he'd heard me rehearsing downstairs."

"Does he live here?"

"No. Not officially. I think he does keep a cot down in his lair."

"What is his lair?"

It was McPhee who explained about the boiler room on the lower floor that Angus claimed as his office. "He keeps an old desk in there, a hot plate, maybe even some clothes in the closet."

Carol Scott listened and then spoke again to Cynthia. "Did you check there on your initial search of the gym?"

"No," said Cynthia. "Just the main rooms. So Angus could have been there the whole time I was patrolling."

"And then after he startled you?"

"Then I left."

Carol Scott stopped taking notes and looked at her. Cynthia silently acknowledged that her own editing had been as obvious as Katrina Olson's.

"Please don't leave anything out," said Carol Scott. "If you start boring me, I'll tell you."

"I went out the same way I came in," said Cynthia. "Through Dan Farnham's apartment. I didn't know he was at home then, and I barged in on him while he was doing calisthenics in his living room. It was awkward." She wanted to omit the details of finding him in only his underwear while he was performing those frantic push-ups on the carpet. They had both been embarrassed, Dan more than she.

Katrina Olson listened quietly with the others as Cynthia finished.

"He invited me to stay for a cup of tea, but I declined. I left immediately through his front door and went home to Stratford House."

"So this building had people all over it," said Carol Scott. "And nobody was aware of anybody else."

"It's a big building," said Grayson.

Cynthia shivered.

"What time did you leave?" Carol Scott asked.

"A little after 9:00," said Cynthia. "I went home for just a minute, and then I went back to the mixer. And then we got Pat's phone call."

Cynthia was worried about Ben. When she had left Farnham's apartment at 9:15 and returned home, Ben had not been there. And he was not there now.

A uniformed policeman knocked at the inside door from the gym and entered without an invitation.

"Nobody else in the building, Carol," he said.

"Where's Farnham? The guy that lives in the other apartment?"

"He's outside with some of the other teachers," said the policeman. "We've got him waiting to talk to you."

"And where's Angus Farrier?"

"Who?"

"The old man who looks after the gym. Is he down in the boiler room?"

"No," said the policeman. "I told you, there's nobody else in the building."

"Is he outside?"

Patrick McPhee knew Angus better than the others. "He might have left," said McPhee. "He comes and goes as he pleases."

"What kind of car does he drive?" asked Carol Scott.

McPhee could identify it. "A yellow Pinto. Three or four years old."

"We have a vehicle of that description in the parking lot," said the policeman.

"Check the license number," said Carol Scott. "I want you to find me this Angus Farrier now."

"Angus would never do anybody any harm," said McPhee.

"No?" said Carol Scott. "Was he out here the night the Phillips boy died? And does he ever shop in the Montpelier School Store?"

No one could say.

Scene 35

Thomas thought it had to be the worst Saturday night in the history of the Western Hemisphere. Everything that had seemed so sure and stable at 9:00 was in complete confusion by midnight. It was like a concentration camp, with all the girls from the mixer lined up and marched onto the buses, and the chaperones yelling at everybody whenever someone was missing. Meanwhile the police grilled all the bus drivers, all the people who worked in the kitchen, all the people in the bands. Anybody could have driven onto the campus. And when they found out that Staines had used the Richard Blackburn method—the rock in the back door—to enter a locked building, then the police decided that anybody could have gotten into the damn gym, too.

Then Angus turned up missing. In two seconds every student on campus decreed that Angus had killed Russell Phillips and Robert Staines and was lurking around to kill more students. Angus! It was impossible.

While the girls were getting herded onto their buses, all the Montpelier boys had to go back to their dorm rooms. The councilmen and the faculty tried to take attendance and squelch rumors and generally keep everybody calm, and they did it by making everybody mad. If you dawdled around the girls' buses or even took your time going back to the dorm, somebody was there yelling at you to get inside. It was like the penitentiary. The thing was, though, it was reassuring, too. You felt safe. It was scary to think about one of the guys on your dorm getting killed.

After about an hour or so of scouring the campus, the faculty members managed to account for everyone. Robert Staines had been the only casualty. Thomas felt as though Hesta were trying to kill by a different method. After the chaperones had started screaming for order, she had gone and sat on her bus with Susie Boardman. She hadn't even looked at Thomas when he'd said good-bye.

Part of him said she was overreacting, that he hadn't even gone all the way with her, that she was just playing the tease. He replayed how far he'd gone, farther than he'd ever been before, and that was exciting, a grim sort of pride, a wonderful, awed glimpse of the mysteries behind the door of adulthood.

And part of him said he was a selfish, insensitive jerk. Robert Staines might have gotten laid more times than he could count, but he didn't know everything about women. Thomas had hurt Hesta, hurt her inside, and he hated knowing that.

He was confused and guilty about everything. When he would stop thinking about Hesta, he would start thinking about Staines, and that would tear him up, too. He tried to explain it to Greg somewhere around 1:00 in the morning.

"I feel terrible because I don't feel sad enough," he said.

Greg said to try that one again.

"The guy's dead. He was my teammate and my neighbor and my classmate, and you'd think I'd feel sorry about it. I don't, though. With him being dead, my life gets a lot easier. I don't have to testify against him to the councilmen, I don't get accused of being a narc."

Greg said that was understandable.

"I even wish I hadn't turned him in now," Thomas said. "If I'd just waited, the problem would have taken care of itself."

"Then your conscience would have hurt you."

"I guess. I just feel like I ought to be reacting differently."

"Like what?" Greg said. "Bursting into tears? Starting a memorial fund for him? Dedicating the rest of the basketball season to his name?"

"Yeah."

"I'm supposed to be a good Christian," Greg said, "but I'm glad that bigoted bastard is off my dorm."

That helped.

But Greg had nothing to say about his treatment of Hesta.

Scene 36

Eldridge Lane returned Felix Grayson's long-distance call at 11:05 P.M. and reviled Carol Scott on the telephone five minutes later.

"Angus Farrier has been an employee of this school for forty-eight years," said Lane. "He started working here when he was fifteen years old. Do you realize how many alumni know him? Are you absolutely certain he's your man?"

Carol Scott told Lane to judge for himself.

"I've heard from the police in New York," she said. "They have matched the cash register receipt with the sample from your school store. We're not talking about coincidence anymore." The psychologist she'd consulted had told her the behavior they were witnessing was impossible to predict, but that it appeared someone was on a random killing spree. She wanted to ask Mr. Farrier about the so-called hunting trip he went on over the holidays.

Eldridge Lane declared he trusted Angus Farrier unconditionally.

"We searched the desk down in that lair of his," said Carol Scott. "We found a used ticket from an Amtrak Metroliner, New York to Washington, for Sunday, November 28. That puts Angus Farrier in New York on the day the kid died in the movie theater."

Lane shifted gears immediately.

"Then why haven't you found him?" he said. "We can't

have a lunatic roaming free through the campus or the surrounding countryside."

She said they were looking.

"You should have the state police here, the FBI, anybody who can help," said Lane.

She said he'd be surprised to know who was working on it. And then she hung up.

Scene 37

Benjamin and Cynthia Warden walked back together from the gymnasium. It was long past midnight. The rain had stopped, but the weather was colder. Two police cars remained on the campus. All the buses had left, and the van carrying the body of Robert Staines as well.

"Angus. I still can't believe it," said Cynthia.

"Nothing's definite yet. They still have to find him."

They walked in silence for a way.

"He could have killed me," she said. "He could have strangled me in that very room."

"He wouldn't do that," said Warden.

"How do you know?"

"Obviously he was only interested in killing boys."

Cynthia wept for the fifth time that night. "So he killed the first boy, the Phillips boy, too," she said.

"Apparently."

"He'd been here forever and ever," she said. "Why would he suddenly crack? Why now?"

"Who knows?" said Warden. "Some little blood vessel in his brain broke open. Some little gland produced too much of its chemical. It could be anything."

"So if he's crazy, then how is he smart enough to get away? If his car's in the parking lot, how did he get off campus?"

"He could have called a cab. There were plenty of cabs

going back and forth taking students to dinner in town. Or he could hitch a ride."

"Why would he hitch a ride? Why not just drive himself?"

"I can't answer that, Cynthia. The man is insane, if he's the one who's guilty."

"He's the one," said Cynthia. "He sneaked up on me in the wrestling room. I don't know what would have happened if I hadn't turned around and seen him." The more she considered the implications, the more horrified she became. It was as though the truth were being revealed to her gradually, like a photograph slowly developing.

"What if he's still on campus?" she said.

"Then they'll find him."

"What if he's hiding somewhere? He knows the school better than anyone. What if he's here on campus in some obscure cubbyhole?"

Warden reminded her that the police were efficient. "Don't start rumors about obscure cubbyholes," he said. "The boys could panic."

"Poor boys. And poor Angus, I suppose."

"Poor Montpelier School," said Warden. "This is going to be a tough one to weather."

He reached over and wiped her tears with his gloved fingers.

"I don't feel safe," said Cynthia. "I'm assaulted from within and from without."

Warden took her hand.

"If Angus can go mad, then anybody can," she said. "There's nothing reliable anywhere anymore."

"Calm down," said Warden. "It will seem better in the morning."

"I can't calm down," she said. "Nothing is stable. I can't count on anything to be the way I left it."

"You can count on me," he said.

"I can't," she said. The tears resurfaced. "I needed you tonight, and I came home to get you, and you weren't there."

"When?" said Warden. "I was at home writing. You know that."

"You weren't home at 9:15," she said. "And you weren't home at 10:00 when I tried to phone you."

"No?" he said. "I did go out for a walk, didn't I?" He paused. "I remember saying good-bye to you after dinner. Then I remember hearing sirens and walking over to the gym. I might have been out for a stroll when the police arrived on campus."

"Did you ever find Kevin's key?"

Warden reached into his pocket and produced the key. "I found it in my pocket while I waited for you at the gym," he said.

She squeezed him with relief. "I was so worried that we'd lost Kevin's key and that some student had found it," she said. "And I was worried about where you were."

"I'm sorry to be such an absentminded professor," said Warden. "I guess the only thing you can count on is that I'll be undependable." He tried to sound jocular, though he felt almost drunk with fatigue.

They were nearly back to Stratford House. Warden noted that there were too many dormitory room lights on; he would have to make a patrol through the building before he went to bed. Cynthia wanted to blow her nose.

"Damn," she said. "Katrina Olson still has my handkerchief."

"You've got others," said Warden. "Let the girl keep it."

But Katrina Olson did not have her handkerchief.

THE FOURTH ACT

Scene 1

On Sunday morning Thomas Boatwright heard someone enter his room. He sat up in his bed in a rush, his heart pushing the speed limit, his breath reduced to one audible inward gasp.

Standing in the doorway, Nathan Somerville laughed. "Sorry to scare you, Boatin' Shoes," he said.

Greg rolled over and jerked his head up. "What's wrong?"

"We're having a special room search for dead squirrels," Nathan said.

Greg told him to ask Richard Blackburn about those.

"Do I still have to testify in front of the honor council?" Thomas asked.

"Of course," said Nathan. "But don't worry. Nobody wants to hold an honor trial for a corpse."

Thomas felt relieved, and then he felt guilty for feeling relieved.

Nathan told them there would be a special chapel service this morning at 10:00. Everyone was required to be there. Then he shut the door behind him and went on to the next room.

That was at 8:30. They considered it a duty to stay in their beds for another forty-five minutes; you didn't waste your one morning to sleep late by getting up too early. They passed the time by commiserating about their respective errors of the night before.

"It was like we were out on the playground again, you know?" Greg said. "I felt like such an idiot."

"Think of how Ned Wood must have felt. Mr. Senior getting caught with his pants down."

"They weren't down yet. But his shirt was off."

Little boys and their fascination with dark, secret places, Thomas thought. All the pain of last night's departure from

Hesta had returned. He decided he wasn't ready to call her. But he did get up and join others in the bathroom down the hall. On the way he had to pass Robert Staines's door. It was shut tight.

Throughout the morning the telephones in the halls rang almost nonstop, always with calls from nervous parents. A couple of guys on the hall were talking about going home. Neither Thomas nor Greg spoke with their families, but Greg declared that he was staying at Montpelier as long as the play was still on. Thomas didn't know what he'd say if his parents called him and offered him a chance to come home. Most of the time being at Montpelier was good, even if it was a lot of work and a lot of pressure. Sometimes, though, Thomas was overwhelmed with the sameness of it all: the same schedule, the same people, the same buildings. Today nothing at all was routine, and yet he wanted desperately to see his family. He wanted to call them. Maybe his dad would even drive down for the day; it wasn't that far. But there was never a telephone free.

At 9:50 both boys were nearly dressed. Greg put on his blue wool blazer and checked himself in the mirror. "I wish I had a gun," he said. "If Angus tried to get me, I'd shoot him."

"You've seen *Beverly Hills Cop* too many times," Thomas said. He was eating a bag of potato chips for breakfast.

"You're going to get copped if he finds you," Greg said.

"I'm not scared of that old pervert," Thomas said. He brushed off the potato chip crumbs before he picked out his tie. When they left for the chapel, however, he slipped his red-handled Swiss Army knife into his pocket. Just in case, he thought, although he wasn't sure how much protection you could get from a pocketknife.

Chapel turned out to be not chapel service at all, but a plain old assembly with Dean Kaufman in charge. He told them that Dr. Lane was on his way back from Philadelphia and that they would be holding classes as usual tomorrow. He said that several parents had called the school to express their concerns about recent incidents on the campus and that five boys had even withdrawn from the school.

"But there is no need to panic," he said. "The school is secure, and you are all perfectly safe."

Thomas knew his parents would believe it if Kaufman or Dr. Lane told them so. Hell, that's why they sent him here; they trusted the damn place.

"And now," said Dean Kaufman, "a few words about the events of yesterday evening."

He told the students about Robert Staines's death. Then he said that they were to alert a member of the faculty if they saw Angus Farrier anywhere on campus.

"I do not mean to suggest that Angus is guilty of any crime," Dean Kaufman said. "In the American system, which I fully endorse, a man is innocent until proven guilty. The police are interested in talking to Angus only. Still, there are indications that he might be somewhat confused, so I insist that you do not talk with him yourselves—"

What followed was the kind of commonsense advice that Thomas thought even an inanimate object could have figured out. Kaufman had obviously written the speech down on paper because he finished every sentence.

"—and, of course," he concluded, "you must continue to use prudence when you roam the campus after dark. No boy—I repeat, no boy—is to be off dorm alone after 5:30 P.M. A violation of that policy will be considered a major disciplinary offense."

Richard approached Thomas and Greg after the assembly was over. "Which altar is it they use to sacrifice the virgins?" he said.

Thomas told him to shut up.

"Come on, let's have a full report," Richard said.

"It's not funny."

"This whole fiasco is funny as hell," Richard said. "They're too cheap to close down the school and find the guy, so they're asking us to pair up like Little Men."

Thomas reminded him that they had seen policemen all over the campus all morning. "It's not like they've lost interest in us," he said. The three boys were walking back to Stringfellow in a crowd of students, Thomas in the middle between Greg and Richard. The weather was clear and cold.

"The cops haven't found diddly," Richard said.

"That means Angus is off campus," Greg had said. "If he were here, they'd find him."

"Bull," Richard said. "He's hiding in the secret tunnel."

Greg said there was no secret tunnel. "The cops looked all over the basement of Stringfellow Hall and the gym and the Homestead, and they found nothing," he said.

Richard asked how they could ignore the blueprint that showed a passageway.

"I figure somebody messed with that diagram," Greg said. "They must have drawn the tunnel in as a place it might have gone, not where it was."

"You've changed your mind?" Richard said. "No more search for the road to Shangri-La?"

Greg said the blueprint had been in the library for years. "If it had been legitimate," he said, "somebody would have found out before now."

"So," said Thomas, "you end up with a sackful of squirrel."

"While you end up with a handful of heaven," Richard said. "Now tell us about how you knocked back McCorkindale in the chapel last night."

Thomas could not tolerate Richard any longer. "Go away," he said, and he pushed ahead to enter the building alone. Up on his dorm, he tried his home number in Georgetown. No answer. He tortured himself by picturing his parents and Jeff out for brunch somewhere, forking in the eggs Benedict and the fresh melon. It was more likely his mom was catering a brunch and his dad was down at the newspaper writing. He wished they had invested in an answering machine.

Maybe he could call his sister, Barbara, at Mason.

Or maybe Hesta.

Okay, practice. She gets on the phone and you say *Don't hang up. I have to apologize* and she says something like *Make it fast* and you say *I don't know what got into me last night but all I know is I love you and I wish you wouldn't be mad.* And there'll be a long pause, and then she'll sigh and say *Oh Thomas of course I love you too.*

But when he called, he spoke to a very unsympathetic Susie Boardman, who told him Hesta was not available to talk.

"Would you tell her to call me?" He was trying hard to be cool.

"I'll tell her you called. Got to go," she said.

Thomas hung up the telephone and wished he could push the reset button, delete the file, erase the disk, and boot up the computer to start his life all over again. He returned to the room ready to crawl into bed forever.

Then Greg asked him if he was ready for play practice.

"Hell," said Thomas. He had forgotten about his 3:00 play rehearsal. "I'm not going," he said. "I'll quit."

Greg pulled a chair over to the bed where Thomas was lying on his back.

"Everybody says you were good at the audition," said Greg.

"Bullshit."

"I was hoping you'd help me with my lines," said Greg. "I'm having the hardest kind of time with them."

"Get Farnham to help you. He's the pro."

Greg said Thomas was more convenient. Thomas would not oblige any attempts at cheering him up.

"You just say it the way Othello would say it," said Thomas. "It's no big deal."

"Show me." Greg had the white paperback in his hand. "There's a hard place in Act IV."

Thomas snatched the book away from him and started to flip through the pages. "Do something we've covered in class," he said. "I haven't even read the whole play yet. We just finished Act III."

"Okay. There's a tough place in Act III, too."

"Where?" Thomas was sick of school.

"Scene 3." Greg explained that he didn't understand whether Othello was angry at Desdemona or not at the beginning of the scene. Desdemona keeps asking Othello to invite Michael Cassio for dinner, and Othello keeps putting her off.

"He sounds mad," said Greg, "but Desdemona doesn't seem to think he is."

Thomas read through the scene. As angry as he was, he couldn't help getting interested in it.

"You're mad at her," he said. "But you're also mad at yourself for being mad at her. The only thing you can do is to tell her to get the hell out of there. Politely, so that you can maybe get yourself under control."

"But I'm not alone. I'm left on the stage with Iago."

"Exactly. You tell the wrong person to leave. It's the turning point of the play."

He was surprised by his own insight.

"Damn," said Greg. "You should take over from Farnham."

"Shut up and read the lines," said Thomas, though the compliment pleased him. He forgot his earlier threat to skip rehearsal. "If you do this right, you can get the audience scared to death."

"Why scared?" said Greg.

"Scared because they know what you don't know," said Thomas. "They know there's a maniac loose, and they're dreading that you're not going to recognize him."

"Everybody knows what happens in this play," said Greg.

"Not everybody," said Thomas.

Scene 2

There were all kinds of residue backstage from the mixer the night before, and Mr. Farnham was furious about it.

"I told people that the stage was Red Flag," he said. "I put up signs on the doors. Red Flag. Off Limits. It did no good. Look at this mess."

Somebody had spilled a Coke on the black boards of the stage and had tried to blot it up with those little napkins from the refreshment bar. A fourth of a cinnamon doughnut was stuck to the goo.

Nobody wanted to remind him that a band had been playing on the stage last night.

"I'll get it," said Nathan Somerville. Like the other boys, he had changed from his chapel clothes into jeans. You didn't want to wear your good clothes backstage.

Thomas would have been crazy to skip rehearsal. He was learning to love it back here in this big empty space where you abandoned reality and became somebody else. He knew enough about theater to appreciate how big a stage it was for a high school theater, thirty feet from one end of the proscenium to the other, additional fifteen-foot wings on each side, and twenty-five feet deep. The place had two stories of fly space overhead, with ropes at the wings controlling flats for backdrops. There was an electric winch for raising and lowering the light bar, and there were more lights out front, in the ceiling over the heads of the audience. A light booth at the back of the auditorium held a big spotlight plus controls for all the other lights in the room. For rehearsals they used the full stage lights, not the smaller work lights lining the walls backstage. It was not economical, but Mr. Farnham said it helped you get used to the glare.

They were there to block the end of Act II, Scene 1, when Othello and Desdemona arrive in Cyprus. Greg and Thomas had been there for fifteen minutes. Mrs. Warden was also there, sitting in a chair and looking as worn out as the bits of trash from the mixer scattered backstage. Nathan Somerville was the only other student there except for Landon Hopkins, who was up in the light booth. Everyone was waiting for Bud Gristina, the senior playing Cassio, to appear. The boys clowned around a little. Greg wound an old scarf around his head to look like a miniature turban, and Thomas found a wooden stick about a half-inch in diameter and three feet long he could use as a sword.

"Don't play with that dowel," said Farnham. "We're using those for the banners." Thomas put down the dowel and helped Nathan Somerville clean up the trash on the stage.

The telephone backstage rang. It was on the wall of the right wing. You couldn't dial outside on it, but you could call the light booth or the prop room downstairs or even a dorm if you wanted.

"Maybe that's Gristina now," said Mr. Farnham. He walked over to pick up the receiver on the wall, and then he replaced it immediately. "They hung up," he said.

Across the auditorium, high up in the light booth, Landon Hopkins shouted down.

"Did you just call me, Mr. Farnham? The telephone rang but nobody was there."

The backstage telephone rang again. Again Farnham picked it up, again no answer. He shouted back up to Landon.

"Did you just call me?"

Landon shouted no.

"What the hell is going on with the telephones?" said Farnham. "Let's set up the scene."

Mr. Farnham had taped off places on the stage where the set would be. They would have two large columns flanking a set of three stairs across the back of the stage, and a series of shorter columns projecting to the edge of the proscenium on either side. Desdemona's bedroom was going to be trucked in from stage left, but the dolly had not yet been built. The columns were now just little squares of tape on the stage; the stairs were parallel strips of tape a foot apart.

Cassio still wasn't here, so they decided to start at the end of the scene, where Othello first lands at Cyprus.

"Othello enters from up here," said Farnham, indicating a place at upstage left. "Desdemona is already here with Michael Cassio"—he pointed to a spot downstage right—"and Iago and Roderigo are opposite them, there, downstage left." The actors took their positions.

The telephone rang again. This time Greg, who was offstage and already in position, answered.

"Heavy breathing," he said. "Then they hung up."

"Just take it off the hook," said Farnham. Greg obliged.

Farnham said to get started. He read Cassio's line himself: "Lo, where he comes!"

"O my fair warrior!" said Greg, striding into center stage.

"Not so breathless," said Farnham immediately. "Try it stressing 'fair' rather than 'warrior.' "

Greg did it again.

"My dear Othello," said Mrs. Warden.

"Perfect," said Mr. Farnham.

Othello and Desdemona had another exchange of pleasantries, and then Mr. Farnham interrupted again.

"Kiss her," he said.

"I can't," said Greg.

"You have to kiss her," said Mr. Farnham. "It's in the text. You'll kiss her again when you kill her."

"I can't do that."

"Why not?" said Mr. Farnham. He was getting mad. After four months of learning to read the signs in his English class, Thomas could see that Farnham was on the verge of a tantrum.

"I am ill, Greg, but what I have is not catching," said Mrs. Warden.

"It's not that," said Greg.

"Then stop acting childish and start acting," said Mr. Farnham.

Before Greg could answer, Landon Hopkins called down from the light booth.

"Mr. Farnham," said Landon, "the switchboard just called and said we had a phone off the hook down here. It's screwing up the other lines somehow."

"Tell the switchboard to go to hell," shouted Mr. Farnham. "I'm trying to run a rehearsal down here." He looked cornered. "Put the phone back on the hook, Nathan." Nathan replaced the telephone.

"Greg," said Mr. Farnham, "what's the problem here?"

"I've never kissed a white woman before," said Greg.

Thomas was about to die from frustration. That was so damn typical of Greg. There were only about 350 boys in the school who dreamed all night about the chance to kiss Mrs. Warden, and the one who finally got the chance to do it was unwilling.

"Kiss her now," said Farnham.

"I can't, Mr. Farnham."

Mr. Farnham's voice got tighter.

"I have been told to continue with business as usual," he said. "It was as rough a night for me as it was for you guys, and I wish you would try to cooperate just for a second on a matter that's absolutely vital to this production."

"Maybe we should just skip the kiss for now and go on," said Mrs. Warden.

"We can't skip anything," said Farnham. "We're just postponing the problem if we do. Othello, if you want to do this part, you will kiss your wife right now."

The telephone rang, and that was it. Farnham popped.

"Which one of you is doing this?" he said. He looked at

each one of them in turn, and Thomas could feel his own face heating with embarrassment when Farnham's eyes drilled him.

"This is some practical joke, isn't it, Boatwright?" said Mr. Farnham.

"No sir."

"Why are the phones ringing so frequently?"

"I don't know, Mr. Farnham."

"Who would want to disrupt our rehearsal?"

"I don't know," Thomas said again. "Maybe it's Landon calling from the light booth." All this time the telephone was still ringing. Nathan Somerville crossed to answer it.

"Landon!" Mr. Farnham shouted up to the light booth. "Is that you?"

Landon shouted no. Nathan picked up the ringing telephone. "They hung up," he said.

"Start the scene again," said Mr. Farnham. But then he froze and looked down at the stage as if he were trying to see through the boards. He ran upstage and out into the hallway. The door shut softly behind him.

"Where's he going?" Thomas asked Mrs. Warden.

Mrs. Warden said she couldn't imagine.

The telephone started to ring again but stopped abruptly. And a second later they heard a shriek from under the stage.

Thomas recognized the voice.

It was Richard.

Scene 3

Mr. Farnham brought Richard upstairs holding him by the upper arm, like a prison guard, and roughly pushed him onto center stage. He told the rest of the group to gather around. Nathan Somerville, Greg Lipscomb, and Thomas Boatwright stood next to Mrs. Warden, who sat in a folding chair between Richard and the lip of the stage. Landon Hopkins, who was still resentful over Richard's damage to his

Shakespeare anthology, came down from the light booth and watched from the auditorium. Richard stared at the floor and waited for his cue under the glare of the stage lights.

"I don't know why it took me so long to catch on," said Mr. Farnham. "All of you know, I assume, that the floor of the stage is also the ceiling of the prop room? Anybody down there can hear every word spoken up here."

Richard's face was shiny with tear tracks, his eyes bright with anger. He wore a black tee shirt covered with brown dust, his favorite old jeans, and black Converse basketball shoes with holes in them. He breathed unsteadily, but his voice was strong when he spoke.

"I'd like to apologize to the group for disturbing your rehearsal," he said.

"Go on," said Mr. Farnham. He stood a little behind Richard.

"I have behaved immaturely and inexcusably," said Richard. He would not look directly at anyone.

"That's enough," said Mr. Farnham.

Richard started to walk upstage toward the door at the stage wall.

"Where are you going?" said Mr. Farnham. Richard did not answer; he continued to walk.

"I asked you a question," said Mr. Farnham.

"Let him go, Dan," said Mrs. Warden. He ignored her.

"Blackburn, answer me."

"I'm going back to my dorm," said Richard as he reached the door and exited.

"Go get him, Boatwright," said Mr. Farnham.

"Let him go, Dan," said Mrs. Warden.

"I have some cleanup chores for that boy," said Mr. Farnham. "Go get him, Boatwright."

Thomas ran after Richard and caught up with him in the hallway.

"He says you have to stay," said Thomas.

"Bull."

"It's a school rule," said Thomas. "You don't disobey a teacher." He felt sorry for Richard, and also disappointed that he would carry on such a childish vendetta. Thomas didn't want him to get into more trouble.

Richard turned and faced him.

"He's berserk," said Richard. "He scared me. He pushed me up against the wall so hard I hit my head. Do you have any idea of how strong he is? He's strong and he's crazy."

"You were driving him crazy with those phone calls."

"You didn't see him downstairs," said Richard. "I'm telling you, the guy was berserk. He is not normal."

But he came back to the rehearsal with Thomas, where Mr. Farnham told him to mop the stage. Then Bud Gristina showed up and apologized for napping during rehearsal time. Instead of raving, Mr. Farnham decided to start the whole scene from the beginning. They never got back to Othello's entrance.

Greg thanked Richard afterward for allowing the kissing issue to go unresolved.

Scene 4

It was no good. Warden tried to be rational, tried to be objective about it all, but he could not dodge the issue. The question of Daniel Farnham's behavior was a mosquito buzzing around his head, and he knew that sooner or later it would land and bite.

He sat in his study on this Sunday afternoon ostensibly reading a letter from the editor of a magazine. He had received it yesterday. Today he distracted himself by reading it again. It was the nicest sort of rejection letter to get, a personal, detailed response to the poem and explanation of what wasn't working in it and why. He liked this editor and respected his opinion, but Warden thought the man was wrong in this case. He would instruct his agent to keep submitting the poem in its current form.

In front of him on the desk was a pile of essays, folded longitudinally and signed with various scrawls identifying each student author. He should be writing them their own forms of personal rejection slips, comments on what was wrong with their thinking and their writing, encouragement to develop whatever might be worth salvaging in their work, harsh condemnation for anyone who continued to make the same error each week.

Was he making the same error each week?

Cynthia had just returned from play rehearsal to report another incident involving Daniel Farnham. Warden had lost track of how many that made over the year, but it was too many. What made this one extraordinarily bad was that Farnham had apparently struck one of the boys or had threatened him so strongly that he might as well have struck him.

What was it with the air over in that gymnasium anyway? Were they being poisoned by some toxic wastes buried under the building a century ago? Angus Farrier first going mad and killing two boys, McPhee's wife moving out, Farnham flying into rages at the slightest provocation. Warden shook his head at himself; his thoughts were outrageous. Still, it was an odd coincidence that so many bad events could be associated with one building. It was as though the place were cursed.

Cynthia entered the study in a blue dress.

"Hurry," she said. "We have dinner in fifteen minutes."

He looked at his watch; it was 6:15. Where had the afternoon gone? He could remember saying good-bye to Cynthia when she went off to her play practice, and then he could remember hearing her report when she got home. What happened in the interim?

He stood up and reached into the pockets of his trousers to empty them and found that he still had Kevin Delaney's key to the gym.

"Is it normal for people to forget as much as I do?" he asked her.

"No," she said. "But you don't forget. You just don't notice."

"All right," he said. "Is that normal?"

"No," she said. "Nor is it normal to write such beautiful poetry."

"These days my poetry is as bad as my administrating."

Cynthia said that was true, but that it made no difference to her.

Warden embraced her. He loved the feel of her delicate body next to his big clumsy rough bulk, loved the way she squeezed him so hard in return.

"You make it tough to forget how much I love you," he said.

"Don't ever forget it," she said.

"Dan Farnham loves you too."

He felt her go limp in his arms, but he held on tight for another moment before releasing her.

"Dan is a boy," said Cynthia.

"I'm going to have to fire him," said Warden, "if he's going to continue to lose his temper."

"He's a good director and a good teacher."

"You know we can't have the faculty manhandling the students," said Warden.

"Come to a rehearsal and watch him work," said Cynthia. Either he would see something good and worth salvaging, or he would catch Farnham in the middle of an explosion and have a valid reason for terminating his contract.

"He won't lose his temper with me there," said Warden.

"Sit in the back of the auditorium. He won't notice you."

"With this beacon lamp of a face?"

"Stop it," she said. "You could hide in the prop room under the stage like Richard Blackburn. Apparently the acoustics are marvelous."

"No," said Warden. "I can't spy on my colleagues. This confrontation will be tomorrow. Face-to-face."

He had put it off for months, but now that he had committed himself, he looked forward to it.

Scene 5

On Sunday evening Thomas Boatwright had to appear before the honor council. It was easy. They heard his story, lectured him about his tardiness in speaking the truth, praised him for coming forward, and sent him back without punishment to study in his dorm room.

By 9:00 he was concentrating intensely on the art of shooting a free throw.

"I don't see why I'm not improving," he said. He lay on his bed and watched Greg finish the geometry homework.

"Show me how you've been doing it," Greg said.

"In here?" Sports on the dormitories were strictly prohibited.

"Just go through the motions," Greg said. "Here's the line." He stood and marked with his toe an imaginary free throw line between the ends of their beds. "The basket's up there above the window. Do everything but dribble and shoot."

Thomas fetched his basketball from the closet. He stood at the line, pretended to dribble twice, and then mimed a shot.

"You're holding the ball wrong," Greg said immediately. "You got to have the lines of the ball perpendicular to your fingers." He took the ball from Thomas and showed him how to hold it. "I'm surprised McPhee never told you that."

Thomas stepped up to the line again.

"Where's the line?" Greg said.

"Right here." Thomas pointed to the imaginary line on the floor.

"That's right," Greg said, "so why are you standing two inches farther back than you were the first time? You got to stand in exactly the same place. Put your toes exactly one inch behind the line. Every time."

Thomas stepped up to the line again, mimed dribbling

twice, and then adjusted the ball so that its lines were balanced horizontally. Then he pretended to shoot.

"That's the way," Greg said. "Just remember when you do shoot to follow through."

Thomas said he'd try it tomorrow after practice.

"This is the first productive thing I've done all day," he said. "I just can't concentrate." Everything was cleared up with the councilmen. Now he wanted to do the same with Hesta.

They spent the rest of study hours talking about everything but schoolwork: Angus Farrier, girls, the taste of beer, the winter play.

"Here's a question for you," said Greg. "Why doesn't Othello go after Cassio? If he thinks Cassio is the one fooling with his wife, why doesn't Othello confront him? Why doesn't he kill Cassio instead of Desdemona?"

Thomas had to think about that one.

Scene 6

Warden invited Farnham to his classroom on Monday before lunch to discuss the outburst at yesterday's play rehearsal. At first Farnham was defensive and resentful that Warden did not take his side. He sat in a student's desk and spoke like a wronged adolescent.

"I pushed him once against a wall," Farnham said. "The boy is incorrigible."

Warden hated resistance but did not retreat. "The boy's behavior is irrelevant," he said. "We have a disciplinarian to handle such cases. You ought to know the rules by now."

Farnham sat silently and combed his mustache with an index finger. "I thought it was all right to take immediate action with problem students," he said.

"It is not all right to humiliate them," said Warden. "I've

heard reports of these outbursts all year. If you cannot control your temper, you will need to find another job."

Farnham was not visibly shaken by the threat. "Why did you never bring this up before?" he asked.

A valid question. Warden said he had hoped Farnham would come to control himself. Farnham brushed aside the answer.

"It's not professional of you," he said. "I've heard nothing all year, and suddenly my job is on the line. Why didn't you mention these reports the other day, when I was helping you with your lesson plans?"

That was a direct hit. Warden had to respect the bastard for launching an effective counterattack.

"I had other things on my mind," said Warden.

Farnham responded by cataloguing Warden's administrative errors for the year to date: the lost student essays in September, the forgotten departmental meeting in October, the failure to order all the books needed for the fall semester.

"You're permitted to make mistakes all the time," said Farnham, "and then you defend yourself by claiming outside distractions. But I've got to be perfect, is that it? Has it occurred to you that I might have something on my own mind as well?"

"Yes," said Warden. "Do you wish to divulge it now?" Here we go, he thought. He's going to confess to me that he's hopelessly in love with my wife. What am I going to say?

"It's this play," said Farnham. His manner changed. He was less hostile, more defeated. "I want it to be perfect. This is my very first time to direct Shakespeare, and so far it's a mess."

It was a radical departure from what Warden had expected to hear. The play? Could the man become so unhinged over a play?

"This play provides my opportunity to make a reputation for myself at Montpelier," said Farnham. "If it goes well, I've proved my competence. If it doesn't, I'm a public failure. At this point nothing has gone right." He listed his casting problems, rehearsal problems, staff problems. "What gets me is that I have to do it all by myself. You haven't been down once to check on a rehearsal. You haven't once asked whether you could do anything to help. Shouldn't the department chairman take a little more interest in the activities of his department?"

Yes, damn it, all right, he had a point.

"Everything you say is true," said Warden. He considered himself a terrible administrator. If Eldridge Lane had spent more time on the campus, Warden would probably have been eased out of the chair anyway. But it was not fair of Farnham to change the subject of their meeting. "Nevertheless—"

"Nevertheless," Farnham interrupted him, "these outbursts are unforgivable."

"Yes," said Warden.

"I agree," said Farnham.

They sat in silence for a moment. Warden recalled Kevin Delaney and his fanatic devotion to basketball, and Kemper Carella and his late-night training sessions for wrestlers. He acknowledged his own enslavement to poetry.

"I never considered how important the play might be to its director," said Warden. "That was literally thoughtless."

Farnham said he had been cutting the text and planning the blocking for months. "The only comment you ever made to me," he said, "was that you thought we should do another play. Now today you've called me in and blindsided me with a threat of firing me."

Guilty, guilty, guilty. "You've raised some sensitive issues," said Warden. He was unsure of what to say next.

"I know I've been irresponsible," Farnham said, "but you've given me no support. Your wife has been much more understanding."

That hurt, but Farnham was right. Warden had never warmed up to him. "I apologize," said Warden. "I offer no excuse."

Warden's apology took the last heat out of Farnham's voice. "Thank you," said Farnham. "And I apologize in turn for my rudeness. I'm not always so outspoken."

After the storm, both men relaxed into the spirit of mutual disarmament.

"Have you always had a temper?" asked Warden.

"Ever since I was born."

A birthmark. Neither man used the term.

Farnham told him of learning to cope by expressing his rage externally. "I used to keep all my anger suppressed," he said. "Then I developed an ulcer when I was thirteen years old. I've learned that I can avoid irritating the ulcer if I go ahead and ventilate my anger. When I'm alone, I'll even throw things. My internist encourages that. Push-ups are good, too." He said he was also trying more long-term solutions, like counseling.

"I've met with Chuck Heilman a couple of times informally," said Farnham. "My problem is that I lose my temper too quickly. It's the short fuse syndrome."

"Do these informal counseling sessions help?"

"Not really." He smiled. "Heilman says the best solution is for me to find a wife. It's all sexually oriented, he says."

"That sounds like Chuck," said Warden. He thought Heilman was an aphoristic imbecile in most cases, but he wondered whether their minister had stumbled onto the truth this time. It was the moment to talk about Cynthia, about Farnham's notorious infatuation with her, but how could he?

"Do you have a steady girlfriend?" Warden asked.

The question flustered Farnham only for a moment. "You might say I'm coming to terms with that issue," he said. "My fiancée broke up with me in Alabama when I took a job at a rural, all-male boarding school. She wanted to practice law in a big city."

Warden asked him why it was so important to him to work at Montpelier. "Didn't your future wife matter more to you than the place you taught English?" he asked.

"I was ambitious. Maybe I made the wrong choice," said Farnham. "But this was an opportunity to work with a nationally prominent poet."

"Me?"

"I chose working for you over marriage," said Farnham. "It hasn't been what I expected."

Warden was flattered, flabbergasted, stunned.

Farnham told him about discovering Warden's poetry in little magazines when he was in graduate school, then finding the books, sharing the poetry with fellow fans.

"I used to write imitations of your poetry to my fiancée,"

he said. "Pitiful imitations. When the placement service told me there was a job at Montpelier School, I had to go for it. You intimidated me when I interviewed, but I got the job anyway. When I came here, I don't know, you seemed even more distant."

"So," said Warden, "you found it easier to be friends with Cynthia."

Farnham flushed. "It hasn't been all that easy," he said. "I see her and she reminds me of Johanna, and I think of what I gave up to come here. It's frustrating."

Was this his way of confessing a crush on Warden's wife?

"In a way," said Farnham, "I've fallen into a kind of rivalry with you."

At last he had admitted it. But then he confounded Warden by explaining exactly what sort of "rivalry" he meant. It was not a competition over Cynthia.

"I'm a perfectionist," said Farnham, "and I want to be the best at my job. But I'm working for Benjamin Warden. Don't you realize how awful that is?" He perceived Warden as having the perfect career, the perfect job, the perfect wife, in contrast to Farnham's own mediocrity. "I can't even run a classroom without having some kid like Richard Blackburn misbehave. I can't command the respect you do. This entire year has been a series of reminders of how much better you are than I am."

Warden was incredulous. "You're envious," he said.

Farnham nodded. "I'm jealous of your success."

Warden wanted to laugh at the irony, but he did not. He said that he had taught for over a decade longer than Farnham, that he was older, that he had committed an abundance of faux pas in his career.

"I understand that," said Farnham. "But I don't see myself as ever reaching your plateau of achievement. I want to be as great a play director as you are a poet. I want to attract as wonderful a wife. So far I can't imagine myself ever getting as good at this job as you are."

Then Warden did laugh. He reminded Farnham of all the forgotten meetings, the misplaced papers, the lost book orders.

"I envy you for your organization," Warden said. "You're always so well prepared, so academically dependable."

Farnham admitted that he could run the department more efficiently. But he complained that he still had little rapport with his students. "I try to be upbeat and pleasant," he said, "but the boys seem wary of me."

"Learn to control your temper," said Warden, "and see what difference it makes."

Farnham said he had improved from his days of teaching in Alabama.

There was no need to discuss his temper further. It was time for Warden to build the man's confidence.

"You've managed to get Greg Lipscomb to play Othello," said Warden, "when I can hardly get the boy to speak to me. That's just one case where you've outshone me."

Farnham was grateful for the example. It was true that Greg had been weak at first, but had come along well in the last few days.

They finished their meeting agreeing that Warden would come to rehearsal today to watch, to suggest, to react. To encourage. It was a pleasant adjournment.

Both men said so to the police later that day.

Scene 7

For basketball practice on Monday, the coaches had put out baskets of towels and jocks and shorts and jerseys.

"No more special service in the locker room for now," said Coach McPhee. He was trying to be as cheerful as possible. "Do your own work, fellows, until we get a replacement for Angus."

It was so weird to be getting ready for practice again. Saturday they had had that terrible game, and two days later they were back, getting ready to practice for another game on Friday, only one of their players was dead, and the man who had killed him was missing. The unsettling thing was that the man who had killed him was somebody they knew. His car had still been parked in the gym lot until this morning, when the police had gotten tired of watching it to see whether he'd return for it and had towed it into town.

Seven sets of parents had pulled their kids out of the school, and it seemed like a hundred more kept threatening to do so. Dean Kaufman had composed a special letter of reassurance to send to all the parents and all the students and all the alumni bombarding the school with questions. Thomas had told his parents he would stay. He wasn't sure why. He didn't think Angus would hurt him, and he didn't want to seem cowardly.

"It's strange to be down here, you know?" said Ralph Musgrove as he pulled on his tube socks. "Think of how Angus must have been spying on us all the time, watching us take our showers and stuff."

Thomas said he had been thinking the same thing.

"Once when I was about nine or ten my mother pulled into the 7-Eleven to get us some milk," said Ralph. "My brother climbed up on the roof of the car and dropped his pants. He was about four, I guess. Just one of those stupid things little kids will do. It was funny until I looked over and saw this old man—he must have been about forty or so—just staring at my brother. Steve didn't even see him. And it only lasted half a minute. My mother came out of the store and grabbed Steve off the car and threw him inside. She was mad and yelling at me for letting him get up there, and she never saw the man either. I never told her or my dad about it. But he was scary, you know?"

"Nobody in your family has much to show off anyway," said Thomas. Ralph punched him in the upper arm. Thomas did not respond. He was thinking of Saturday night with Hesta, of that power he had glimpsed briefly with her in the chapel, of that awful urge that had driven him past where she had wanted him to go. But that had been okay sex, hadn't it? Hadn't that been normal? And yet he could imagine how Angus could have taken such a pleasurable instinct and twisted it into the perversion it had become.

"I hear you were swinging your pole vault in the chapel," said Ralph.

"Not really," said Thomas. He felt that irritating mixture of anger over being the subject of gossip and pride that he'd impressed his friends. He was also ashamed of feeling proud; it was like he was hurting Hesta more. He had tried to call her again after classes today, but Susie Boardman had said she wasn't on the dorm.

Coach McPhee motioned through the glass door of the locker room for them to hurry up.

Before they started, he had everybody on the team sit on the court while they talked about Staines's death.

"I've experienced death up close," said Coach McPhee. Thomas figured he was going to go into the story of his baby brother's drowning in the bathtub again, but he kept his remarks generalized. "You never get used to it. You never stop being surprised by it. The important thing is to avoid it yourself. You guys need to make sure that it doesn't do anything to you. You want to make sure that you don't let somebody else's death affect you."

Everybody talked about Staines as if he were Mister Perfect.

"He was our leader, man."

"The best damn quarterback in the league."

"He would have gotten a scholarship for sure."

"The guy was always making me laugh."

"It'll never be the same without him."

Thomas couldn't understand it. He had always thought Staines was a cockroach, and while he was sorry he got killed and all, it was hard to feel genuine remorse. But he joined in. He felt a little weird for pretending to mourn, but he felt even weirder for feeling sorrier for Angus than for Robert Staines. For Thomas, Angus was the loneliest person he could ever imagine.

Practice was bad. They had to rearrange the team to take Staines's place, so nearly everybody was learning a new position. What made it even more complicated was that Coach McPhee had lost his whistle, so there was a lot of yelling whenever he wanted them to stop one drill and start another one.

"Some souvenir hunter picked it up over the weekend," said Coach McPhee. "We had too much traffic through this building."

After practice Thomas stayed behind to shoot free throws.

Coach McPhee stayed with him and rebounded. He threw the ball back to Thomas with sharp bounce passes and an occasional chest pass that made Thomas feel like a pro.

"Same routine every time," said Coach McPhee.

Thomas stepped up to the line, left foot first. He put the toe of his left shoe exactly one inch behind the free throw line. Then he positioned his right foot so that it was also one inch behind the line. He dribbled the ball exactly twice, placed it so that the lines on the ball were roughly perpendicular to the splayed fingers of his right hand, looked at the basket, and shot.

Swish through the net.

"Good shot," said Coach McPhee. "Try it again."

The ball bounced off the front of the rim.

"You didn't follow through," said Coach McPhee. "Wave the ball into the net. Extend your whole arm, and just wave that ball right into the basket."

Thomas tried it again. Same routine. Looked at the basket. Shot. Swish.

"Good. Try it again."

The ball bounced off the right of the rim.

"Don't rush it. Take your time. Concentrate."

Swish. Swish.

"Good," said Coach McPhee. "Go for ten in a row."

Three for three. Four for four.

"You'll probably be playing more for us now," said Coach McPhee.

"Yes sir." Five for five.

"Anybody can have one bad game."

"Yes sir. Thank you," said Thomas. Six for six.

"You have a girl down this weekend?"

The ball bounced off the rim.

"Yes sir," said Thomas.

"You lost your concentration," said Coach McPhee. "In a game you're going to have people screaming at you to miss it. You're going to have some guy on the rebound line whispering crap at you. You're going to have your parents or your girlfriend in the stands. You got to block all of them out and concentrate on your routine."

Thomas started over. One for one. Two for two. Miss.

"Shake it off," said Coach McPhee. "You can't be perfect. See how well you can do."

Three for four. Four for five. He finished at eight out of ten. The free throws toward the end felt really good.

"Eighty percent's a winner in any league," said Coach McPhee. "You'll do well as soon as you learn to control your emotions."

"You threw me off when you mentioned girls," said Thomas.

"My point exactly," said Mr. McPhee. "Let me tell you a true story. A very embarrassing story. When I was a kid, early teens, I used to watch a girl in the apartment across the alley get dressed. Every day at the same time she'd be in that room with the shades up, and she'd take off every bit of her clothes, and then she'd brush her hair by the window."

It was funny to imagine Mr. McPhee as a peeper.

"She'd brush it and brush it and brush it," he said, "and I'd watch her the whole time. I got into so much trouble for that." He paused.

"And?" said Thomas.

"And I got into trouble," McPhee said. "That's the moral of the story, Boatwright. If you fool with girls, you're going to have trouble. Take my word for it."

"How'd you get caught?" said Thomas.

Mr. McPhee laughed. "I'm the type who always gets caught," he said. "Go get your shower and then I'll walk you over to play practice."

It was 5:35. Thomas showered and dressed in ten minutes while Coach McPhee put away the basketballs and turned out the lights. They stood together outside in the cold while Coach locked up the gym. He had his key to the gym on an old Boston College key ring.

"Supposed to snow tonight," said Coach McPhee.

It was good to have the coach along as they walked across the dark campus to Bradley Hall.

"Mr. McPhee?" asked Thomas. "Why does somebody like Angus do what he did?"

They walked in silence for a time, and Thomas thought that Coach McPhee was not going to answer.

"It's that damned passion," said Coach McPhee. "It brings

us into marriages and splits us into divorces. Sometimes it goes bad. It's a tricky force, Thomas. Right now in your life it would be better for you to stick to basketball and stay away from the ladies."

He sounded just like Dad. You asked him a question about somebody else, and he gives you a lecture about yourself. It was always sensible advice, impossible to follow.

Scene 8

They were having a terrible time killing off Desdemona.

It was Monday afternoon, and Benjamin Warden watched from the back of the auditorium. For such a brief and famous piece of stage business, the smothering scene presented an astonishing set of complications.

The blocking would not work. If Cynthia as Desdemona lay in bed, then her lines were inaudible to the audience, and nobody could see the anguish on her face. If she sat up in bed, then the Lipscomb boy as Othello had to push her down before he could smother her with the pillow, and the effect was more comic than horrifying. If she got out of the bed to have her final speech with Othello elsewhere in the bedroom, then the imagery of the scene disintegrated.

"Shakespeare wanted it to occur in bed," said Dan Farnham. "He wanted to show an act of violence between a man and a woman in a bed. The parallels between Desdemona's death and the sex act are obvious and disturbing. The only thing is, I don't see how the hell it's been blocked. People have been doing it for 350 years, and I can't figure how to set it up."

Warden was there to help and could offer none. Stagecraft was a mystery to him; what looked perfectly natural up close was either invisible or ridiculous from the viewpoint of the audience.

So far Farnham had been remarkably patient with the

logistical problems. Warden was worried more about Cynthia, who seemed increasingly fatigued and desperate with each run-through. She really wants it to work, he thought. But she is exhausted.

Patrick McPhee and Thomas Boatwright entered the auditorium from the lobby. Farnham explained to McPhee why the blocking was forcing them to run behind with rehearsal.

The coach understood the problem immediately. "It's like putting in an offense in basketball," he said. "The one that works one season with one team just isn't right for another."

"You sound terrible," said Farnham. "Are you getting a cold?"

"Lost my whistle," said McPhee. "Too much yelling at these renegades." He gave Thomas Boatwright a soft slap on the head.

The actors stood on the stage waiting for Farnham to get back to them. They were nearly motionless in a series of poses that the director might have carefully arranged to look casual. Cynthia sat Indian style on the bed, which had just been finished that afternoon and supported an old mattress from Stringfellow Hall. Greg Lipscomb leaned against the bed with his arms folded across his chest. Ginny Kaufman, wife of the dean and cast as Emilia and understudy to Desdemona, sat in a folded chair at the edge of the stage and read. She had graying hair which she wore in bangs, and she used large round tortoiseshell glasses to read. Nathan Somerville had on a white tee shirt and lounged back on the balls of his hands as he sat on the stage itself next to her chair. Thomas Boatwright sat in the front row of the auditorium. He wasn't in this scene; his character was dead by now.

"Any suggestions, Pat?" asked Farnham.

McPhee asked why they had given up on kneeling.

"We've never done it with Desdemona kneeling," said Farnham.

"Maybe that was Maggie Smith in Olivier's version," said McPhee. "I've seen somebody do it somewhere."

Farnham said Olivier's was a good blocking to steal.

"Why not? I steal basketball plays all the time."

Cynthia asked McPhee to show her how.

He still wore his gray sweatsuit and basketball shoes from practice and vaulted easily up onto the stage. "Desdemona kneels at the edge of the bed. Othello faces her. She holds out her arms as if to embrace him. He grabs her by the throat and chokes her. Then he forces her down onto the bed, all the time climbing onto the bed himself, and finishes her off by smothering her with a pillow."

They tried it.

"That feels right," said Cynthia.

"No problem for me," said Greg.

"It feels exactly right," said Cynthia again. "I've tried it this way on my own. It's what Desdemona would do. I should have thought of it myself."

"The basketball coach sets us back on schedule," said Farnham. "Of course, the smothering isn't going to be enough. We want Othello to stab her, too. Get the knife, Greg."

Greg left the bed and walked over to the props table offstage.

"I can't find it," he said.

Farnham groaned, not angrily. "Who has the knife?" he asked the group. Then, calling up to the light booth, "Landon? You got the knife?"

Landon replied that he did not.

Thomas reached into the right front pocket of his jeans and pulled out his red Swiss Army knife. He held it up from his seat.

"You can borrow this if you want," he said.

Farnham waved it away. "We need something more authentic," he said, and he walked over to join Greg at the props table. He found the dagger stuck to the taped handle of a fencing blade.

"Put this back in its spot when you finish," he said to Greg. The dagger was about eight inches long and ended in a thin, tapering point. From Warden's seat in the auditorium, it looked like a dangerous crucifix. Greg Lipscomb was wearing large floppy boots—part of his costume—and he stored the knife in the right-hand one.

"Not there," said Farnham. "You're going to be barefoot by this point of the play. You get more and more African."

Greg put the knife up his sleeve.

"Othello must have a knife hidden on him," Farnham said to McPhee. "That solves two problems for us. First, how Desdemona seems to come back to life just before she dies. We can have her succumbing to loss of blood rather than suffocation. Second, how Othello manages to stab himself after he's supposedly been disarmed."

They were doing the business with the knife now. *Emilia calls from the door to the bedroom. Othello has the pillow over Desdemona's face. Her arms are waving frantically. Othello has to hurry now because of the approach of the lady-in-waiting. He pulls the knife out of his sleeve and speaks: "I would not have thee linger in thy pain:/So. So." On the first "so" he stabs her in the heart. On the second he twists the blade. Desdemona arches her back in an agony that looks also like sexual ecstasy.*

Warden played with Othello's words: "I would not have thee linger in thy pain." It was the voice of one who loves intensely.

He was surprised when his throat thickened and tears burned his eyes. It was only a rehearsal of a high school play, and yet it had awakened an urge within him that had to be satisfied now.

Scene 9

It was 6:15 before they got the damn death scene figured out. Thomas had sat around for over half an hour watching Farnham and McPhee screw around with the blocking while everybody else got bored out of their gourds. Teachers were always asking students to get to places on time so they could make them wait after they got there. It was nice of Mr. McPhee to be so interested in the play, but hey, come on, some of us have work to do. Farnham should have been getting as irritated as Thomas was over McPhee's interference, since McPhee was out-blocking the director. But Farnham seemed glad for the help. Maybe McPhee would invite Farnham to basketball practice to put in new options for the offense.

What Thomas wanted more than anything was to do his scene. This acting business was okay, better than basketball even, except for the unpredictability of Mr. Farnham's rehearsals. Thomas knew theater. His dad had been reviewing plays since before Thomas was born, and three years ago they had gone on a backstage tour in Stratford, England, where they had seen how slanted the stage was and how small the auditorium looked from the stage side. They had met one of the directors of the Royal Shakespeare Company, and he had seemed just like a regular person you'd see at a cocktail party. But he'd been in a hurry to get to his rehearsals. Everything in the professional theater seemed to run on schedule. Mr. Farnham was too temperamental to be prompt.

In the back of the room Mr. Warden sat and watched. Thomas had waved to him from his seat on the front row, and Mr. Warden had waved back. Thomas had thought about going back to sit with him. He was a good advisor, really interested in what you were doing. But Thomas knew that sometimes he liked to be alone. If Mr. Warden wanted to see him, Mr. Warden would come down to the front.

Mr. McPhee jumped down off the stage and landed softly in his white basketball shoes. He sat beside Thomas in the cushioned theater seats. Thomas asked him how he knew so much about Shakespeare.

"Being a coach doesn't mean you have to be ignorant," said Mr. McPhee. "Remember, I'm a teacher, too."

Thomas watched Mrs. Warden as Desdemona. She lay on the bed on her side, facing the audience, pretending to be asleep. Greg entered from upstage left, miming the holding of a lantern in his right hand. In his left hand, he was holding his book.

"Put out the light, and then put out the light," Greg read.

When Desdemona awakens, she springs up into a kneeling position, her legs tucked beneath her on the sheets. Her husband is pacing. He's literally insane with jealousy. He accuses her of infidelity with Michael Cassio; she is shocked for a moment into silence, and then she swiftly denies any such treachery. He tells her to prepare to die.

"Kill me to-morrow," says Desdemona in desperation. "Let me live tonight."

"Nay, if you strive—"

"But half an hour!" she pleads. She has reduced her request to a mere thirty minutes, but her pleading only strengthens his resolve.

"Being done, there is no pause," says Othello.

And it is here that she lifts her arms in pleading as he comes toward her. She is asking now not even for half an hour, only for enough time to speak to God: "But while I say one prayer!"

"It is too late," Greg replied, and his hands closed around her neck. With Greg it was only one hand and a book pressing against her throat, but the result was amazing. She started to scream.

Greg jumped back and dropped his paperback. She had scared him. The screams subsided into sobs. Nobody moved. Farnham was on the apron of the stage; Mrs. Kaufman and Nathan Somerville were backstage but visible in the wings.

"I just started thinking about Robert Staines," said Mrs. Warden. "The hands on the throat, the choking. I was in that room on the night he died, rehearsing this part. It all just caught up with me for a minute. I'm sorry."

Mr. Farnham walked up to her and placed a hand on her shoulder. She got up from the bed and moved away from him.

"I'm all right," she said.

Nathan Somerville looked at his watch. Mr. Farnham saw him do so and looked at his own.

"It's 6:25," said Mr. Farnham. "We'll have to break for dinner now anyway." He turned to Thomas. "Roderigo, can you come back at 7:00? Iago?" He asked Nathan with a swivel of his head.

That was so damn typical. Thomas had hoped to call Hesta after dinner and before study hall.

"I'll be here," said Thomas.

"Me too," said Nathan.

"You, too, Othello," said Mr. Farnham to Greg.

Mrs. Kaufman walked up to Mrs. Warden and tidied her long blond hair the way she might smooth out a bedspread. "Can I walk you to dinner?" she asked.

"I'll be up in a minute," said Mrs. Warden. "I need to think."

"Do you want to stay down here alone?" asked Coach McPhee.

"Ben's here," she said, but when they looked to the back of the auditorium, Mr. Warden was gone.

Thomas wondered whether he had been there to see his wife break down.

Mr. Farnham called to Landon to leave the stage lights on. They'd be back in less than an hour.

"I'm going to skip dinner and work on my lines," said Mrs. Warden. "I'll be here when you return."

Mr. McPhee and Mr. Farnham walked out together. Mrs. Kaufman asked Landon Hopkins to walk with her. Thomas, Greg, and Nathan left together. Outside the building they bundled up against the cold and walked straight for Stringfellow Hall.

They did not see Kemper Carella in the dark of the sidewalk to their right, nor did they notice him enter Bradley Hall.

Scene 10

It would be crazy to make a move here, now, early evening in a lighted theater with the woman lying in bed on the stage of all places, but Carella was tempted. She was so hot-looking. He had seen everybody associated with the production leave the theater building, and he knew where the husband was—hell, Carella had just run into the old astronaut pacing the campus sidewalks and mentally orbiting somewhere around Uranus.

Carella stood for a minute inside the door of the auditorium and watched her work on her lines. She would mumble the words, kneel on the bed, hold out her arms, melt her face into a *sprezzatura* seizure of terror. She was hot to watch, those titties bouncing up and down, that long foxy hair. What if he climbed up on the stage and tied her up?

"Who's there?" she called from her bed.

She must've spotted him.

"It's me," he said.

She looked surprised to see him out among the seats. "The acoustics in here are strange," she said. "I thought I heard a noise backstage."

He walked down the closest aisle of the auditorium and hopped easily up onto the stage. She looked even better up close.

"Hi, Cindy," he said. She didn't like that name, he could tell.

"What do you want, Kemper? I don't have much time."

This won't take much time, babe, he thought. Oh, how good it would be to peek under those blue jeans of yours.

"You're working awfully hard on a play that doesn't happen until March," he said.

She asked him again what he wanted.

Before he could answer, the telephone rang. Carella answered it.

It was Patrick McPhee. "I'm at the gym looking for Dan Farnham," he said. "Have you seen him over there?"

Daniel Farnham was nowhere in sight.

Carella hung up the telephone and turned back to Cynthia.

"Well?" she said. "What's going on?"

He told her.

Scene 11

After a dinner like that, you felt like getting something to eat.

It had been the worst ever—lasagna charred on the outside and cold on the inside, a salad that was nothing but lettuce and no dressing, stale bread, and canned fruit cocktail for dessert. The rumor was that everybody working in the dining hall had quit because they were scared that Angus Farrier would murder them. The truth was that the electrical power in Stringfellow Hall had gone out for the crucial half hour before dinner, so everyone on the staff had valiantly carried casseroles of lasagna to faculty apartments and common room kitchens around the campus to heat up the food. It had meant that everyone had a buffet dinner instead of a sit-down, family-style meal at assigned tables. That part had been good; it had meant that Thomas and Greg could eat together instead of with their advisors. The bad part was that the power had come back on in time for them to see clearly what they were eating.

"They could have at least put out butter and salad dressing," said Thomas.

"Or heated up the bread," said Greg.

"Or put out some breakfast cereal."

"Or driven us to McDonald's."

"Or given us the cheese and let us make our own pizza."

"Do we have any food back in the room?" Greg asked Thomas.

"Just some crackers and some of that aerosol cheese."

"I meant food," said Greg.

They were walking in the cold from Stringfellow to Bradley Hall, where they hoped to finish their rehearsal before the 7:30 study hall.

"Why wouldn't you kiss Mrs. Warden?"

Greg didn't answer.

"I'm sorry I brought it up," said Thomas.

"It's her husband," Greg said. "He scares me."

Thomas was surprised. "Mr. Warden? He's really nice."

"I know he is," said Greg. "But he's got that mark on his face. I can't kiss a lady who's been kissing him. It's like it's contagious."

They walked on a little farther.

"That doesn't make sense," said Thomas.

"I know it doesn't make sense," Greg said. "It just is. That's just the way I am."

It was starting to snow, though no flakes stuck to the ground yet. The boys were fifty yards from the light and warmth of Bradley Hall when a figure jumped suddenly in front of them from behind a tree. It was someone dressed in a hooded ski jacket. A ski mask covered his face, and the thick gloves he wore made his hands look huge. The person shrieked a loud death yell and surprised them so badly that they joined in the shriek, like dogs hearing a siren. Then they recognized the figure as Richard, who was leaning against the tree and laughing helplessly.

Thomas had to admit it was pretty funny. His older sister, Barbara, used to scare him when they were little, and he would do the same thing to his younger brother, Jeff. He thought it was strange that something as bad as fear could be so entertaining as long as there really wasn't anything to be afraid of.

"How'd you like dinner tonight?" asked Richard.

They repeated their complaints.

"Yes, I'm afraid I didn't think things through when I pulled the old plug this afternoon," said Richard. "I should have realized that we'd all be paying the price in medical bills."

"You're the one who caused the power shortage?" Thomas said.

Richard explained that he had returned to the basement of Stringfellow Hall to search for Greg's tunnel.

"I couldn't find it anywhere," he said. "I think the place is sealed off, if it ever existed in the first place. But I did find the breaker panels for the building. Just push a few buttons and instant blackout."

"What for?" Thomas asked. Despite the dim light, he could see Richard's eyes roll behind the ski mask.

"Inconvenience," said Richard. "Variety. Self-amusement. All of the above. I didn't realize you were running for councilman now."

"It seems pretty stupid to be out here by yourself," said Thomas.

"Oh, Dad, please let me stay out for just a few more minutes."

Thomas said they had to get to play practice.

"Farnham's not there," said Richard. "I just saw him leave the building before you came along."

"Farnham?" said Thomas. "Are you sure?"

Richard said it was either Farnham or O. J. Simpson sprinting to catch a plane.

"He'll be back," said Thomas. He was tired of Richard. Thomas and Greg walked on to Bradley Hall.

Inside the building it was quiet and bright. Thomas didn't know whether to believe Richard or not about Mr. Farnham's absence. Richard was getting strange these last few days; he seemed to be doing everything but growing up.

"Damn," said Greg. "I left my book up in the dining hall."

"We have time to go back," said Thomas. "It's still only five minutes to 7:00."

"Don't bother," said Greg. "I can run."

"You sure?"

"Yeah. Look at Richard. Nobody around here's going to be messing with us."

It was fine with Thomas to wait. Bradley Hall was warm, and furthermore, Mrs. Warden was around somewhere. He unzipped his jacket and removed his hat as he turned to the right to enter the auditorium. He wanted to see whether Mrs. Warden was still practicing her lines, and he thought he might get a chance to watch her for a minute before she noticed him.

The houselights were out when he entered the auditorium, but the stage lights were still up, as if there were an actual performance in progress. From the doorway he saw Mrs. Warden lying on the bed, and he jumped. He felt his heart pound and his insides lurch, and then he laughed. She was lying on the bed like a real corpse, her head lolling back over the front of the mattress so that her face was upside down from Thomas's view in the audience. Her eyes were open and seemed to be staring directly at him, and the very tip of her tongue was poking out of the side of her mouth. Her arms were splayed out toward him, palms down. After Thomas recognized her, he realized that she must have turned down the houselights so that the effect on the stage would be more dramatic.

"You got me," he called to her. He walked up toward the stage.

She made no reply.

"How do you keep your eyes open like that without blinking?" he said again.

She still did not answer.

Thomas arrived at the apron of the stage and stopped. He saw and understood and reacted all at once. She was only ten feet away. He could by now see the red bruises on her neck, could see that her body was lying on its stomach, could see that her head had been twisted around to a place it never belonged. He started to tremble and to shriek as he stared into her glazed eyes.

Desdemona was dead.

Scene 12

She was dead, and she was never coming back. He had been ready for her death, but it was not supposed to come for at least twenty years.

Warden sat in his favorite wing chair in Horace and Kathleen Somerville's living room in the Homestead. It was almost like reality. But it wasn't real, because everyone kept telling him how sorry they were that Cynthia was dead, and he knew that could not be true. When Cynthia died, then chaos would come again; this was a perfectly ordinary gathering of people he knew, friends of his, and a few strangers, too, members of the police department, but that was all right, Kathleen Somerville was here serving coffee, and Horace was sitting nearby. And Dr. Lane the headmaster was here, as was that new biology teacher, Kemper Carella.

There was one of his advisees, too, Thomas Boatwright, sitting on the couch next to Felix Grayson, Felix the disciplinarian who wore his Paul Bunyan boots and his Ernest Hemingway sweater and listened as Thomas wept and talked to him quietly. Why was Thomas Boatwright crying? Oh, yes, now he remembered, it was because Cynthia was dead.

Every time he said it to himself, Warden felt it sink in like a cold blade. He was numb, but he knew enough to realize that he was numb, and he also knew that very soon the horribly poisonous news of his wife's death, the news that had reached his brain some time ago but had not yet trickled down to his heart, was going to register with him fully. And then, he supposed, he would break down.

For now, though, it was a curious experience. He could carry on a perfectly rational conversation with Horace Somerville, and at the same time he could be completely oblivious to what either of them was saying. He could hear again and again that Cynthia was dead, that Cynthia had in fact been murdered right here on the campus, and yet he could look up each time the door opened and expect to see her walk in. It was like being in a play; he had a set of speeches to deliver, but they were not really his words, and he concentrated more on the activities around him than on the words of the script he seemed to be following. None of it was real, but he could sense with growing dread that it was becoming real, that very soon he would say it, say that Cynthia was . . . dead, and that he would believe it.

The news of her death had caught up with him half an hour ago. He had been out walking on the campus composing a poem when he had been interrupted by the noise of sirens and the flash of blue lights.

Dr. Lane had been angry about the sirens and the lights. Across the room Lane talked with Kathleen Somerville, and he voiced the same complaint he had expressed to anyone who would listen for the past hour.

"I told them specifically not to advertise their presence," he said. "I told them we did not need lots of noise and excitement on this campus." Kathleen sympathetically shook her head and issued little hums now and then to indicate she was listening.

The noise from the police cars had attracted to Bradley Hall what appeared to be everyone on the campus, a couple of hundred boys anyway, some of them silly enough to come out in the cold without coats and hats. Warden had walked down among them, and they had known somehow to let him through. They had greeted him in sympathy, some of them even reaching out to touch his arm or to pat him on the shoulder, as he walked to the door of the building where the police stood. How had they known? The phenomenon of rumor had always amazed him on this campus. Something would happen, and then instantly every student would simply know, would have the facts and the details, and would gladly explain them to an ignorant adult. Someone was always being a teacher.

They had taken him inside and had shown him her body. That was the worst part, the part that he did not want to remember. But had he not seen her lying dead earlier? Of course, that was just the play, the rehearsal of the part she had been playing. This other was true, outrageous, premature, horrible . . . death.

He trembled. Cynthia was dead. And what of the man who had killed her? When were they going to find him? And why did it already smell like a funeral in here?

Kathleen had lighted an incense stick.

"I hope the smell doesn't irritate anyone," she said. "We're just having a little odor problem in the basement."

The incense reminded Warden of church. He had not been to church for years.

"More coffee? Ben?" It was Horace Somerville. He was reaching out for Warden's cup. Warden handed it to him obediently, thanked him, smiled.

The investigator, Carol Scott, was an attractive woman who was kind and businesslike simultaneously. They had met each other last Saturday night, and Warden astonished himself by remembering that she wore exactly the same clothes—a gray woolen suit, black nylons, and low-heeled shoes.

"Mr. Warden?" she said. She approached his chair and demurely squatted so that she could look him in the eye. "Are you ready for a few more questions?"

He responded with one of his own. "Have you found Angus yet?"

"No," she said. "We are searching every building on this campus. It will take some time."

"May I speak to him when you find him? I want to ask him why."

She stood and asked for a chair, which Horace provided. "No one has seen Angus Farrier since your wife saw him last Saturday night," she said after she was seated in the ladder-backed chair. "I'm having a hard time believing that a man could live on a campus as busy as this one without being spotted by somebody."

Warden asked her what she was suggesting.

"I'm suggesting that we may want to test a few other options," said Carol Scott. "It's perfectly possible that Angus Farrier was hiding in the building during the rehearsal and killed your wife. People like this have their own crazy reasons for doing what they do. He could have thought of her as a witness who needed to be eliminated. Or maybe he had an obsession. We'll ask him when we find him. But right now, we'd like to compare your story with Mr. Carella's." She waved Kemper Carella over. Horace Somerville pulled up another chair. This was like a cocktail party, Warden thought. We're all going to discuss Updike's latest novel.

Carella was nervous, trembling, and fidgeting as he joined the group. He wore one of those pullover sweatshirts with a hood, and to Warden he looked as young as Thomas Boatwright, who was still sitting across the room on the couch.

The boy had been the one to find her. That had been bad. Warden felt pity for Boatwright, who was rubbing away each tear as it appeared on his cheek and was trying to breathe evenly. The boy had found her, but he had not been the last one to see her alive. That had been Angus, of course, hadn't it?

"Mr. Carella," said Carol Scott. "You were in Bradley Hall shortly before Cynthia Warden died."

"That's right," said Carella. "About 6:30, like I told you."

"Why?"

"To deliver a message from her husband."

"Yes, that's right," said Warden. "I got an idea for a poem while I was watching the rehearsal, so I left. I had to work it out then, while it was hitting me. I don't know where I walked, but I do recall now running into you—we were there on the sidewalk down from the library, weren't we?—and asking you please to deliver a message to Cynthia, to tell her that I would be writing and wouldn't be going to dinner."

Carol Scott wanted to know why he hadn't told his wife himself.

"I wasn't exactly aware of leaving," he said. "And after I had, I didn't want to interrupt my train of thought." It was a poem about a dying child. He could see a little girl step on a poisonous snake when she was in the woods with her father. He saw it from the father's point of view.

"Who was there for the rehearsal, Mr. Warden?"

Warden closed his eyes to picture the participants. She had asked him this question before. "Dan Farnham, the director. Cynthia. Four of the boys. Pat McPhee was there for a while."

Carol Scott checked her notes as he spoke. "Where did you go on this walk, Mr. Warden?"

"I'm not sure."

"Did you go back to the theater building?"

"I don't think so," said Warden.

"You'll have to do better than that," said Carol Scott politely.

Warden said he did not know how to explain the creative process, how it was like going into a trance, like entering a different dimension. It was like going into anesthesia. Literally like losing one's mind.

"I was thinking," he said. "I was not aware of time or place when I left the auditorium. I became aware when I encountered Mr. Carella here, and he asked me how Cynthia was."

He felt like a fool. He was not even able to produce a draft of the poem to show the police that he had been working; there had been no time for writing it down. He could tell them only what he had already told them, had already said to this polite but very persistent woman from the police department who had interviewed him at length in Horace Somerville's private study.

She had taken him just thirty minutes ago back to the paneled study with the brass desk lamp and had asked him the same questions again and again.

"Mr. Warden, your wife was ill, was she not?" she had said.

"She had multiple sclerosis, yes." It had hurt to fall into the past tense.

"Did that upset you?"

"Of course it did," Warden had said. "We were both devastated."

"Did you hate the idea of seeing your wife suffer?" Carol Scott had asked.

"Yes."

"Did you want to help her end her pain?"

Warden had known what he was saying. "Yes," he had said.

"Mr. Warden, did you kill your wife?" Carol Scott had said.

Warden had not answered.

"Mr. Warden?"

"I thought about it," he had said.

"A mercy killing?"

"Yes," he had said.

"Because you loved her?"

"Yes."

"Did you do it, Mr. Warden?"

He had shaken his head. "No," he had said. "I could never do that."

She had watched him and listened to him and asked him about his trip to New York at Thanksgiving and his schedule for working out in the gym and his acquaintance with Robert Staines. But she had finally said okay and had returned him to the living room. "That will be all," she had said.

But it was not all. She was back now with Kemper Carella and she was starting in again with more questions.

Carol Scott turned and asked Carella whether Cynthia was alive when he got to the theater.

"Of course she was alive," said Carella. He sat in a wooden chair to Warden's right. "She was there practicing her lines. She laughed when I told her about Ben, and she said something like, 'He'll be all right,' or 'He'll be fine.' "

"Was anyone else in the building?"

"Not that I could see," Carella said. "It was just Cynthia and me." His eyes jumped from face to face.

"Did you see Mr. Warden return to the theater?" asked Carol Scott.

"No."

"Did you like Cynthia Warden?"

"Not especially," said Carella. He waved his hands as if to cancel the answer, to erase it in the air. "I mean I liked her all right, but I didn't have a thing for her the way some people did."

"Who were those people, Mr. Carella?"

"A lot of the boys did," he said. "And everybody knew Dan Farnham was going crazy over her."

"But not you?" asked Carol Scott.

"No."

"You don't like women?" she asked.

"I didn't say that," said Carella. "I like women just fine."

"Yes," said Carol Scott. "Your friend in New York finally told the truth about how you spent your latest Sunday afternoon there."

Carella's face turned pale. "That has nothing to do with this," he said.

"What does a woman charge you for services like that?" said Carol Scott.

"That has nothing to do with this," Carella said. "Nothing at all. What are you trying to do?"

Carol Scott did not pause.

"Did you see Daniel Farnham at the theater this afternoon?"

"No."

"What time did you leave?"

"I was there only a couple of minutes. It must have been 6:30, 6:35."

"And you saw no one besides Cynthia Warden."

"No."

"So nobody can confirm these times."

"Yes," said Carella. "Patrick McPhee. I talked with him on the telephone while I was there."

"Why did you telephone Mr. McPhee?"

"I didn't," said Carella. "He telephoned me. Or rather he called backstage. He said he was at the gym and was looking for Farnham, and thought maybe Farnham had come back to the theater."

Thomas Boatwright spoke up from his seat on the couch.

"Mr. Farnham did come back to the auditorium," he said.

"Richard Blackburn saw him come running out the front door right before Greg and I got there."

"What time was this?" asked Carol Scott.

"A few minutes before 7:00."

"And where is Mr. Farnham now?" asked Carol Scott.

No one had any idea.

Scene 13

They found Farnham in Patrick McPhee's apartment. He was drinking coffee and eating a sandwich, and it was clear that he had been weeping. Carol Scott was with three uniformed police officers and another investigator, and the first thing she asked was for permission to search his apartment in the gym.

"For what?" said Farnham. He sounded astonished. He had removed his tie and had slipped on a navy blue crew-necked sweater.

"I have probable cause," said Carol Scott. She had said the same thing to Warden and Carella before she had searched their homes. "Will you allow us to search it now?"

Farnham said yes.

"May I have a key?"

"It's always unlocked," he said.

She sent three of the four men to his apartment and remained to question him herself.

"Should I leave?" asked Patrick McPhee. He, too, had changed from coaching attire to a sweater and slacks. His sweater was red with green horizontal stripes.

"No," she said. "I want you to be here."

The light was warm and comfortable in McPhee's apartment. One uniformed policeman stood by the door. Farnham sat in the easy chair near the floor lamp; McPhee sat on the couch; Carol Scott pulled in a wooden chair from the dining room and sat facing both men. She asked Farnham where he had gone after the rehearsal.

"To get some dinner," he said.

"No one reported seeing you in the dining hall," she said.

"I didn't go to the dining hall. I came back here."

"Here? To Mr. McPhee's apartment?"

"No, here to the gym. To my own apartment."

He said he arrived at his home around 6:30 and decided to make himself a bowl of soup for dinner. McPhee interrupted.

"It was a few minutes before 6:30, actually," said McPhee. "Don't you remember, Dan? We walked as far as the dining hall together. We commented on how they were having a buffet supper tonight."

"Okay, sure," said Farnham. "A few minutes before, then."

Carold Scott asked why he did not eat in the dining hall, where the meals were free.

"My stomach was bothering me a little," he said. "I wanted a blander diet."

"So you were alone from 6:30 until when?"

He said he walked back over to the theater around 6:50.

"I wanted to be on time," he said. "So that we could be ready to go when the boys arrived. And I also wanted to check with Cynthia Warden about why she seemed so distressed during rehearsal. She was uncharacteristically upset."

Carol Scott asked him to go on.

"I got to the theater and was annoyed to find all the lights out—the houselights, the stage lights, everything."

"The lights were off in the entire building?"

"No, not in the lobby area. But the theater itself was completely dark. I called out loud for Cynthia and got no answer, so I climbed up to the light booth to turn the stage lights back on, and when I got there, I discovered that they were already on. That is, they were turned on, but they weren't casting any light."

Carol Scott asked how that could be.

"It took me a second to figure it out," said Farnham. "Then I realized that somebody must have thrown the blackout switch from backstage. Our theater is built so that the stage manager in an emergency can turn out all the lights on the stage from backstage if he needs to. He can also turn on and off the houselights. All the master controls are of course up in the light booth at the back of the auditorium."

"So how did you relight the stage?"

"It was simple," he said. "I just pushed the reset button on the master control panel. It overrides the backstage controls. The stage lights surged on, and that's when I saw Cynthia." He started to tremble. "Even from the back of the house, I could sense she was dead. But to make sure, I came down to the stage and took her pulse. Then I don't know what happened. I just freaked out. I had to get out of the building right away, you know? I should have called the police or the switchboard from the phone backstage, but I didn't think of that. I just thought that whoever had done it might still be in the building, and I wanted to get away."

"And where did you go?"

"I ran all the way back here and saw Pat's lights on. I pounded on his door. I told him what had happened, he told me to calm down, and then he offered to call the police for me."

"But when I called," said McPhee, "I heard that you were already on the way."

"That's when I remembered the boys who were on their way over for rehearsal," said Farnham. "To my everlasting shame, I confess that I forgot all about the students. I behaved very selfishly."

"And you had no curiosity about returning to the theater?"

"I did," said McPhee. "In fact, I mentioned a couple of times that we should perhaps go over there."

"I couldn't," said Farnham. "I couldn't see Cynthia like that again. I touched her, and she was dead." He held his fists to his temples as though his head might explode.

"I thought it was best to wait here with him," said McPhee.

"I understand," she said.

The other investigator and the two policemen knocked and entered through the door to the hallway of the gym. The investigator was carrying a tan cardboard shoe box. He conferred for a moment with Carol Scott, opened the box, showed her the contents. She took the box from him.

"Mr. Farnham, is this yours?" she asked.

"Yes," he said. "I keep my bank statements in it. What do you want with those?"

"These are not bank statements," said Carol Scott.

She walked over to the chair where Farnham sat and held the box under the light of the floor lamp. Inside were several random items: a ticket stub from a theater in New York, a pair of athletic socks, the button from a shirt, a signet ring. And an embroidered handkerchief—two Cs on either side of a large W.

She did not touch the handkerchief but pointed to its monogram with a pencil.

"Whose handkerchief is this?" she asked.

"I don't know," said Farnham.

"Cynthia Cunningham Warden," said Carol Scott. "Isn't this her monogram?"

"What is all this?" said Farnham.

"They found this on the back of the top shelf in your bedroom," said Carol Scott.

"That's not mine," said Farnham. He looked around the room for confirmation. McPhee spoke quietly.

"Dan," said McPhee, "I got an idea about the blocking and left the dining hall without eating. I knocked on your door at 6:30. You weren't home. I called you at 6:40. You still weren't home. You were never home when you said you were. I tried calling the theater and couldn't get you there, either. Where were you?"

Farnham shook his head and swallowed and held his hands out in front of him as if he were trying to settle down an unruly class of students.

"Now wait a minute," he said. "I was at home when I said I was. Something is wrong here."

Carol Scott asked the policeman who had brought the shoe box whether he had seen any sign of dirty dishes in Farnham's apartment. He had not.

"I always do my dishes immediately after I use them," said Farnham.

"You went back to the theater, you made a pass, you were rebuffed, you lost your temper, you killed her. Isn't that what happened, Mr. Farnham?"

Farnham said no.

"Mr. Farnham, I should advise you at this point that you have the right to remain silent," said Carol Scott. She recited the standard list.

"Hold on," said Farnham. "This is all going too fast."

"Mr. Farnham," said Carol Scott, "I would like for you to come with me to police headquarters."

"No," said Farnham. "This is a mistake."

Carol Scott held out the shoe box they had found in Farnham's apartment. "The Staines boy's shirt was missing a button," she said. "The Phillips boy's body was missing the socks. These are souvenirs."

Farnham had an immediate reply. "Angus must have planted them there," he said. "He could have. I never lock my apartment."

"You were in New York over Thanksgiving," said Carol Scott.

"Yes, I was," said Farnham. "Anyone at the hotel could vouch for me."

"The police in New York found a receipt from the Montpelier School Store on the floor of a pornographic movie theater last week. It was lying near the body of a boy whose neck had been twisted one hundred and eighty degrees."

"I don't know what you're talking about," said Farnham.

"Your school chaplain told me last week that he was concerned over your violent outbursts," said Carol Scott. "Psychosexual, he called them."

Daniel Farnham's teeth ground against one another so hard that the others in the room could hear them. Then he opened his mouth as wide as a baby bird's and screamed one loud continuous inarticulate noise.

Carol Scott produced a set of handcuffs, and two of the uniformed policemen took hold of Farnham's arms.

All at once he collapsed into limpness and began to sob. "Heilman," he said. "That son of a bitch betrayed me."

Carol Scott held the shoe box out for McPhee to see. "Don't touch," she said. "Just look. Do you recognize that ring?"

"Yes," said McPhee. "It was Angus's."

"Then we're still looking for Angus Farrier," she said, "only now we're looking for a corpse."

Scene 14

Richard waved the edge of his Reuben sandwich as if it were a weapon.

"I'm telling you, I was on to the guy from the beginning," he said. "Didn't I tell you he was crazy?"

"I'm the one who told you," said Thomas. "Remember, I'm the one who saw him pounding the floor in the tech room last week."

"Pass the salt," said Greg. They were sitting at lunch on Tuesday, the day after Cynthia Warden's death. It had been a busy morning. Right after breakfast the whole school had met in the chapel once again; special assemblies were becoming part of the daily routine. Heilman had read some stuff from the Bible, and then Dr. Lane had talked to them about how sad all these events were and how it was important not to let their grief for Mrs. Warden and Robert Staines get the best of them. He had also stressed how it was better not to talk to any reporters who might visit the campus. Richard had asked Thomas whether that meant he couldn't talk to his own father.

"I already have," Thomas had said. "I talked to him last night." It had been great to talk to his parents. They had offered to come and get him on the spot, and while it was tempting, he didn't want to miss any of the excitement here. Now that they had caught Farnham, the campus was in an uproar. Montpelier was much more lively than Cathedral Academy ever would have been. His parents were coming down this weekend to see his basketball game and to take him home Saturday for an overnight.

"Won't Lane get mad that you spoke to your dad, since he works for a newspaper?"

"He's not writing a review of this stuff, Richard."

Mr. Warden was gone from the campus, and Mr. Farnham

was of course also gone, but they couldn't cancel classes, not at the fabulous Montpelier School for Boys, not even just for one day. The teachers, however, were being cool about it. Mr. Carella had held biology class, but he hadn't made his students take any notes. He'd let them discuss the events of the day before.

"It's better to talk now and get it out of your systems right away," he had said. "It's not healthy to store things up."

Richard was still on the subject at lunch.

"I was lucky not to get killed when he caught me downstairs making those telephone calls during your rehearsal Sunday," said Richard. "He would have wasted me if he could have."

"You're just trying to get your name in the paper," said Thomas.

Dr. Lane, exempting himself from his own injunction, had been talking to reporters all day. Television stations from Washington and Richmond had sent film crews, and a few more parents had withdrawn their sons from the school. For most, however, it was considered the end of a string of bad luck. The only missing piece was Angus, and the police were now saying that he was probably dead.

"I'd like to think he's still alive," said Greg. "He might be, you know."

"Farnham probably cooked him and ate him," said Richard. "It's a good thing he's not in charge of the dining hall."

"I wish we could get him back," said Thomas, "Since he's been gone, our locker room has started to stink."

"That's what happens to you athletic types," said Greg. "All those stinky clothes get ripe."

Richard started to laugh.

"Maybe there's more to it than just clothes," said Richard. "But don't blame me. I don't know anything about a dead squirrel getting thrown down the ventilator shaft outside McPhee's apartment."

Thomas said Richard was the most vindictive person he'd ever seen.

Richard looked at Thomas impatiently. "You've turned awfully outspoken lately," he said.

"I have a new policy since Staines died," said Thomas. "I always tell the truth."

"That'll last until your next date," said Richard.

Thomas had tried to call Hesta last night and again this morning, and each time they told him that she wasn't on dorm. He was beginning to fear that he would never talk with her again. He had killed all the affection she had once had for him.

"I'm not anticipating any more dates," he said.

"How touching," said Richard. "You and Robert Staines had your last dates on the same night."

They talked about how Farnham had been taken to the jail in Charlottesville, how he was denying any wrongdoing, how they didn't blame him for trying to lie his way out of it.

"I heard they found all these souvenirs," said Richard. "There's probably a scrapbook with pieces of hair and pictures of all the victims."

The other two said that was disgusting.

"I feel right rotten inside for not wanting to kiss her that time," said Greg. "Do you think it hurt her feelings? I'd do it if I had the chance again."

"It didn't hurt her feelings," said Richard. "She just thought you were crazy. Boatwright's the man in the hurt feelings department."

"Shut up, Richard."

Richard said Farnham had been madly in love with Mrs. Warden. "I heard him try to put the moves on her before rehearsal one day. Back before I got fired from the play. It was a crime of passion."

"How come we never heard that story before?" asked Thomas.

"Okay, so I didn't exactly hear it myself. But Landon Hopkins was telling everybody about it today."

Thomas felt pity for Farnham unexpectedly overwhelm him. It was so easy to talk macho, to say that you never let a woman get to you, that it was a sign of weakness. He figured people like that had never been in love.

"He's just like Othello," said Greg. "He killed the thing he loved."

"Jealous because she was married to somebody else," said Richard.

Thomas said he seemed more like Roderigo than Othello.

"That's because you play Roderigo, dork," said Richard.

"No," said Thomas. "He just seems more like the dumb guy with the crush than the man with the great love. If it's going to be like Othello, then Mr. Warden would be the one to kill her."

"It's not like Othello, then," said Richard.

Horace Somerville, who sat with his back to them at the adjacent table, was fascinated by every word.

Scene 15

Although it had only been a couple of hours since lunch, it seemed to Thomas Boatwright like two decades. Today's English class had been unbearably boring, even with McPhee teaching, but in just a few more seconds the class would end. It would be 3:00, and Thomas could get the hell out of there.

Three . . . two . . . one . . . the bell rang. Thomas already had his books packed and was up and out of his seat when Mr. McPhee stopped him.

"Hold it, Boatwright," he said. "Get the homework first."

The rest of the English class laughed. Mr. McPhee had been their substitute only one day, but they were already comfortable with him. He was so much more relaxed than Mr. Farnham had been, and he was still a good teacher. By this last period of the day, everybody was talked out about Mr. Farnham and Angus Farrier and Mrs. Warden, so Mr. McPhee had gone over the way Aristotle defined a tragic hero: a noble character who was brought down by one fatal flaw.

"Adam was the first tragic hero," McPhee had said. "He was a good man who let his passion to please Eve get the best of his reason."

Talk about tedium. Aristotle and the Bible in one day.

"A tragic hero is a good man," McPhee had said over and over. That was all Thomas could remember of the whole class period. Nobody had mentioned Farnham's coverage of all that tragic hero stuff during their unit on *Oedipus Rex*.

Now they were free as soon as they got the homework assignment.

"Read Act V," said Mr. McPhee.

"The whole thing?" asked Richard.

"The whole thing," said Mr. McPhee. "That's the final act. Then you'll be all finished. Good-bye."

Thomas practically screeched out of the room. He was headed to the dorm and to the telephone; he was going to get all his problems straightened out. After lunch he had checked his mail. There had been a letter from Hesta. At first, when he'd seen the envelope, his heart had beat like a fire bell. Then he had read the letter.

> Please stop calling me on the dormitory. Didn't you hear what I told you on Saturday night? You hurt me. You are not the person I thought I knew. I don't want to see you any more. We are all sad that so many people at your school have died. I am particularly sad that, as far as I am concerned, you are one of them.

He wondered how long it had taken her to come up with that last line. She'd probably been practicing it for days. He tried to work himself into indignation, but he couldn't get it to stay. He was building it on a shaky, soggy bog of guilt and self-disgust, and his anger was only an illusion. He felt sick and ashamed and very lonely.

On the dormitory he called the familiar number for Mason, only this time he asked for his sister's dormitory.

"Thomas!" Barbara said. "How are you? What is going on down there? I hear you had some mad slasher on the loose."

"They caught him. He was my English teacher."

"Gross!" she said. "Does it make you feel weird?"

Thomas said he supposed so. It was so comforting just to hear Barbara's voice. She talked like a damn air-head but was only about the smartest person in the eastern United States. She was going to be valedictorian of her class and was going to hear any day from Amherst about her early application. Ever since he'd been a little kid, Barbara had been there as his protective older sister, showing him around, spoiling him probably, but there. He could imagine her there by the telephone, her long black hair pulled back by her right hand into a makeshift ponytail while her left hand held the receiver. She'd be wearing some sweatshirt, jeans, and sneakers, and she'd have on her favorite little gold pegged earrings.

"Have you talked to Hesta lately?" he asked her.

"Thomas, that's bad," said Barbara. He felt himself going weaker and colder with shame. "She hasn't said anything to me at all since Saturday. What happened?"

"I guess I was stupid," he said. "Could you talk to her for me?"

"Did you do something wrong?"

"I guess so."

"I could tell her you're sorry," said Barbara. "That's not much."

"That's why I'm calling you," said Thomas. "What else can I do?"

"Wait and see," said Barbara. "She may never forgive you. You might just have to learn a lesson the hard way."

Thomas was tired of learning lessons.

Barbara had to go to gymnastics. Thomas hung up and went immediately to basketball practice, where he hit eight out of nine shots from the floor and got called for seven fouls during the intrasquad scrimmage.

"There's a new fire in Boatwright," said Coach McPhee. "I wish we could just turn down the thermostat a little."

After practice, Thomas stayed and shot free throws. He hit thirty-eight out of fifty, and he and Coach McPhee talked about women.

"You remember how you told me about that girl in the other apartment?" said Thomas. "The one you used to watch when you were my age?"

"I knew I'd regret mentioning her," said Coach McPhee. He was joking.

"I was just wondering," said Thomas, "if you ever knew her name."

Coach McPhee was surprised by the question. "I don't think so," he said. "She went to a girls' school. What brought this up?"

"I don't know," said Thomas. "It just seems easier to like girls in general than to like one in particular." It was hard to explain. "If you'd known her name, somehow that would have made it less funny. To be watching her in private like that. To be using her. I don't know what I mean."

Coach McPhee didn't answer. He took a couple of shots himself before he threw the ball back to Thomas.

"So you're still bothered by some girl trouble," said Coach McPhee.

"Yes sir."

"Want to tell me about it?"

"It's embarrassing," said Thomas. He wanted to talk, but he didn't know where to start.

Coach McPhee said it didn't matter. "I've heard the story many times before," he said. "Boy meets girl, boy loses girl, boy wants girl back but she won't come."

"That's it," said Thomas.

"Exercise and abstinence are the best cures," said Coach McPhee. "Take my word for it." He dribbled the length of the court and shot a lay-up, leaving Thomas to rebound his own shots.

Thomas felt like a freak. All the guys just moved from girl to girl without a qualm. Coach McPhee lost his wife and didn't even blink. Nobody at Montpelier seemed to understand how much he was hurting. Maybe if he'd been at home he could have talked about it with Dad, but not over the telephone, not on the dorm with people walking by. The guy he really wanted to see was Mr. Warden, his advisor, who was away to prepare for his wife's funeral. Mr. Warden seemed to be the only one who could understand what it meant to grieve.

Coach McPhee dribbled back up the court.

"You're better off without them," he said. "Trust me."

"You're right," said Thomas. "I'm never going to fool with girls again." He shot the basketball. Coach McPhee rebounded and shot one himself.

"Do you think I'll be able to keep that promise?" Thomas asked him.

"No way," said Coach McPhee.

They both laughed.

"That's the spirit," said the coach.

But Thomas felt like an actor who was only providing his audience what it wanted. He couldn't stand thinking that she hated him so much, and he couldn't find anybody who could sympathize.

THE FINAL ACT

Scene 1

Warden sat in his office and looked out the window at the crusting snow. He knew he would be looking at the same snow in March, even with the inevitable January thaw that would give everyone a false hope of spring before the arctic wind currents shifted and again forced everyone into hats and gloves and scarves.

It was Wednesday, December 15. Cynthia had been dead for nine days. It was over. Lawrence and Margaret had come up from Atlanta for the funeral. Joseph Moore, his literary agent, had flown in from New York. There had been many friends—editors, other writers, people from the university, women Cynthia had known in school. For a week his apartment had been jammed with casseroles and cakes and hams and congealed salads and coffee and beer and wine. He had been surprised at how much publicity there was; *Time* magazine even ran a short piece. People he had never met had written him notes of sympathy. Television crews had come out for interviews.

Warden had received a kind word from every person he knew in the world during the past week, it seemed, except for one.

Harold Cunningham.

His father-in-law had attended the funeral. It was held by the graveside at the Warden family's plot in Charlottesville. Harold had come, had rebuffed Warden's invitation to sit with the rest of his family, had left after delivering only one brutal line to Warden.

"She would still be alive today," Harold had said, "if she had not married you."

Warden had been convicting himself on the same charge for days. Why had he been so selfish as to bring her to Montpelier? Why had he not remained in the theater with her that afternoon? But the result of Harold's accusation was to show Warden the absurdity of such thinking. Harold had accomplished the opposite of his mission; he had helped Warden start to forgive himself.

That was the past. It was Wednesday, December 15. Cynthia had been dead for nine days. It was over.

It was over, he corrected himself, except for the legal aftermath. Carol Scott had come out with a woman from the district attorney's office to ask him questions about Daniel Farnham, who was still in police custody but was now in the hospital with anemia and a bleeding ulcer. The man continued to claim that it must have been the still-missing Angus Farrier who had set him up. Warden was certain that Angus was dead—there was no other explanation for his extended absence—but his missing body complicated the case against Farnham.

Warden shook the memory out of his head. It was Wednesday, December 15. Cynthia had been dead for nine days. It was time for him to get on with his own life. It was time to remember the rest of the world. Now it was time to remember his vocation.

He looked at the blank paper in front of him. He was trying to write, but there was nothing to write. His wife was dead and buried. He had thought that nothing could be worse than knowing she was ill, and he had been wrong. This absence was worse. Two days ago he had read that most wives stay with husbands who have multiple sclerosis while most men leave their sick wives. Such betrayal was inconceivable to him, as untenable as the abstract thoughts of euthanasia he had abandoned after the briefest of flirtations. He had chosen to stay with Cynthia for better or for worse. But she had left unexpectedly.

It was 10:15 in the morning. Boys walked to dormitories. A normal life occurred in the hallways and on the sidewalks around him. In half an hour he had a class to teach. And he was numb.

He heard a knock. It was Thomas Boatwright, his advisee. Warden had forgotten that he'd asked the boy to come by today. He seemed to be forgetting everything except his life with Cynthia, which he recalled constantly in agonizingly fresh detail.

For the moment, however, he turned his attention to the boy. Boatwright had been just as depressed as Warden himself for the past week. You could tell it in everything about him, from the way his head drooped to the way he dressed. Even today Warden noticed the grime on his jeans and the dirt on the old sweatshirt the boy had on. The kid's hair was poorly washed and unkempt—unkempt for Boatwright, who was usually tidy—but his eyes still looked okay. No glaze, no hostility. This was a boy who wasn't turning to drugs, Warden decided. He was a boy in some kind of spiritual pain, and it was Warden's duty as Boatwright's advisor to help if he could.

"Sit down, Thomas." The boy took a chair beside the desk and sat with his blue hardback notebook and three thick textbooks in his lap. Warden caught a faint odor of funk. He decided not to ask about the last time the sweatshirt had been washed.

"I owe you an apology," Warden said. "I've been so wrapped up in my own problems that I haven't paid any attention to yours. Is there anything bothering you? Anything you'd like to discuss with me?"

He saw the boy's eyes brim with tears, saw the lashes blink them back before they could trickle onto his cheeks.

"I've been wanting to talk to you for so long," said Boatwright. "But I thought it would be so unfair."

"Why unfair?"

"Because of what happened to Mrs. Warden. It would be selfish of me to ask for your sympathy."

Warden's fingertips casually brushed the birthmark on the left side of his face.

"I can appreciate your thinking that way, Thomas," said Warden. "But you're doing me a favor right now. You're giving me a chance to think about somebody besides myself."

Boatwright managed a rueful grunt of recognition. "That's all I've been thinking about, too."

"What's the trouble?"

The boy was hesitant at first, hard to get started in his narrative. But once he began, the whole story cascaded like effluvium out of his mouth. Warden could watch the weight depart from the boy's shoulders as he talked, as the words tripped and fell and shoved one another for the chance finally to get out into the daylight.

"I didn't know I was hurting her, you know?" he said. "I called her and then wrote her to apologize. She wrote back and it's like she hates me. I always thought, you know, you could make up for your mistakes. But I can't do anything. I keep calling, she won't talk. I keep writing, she never answers. I feel like such an ass, and nobody around here seems to care. They act like I'm a wimp for even wanting to see her again. And all my dad can say is that there are plenty more fish in the sea."

Warden wanted to tell him it would be all right, but it would have been the same standard conventional wisdom Warden himself had found so unsatisfactory. They had both suffered a loss. They both needed time to recover.

"I'm sorry," Warden said. "I know it hurts. And you know that I care."

"Coach McPhee says the best thing to do is to pour myself into basketball. Physical exercise helps, he says."

"That's good advice. So does mental exercise. Schoolwork can be a fine distraction."

"Yes sir." He pulled out a cream-colored envelope from his notebook. "I got invited to tea at the Homestead tonight by the Somervilles," he said. "Do you think it's a mistake? I was just there two weeks ago."

"I think the Somervilles are trying to look after us," said Warden. "I got an invitation myself. Will you be there?"

"If practice is over in time. Yes sir."

"Good. I'll see you there."

Boatwright stood up to leave as though he had just been unshackled.

"Mr. Warden?"

"Yes?"

"Who's going to be taking Mr. Farnham's classes for good?"

Warden explained that they were looking for a qualified substitute, that if they could find none, the rest of the members of the department would divide the duties. "Or maybe Dean Kaufman and his wife," he added.

"Could I make a request?" asked Boatwright.

"Certainly."

"I'd really like to have you."

"You're not enjoying Mr. McPhee?"

"He's great," said Boatwright. "Everybody just says you're the best when it's time for poetry."

"We'll see what happens," said Warden. The boy left. There was something warming about genuine praise devoid of all sycophancy. The surge of joy Warden felt surprised him, like a warm current in a cold lake. And then he felt terribly guilty. He had forgiven himself for marrying Cynthia and bringing her to Montpelier, but he was not entitled to know happiness. How could he be happy with Cynthia dead? How could he dare be happy? What an insensitive, selfish lout he was.

He turned his attention back to the blank sheet of paper on his desktop and picked up his pen. Then, instead of writing, he drew a human face, a face blotched and disfigured down the left side, a face that was ugly and frightening and evil.

Scene 2

At 4:00 on the afternoon of Wednesday, December 15, just a few hours after Thomas Boatwright had his conference with Benjamin Warden, Horace Somerville found Kevin Delaney in the art room in Bradley Hall cleaning paintbrushes at the sink.

"I tried the gym first," said Somerville. "I thought you'd be having practice."

"Yeah," said Delaney. "With two cases of the flu, one separated shoulder, three sprained ankles, a knee with the ligaments twisted, and at least four people with a major history test tomorrow, I guess I could have had practice with the single available boy left on the team, but I decided to give him the day off. Yesterday's game demolished us. I'm too old for this."

Somerville had long ago decided Delaney was the kind of art teacher who would have been sculpted by Henry Moore: heavy and rounded everywhere, with a double chin and drooping eyelids, arms like a blacksmith's, and a beach-balloon belly. He wore socks that rarely matched and occasionally even two different kinds of shoes. A man of his size belonged in the art room, which was the largest single classroom on campus, at least fifty feet square, with one half given over to blackboards and four large tables with chairs, and the other half to easels, boards for working clay, and a pottery wheel. Shelves throughout held residue from the past decade of students: figurines of every medium from clay to alabaster, charcoal drawings, acrylics, oils, watercolors, misshapen pots with peculiar glazes, broken mobiles awaiting repairs, plaster models of bizarre buildings.

Somerville had a rolled tube of paper. He took off his topcoat and laid it, folded, on a nearby stool. He held on to the paper.

"Look at this place," said Delaney. "I still can't find my pastel crayons. I am never letting them hold a mixer in here again."

"It looks neater than my classroom," said Somerville. "Can you talk while you wash?"

He could.

"Tell me about this secret tunnel."

Delaney laughed. "You've been here longer than I have," he said. "You tell me."

"There have always been legends around here," said Somerville. "What exactly have you heard?"

Delaney said he'd heard stories about secret escape passages and hidden rooms and ghosts when he'd come to Montpelier twenty years before, and so he had decided to turn the rumors into an assignment.

"I told the kids to see if they could find a secret tunnel built by the Stringfellows from the Homestead to Stringfellow Hall."

"Under the entire length of the Quad?"

"Sure."

"But you knew all the time that there was no such tunnel."

"I never told them exactly that there was a tunnel. I just encouraged them to find it," said Delaney. He was shaking off the brushes.

"So the rumor of that particular passage started with you," said Horace Somerville. "I thought so. I'd never heard of any tunnel from the Homestead to Stringfellow until you arrived here."

"Okay," said Delaney. "What's the harm? It gets the boys looking at buildings, it gets them thinking about design. Who gets hurt?"

"I didn't come here to file charges, Kevin."

"I'm not the one who originated all the old tunnel lore, you know," said Delaney. "I just embellished it a little."

Horace Somerville admitted that the rumors about secret rooms and ghosts had preceded Delaney by decades.

"I've been thinking about those old stories recently," he said. "A stray conversation I heard in the dining hall a week and a half ago started me off. Some boys were saying that there was an unpleasant odor in the basement of the gym. Kathleen and I have been having a terrible time with an odor in our own basement. I started to wonder whether the two odors could have the same source."

Delaney said he didn't follow.

"Have you ever considered there being a passage between the gym and the Homestead?" asked Somerville.

"Of course," said Delaney. "That's the one that makes the most sense, with part of the gym being your old kitchen for the Homestead. I've considered every permutation at one point or another. There's a blueprint in the Archives Room of the library. Some kids have tampered with it, I think. It's got some pencil marks showing a tunnel leading from the gym. But that particular tunnel seems to lead to Stringfellow."

"This blueprint?" Somerville unrolled the tube in his hand. It was the diagram that Greg Lipscomb had come across on the night of the mixer.

"Yeah," said Delaney. "How did you sneak that past Janie Shepherd?"

"She trusted me to return it."

Delaney dried his hands on several paper towels at the sink. He held the blueprint down on a tabletop with his huge round fingers.

"See," said Delaney. "Here's the supposed tunnel coming out of this lower floor. It's labeled GYMNASIUM on the reverse side, so I'm assuming it's the old library. You match up this fireplace to any of the three fireplaces on the gym, and the only one that works is the one in Farnham's old apartment. The other two point across the Quad or into the playing fields. Every couple of years a boy will find it and get excited about it, but there are no tunnels in Stringfellow Hall. There's just nothing to find."

"I'd always believed the same thing," said Horace Somerville, "until the Lipscomb boy got me thinking about it. I believe we have been jumping to conclusions, Kevin. Why should we assume that any one of those chimneys at the gym is the chimney in this diagram?"

"Only because of the label on the back. It says it's the gym," said Delaney.

"Aren't we making one false assumption? Isn't it possible that there could have been a fourth chimney, attached to a fourth fireplace, one that would be big enough to serve a provincial kitchen? A fireplace that no longer exists?"

Delaney said that was possible.

"I've seen photos from the time when that gym was being built," said Somerville, "and I can still remember my brother Virgil talking about a huge pile of old bricks. What would stop them from taking down the chimney from the old fireplace and rebuilding it here, on the east end, where McPhee's fireplace now is? All you have to assume is that the original fireplace for the kitchen was on the south side, on what's now an inside wall. And if you do, you can take this diagram and see—"

"—that the pencil marks lead straight to the Homestead," said Delaney. "So you think your basement is directly connected to McPhee's apartment by this tunnel."

"Actually, it would have to be the boiler room," said Somerville.

"Angus's lair," said Delaney.

Exactly.

"It's the coincidence of the smell that persuades me I'm right," said Somerville. "I'm sure there's a dead animal in there."

"How does a dead animal get into this sealed tunnel, Horace?" asked Delaney.

"It burrows up through the ground. Or it slips in through a crack in the wall. Or some prankster drops it down a ventilator shaft."

"That's quite an assumption."

"Of course it is," said Somerville. He rerolled the diagram. "It's only in the theory stage right now. We need facts."

"And when are you going to get the facts?" said Delaney.

"Right now," said Somerville, and he put on his coat and left.

Scene 3

Toes on the line, two dribbles, face the basket, bend the knees, shoot.

"Follow through," said Coach McPhee. "You aren't following through."

It was 5:30 P.M. McPhee and Thomas were the only ones left in the gym. The coach flipped the ball back to the shooter, who bounced it hard with both hands off the shiny floor in disgust. He was never going to master this skill.

"Come on," said Coach McPhee. He had gone all the way through practice wearing his school clothes, a white button-down with a loosened tie. His face was misty with perspiration. "You've lost your concentration. What's the matter? We won, remember?"

After the death of Robert Staines, they had lost their next two games. But yesterday they had won by two points. It had been despite Thomas, however; he had missed two free throws in the last quarter.

Coach McPhee tried a different topic. "Not still woman trouble, is it?"

Thomas smiled briefly. His talk with Mr. Warden had helped with the woman trouble. "Not really," he said. "I've accepted my doom. I'm always going to like girls, but they're never going to like me."

Coach McPhee said that plenty of them would like him. "You'll have to keep them away," he said. He held the ball for a second before he threw it. "How intimate were you and this lady friend of yours, anyway?"

"We didn't do it," said Thomas. "But almost." It wasn't so hard to talk about it since he'd confessed to Mr. Warden.

Mr. McPhee, however, did not want to hear any details. "Now you can concentrate on basketball," he said.

But that was the problem. Basketball wasn't Thomas's game, and he figured he would try something else next year. Maybe wrestling on Mr. Carella's team. Or maybe theater full-time. Basketball was too frustrating. But Thomas didn't want to get into all that with Coach McPhee. He should change the subject.

"Hang on," said Thomas. It was time to produce the Christmas present. He dropped the ball and ran over to the sidelines where his warm-ups were. He pulled out the small paper bag that he had hidden inside his sweatshirt and ran back to the coach. He'd bought the gift in the school store just this afternoon.

"I didn't have any paper to wrap it or anything, and I didn't want to give it to you in front of all the guys," he said.

"I understand," said Coach McPhee. He was touched.

He looked inside the bag, grinned, and pulled out a new coach's whistle on a strong black cord. He blew one shrill blast and then put it around his neck. "And I was just getting used to yelling at you guys," he said. "Thanks."

"Practice just hasn't been the same without your whistle," said Thomas.

"Nothing's been the same, has it?" said Coach McPhee. He folded the paper bag and put it into his pocket.

Thomas agreed that it had been a weird month.

"You know, one of the nicest parts of my life has been these times we've been able to spend together after practice," said Coach McPhee. "My stepson, Michael, is gone, you know. I've often wondered what it would be like to have a son like you."

This was getting embarrassing.

"Let me try ten in a row," said Thomas.

Coach McPhee watched while he started his shooting routine. "You're not exactly a natural, but you're a fighter, I'll give you that. Go for your ten, put the balls away, and then hit the locker room. I've got something to give you, too." He blew one more quick jolt with the whistle and then departed.

Thomas remained to take the last free throws he would ever shoot in his life.

Scene 4

The killing of Cynthia had supposedly been the last one. He had needed to kill her, she was on to him, he had had to protect himself. It had been easy to plant the evidence on Farnham and to let the police come to their natural conclusions. He was safe, safe from everyone but himself.

It had been over a week since the high tide of passion had last drowned his self-control. He had been hoping that the flood had peaked, that the urge had been flushed out to sea, that he could return to being a normal citizen of this model community. But life kept intervening. This Boatwright boy, for example. He found himself thinking again and again about the Boatwright boy. This boy was different from the others. The kid liked him. Why? There was no valid reason. It was an irrational affection, but welcome just the same.

And yet the kid also liked girls. It was only a matter of time before Boatwright found himself another girlfriend.

With dread and yet with grim recognition and acceptance, he felt the old urge pump into his veins again. So this was the way it would be. This thing was a part of him; he had to admit his ties to the passion. It was here, it was ready, and it was going to goad him into action again.

Only after this time, it was going to disappear for good. He could promise himself that.

He had to kill once more before it could be finally over.

Scene 5

Kathleen Somerville had been amused at first, but when Horace started to remove all the crystal and china from her storage closet in the basement, she decided that it was time to arrest this latest passion of his.

"You aren't serious about this tunnel thing," she said. "Horace, we have lived in this house for thirty years. We know everything about it."

"Listen," he said. He tapped on the back wall of the closet. "Doesn't that sound hollow?"

The basement of the Homestead comprised a substantial portion of the living area of the house: kitchen, dining room, guest bedroom, den with a television set. Horace and Kathleen were in their dining room, which sat in the southwest corner of the house. Its walls were painted pale Williamsburg blue with white trim, and it was lighted by electric candles in sconces and in the chandelier. In the center of the room was a finely polished oval mahogany table on a brightly patterned Indian rug. Kathleen stored some of her china in the sideboard along the east wall, and the rest in the closet on the west wall. Now, however, Horace was un-storing it.

Horace tapped again on the back wall of the closet. Then he lifted the last stack of dishes off the bottom shelf of that closet and placed them on the table.

"Of course it's hollow," said Kathleen. "There's probably half a foot of space between the lumber and the brick foundation."

"Let's find out," said Horace Somerville. He lifted the top shelf from its metal brackets and set it gently outside the closet.

"What are you doing?" she said.

"Taking down the shelves before I pry loose the boards," he said. "I don't want to start right in with the crowbar."

"Horace, this building is a national historic landmark," said Kathleen.

Horace pulled down the second shelf. "I know," he said. "If I'm wrong, I hope they don't charge me damages by the year."

Kathleen was glad that her children were not here to see this.

"If you're right about a dead animal, then you're going to need some gloves," she said. "The smell is just awful."

"Getting rid of it is worth a little vandalism." He picked up the eighteen-inch crowbar and carefully inserted it into a seam between two boards at the back of the closet.

They both smelled the putrescence more intensely as soon as Horace pried the first board loose from its supporting studs.

"There's a dead horse back there," said Kathleen. "Horace, if you let one living creature into my house, I'll leave you."

"Bring me a flashlight," said Horace. "One more of these, and I can get through." The boards were eight inches wide and were nailed vertically across the back of the closet. He gently worked at the second board. Already there was a space wide enough for a child to slip through. Behind it was darkness, nothing as far in as he could reach.

Kathleen went to the kitchen and returned with a flashlight. The smell was worse. Horace had his handkerchief to his face.

"It's awful," she said. "You can't go in there."

He turned on the light, stuck his right leg into the hole and entered sideways. The inside was lined with dry brick. It was a narrow passage, perhaps four feet wide, and seemed perfectly secure. Its ceiling was arched and also lined with brick, and it reached almost eight feet high. It stretched away from him into the earth.

"It's a tunnel," he said from inside.

Kathleen said she would wait to hear him fall into an old well or whatever was in there.

With the light from the hole in the closet and the beam of the flashlight, Horace could see virtually the length of the tunnel. He had intended to walk through to see where it led, but he changed his mind once inside. Fifteen feet from where he stood, he found the source of the stench. He walked only as close as necessary to confirm what he suspected, and then he quickly retreated. He knew that he had to leave immediately, that he had to exit that close, stifling tube before he became ill.

It was not a dead squirrel. It was larger. A hideous form recognizable as human despite eleven days of decay. A white tee shirt. A head with short-cropped hair.

Angus Farrier.

Scene 6

Eldridge Lane arrived before the police, but barely. It was 5:25 in the afternoon when he rushed into the vestibule of the Homestead.

"Good Lord, I can smell it up here," he said. "You're going to have to sleep somewhere else tonight."

"An hour ago my life was perfectly normal," said Kathleen. "Now—"

"Please tell me later," said Lane. "I was just ahead of a large group of students. How did they find out already?"

"Good heavens," she said. "Our Wednesday afternoon tea." They could hear the footsteps on the porch, the prompt ring of the doorbell. Before Kathleen could move, Benjamin Warden let himself and a dozen boys into the foyer. Eldridge Lane blocked their path.

"Not tonight, boys," said Lane. "Ben, if you'd like, you may stay."

The students resentfully turned back toward the dormitories. As the pack of boys departed, Horace Somerville emerged from his bedroom, where he had taken a shower and changed his clothes. At that moment Carol Scott arrived with four men. None were in uniform. They had sounded no sirens on their way to the campus, but the boys had seen and recognized them. Lane suspected the rumors would be circulating again.

It took a moment to sort it all out as the four policemen, one female police investigator, two Somervilles, the headmaster, and Benjamin Warden stood in the foyer.

"We've had a little discovery here," said Horace Somerville.

Eldridge Lane told Carol Scott he hoped this was an end to the matter.

"It's disgraceful that a member of my faculty should have had to do your job for you," he said. "Close it up quietly."

Carol Scott was not in a frame of mind to tolerate Eldridge Lane. "Your people called me," she said. "Do you want me here or not?"

Lane told her that he wanted her here for as brief a period as possible. Then he left.

"What's going on?" Warden asked.

"Sit in the living room while the police go downstairs," said Horace Somerville. "I'm going to fetch us some whiskey."

Somerville had been glad to see the boys leave a few minutes ago. Until this moment he had never realized how tired he had become of spending every Wednesday afternoon performing the same rituals over teacups. It was a shame about Angus, but Somerville had to admit the truth: uncovering that tunnel had been downright fun. He had not felt this lively in years.

Scene 7

Thomas made eight of his ten shots and headed downstairs. As usual, everyone else had left the locker room before he arrived. It had been a regular routine for the past week or so, Thomas staying to shoot baskets and talk with the coach, and then the two of them locking up the gym. He didn't see Coach McPhee or anyone else as he pulled off his damp practice clothes and stepped into the shower.

It was nice to be the last one out of the gym. You hardly got any privacy at Montpelier, hardly any time to yourself. There was always some pressing appointment. Like special assemblies. Or tea at the Homestead.

"Hell," Thomas said out loud in the echoing shower room. He had forgotten about his invitation for tea this afternoon. It was past 6:00, too late now to show up without looking stupid. He would have to write the Somervilles a note of apology.

When he emerged from the shower into the locker room, Coach McPhee was sitting on the bench in front of Thomas's cubicle. Thomas's school clothes, which had been hung on the hooks inside the cubicle, were piled untidily on the bench beside Mr. McPhee. Thomas held up his towel self-consciously and wrapped it around his waist. Mr. McPhee straddled the bench. He held the edges as though he were on a steel girder twelve stories high.

"I've just locked all the outside doors to this building," he said. "Do you know that we're the only two people in it?"

"We stayed late," said Thomas. He waited for McPhee to get up from his seat in front of the locker, but the coach remained in his spot. Thomas started to dry himself tentatively, about five feet away from his clothes.

"Did you have a nice bath?"

That was a weird question. "A good shower," said Thomas. "Yes sir."

"Shower," said Coach McPhee. He shook his head with friendly impatience the way Greg did when Thomas had corrected his lines for him. "I've decided to give you something very special, Thomas. Do you know what that is? It's my confidence. I want to talk to you about something I've never discussed with anyone before, about my wife and my stepson. Do you feel like listening?"

"Sure," said Thomas. He wished the coach had left his stuff hanging the way he'd had it. "Why did you take out my clothes?"

"The clothes don't matter," said Coach McPhee. "What matters is that you hear me out."

"I'm listening," said Thomas. But Coach McPhee simply stared at him with those intensely green eyes.

"Maybe it would be better if we didn't talk," said Coach McPhee. "Let's just get out of here and go to dinner." He stood up quickly and moved to the glass door of the locker room. He pushed, but the door did not open. He turned to look at Thomas again. "I locked it," he said. "I wish I hadn't locked it." He pulled his keys out of his pocket, then replaced them. "I don't know which way to go here." He coughed gently and rubbed his hands on his trousers. "Do you think it's hot?"

"Not really."

"That's because you don't have any clothes on." This was not the way Coach normally behaved. He returned and sat down on the bench beside Thomas's clothes again. He lifted Thomas's blue boxer shorts. "Here's a nice pair of underwear," he said. "What can you give me for these?"

Thomas decided it was all a joke. "I'll give you a hundred free throws tomorrow after practice," he said. He reached for his underwear. Coach McPhee jerked the boxers out of his reach.

"Conversation," said the coach. "What kind of conversation can you give me for something to wear? Something basic. We're talking about getting back to the basics here."

"Coach McPhee—"

"I need to talk to somebody," said Coach McPhee. His voice was calm and level, and he was looking straight at Thomas as if they were having a theme conference in the classroom. But his face was still wet from perspiration.

Thomas felt his own hair drip down his back. He continued to dry himself as the coach talked.

"I've chosen you to talk to," he said, "because we know each other. I used to talk to my wife, but she left. You knew that, didn't you? Did you know that I went to Boston over the Thanksgiving holidays to see her? I flew from Washington all the way to Boston to see my wife and to talk to her, just to talk to her, and she wouldn't listen. She wanted to do all the talking herself. She's like you kids here, you guys talk a lot when you have a problem, but you never want to listen to anybody."

Thomas was dry now. He could feel a cold drop of sweat roll down his ribs, and he shivered. What kind of game was the coach playing?

"All right," said Coach McPhee. "Put on your underwear." He threw the boxers at Thomas. They landed on his chest, where he grabbed them and quickly put them on. Then he put his towel on the bench and moved for the rest of his clothes.

"Not so fast," said Coach McPhee. "I'm not finished with my story. Did I tell you already we're the only ones in the building? Dan Farnham used to live here, but he's away now. He got arrested for killing Cynthia Warden and Robert Staines and Russell Phillips and that boy in the movie theater in New York. I never knew that boy's name."

Why was he going through all this old business? Thomas felt his face go hot with dread. He was about to learn something terrible. He stood still in the locker room and listened.

"The mind is a delicate thing," said Coach McPhee. He picked up Thomas's jeans from the bench and flicked the zipper. Thomas remembered the knife he had in the pocket.

"A very delicate thing," said McPhee again. "The rational part sometimes succumbs to the emotional part. My wife in Boston was very emotional. She was not rational at all. Do you understand what I'm saying?"

"Yes sir," said Thomas. "I understand."

"Reason gives way to passion," said McPhee. "My wife would not listen to reason. She said that she was going to leave me because of my abuse of her son. She said that I hit him too hard. Did you know my stepson?"

"Yes sir."

"Did you ever know him to have any bruises? Did he ever look unhappy to you?"

Thomas could remember the broad-shouldered, pimply, quiet boy with the scraggly blond hair and the nervous eyes who turned away whenever you walked up to him and tried to talk. At lunch in the dining hall he would sit by himself.

"Did you ever see him looking the least bit unhappy?" said McPhee again.

"Yes sir," Thomas said. Maybe he should have lied. But he had told himself that he was not going to lie anymore.

To Thomas's relief, McPhee said he was not surprised to hear that.

"Michael was undisciplined. He was spoiled," said Coach McPhee. "His mother spoiled him before I met her, before we were married. I told Angus about it. He was never married himself, old Angus. I never met my stepson until he was fourteen years old. By then it was too late. Diane had spoiled him. Discipline is a tough form of love, don't you think?"

"Yes sir." Thomas just wanted to forget all this, to put on his clothes and get out of here. It was way after 6:00. Would anybody miss him at the Somervilles' tea and come looking?

"We disagreed over how to train that boy. Diane was too easy on him. I know the kinds of urges that young boys feel, and I know how dangerous they are. You need to discipline those urges out of them. You need to keep the filth out of their minds. Diane used to take him into town for Sunday night meetings at the church. And why? So that he could meet girls. Can you imagine? The boy's own mother contributing to his corruption?"

Thomas said he found it tough to imagine the Sunday night youth group at the Presbyterian church in Montpelier to be all that lurid an evening. Coach McPhee was not interested.

"One day this past Thanksgiving break I found Michael in his room with a girl," he said. "I blew up. In my own home on this very campus, this stepson of mine had imported some female playmate. I suppose I did shout at him. Is that so bad? Does your father ever shout at you?"

Thomas said yes.

"Diane wouldn't listen to reason," said McPhee. "She defended them. She said they were doing nothing wrong. But that was typical of a mother, don't you think? To defend her child? She said they were simply having an innocent visit in a quiet place. But in his room? They were fully dressed, yes, at that point they were dressed, but they were touching each other. She was sitting in a chair in Michael's room, and Michael was brushing her hair."

Thomas felt as though he ought to understand how serious that was, but he could not.

"So after I hit him, Diane took him with her to Boston," said Coach McPhee. "I was wrong to hit him, I admit it. So I flew to Boston to apologize and to ask her to come home, for both of them to come home. And they refused. They simply refused. I was humiliated, and I sold my plane ticket and went to New York. I got a ticket for the biggest, loudest musical I could find. It was terrible, nothing but noise and spectacle. I know a lot about theater, you know. I was an English major in college. I would have graduated with distinction if one professor hadn't hated my honors thesis."

"Yes sir." Thomas could not see why he needed to hear all this right now, but if Coach McPhee wanted to talk, he would listen.

"You see, the traditional way of reading the story of Adam and Eve is that Eve tempted Adam into sin. But I don't believe it was Eve's fault. Women can't help being sensual or attractive. That's just the way they are. It's up to the man to maintain control, to hang on to his self-discipline, to resist the temptation. I argued in my thesis that Adam could have lived forever in paradise if he hadn't wanted Eve to be anything more than a companion. That's all Diane and I were. We lived in separate bedrooms. I insisted, because to have been in the same room with her I may have been tempted, like Adam. And then Michael the serpent came along and ruined everything. It was perfect companionship until we argued over him. I dreamed one night about breaking his neck and throwing him off the gym roof."

A dreadful suspicion shook Thomas, a suspicion so inconceivable that he could not articulate it. Farnham was the killer, wasn't he? Farnham was the one they arrested. Farnham was the one with the bad temper and the bloodlust. Not someone else?

"When I saw the boy outside the movie theater in New York he reminded me of my stepson a little. Or maybe not. Maybe he reminded me of somebody else. This boy in New York was performing unspeakable sex acts for money, and when I saw him, I don't know, I just went after him. I was going to stamp out sexuality at its source—not the females, they can't help it, but the males, the undisciplined adolescent males. I twisted his neck. And you know, I imagined that I had solved a problem for just a little while. Put on your pants."

He threw the jeans to Thomas, who missed the catch. He was trembling, though he was not even conscious of being afraid, only of needing to flee. Maybe he could break the glass in the door and get out that way. What could he use? Everything in the locker room seemed to be bolted down. He fumbled for his trousers and felt for the knife as he pulled the jeans up over his boxers.

"Are you missing this?" said McPhee, who reached into his own hip pocket and pulled out Thomas's knife. He flipped open the largest blade. "You have to be careful with these little pocketknives," he said. "You can cut in only one direction. If you try to pull the blade back and forth, it will close on you." He lunged forward and grabbed Thomas's towel off the bench. McPhee punctured the towel with the knife and pulled the blade along for a few inches.

"It's sharp," he said. "That's good." He threw the towel onto the floor.

"Do you understand what kind of danger you are in?" he asked.

"Yes sir." Thomas sobbed once, trying to fight off the tears. He understood all at once that he was going to be killed here by a man who he had thought was his friend.

Scene 8

At a few minutes past 6:00 in the afternoon Carol Scott stood in the living room of the Homestead and told the Somervilles what they had found.

"It's not a long tunnel," she said, "maybe twenty feet. It probably does come out in the boiler room of the gymnasium, but I can't get through. The other side seems to be sealed off the way yours was. We can search for the door on the gym side before we resort to breaking it down. Whoever did it must have killed him outside the tunnel and then dragged him inside. We could see where he was dragged. So it was somebody who knew that this tunnel existed."

Benjamin Warden sat silently and listened.

"Nobody knew about it," said Horace Somerville.

"Farnham must have," said Carol Scott. She had on jeans and a brown sweater and looked like someone from Middleburg who might have been out for a canter. "The place was just like his apartment. Too clean and tidy. No cobwebs, no dirt balls, no bugs to speak of."

"Maybe Angus knew," said Horace Somerville. "He liked to keep everything in the gym clean."

The police had telephoned a mortician in town who would take the remains of Angus Farrier away in a heavy rubber bag. They were airing out the basement of the Homestead.

"He's been dead for several days," said Carol Scott. "I'm sure he died on the same night he disappeared. The night of the Staines boy's death."

Horace Somerville asked if it was another broken neck.

"No," she said. "I think Mr. Farnham strangled him." She held up to them a clear plastic bag. Through the film of the plastic they could see a thick cord crusted with brown. At the end of the cord was the dull metallic shine of a whistle.

"Angus Farrier was garroted with this cord. Does it look familiar to you?"

It was a coach's whistle on a thick corded loop. They could see the crust clearly. Benjamin Warden turned away.

"I'm sorry about its appearance," said Carol Scott. "It was stuck to his neck. Do you recognize it?"

Horace said he'd never seen Angus wearing a whistle.

Whistle. Warden could remember something about a whistle, somebody speaking, somebody complaining . . .

"Patrick McPhee lost his whistle," said Warden.

"When?"

Warden was not sure. "I heard him mention it when I went to play practice. That was the day Cynthia died."

"That's it, then," said Carol Scott. "Farnham stole McPhee's whistle and used it to kill Farrier. Maybe the old man caught him killing the boy."

Horace Somerville liked Carol Scott but did not like her reasoning. She was typical of young people, always wanting to finish the job in a hurry.

"Carol," he said, "I would ask you to reconsider. How could Farnham have stolen this whistle when McPhee had it around his neck almost constantly?"

No one said anything for half a minute.

"I suppose he could have misplaced his whistle," said Kathleen.

"Patrick McPhee has been on the scene of every death on this campus," said Somerville.

Carol Scott had interviewed McPhee. He had flown to Boston over the Thanksgiving holidays. She had seen the records. Had she seen anything about his flight back? How far was it from Boston to New York?

"He lives on this side of the gym," she said. "Could he have known about this tunnel?"

No one spoke.

"Your wife's handkerchief," she said. "The one we found in Farnham's apartment."

"What about it?" said Warden.

"The girl Katrina Olson was using it to wipe her face. That was in Mr. McPhee's apartment. Farnham wasn't there."

They looked at one another.

"I wonder why Pat McPhee never complained to anyone about the smell around his apartment," said Somerville.

"Perhaps I'd better talk with Mr. McPhee," said Carol Scott. "What is he doing now?"

Scene 9

"It's the mind," said McPhee. "I'm observing myself and knowing how much I'm scaring you and hating myself for it. I like you, Thomas, and I don't want you to be afraid. But there's a passion in me that keeps welling up. Welling up, that's an old-fashioned expression, but that's the only term I can think of. Sometimes the passion takes over, and once it starts, once it becomes dominant, then I have a hard time getting my control back. Is this making any sense at all?"

"Yes sir." Thomas stood with his jeans on and trembled.

"The worst time was right after I got back from New York. I was so calm at first, taking the train back to Washington and then catching the Metro out to my car in the airport parking lot. But I was like an alcoholic on a binge. Russell Phillips was just there, with tales of sexual conquest and his flippant attitude. It was his hair, you know? It looked so long and brushable. Russell was already corrupted, he needed to go. I figured I was bound to get caught after Russell, and I should have been. They thought somehow he had killed himself, should have known better, don't you think? I was ashamed of myself and hoped maybe I could stop. Saturday night I went back up to the wrestling room just to punish myself, just to remind myself of what I had done, and I admit maybe to relive the moment a little, maybe to try to recapture that sense of satisfaction, of knowing that I'd made the world a little cleaner. Cynthia Warden came upstairs and had sex with Robert Staines."

He paused, shook his head. "No, wait, that's wrong," he said. "Cynthia was there by herself, and then Angus found her, and Staines showed up later with that other blond girl. So many blondes. Staines showed up with a girl and had sex with her right there on the pad. Can you imagine? He had no self-control whatsoever. He just took that girl on the floor, showed no respect for her at all."

Thomas thought of himself with Hesta in the chapel.

"I didn't deserve to get caught for Staines's death. He was entirely too undisciplined. So I got Angus and choked him and that worked just fine, especially when I hid my train ticket in Angus's desk so the police would think he'd been to New York. But then I got wrapped up in the play. I went over and watched them trying to block Desdemona's death scene, and I gave myself away. I said they ought to do it with Desdemona kneeling, and the only time Cynthia Warden had knelt was that night in the wrestling room. She had been up there before Staines arrived, and I had watched her from my hiding place among the mats rolled up against the wall. She guessed that I'd been there. In fact, when I showed back up at the theater she was expecting me. She knew I was going to kill her. I think she wanted it."

He threw Thomas a white tee shirt. Thomas could barely hold it because of his trembling.

"I wouldn't have gotten mixed up with the play if it hadn't been for you," said Coach McPhee. "You needed someone to walk over there with you."

"Coach McPhee," said Thomas. "Please let me go."

"I will," said McPhee. "I won't hurt you. If I can possibly help it."

Thomas would run if he had to. He didn't have any shoes on, but he would kick at the glass door if he could get to it.

"I want you to hear the entire story, Thomas. And then I want you to answer a question for me. The answer to the question is very important. Would you do that?"

"Yes sir."

"Would you care to sit down? You've been standing an awfully long time. I'm almost finished."

"That's all right," said Thomas. "I'll stand."

"Sit down," said McPhee. "Sit here on the bench."

Thomas sat.

Scene 10

Carol Scott pulled on her mittens and her knit hat and walked in the cold with two of her men from the Homestead to the gym. The main entrance was locked.

"Try the other doors," she said to the men. "I'll try the outside entrance to McPhee's apartment." She circled around the building to her right, past the chimney at the end of the building, and knocked at the darkened door to McPhee's apartment. There was no answer. She tried the knob. It was locked.

This had been a bitch of a day for Carol Scott. One of her kids was sick with whatever flu was going around, and she still hadn't done a bit of Christmas shopping; she'd asked for some time off, but Stuart had called at noon saying that they were two cops down and that he needed her to check out a burglary out on Blue Ridge Drive. It had been one nagging little thing after another all afternoon, then the call from Montpelier School. Crap. This was her first murder case since her maternity leave, and she was pleased at the way it had gone, even with that headmaster bitching at her. Now there was a chance she had a false arrest on Farnham. That would be just groovy. Eldridge Lane would be all over her butt if she'd arrested the wrong man. She would hate to give him that satisfaction.

It couldn't be McPhee. It had to be Farnham. She just needed to find out how he got that whistle.

But she was a good enough cop to admit that the whistle, if it did turn out to be McPhee's, weakened her case. It couldn't be McPhee, could it? He'd said he was asleep when the Staines boy got killed.

She walked back to where she had left the men. The campus was quiet and cold, lights on in the buildings, but not many people about. Why should anybody be out? It was freezing. She should be at home herself, instead of begging the flu bugs to assault her.

The men returned from different directions in a couple of minutes.

"Every door locked," said the older one.

She thought for a minute. "Do you think anybody's even in there?" she asked.

The younger one said he'd seen a light on down in one of the window wells.

"A locker room," she said.

She told them to wait and watch the building in case McPhee came out. She herself would return to the Homestead and call Felix Grayson, who had a pass key to the gym.

"If I had my tools, I could jimmy it," said the older one.

"Why don't we just kick it down?" said the younger one.

She was tempted. She felt like kicking somebody's tail. But then what would that headmaster say about the unnecessary damage to his facilities?

"No," she said. "We just want to question the guy. It's not as if we've got some emergency."

Scene 11

Coach McPhee had the knife out as he talked to Thomas.

"Angus and I used to drink some together," he said. "Not a lot. Neither of us was much of a drinker. But we'd talk, you know, about basketball or about the school. Did you know he went deep-sea fishing in Cuba every summer before it went Communist? Said he never saw Hemingway. There was a lot to Angus."

Thomas had been permitted to put on his shirt. It had not helped his trembling.

"One night he showed me an old hidden tunnel," said McPhee. "It opened out the back of one of those closets in his lair. Made me swear I'd never tell anybody. This is the first moment I have violated that oath. I want you to know that."

So there was a tunnel, Thomas thought. And with nauseating insight he realized that McPhee had told him because he would never have an opportunity to reveal the secret.

"I think Angus knew I was slipping," said McPhee. "He'd encouraged me to resign before Thanksgiving. He was more observant than you'd think. That night of the mixer, he was over here hunting for me. He'd looked at me awfully funny when Russell Phillips died, and I think he figured maybe he could prevent any more trouble. Angus was tough, but he was no match for me physically."

Thomas said, "I'm going to be sick."

"Go ahead," said McPhee. "It's going to be messy enough in here in a minute anyway."

That was when Thomas started to cry.

"Angus had been patrolling the building. I was hiding in the wrestling room when he came in and scared the hell out of Cynthia Warden," said McPhee. "After she left, I found him downstairs and had it out with him. He was a tough old bastard, toughest neck muscles I've ever seen. I finally had to improvise a strangulation with my coach's whistle. It's horrible, isn't it?"

"Let me go," said Thomas.

"I'm not finished." McPhee slid the blade of the knife across his left palm as if he were honing it. "I want you to hear all of this so you will know that I'm aware of just how awful a monster I am. Do you understand me?"

Thomas said he did.

"I dragged Angus's body into the tunnel, thinking that it would just be there for a couple of hours, until I could drive it off campus in his car. You can see how I was thinking then—a fake automobile accident, an unfortunate fire. I'd have taken him off campus right away if it hadn't been for all those people around for the mixer. Instead—I don't know why I did this, really I don't—I went back upstairs. I unlocked the weight room and thought maybe I'd work out in the dark up there. You know how physical exercise is good for releasing tension? And then I heard a couple of kids sneak in downstairs. I ducked over to the wrestling room. I didn't want to go home. The wrestling room was nice and peaceful. And then Staines showed up. He took that girl straight to the room where I was hiding. I wonder what would have happened if his date hadn't wanted to go to the bathroom. I should have killed her too, but I didn't. I think part of me wanted to get caught. That's why I saved all that evidence—the socks, the button, the ticket stub. The handkerchief I picked up in my own apartment in front of half a dozen people, and nobody noticed. I've given them so many opportunities to catch me, really, but I've been smart, too."

He stopped moving the knife. "You see, I have a strong survival instinct as well."

Scene 12

Warden sat in the living room of the Homestead with Horace and Kathleen Somerville and told them about his telephone call earlier today from the chairman of the English department at Columbia University.

"He wants to hire me," said Warden. He took a sip of his coffee. "I'd be writer-in-residence and teach one course per term."

"That's terrible," said Horace Somerville. He had started his second scotch and water.

"Horace," said Kathleen.

Somerville said it was terrible for Montpelier School. "It's a fine personal opportunity, if that's all you care about," he said. Warden could see he was pleased.

Kathleen asked if this offer came unexpectedly.

"No," said Warden. "He'd made me the offer before. I've been keeping secrets from you." He told them that it had started a few weeks ago, when he was in New York over the Thanksgiving holidays. "I interviewed with him before the reading on Saturday. Then several of them had a party for me that night. It was flattering."

Somerville asked him why he had not told anyone.

"It was because of Cynthia," Warden said. He had specified that such an appointment was contingent upon Columbia's also hiring Cynthia as an instructor. Negotiations had lapsed into friendly limbo when her illness had threatened to delay the completion of her dissertation. Warden had never told her of the opportunity. He had not wanted her to think that she was holding him back.

Horace Somerville was relieved. "I knew there was something distracting you since that trip to New York." He had tried to explain it away as concern over Cynthia's illness.

"I've felt guilty all day," said Warden. "The offer is appealing, but to take it would seem like a betrayal. She's dead. I should be mourning."

"That's normal," said Kathleen. She told him they had suffered the same pangs when Alfred died. "One day you find yourself smiling, and then you remember his death, and you force yourself to stop smiling, as though you don't deserve to be happy."

Horace told him to consider the facts. "You think you're showing respect by keeping yourself miserable," he said. "Makes about as much sense as our showing respect for Angus by spending tonight here with this damned smell."

Warden invited them to stay with him at Stratford House.

"It's about time you asked," said Somerville.

They heard the front door close. Carol Scott entered and asked to use a telephone. "I need to call Felix," she said. "We need a pass key to the gym."

Pass key. Something about a pass key. Warden reached into his pocket. There it was—Kevin Delaney's key to the gym. He must have been carrying it around for over a week now.

He showed it to Carol Scott, who put down the telephone.

"Fine with me," she said. "You can save me a couple of minutes."

Scene 13

Thomas Boatwright had never been more alert. He could feel the hardness of the bench through his jeans, the roughness of the carpet with the bottoms of his feet. He could hear the quickness with which Mr. McPhee had started to speak.

"When I saw we were having a buffet dinner that day, I just slipped back to the theater building. I was heading backstage when Kemper Carella showed up. I figured that was it, I'd never get a chance at her, but then I got an idea. I went downstairs and called Carella from the telephone under the stage and pretended to be at home looking for Farnham. Not only did it make Carella think of me at home, but it also made Farnham look missing. Farnham was the logical one to set up, you see. Everybody knew what a terrible temper he had, and what an awful crush he had on her. After Carella left the theater, I went upstairs. She was waiting for me on that bed. She fought me off, or tried to, but not very hard. She was not very strong. Afterward it was easy to go home and collect my little souvenirs. I waited until Farnham finished his bowl of soup, and then I hid the pieces of evidence in his apartment. Even if he'd locked the place, which he didn't, I could have used my pass key."

Thomas heard a door open in the hallway outside. He could hear voices.

McPhee stopped talking and listened, too. It sounded like several people who had just come out of a meeting.

"That's impossible," said McPhee. Before Thomas could react, McPhee was up and had Thomas standing in front of him like a shield. Thomas's arms were twisted around behind his back and held in place firmly by McPhee's left hand. McPhee's right arm stretched halfway across

Thomas's chest, and his right hand held the open knife at Thomas's throat.

"We will not be interrupted before I'm finished," said McPhee. They both faced the door to the locker room. They could hear the voices and the footsteps approaching. Then they could see through the glass several faces—Benjamin Warden, that lady police detective, a couple of male cops. All the voices went silent; all the mouths hung open in shock.

Benjamin Warden pushed on the door handle. But the door was bolted. He fumbled for the key and eventually managed to open the door. The police had drawn their guns.

Nobody spoke. Mr. McPhee held Thomas tight.

Scene 14

Richard Blackburn was on the telephone in Stratford House.

"McBain House," said the girl on the other line.

"Katrina?" said Richard.

"Yes."

"Katrina Olson?"

"No, Katrina Murgatroyd from South Philly," she said. "Who is this?"

"My name is Richard Blackburn," he said. Damn, his palms were sweating all over the telephone. "I got your message, and the answer is that I would love to."

"Love to what, Richard?"

Oh, no.

"Come up to your Christmas dance this weekend?" he said. He did not like the way she sounded.

There was a pause.

"I didn't leave you any message, Richard," she said.

Another pause.

"Oh, damn," he said. "I found this note on my door. I thought—"

"No," she said. "Somebody has played a joke on you."

"Yeah," he said. He felt like hopping a bus to Alaska.

"You're from Montpelier, right?" she said.

"I'm sorry," he said.

"It was a rotten trick," she said. "Typical."

"Yeah," said Richard.

"Why don't you little jocks just stick to your own balls and bats?" she said. She hung up.

Richard walked back to his dorm room and told Ralph Musgrove what had happened.

"It was probably Boatwright that did it," said Ralph.

"Yeah," said Richard. "The next time I see that bastard, I'm going to kill him."

Scene 15

Thomas allowed McPhee to walk him backward away from the door toward the showers when Mr. Warden and everybody entered the room. He could feel the sharp point of the blade pushing directly into his Adam's apple; he was scared to swallow for fear that the motion would cut. Both his arms hurt, but what he could feel more than anything else was the pounding of Mr. McPhee's heart through his shirt. It was going so fast that Thomas thought it might break.

"Stop there, Ben," said Coach McPhee.

Mr. Warden and the rest of them stopped walking. Then one of the policemen started to move around to the right, behind the island of cubicles in the center of the room.

"I said stop," said McPhee, and he pushed the knife just a fraction. It was enough to cut Thomas's skin.

Nobody in the room moved. Thomas could feel a wet ooze on his neck.

"I was in the middle of explaining to this boy," said

McPhee. "Now you've interrupted me." He paused. "This is one of those great moments of decision, isn't it? What I decide to do in the next few minutes will matter a lot, won't it? I've made some very bad decisions in the past couple of weeks. Thomas Boatwright can tell you all about them. I've made some terrible decisions."

Thomas was still crying, without any noise.

"When I was this boy's age," said Coach McPhee, "I used to look out of the window at a girl across the alley. She would take off all of her clothes and stand by the window and brush her hair. Every day at the same time, I could count on her. It was like watching a regular afternoon television show. I would indulge my sexual appetite and gaze at her."

Everyone in his audience listened.

"One day I was supposed to be baby-sitting for my little baby brother," said Coach McPhee. "He was in the bathtub. I had helped him undress and had put him into the bathtub. I knew I was supposed to be watching him, but it was time for the show, so I left. I left the bathroom, left the little boy in the tub all by himself, all his clothes laid out in a little pile where I would help him get dressed, and went to watch the girl in the window brush her beautiful hair. I could hear him in the tub, he was all right, but then I realized when the girl left the window that the bathroom was silent. I couldn't hear him anymore, and I went rushing back in, and he was dead. He was dead because of my own sexual appetite. All his clothes lay there in a little pile. I promised myself that from that moment on I would live in utter purity. I would never indulge my sexual urges again."

There was a silence.

"Patrick—" said Mr. Warden.

"Shut up, Ben," said Coach McPhee. "It wasn't Michael I hated. It was that irresponsible fifteen-year-old me. All those boys, they just reminded me of myself."

He started to sob. Thomas was so scared now that his own tears stopped. This is it, he thought. He couldn't move. He was going to die.

"What I wanted Thomas to tell all of you was that I was sorry," said Mr. McPhee. "I wanted him to be the messenger,